MW01049018

Praise for *Shadows of Berlin*

"I have been a fan of David R. Gillham's work since *City of Women*, and his latest, *Shadows of Berlin*, is his best yet. The story of Rachel, a Holocaust survivor, who seeks to start a new life in New York City with her American-born husband, Aaron, but cannot outrun the secrets of her past and what she did to survive, is haunting and enigmatic. Gilham writes about both the war and its aftermath with a sure hand, placing readers in the shoes of his memorable characters and compelling them to ask what they would have done. Reminding us that history is made up of infinite individual choices, *Shadows of Berlin* is a masterful story of survival and redemption."

—Pam Jenoff, *New York Times* bestselling author of *The Woman with the Blue Star*

"David R. Gillham has written a deeply moving story about an aspect of the Holocaust that few people know about—how thousands of survivors came to New York City to restart their lives and escape demons from the past. But some have a hard time dealing with the guilt, shame, and anger caused by the terrible experience. Gillham paints a vivid picture of their life in post-war New York while imaginatively linking it to their ordeal in wartime Berlin."

—Charles Belfoure, *New York Times* bestselling author of *The Paris Architect*

"Straddling the ragged line between guilt and tender mercy, *Shadows of Berlin* is Gillham at his best, writing compelling, evocative history. He is a master wordsmith who deftly pulls us down winding corridors riddled with broken spirits and haunting ghosts on a quest for absolution. An unspeakable past unspools in spits and sputters. Gillham nimbly sews the scraps together. The result is a riveting story that is unputdownable."

—Leah Weiss, bestselling author of *If the Creek Don't Rise* and *All the Little Hopes*

Also by David R. Gillham

City of Women
Annalies

SHADOWS

of BERLIN

SHADOWS
of BERLIN

a novel

David R. Gillham

sourcebooks
landmark

Published by Sourcebooks Landmark, an imprint of Sourcebooks
P.O. Box 4410, Naperville, Illinois 60567-4410
(630) 961-3900
sourcebooks.com

Library of Congress Cataloging-in-Publication Data

Names: Gillham, David R, author.
Title: Shadows of Berlin : a novel / David R Gillham.
Description: Naperville, Illinois : Sourcebooks Landmark, [2022]
Identifiers: LCCN 2021037069 (print) | LCCN 2021037070 (ebook) | (hardcover) | (epub)
Subjects: LCGFT: Novels.
Classification: LCC PS3607.I44436 S53 2022 (print) | LCC PS3607.I44436
   (ebook) | DDC 813/.6--dc23
LC record available at https://lccn.loc.gov/2021037069
LC ebook record available at https://lccn.loc.gov/2021037070

Printed and bound in the United States of America.
WOZ 10 9 8 7 6 5 4 3 2 1

To my wife, Ludmilla

Every angel is terrifying.
—Rainer Maria Rilke

PART ONE

The Dead Layer

NEW YORK CITY

1955

1.

All Is Perfect

S HE IMAGINES THE FINAL MOMENTS AS WHITE, PURE WHITE, AS the plane plunges through the blizzard. The snow obscures the cockpit glass until the mountain emerges in a split second of clarity, the cliff face surging forward in the instant before impact.

Her shrink tilts his head. Slightly. "Why only plane crashes?" he wonders. "Why not floods or train wrecks or any number of other disasters?"

She recalls the headline of the story that she had carefully scissored from the newspaper that morning with her sewing shears. JET HITS MOUNTAIN IN SNOW SQUALL. Below the headline, a photo of the wreckage revealed the result. A twisted, torn fuselage in pieces. Chunks of smoking steel.

"I think the crash of an airplane is different," says Rachel.

Dr. Solomon frowns reflectively. An arm and a leg he's being paid, so it's his job to ferret out this young woman's madness, isn't it? Just as it's her job to be just mad enough to be cured. "Different?"

"Because they are so sudden," she explains. Quietly. "So complete. And so very few survive it. How is the decision made?"

The man tilts his head again. She can tell he's not quite sure what she means. How is *what* decision made?

"Only a handful may live through it when most do not. How is that decided?" she asks. She began collecting the clippings from the newspapers sometime after she and her uncle had arrived in the States and taken up residence in the hotel for refugees on Broadway. She was always buying newspapers at her uncle's insistence. To improve their English, he maintained, though what did he end up reading, her Feter Fritz? *Der Forverts* in Yiddish. Sitting at the little café table with his cup of Nescafé. But was that really when she began snipping out the headlines of aerial catastrophes?

She was twenty-one the year they arrived in the Port of New York aboard the *Marine Sailfish* in 1949. Over six years ago. The few photographs of her taken at the time show a haunted, dark-mopped waif. She was an open wound at that point. Bundled in ill-fitting castoffs, thin as a matchstick, and still faintly stinking of a continent burnt to ashes. Stumbling over her English, she was boiled by the summer's heat and overpowered by New York's towering intensity, the skyscraper architecture, crush of people, and blare of traffic. Berlin's Unter den Linden was famously perfumed by the sweetly honeyed scent of the linden trees, till the Nazis ordered them cut down, but New York City stank of exhaust and ripening garbage. It was deafening, smothering, and teeming with pedestrians trying to trample one another. Simply keeping up with sidewalk traffic was exhausting. Also exhausting was contending with the city's abundance. The lavish variety of produce, the sumptuous profusion of color filling the shelves of a corner market were so taxing to her senses that buying cabbage and cucumbers was enough to cause her to panic.

But surely it was after those first dizzying months had passed that she first started her collection of clippings. It had to be after the Hebrew Immigrant Aid Society had helped them find the tiny apartment on Orchard Street. A tenement house populated by mobs of homeless refugees. Jews like themselves, just off the boats from the displaced persons camps. She remembers stowing the clippings in an Endicott Johnson shoebox. But she didn't start pasting them into scrapbooks until she married Aaron. That's when she began treating the clippings like a secret, a shameful secret, hiding them in the rear of the closet behind the vacuum cleaner, where she knew her new husband would never look. After all, why would he ever touch a vacuum cleaner?

"So am I here to make a confession, Doctor?"

"You'll have to decide that for yourself," the doctor tells her.

She nods. So that's how it's going to be, is it? All up to her? Should a sinner willingly confess to sin? Jews don't make confessions inside little booths. They must expiate their sins on earth through good deeds, but she is not much for mitzvot these days. Last Christmas, there was a brass band from the Salvation Army playing outside Macy's. On an impulse, she dropped a five-dollar bill in their pot, but she still couldn't find a cab. Her bet is that God just pocketed it.

"I'd like you to consider painting again," says Dr. Solomon.

Rachel stares. "Painting."

"Yes."

She feels a sickly terror and has to look away, glancing at the leather sofa to see if Eema has arrived, but it is empty of mothers. "And why should I want to do such a thing, Doctor?" she asks. To push a brush into the crazy woman's hand. To shove her at a canvas and order her to *paint*? It's dangerous. What raving madness might explode from her body and bloody the canvas?

And yet! "It could be very helpful," the good doctor submits. "Creativity can often provide emotional relief." But he does not press the matter. "Give it some thought," he suggests. "That's all I'm saying. Your art," he tells her. "It seems to me that it plays a large role in forming your self-identity."

Her self-identity. That ragged patchwork of truths and untruths. In the war, her identity was dependent on forged documents. It was her ersatz self that she clung to, because her true identity could murder her.

⌐•⌐

One of the first things that shocked her about New York City, apart from the looming towers of Midtown and the crowds swarming the sidewalks, were the filthy streets. Berlin was a clean city before it was pummeled into ruin. No one dared drop trash in the street; it would have been unthinkable! Undenkbar! But New York is a pigsty in comparison. The gutters are clogged with trash. Ash bins and garbage barrels overflow. Dogs are permitted to soil the sidewalks with impunity.

Last year, the city government erected a gigantic wire bin in the middle of Times Square, loaded with trash collected from the streets. The accusation was clearly printed in huge letters: THIS LITTER BELONGS TO *YOU*! YOU MISS THE LITTER BASKET WITH 1,200 POUNDS A DAY IN TIMES SQUARE ALONE! Going down into the subway is not better. Squashed cigarette butts everywhere. Sandwich wrappers, crumpled bags, discarded pop bottles, fruit peels, and half-eaten hot dogs crawling with ants. Of course in Berlin, there was a time when she was one of those ants, trolling the gutters and bins for food.

Advertising cards on the Lexington Avenue Local provide a lesson on Good Subway Citizenship as the train bumps through the tunnel: PLEASE, DON'T BE A SPACE HOG, A DOOR BLOCKER, A FEET RESTER, A LEG PEST, OR A LITTERBUG! All instructions that are generally ignored by passengers. This is also a difference between New York and Berlin. In Berlin, who would have dared smoke where the sign commanded RAUCHEN VERBOTEN! Or dared be a Jew where the notice declared JUDEN VERBOTEN!

The crowd in the car thins out. It's then that Rachel notices a child staring at her. A little girl, four or five years old, with a knit hat and silky brown bangs across her little forehead. Her eyes are shiny buttons, and she gazes at Rachel with innocent interest. A contented little fox caught out in the open, yet who can look through a person to spot the animal truth of them.

It's not that Rachel does not *want* children. She *does*, or at least there are times that she does. The desire for a child of her own strikes her in moments of urgency. Perhaps that's how she herself was conceived. In one of her eema's moments of urgency. God knows it's difficult to imagine Eema actually planning for such a process as conception. Drafting out a child in her mind, laying down the sketches in her heart before a child filled them in, filling up her womb. Before a child stretched out her body and confounded her life. Before it ruined her punctuality, disrupted her routines, drained the color from her lips, and demanded strict attention on a tyrannical scale simply to survive the day. Would she have ever actually agreed to such a disruptive intrusion with the benefit of forethought? Doubtful. Her daughter must have been an accident of the moment.

Gazing back at the girl with the straight brown bangs, Rachel can only view motherhood as a foreign concept. Like the moon or like the American Dream. To dream like an American? What does this mean? Even after becoming a citizen, she does not know. Perhaps because she is still only partially here in this country. Part of her is still buried in the cinders of Berlin. Before she was Rachel the American, she was Rashka or Rokhl or Ruchel, or her mother's Little Goat. And it is little Rashka's terror that punctures any urgent moments in Rachel's life that might lead to conception. Any true desire for a child of her own is restricted to a wistful reverie, in the same way she might imagine what-if. What if her mother had loved her as much as she loved art? What if she had remained an innocent? What if she had never shared a table with the red-haired woman in a Berlin café? What if horses could talk and pigs could fly? What if.

At home, they don't really discuss the Episode.

She and her husband, Aaron, that is.

It's not really on their agenda for conversation. Rather they talk around it, as in Aaron's refrain: "We don't want a repeat of *the Episode*."

The Episode being the night she ended up in a straitjacket for her own protection, locked up in Bellevue's psychiatric wing. The doctor there stitched and bandaged her hand slashed by the shattered glass so that no visible scar remains. But scars are often not so visible. Since that night, the surface of the wound has healed over. Already, more than half a year has passed, and both she and Aaron have returned to the routines of their daily lives, except for one thing. One thing hardly worth mentioning really. The thin layer of dread that gives an undertone to the everyday colors of every moment. The Dead Layer below all her exteriors. Other than that? Altes iz shleymesdik. All is perfect.

For their first anniversary, Aaron's mother wanted to buy them a T.V., but Aaron is dead set against television, so it was a radio instead. A Philco 51–532 table model that sits on a shelf. If Rachel wants to watch T.V., she must drag her husband down two blocks to the window of an appliance store on West Twentieth. There's often a crowd when *The Lone Ranger* comes on, though it's hard to hear through the glass. Rachel doesn't care. It's an American western. Everyone climbs into the saddle. All the men have six-guns on their hips and are all expert shots, picking rattlesnakes off the rocks. The women wear long calico dresses, but even they can handle a rifle.

"We could buy a T.V.," she tells Aaron.

"Who can afford one?" he asks without looking up from the kitchen table, smoking as she cleans up the supper dishes. "Besides, T.V. is for suckers. It's all about moving the merchandise."

Rachel doesn't care about that. She *likes* the commercials. The cartoon giraffe with the sailor's cap selling the Sugar Frosted Flakes. You can eat 'em right out of the box! And she would like to be able to *sit down* while watching *The Lone Ranger* instead of standing outside a storefront. Or maybe watch an entire episode without Aaron nagging her about how his feet hurt after working the Thursday all-you-can-eat shrimp cocktail special lunch shift at the restaurant or that his back is getting to him standing there like a schmuck for half an hour. Aaron says, "Who needs a picture tube?" He liked Jack Benny better on the radio, 'cause he likes to use his *imagination*. It's cheaper.

"We could put it right there," Rachel tells him.

"What?"

"A television set. We could put it right there, across from the sofa."

"Hasn't she been listening?" he wonders aloud.

"It would fit."

"But there's a chair there."

"So we move the chair."

"No room."

"Then we give the chair to the Salvation Army."

"Thank you, no. That chair belonged to my mother's aunt Shirley and has great sentimental value."

"It was here when we moved in."

"And I've gotten very attached to it since. Besides, isn't there some *Jewish* charity, by the way? Doesn't the Joint run a thrift shop?"

"The Joint does not want our chair."

"Maybe not, but my point is this: Why give a perfectly good chair to the goyim? Let them buy retail."

"You're not very funny."

"No? Then go give your own family heirloom to the Salvation Army, why don't you?"

Only she has no family heirlooms. Nothing left of the elegant Klimt chairs or Biedermeier dining set. The silver Shabbat candlesticks or the Italian gilt-wood menorah. Nothing of her eema's Turkish carpets or the Silesian porcelain coffee service. Not anything. Not anything at all. Not even a speck of schmutz has survived from under the rugs. Her uncle Fritz is the only family antique that comes close to qualifying.

In the bedroom, while the ambient fuss of street traffic drifts up from below, the bedside lamps are switched off. Rachel and Aaron climb under the blankets. But it's immediately obvious that Aaron is interested in pursuing a little something other than the nightly routine of good-night pecks. The smell of him as he pulls her closer can still intoxicate her, even after five years of marriage. The feel of his skin,

the hair on his chest, that head of thick russet curls. It's easy for her
to lose herself. The small ceramic night-light she bought for twenty
cents at the hardware store is plugged into the electrical outlet under
the window, and every night, she snaps it on because she cannot tolerate total darkness. In total darkness, she will drown. So the night-light
glows like a petite yellow star.

Aaron has opened her pajamas. The blue silk pajamas he bought
in Chinatown for their fifth anniversary, though probably picked out
by his sister Naomi. Still, they are so luxurious. She slides her fingers
through his hair as his lips brush her skin. His hand moves slowly,
gently, as he slips the Chinese silk from her hips. Exposed, on top of the
blankets, she feels the vulnerability of her body deepen. His lips find
the curve of her neck. She kisses his ear, her desire tightening.

"Aren't we forgetting something?" she whispers softly. "Aren't we
forgetting something?" But he doesn't answer. His hands are moving.
His mouth. She can feel herself warming, her breath expanding. A
void opening. But when she whispers his name, she is still repeating
her drowsy question. "Aaron? Aaron? Aren't we? Aren't we *forgetting*
something?"

Aaron's answer is to shift her body under him, and she feels a liquid
craving, but also an edge of fear. Doesn't the Talmud teach that the
obligation to be fruitful and multiply is on the man? So siring children
is a mitzvah for the husband, which has contributed to Aaron's disdain of condoms. And Rachel would rather be in control of the process
anyway. Women have more leeway. So she whispers sensibly, intimately.
"Aaron, I don't have my *shield*."

She means her diaphragm. A word she mispronounces enough
to elicit an indulgent correction: *Die*-a-fram, says Aaron. Like *die*-a-
thousand deaths. Not *dee*-a-fram. So instead of *die*-a-thousand-deaths
diaphragm, she calls it her shield, because that's what it is, isn't it? Her
shield to keep her safe from her own body. She can slip through Eve's
loophole and escape her own biology. Her own history. "*Aaron...*"

"Would it be so terrible, honey?" her husband wants to know. "Would it be so terrible if we made love like man and wife? Think of Ezra Weinstock," he tells her. "He has three little Weinstocks already, with a fourth in the hopper."

"Aaron."

"My own cousin, that fucknik Ezra, *is ahead of me*, Rachel. Ezra Weinstock from Coney Island Avenue, so fuckin' smart that, when he was ten, he stuck a pencil up his nose—*is ahead of me*. Do you know what that's doing to my *mother*? Every Wednesday, she's playing mah-jongg with Aunt Ruth, and *oy* what an earful she gets about the adorable Weinstock grandkids. How much longer can the woman stand the disgrace? She'll have to adopt a different son."

Rachel absorbs the smile in his voice. The spreading warmth of his touch. "Aaron," she repeats.

"She'll have to replace me with Hilda Auerbach's boy. He's a doctor now with his own practice in Prospect Heights. An eye-ear-nose-and-throat man." He is saying this in the funny way, kissing her belly button and breasts once for each specialty: eye, ear, nose, throat. But Rachel can tell that he is also deadly serious. How can he face the world as a man? How much longer can he face himself with no children? Without that gift from his lovely wife? Time is running out.

He is moving into her. Pressing his advantage, exploiting her weakness for him, and she is feeling her resolve melt. "I can't" is all she manages to say, but it's tough to win this debate in the closeness of their room, in the sweetness of their bed. Words are slipping away from her. Sometimes, she thinks that she should just *let him be fruitful*. Let him cook up a baby inside her. Put a bun inside her oven. *Their* bun. But then the elevated West Side freight line roars past, and something in the unrelenting thunder from those tracks panics her. Trains lead to death.

"*Stop it*," she hears herself snap. "*Stop it*." A terror has gripped her, seized her by the bones. She feels like she might suddenly suffocate under his weight. Like her heart might stop. "*Aaron!*" she pleads, frantically now, and this time, he's had enough. He quits, disconnects, and rolls onto his back.

For a moment, they simply breathe roughly into the darkness hanging above them. Rachel feels the tears heating her eyes. Is it really so much to ask? A child for her husband? He never made any secret of the fact that he wanted a baby. "I'm sorry," she breathes, smearing at her tears. "I'm sorry," she repeats, but it makes no difference. Her husband has become a solitary island beside her.

"No, it's okay. I get it." He sighs. "Not angry. Forget it," he tells her thickly. Issuing a quick peck on the cheek, he rolls over, turns his back on her, shifting the bedclothes to his side. Leaving her to the darkness. Alone in her body, her guilt is insistent: What right does a murderess have to create life? Blanketed by the night, only a small halo of yellow from the night-light keeps her from going under.

As far as talent is concerned, she must make do with what she has been able to scavenge. Her mother always encouraged her. Rachel was the daughter of Lavinia Morgenstern-Landau, Portraitist of the Great and Near-Great. One of only two women to be elected to the Prussian Academy of the Arts! The founder of the Berolina Circle! Of course the daughter must show talent.

But only up to a point. She could never be so skilled that she mounted a *challenge* to her eema's hegemony as the supreme painter of the family. Her father, she had learned, had gathered his laurels as a poet, which had been sanctioned because poems were only words, and words were no competition in Eema's mind. And Abba was dead by the time Rashka was a toddler, so she was not old enough to retain memories of him. He survived the war, survived the influenza, but then was devoured by consumption in 1928 when Rashka was only two. Her single memory of her father is shaped by the portrait that hung in the salon. Eema had painted him in shadows not long before his death, a gaunt, handsomely distant face, half in the dark, already partially consumed by the disease that would claim him.

As she grew, people commented on how Rashka had his eyes. Sometimes his nose. Also, they said, his stubbornness and his silence. These ghost features, these traits that she has inherited from a dead father, were always like the spirit of a dybbuk possessing her but in a quietly paternal way. Eyes, nose, stubbornness. Silence. These are her abba's lone bequests to her. All else is Eema. Rashka was permitted to shine as a reflection of her mother's genius. This single fact defined Rashka's development as an artist. Even now, years after her mother's demise, it is there, sewn into Rachel's heart as she scrutinizes her reflection distorted by the aluminum face of the Proctor electric toaster.

Days have passed since their aborted attempt at marital intercourse. The air is growing chilly. The radiator hisses with heat. She is dressed in one of Aaron's old knit sweaters pulled over her pink chenille bathrobe and with wool socks on her feet, because she is always cold. One of her husband's Lucky Strikes smolders in the green glass ashtray on the kitchen table as she sketches her reflection on a pad with a charcoal stick. Her mother shares the table, smoking a rice-paper Gitanes Brune inserted into an elegant amber resin holder. A strong and pungent aroma in the past, but all that Rachel smells is the stink of ash that always lingers over her mother's arrival. Eema's face is a perfect heart shape and her complexion alabaster. She is dressed in her finery of velvet and sable. Her black bob is silvered by the arrow point of a widow's peak. Her face is coldly beautiful. Not exactly the nurturing parent, perhaps. Always happy to judge.

So we are here, you and I, she hears her mother observe. Azoy, mir zenen do. Always, between them, it's Yiddish.

"Yes, Eema. We are here."

Peering at her daughter with her usual mix of curiosity and disapproval, she wonders, *What is this you are doing?*

"I'm drawing," Rachel tells her.

Really? Eema is skeptical. *Is that what you think? This qualifies as drawing?*

"Es iz a shmittshik," Rachel says and then picks out a few words from English. "A doodad, you know? A doodle."

So you may call it. But is it a waste of your God-given talent?

"And now it's about what God gives us, Eema? I thought my talent came from you. Besides, you said you had abandoned God."

Eema replies in a leaden tone, *Of course! This is how a daughter speaks to her mother. Let's be correct, Rashka. I did not abandon God. God abandoned me.* She expels smoke with a certain dramatic aplomb, but Rachel does not react, prompting Eema to frown at the silence. *So this shmittshik? You think it serves art?*

"Degas said that art is not what you see but what you make others see."

Degas, Eema scoffs. *Degas was an anti-Semite and a misogynist, tsigele.*

"Don't call me that. I'm not your little goat anymore."

But still stubborn as one. When will you stop sleepwalking? You've been scarred, yes. We live, we die. But in between, for those chosen, we have a duty to create.

"Very simple for *you* to say, Eema." Rachel's charcoal stick scratches against the paper. "You're dead."

But her eema is deaf to this fact. She clutches at the sable collar of her coat. *When I was your age, Rashka, I was already a recognized artist. My work was highly valued. Hanging in the most important galleries in Berlin.*

"And yet not a single painting survives. They all went up in smoke. Just like you."

As usual, you're missing my point. You have your share of talent, Rokhl. A blessing or a curse? I can't say. But why do you waste yourself?

"I'm not wasting myself, Eema. I'm protecting myself."

Forget these silly drawings. Go! Pick up your brushes. Lay color onto your palette.

"No," Rachel answers.

Open your easel and face an empty canvas!

"*No*," Rachel answers more forcefully. "No, I cannot. I'm sorry, I cannot do it. It will hurt me."

It will heal you!

"No! I'm afraid, Eema," she confesses, her eyes heating with tears. "I'm afraid of what will come out of me." She's startled by her tiger cat leaping up onto the table, and with that, her mother's chair empties. The smell of smoke returns to the cigarette in the ashtray. Wiping her eyes, Rachel seizes the cat. Kibbitz she calls him, because he's always sticking his nose in, always getting into the middle of things.

Escaping to America, surviving the ruins of Europe, she felt she must—*must*—continue as her mother's daughter. So for a period of years, she had dabbed a brush into globs of oily colors and smeared them onto canvases. "Ghosts" she called them. At first, they were only plumes of color. Whiffs of smoke. Nothing human. But gradually they began to take shape into more human forms. Of human memories. Over and over, she tried to capture the essence of what she had lost. The life of her mother? Yes. A life lost to a colorless killer, cyanide gas. The millions of lives lost. But she didn't dare confess this, even when she found a gallery. Even after the gallery was selling those small works on small canvases or Masonite board. A newspaper printed her name and called her work both challenging and promising. She was married by then, yet Aaron didn't seem to mind. He wasn't exactly an art expert, he'd confess, *obviously*. Still, he was impressed that a painting could actually sell for money. He'd joke about retiring to easy street now that his wife could turn a profit!

But really, underneath it all, it was a lie. She was still *pretending* to be an artist. The human plumes of color she was producing were nothing. They were personal without being profound. Their impact was as meaningless as candle flames. A cough could blow them out. And they certainly weren't Art. Not real Art like the Art of her mother. Secretly, she was ashamed of how inconsequential they were. Ashamed but also relieved. Maybe she didn't *need* to be an artist. Maybe she could escape. Leave Eema's legacy behind with the ashes. Maybe she could simply be what her husband expected her to be. A wife and a mother. Those were both acceptable professions in his mind. Maybe she could sign on as a regular American woman. And if she painted a canvas or two on the side? Well, there was a word in English that took the curse off that. *Hobby.* A pastime, a way to pass time. And in the process, if she collected a few dollars doing it? Even better. It didn't mean she *had* to be—that she was *doomed* to be—her mother's daughter. Rachel could avoid a career with the same zealousness that Eema had cultivated hers.

But after Bellevue? After the Episode, there was no question. She had to face the truth. There was a monster inside her. Locked away so that no one could see it? Yes. But painting was dangerous. Painting baited the monster out into the open. It made her vulnerable to herself. Who was she trying to fool? God? History? Herself? She had forfeited her rights as an artist one day while seated in a Berlin café. So returning from Bellevue to their apartment on West Twenty-Second Street, she'd locked away her easel and closeted her Winsor & Newton painter's box. She no longer pretended that any of her soulless plumes of color had purpose. They were meaningless. Nishtik! They were trash, and she simply discarded them like New York litter, one at a time, leaving them behind on the subway or leaned against a fire hydrant in the street for dogs to piss on them.

Now? She confines herself to these scribbles. The Episode was a line of demarcation. After it, she could no sooner pick up a brush and apply paint to canvas than she could sprout wings and fly into the tree-tops. All that remains to her is the shmittshik. The doodle of her face mocking her warped reflection in a toaster. Her avowal of the truth of her inner distortion. The monster crouched so deeply within her.

When she hears the toilet flush, she removes the cat to the floor, then flips her sketch pad closed. "Good morning, Husband," she calls, tamping out her cigarette, rubbing the charcoal dust from her fingers.

Aaron is trim, with a handsomely ordinary face. His curls arc uncombed, and he's dragging his tuchus, as he likes to say, shambling in from the bedroom in his pajamas. He's wearing the plaid flannel bathrobe with matching slippers that she'd given him last May on his thirty-fourth birthday. The robe hangs open, and its belt drags on the floor on one side. Rachel is up, padding toward the kitchen galley in her socked feet to pour him coffee.

"Morning, Wife," he replies and yawns widely.

The coffee streams into a china cup on the sink counter. "What time did you get home last night?" she asks.

"I dunno. *Late*," says Aaron as he plops down at the table. "Leo had a four-top from the U.J.A. who stayed forever. Mr. Big Shot as usual. Is there coffee?" he asks just as Rachel delivers the cup on a saucer. "Ah, great. Thank you."

"I can make you a fried egg on toast."

But Aaron is busy pulling a sour face. "What *is* this?"

"It's instant. Good to the last drop."

"The *last* drop? They should worry about the *first* drop. Where's the sugar?"

Rachel pops a slice of Levy's seeded rye from the bag into the toaster. "We have none. I forgot."

To which her husband can only shrug. "S'okay. I'll suffer." He sips at the coffee and ignites a cigarette with his Zippo as Rachel is busy fetching an egg from the fridge and cracking it into an iron skillet.

"So I heard this story," Aaron begins, exhaling smoke. "This guy, walking down the street on East Thirty-Third, minding his own business, when suddenly—*ka-chunk*! A piece of masonry falls off one of those big apartment buildings and lands right on his kop."

The egg sizzles loudly in the pan. "What happened to him?"

"What *happened* to him? Well, honey, whattaya *think* happened when a hunk of masonry goes ka-chunk on your head?"

"And did it actually make that sound? 'Ka-chunk'?"

"Yes. It made that sound exactly." He smokes, done with this business of ka-chunking and what follows. "So. Any ideas for your birthday this year?"

The question automatically inserts a splinter into Rachel's belly. "My birthday?" she asks and flinches inwardly at the sight of a dead rat sizzling in the skillet. Absorbing the horror, she blinks it away till it is once again a frying egg.

"It's only a couple weeks away," Aaron reminds. "Whattaya wanna do?"

"I don't know. What did we do last year?"

Her husband relives the boredom. "Invited Naomi over for takeout and played Scrabble. Just like the year before and the year before that and on and on back to the beginning of creation."

Rachel replies, defending something. "Okay. Well, I *like* Naomi." The toast pops. Rachel grabs it by the edges and drops it on a plate, which she shuttles over to the table.

"Uh-huh. I like Naomi too," her husband agrees in a flattened tone, scraping the burnt toast with a table knife. "She's my sister, so what choice do I have? Is this butter or margarine?"

"Margarine," Rachel tells him.

Again, he frowns but doesn't complain aloud. "I thought this year we might do something *else.*"

This makes Rachel uneasy. "And what's wrong with Scrabble anyway, I'd like to know? Scrabble is my favorite game." The truth is that the Scrabble games with her sister-in-law make her feel safe. They make her feel as she did as a child in their home in the Fasanenstrasse, playing board games on the card table with school friends, rolling dice and counting off spaces. Walking the skillet over to the table, she scoops out the burnt egg using a spatula, plopping it onto the waiting piece of toast. "Sorry. It's black around the edges."

"S'alright. There's pepper?"

She moves the pepper shaker from the middle of the table to a spot within Aaron's easy grasp. God forbid he should have to reach for something.

The telephone rings. Aaron moves not a muscle to answer it. He only huffs a sigh. "*H'boy.* I wonder who *that's* gonna be."

The telephone is a black Bakelite instrument. It sits ringing on the old gossip bench that came from a flea market downtown. It continues to ring till Rachel picks up the receiver, because who else will answer it? "Perlman residence," she announces.

A familiar voice responds. A male voice, a fatherly Brooklynese voice, greeting her over the noise of a busy kitchen. "Hello? Mrs. Perlman? It's Abe Goldman."

She can picture Abe, the restaurant's majordomo. Aging but still a giant of a man with the kitchen wall phone tucked under his multiple chins, sweating into his tuxedo shirt.

"Can you tell Mr. P. that the refrigerator's gone on the fritz, and we're about to lose a shitload of red snapper, if you'll pardon my French?"

"Hold on, Mr. Goldman," says Rachel, proffering the receiver. "You're about to lose a shitload of red snapper."

Aaron has already left the table and appears beside her to accept the phone, muttering, "Stupid piece of junk." Then into the receiver, he says, "So, Abe, did I mention I hate your guts? *Where's Leo?*"

Aaron's job is managing Charades, a swanky seafood palace opened for the theater crowd by that maven of the Great White Way eateries, Mr. Leo Blume. "Fine dining till curtain time" on Broadway across from the Winter Garden between West 15th and West 51st.

"*Figures!*" her husband shouts into the phone with a kind of sour vindication. "The place goes up in flames, and Mr. Big Shot is nowhere to be found, as usual." His battles with Leo, his battles with the waiters, the busboys, the customers, the whole meshugaas—it consumes him like a flame consumes the candle. But Rachel is detached from his struggle. In fact, she's relieved by it. His obsession with work means less pressure on her. More solitude.

Kibbitz is mewing loudly to be let out, so Rachel shoves up the window sash, smelling the street fumes greasing the chilly air. The cat hops out onto the fire escape and charges upward toward the roof. There's an extravagant depth to the vastness above the buildings. The last ripe blues of November swelling the sky before the drabness of winter settles in. She compulsively breaks apart the color into painterly hues. Van Gogh said that there is no blue without yellow and orange. This sky holds undertones of cadmium yellow and vermillion to give it the proper weight. Then a blend of cobalt and white flattens it into an endless sheet.

"Haven't you heard me *tell him* a hundred times, Abe, that we need a new freezer?" Aaron is demanding confirmation. "A hundred times at least."

"You should tell him to phone the man you bought it from," Rachel calls from the window.

"Okay, okay, I'm on my way," Aaron is conceding into the telephone. "In the meantime, get what's-his-name on the phone. Gruber. The swindler who sold us the piece of crap to begin with." Aaron hangs up with a bang and puffs a sigh, resigned to his fate. "So whatta surprise," he says, frowning his standard frown. "The joint's in chaos, and Leo's uptown smoking a Montecristo B on his terrace."

Chaos! Enough to give him the gastritis. Just the way Aaron likes it! He is on his way to dress when the phone rings again. "If that's Abe," Aaron is yelling from the bedroom, "tell him I gotta put my pants on before they'll let me on the goddamned A Train!"

"You should hail a cab and have Leo pay for it," Rachel yells back to him and picks up the receiver. "Mr. Goldman," she says, "he has to put his pants on before they'll let him on the A Train."

"Rashka!" she hears and feels her grip on the phone tighten.

"Feter Fritz," she says loud enough for Aaron to hear as he reenters from the bedroom now wearing his trousers, his dress shirt unbuttoned. He responds to the mention of her uncle's name with an eye roll. Seizes a brownish banana from the kitchen counter and starts peeling.

"Bistu gut, Feter?" she asks the phone.

"Rashka, ziskeit, tsu hern deyn kul iz a brkhh." Even though her uncle likes to insist that one language is never enough, he seldom speaks to her in anything but the language of their homelife. Not German like the good Yetta Jews spoke, raising up their Christmas trees, trying to be more German than the Germans. But Yiddish! Especially on the telephone, as if a phone call is a kind of spectral connection, voices thrown over distance, not bound by physical proximity, that must be anchored by a common touchstone of their past. Their vanished lives. Vanished in all ways except how they speak, how they think, what they remember or choose to forget.

She can see him in her mind, her uncle, ensconced like an exiled princeling on the scruffy velveteen sleigh chair that he drags out into the tenement's hallway to make use of the pay phone. A lit cigar rib-boning smoke upward to the tobacco-stained ceiling. She is buoyed by his voice, yet she knows that every conversation with her feter has a price attached. He wants to *see* her, he tells her. And not just *wants* to! "It's *essential*, Rokhl," that he sees her. And that she sees him. Normally, these conversations are chock-full of her uncle's ersatz cheer, but this time, a smear of desperation underpaints his jaunty bravado. It makes her wish she had simply let the phone ring. But she agrees to meet him, because what else can she do? It means she doesn't go to the grocery to pick up sugar for her husband's coffee or take his shirts to the cleaners. It means she doesn't use the morning to clean the oven or vacuum the draperies. Those are tasks she'll have to leave to the mice if they want to make time. Aaron is tossing the banana peel into the trash as she hangs up, his shirtfront now buttoned and tail tucked into his waistline.

"So, your *uncle*, huh?" he says, still chewing the last bite of banana but frowning now, as if the mention of her feter has ruined the taste. She knows Aaron believes that her Feter Fritz is an open drain for her. "And how is *he*?" her husband wonders, lifting a wing tip onto his chair to retie a loose shoestring. "And by that I mean what does he *need*?" Licking his thumb to rub clean the toe of his shoe leather.

"Nothing," she assures him. "He doesn't need a thing. Just inviting me for a coffee," she insists and retrieves her husband's coat and hat from the hall tree by the door.

"So you don't think he's after another 'loan.' And I used that word ironically, since we've never seen a dime back."

"No," Rachel replies blankly, holding Aaron's hat. "He's not *after* anything."

"Okay, sorry." An unapologetic apology. "Don't mean to sound insulting. It's just that *usually*? He is."

"Is what?"

"After something."

"He's not."

"Okay," Aaron says again as he shrugs on his coat. "Just don't get bamboozled is all I'm saying."

"How can I be, since I don't even know what this means?"

"It means hold on to your purse."

"I won't even pay for his coffee."

He accepts his hat from her. "Great, so now you're making me sound like a putz."

"*I* am?"

"Just try to keep it manageable is all. Pay for his coffee but make him leave the tip."

"Yes, sir," she says with a small salute.

"H'okay," Aaron sighs, slipping on his hat. The old snood, he calls it. "How 'bout I bring home Chinese for supper? Whattaya want, the lo mein?"

"Surprise me," says Rachel.

"If you wanna risk it." He's ready to go, ready to enter the world beyond the door, but then he wonders something as an aside. Something connected to the pesky problem of his wife's mental stability. "So you're not gonna lose track of time, right?"

"Lose track?"

"Aren't you supposed to see what's-his-name today?"

"Dr. Solomon. Not until three."

"Okay." He gives her a peck on the lips. "Just don't miss him again, please. We're spending a fortune on this genius."

"I won't miss him," she promises.

"I'm just sayin', is all." Another peck on the lips. "G'bye."

Leaving the apartment, Aaron's day doesn't get better. Rachel has closed the door behind him and is leaning into it as if she might need to barricade herself when she hears the easy, challenging voice of Aaron's cousin, Ezra Weinstock, coming up the stairs. The Fucknik. "So, shvesterkind!" Ezra calls to Cousin Aaron. "Off to another day schlepping hash? When are you gonna stop screwing around and *do* something with your life, boychik?" he wants to know.

"Can't say, Ez," replies Aaron. "When are you gonna learn to raise the seat on the toilet before taking a piss? Your wife keeps complaining to mine."

Ezra snorts a laugh. "All I'm saying is a grown man waiting tables?"

"I'm the *manager*, pal."

"Sure, the *manager*. Your mother brags all the time, I'm sure. He's the *manager*."

And now Rachel hears the barely restrained aggression squeeze Aaron's voice, the sure sign of an anger too complicated and dense to be contained by hallway sparring. "So who are *you*? Mr. Big Shot Public Defender, playing footsie with pimps and hopheads all day. I bet all those goyim at the courthouse think you're one superior Jew boy, pal."

She can hear Aaron pounding down the stairs after this, leaving Ezra shouting after him with snide passion. "Right! Big man! You think *you* know what it means to be a *Jew*? Well, I got news, bubbee. What you *don't* know would fill a goddamned ocean!"

Rachel leans into the door till there's silence in the stairwell. Kibbitz at the window has changed his mind, the silly beast, and now is pawing on the glass for entry.

She goes to the window and shoves up the sash, allowing him to hop down to the floor. But the morning air causes a cool shiver to creep through her skin. She shuts the glass and scoops the cat up in her arms, hugging the warmth of this furry feline body against her.

The day had dawned a stony gray on the morning that Aaron had arrived to rescue her from Bellevue. His face was bleached by shock, but it was evident from the deep shame coloring his eyes that it was he himself who felt in need of rescue. It was he who was the suffering one here. Salvaging his wife from the loony bin? More than he had bargained for, was it? God forbid his mother ever hears. All that was unspooling across his face like the headline ticker in Times Square.

There's an old-fashioned claw-foot bathtub in their apartment, with a showerhead installed on a tall pipe and a ring around the top from which a plastic shower curtain droops. Sometimes the water goes cold in the pipes by this point in the morning, but she's lucky that today it's still gushing hot, as hot as Rachel can stand. It brings the blood to her skin. She stands under the showerhead, eyes closed, allowing the steamy water to pour over her.

She and Feter had been permitted to come ashore in America by the Displaced Persons Act of 1948, slipping into the country during a narrow spasm of charity on the part of the American Congress as the mass graves of Europe settled into the earth. Their entry was sponsored by members of a Jewish labor board who also helped them get work. She found a spot at a five-and-dime, and Feter Fritz took a job as a janitor in an office building and sometimes ran the elevator. During the day, he worked with a mop and broom, but in the evenings, he re-created a version of his old self, changing into his baggy second-hand suit and sitting with an espresso. He would give his niece a dime and instruct her to walk down to Michnik Brothers Tobacconist on

Rivington Street to buy a certain brand of sickly sweet cigars because they were sold two for a nickel. In shlekhte tsaytn, iz a peni oykh gelt, Feter would say. In bad times, even a penny is money. This when they were housed in the Hebrew Immigrant Aid Society's refugee house on Lafayette Street, along with a ragged collection of other Jews who had managed to escape the death's-head battalions and the crematorium chimneys.

But even with jobs, their incomes were meager. H.I.A.S. provided a small monthly stipend per head, but generally not much money was to be had. So Feter would attempt to ration his cigar supply, smoking judiciously. Always one cigar with his morning coffee, one after his midday meal of boiled mushrooms on toast, and one every evening after his usual bowl of kasha with a side of chopped eggs and onions. Or maybe the fried cheese kreplach with cream *if* he could manage a two-dollar supper at Ratner's and still afford his niece's lettuce and tomato sandwich for thirty-five cents.

But mostly the food was irrelevant to him. Feter Fritz had been taught to eat to survive by Auschwitz, which meant to eat without joy. The *cigar*, however, was what he savored. The ritual. The strike of the match, the whisper of flame. The rhythmic pace of puffing that kindled the tip into a glowing ruby. The long, low hush of smoke. It was during those few precious moments relishing his cigar that he would return to the man that Rachel had known as a child. The confident, charming, canny Feter Fritz, not the displaced person. Yet it was like watching a ghost inhabit a living body, a dybbuk of hubris that would possess him and then slowly dissipate with the smoke.

Out of the heat of the shower, Rachel's hair is dripping. Chilly air has slipped under the bathroom door as she towels herself down. Because she is always cold, she has bought a heater. An EverHot Ray-Vector space heater that's stationed under the bathroom sink. The heating elements glow in red-gold coils when she switches it on. The wave of heat calms her as she dresses in her slip, the rayon clinging to her skin. She wipes the steamy fog from the medicine cabinet mirror with her palm, gazing into her own reflection. Then she pulls open the mirror that squeaks on rusty hinges.

The shelves of the medicine cabinet are crowded with a half-used tube of Brylcreem, a little dab'll do ya, a packet of razor blades, an aerosol can of Old Spice Smooth Shave, and a bottle of Kings Men aftershave. A Vaseline jar, a pocket tin of Anacin tablets, ten cents on special at Block Drug Store, a roughly squeezed tube of Preparation H hemorrhoid salve, because Aaron has problems with that and often needs more than a little dab. She has to rearrange everything to find the small bottle of pills prescribed by her shrink as a minor tranquilizer. Miltown it is called.

Her mother had sometimes dosed herself with an extraite de l'opium known as Laudanum de Rousseau, because a single teaspoon every three hours reduced the grief of menstrual cramps. It wasn't much of a secret. Women in Eema's circles carried on a love affair with laudanum. Eema decanted her elixir into a rose glass bottle with an elegant crystal stopper. But Miltown? Not so much elegant as commercially manufactured. It's a sedative with an advertising profile.

In the newspaper ads, wives and mothers on Miltown get their husbands off to work and their children off to school calmly and without fuss. Picking up a prescription for Miltown, the ads assured her, is as common and wholesome as picking up a quart of milk from the grocery. Two tablets, four hundred milligrams each, twice a day, morning and night. Rachel unscrews the cap from the bottle and swallows her dosage as fortification against her meeting with Feter Fritz. By the time she boards the Eighth Avenue IND at West 22nd, she should be feeling as relaxed as a cat poised on a sunny windowsill.

2.

Promise Me She Is Dead

AT THE END OF THE WAR, IT HAD BEEN NEARLY IMPOSSIBLE FOR young Rashka Morgenstern to prove that she was actually Jewish. A problem because by the time she had arrived at the gates of the displaced persons camp in the American zone, it had been designated *only for Jews*. So what was she to do? She was an adolescent girl on her own. She had no tattoo on her arm from a concentration camp. No documents stamped with a purple J. Her papers, in fact, said she was an Aryan! But then a young American officer with a fuzzy moustache and a pistol holstered at his hip asked her a question.

Azoy, iunge dame, aoyb ir zent take a eydish, kenen ir redn mit mir in eydish?

Tears flooded to her eyes. She cried with unadulterated joy as she answered him. Ya! Yo, ikh kenen redn mit ir! Ikh ken redn mit dir!

Yiddish had saved her.

It was her heritage. Not the holy tongue but the mother tongue. The language of Eema's parents, Chaim and Freidka Landau, living in the sunny, clement city of Tarnów under the Hapsburg dynasty. They were religious people, Chaim and Freidka. Observant Jews, pillars of the synagogue, but also deep thinkers. And though she never knew them while they lived, this is the way they were always described by both mother and uncle to little Rashka Morgenstern growing up in Berlin. Zey zenen tif tingkerz, deyn zeyde-bobe. Intellectual people. Teachers. Her grandfather taught languages—German, French, also

Hebrew—in a local school, and her grandmother taught piano from
the parlor of a comfortably appointed house on Lwowska Street.

When they left Tarnów for Berlin, so that Chaim could fill an
important teaching position at the Jüdische Mädchenschule, maybe
they spoke German in the streets, the classrooms, the shops and public
spaces. The language of assimilation. But if they retained a comfortable dialect of Yiddish in their own home, who would care? And if
they continued in Yiddish after their daughter, Lavinia, and their son,
Fredrich, were born, who could criticize? Yiddish was the language of
the heart. So when the time came that Eema had her *own* daughter,
was it utterly unthinkable that she share the language mother to child,
just as her mother and her mother before her had done? Just as she
shared the very essence of Jewish blood mother to child since Sarah,
wife of Abraham? Besides, with this child, it was obvious. This was a
daughter with a God-given talent for languages. "If she can hear it, she
can speak it," her eema would say of Rashka. "Just like her grandfather
of blessed memory. If she can see it, she can read it. If she can read it,
she can write it."

Even so, because Rashka grew up in Berlin-Wilmersdorf, that staid
dominion of bourgeois Jewish fortunes, their Yiddish remained concealed as the language of hearth and home.

German only in society! Um Gottes willen! Don't embarrass yourself with Yiddish in front of other Jews. What do you think, this is the
Ukraine?

So it was for her a secret language that little Rashka Morgenstern
spoke with Eema and Feter Fritz alone. Now, however? In the city of
New York? The tribes speak aloud. One is likely to hear all variants and
varieties of Yiddish anywhere and everywhere, at least on the Lower
East Side. Even today on certain street corners, between Canal and
Houston, in certain coffeehouses and meeting spots, outside certain
delicatessens, it is the language of public conversation, for heaven's sake.

The Orchard Café and Dairy Restaurant is one such certain place where Yiddish is king. A Lower East Side institution. It is the domain of the "alter kockers" as Aaron calls these weathered old men. White hair, silver hair, no hair left at all. Many of them men who have transplanted their bodies but not their souls from the old country. They are roosting here on the Lower East Side, bent, round-shouldered, over their chessboards, their backgammon games, slapping down cards and poking pegs into their cribbage boards. They smoke and drink coffee together and deliberate. The State of Israel, the state of Zionism, the state of Jewish socialism, all topics of debate and examination. And they argue. They argue as if they are deciding an ancient biblical grudge over the general decline of everything. Especially literature! Especially art! Especially the Yiddish theater ! Especially the quality of the potato knish now that you can buy it frozen in the grocery like those ummeglich little pizza pies!

Entering the revolving door, Rachel inhales the aroma of stewed cabbage, chopped liver, and boiled kreplach floating in chicken stock. The Miltown had been doing its work. Crossing Orchard Street, she'd felt confident that she could tolerate the stress of sussing out her uncle's ulterior motives. Even on the train, she'd been paging through the catalog of possibilities in her head. Another gambling debt to a bookie has caught him short? ("These are violent men, Ruchel.") Or does he need to parade her as his daughter again? ("Only for an hour to convince the bureaucracy. You'll fill in a few forms and put up a small fee. It's nothing.") Or will it be another *investment*. ("Really, it's an opportunity for *you*, Rashka, as much as me. And for only a few dollars.") She only hopes that whatever it is, she can keep her lies to Aaron about it to a minimum. In preparation, she's already sketched out a lie or two in her head. ("It was nothing. He needed a few dollars for a doctor's appointment. His anemia, you know." Or "He was hoping to make a small donation to the Jewish Immigrant Fund. In repayment for what they did for us.")

But when she spots her uncle seated in the corner, she feels her heart drop, and no dosage of Miltown can deter her grief. In the Berlin of decades past, his hubris had made him a charming rogue of the art world, sleek, well-barbered, and immaculately tailored, the king of every room he entered. A man who could reserve the best tables in restaurants from Kempinski's in the Kurfürstendamm to the Adlon at the Pariser Platz. Now the vacuum left by the disappearance of the Old World has made him a caricature. A shmittshik! Now he is, at best, a charming charity case. At worst? An opnarer. A shifty operator, with the hunger of an alley cur and the cunning of a wounded fox.

He sits, smoking in his chair at the Orchard Café, his face guarded by a blank scowl. He is thin and bony. His clothes lend him the look of a scarecrow. His hair, once lush, dark, and pomaded, is brittle and shot through with streaks of white, and his jaw is carelessly shaven. Still, the moment he spots Rachel, the dybbuk of his past returns, animating Feter's limbs and his character. He leaps to his feet, and his eyes ignite with a bright reflection of the old days when he treated his little niece to a plate of nussecken at Karl Kutschera's Konditorei Wien under a grand, lead-crystal chandelier.

"Rokhl, my treasure," he calls her, and in that instant, she fights the urge to flee, but her mother appears just long enough to scold her for her fears.

Whatever he's up to, Rokhl, your feter is still your family, she reminds. *Your blood.*

Rachel says nothing. She sometimes finds him at his cribbage board, ready to double skunk all comers, but today he occupies his Stammtisch, back against the mural of the old Hester Street Market, alone with his coffee cup and the last bite of an egg cookie tucked into the saucer.

It was a miracle that they were reunited after the war, Feter and Rachel. For months, she had assumed that her uncle was farshtorbn. Mausetot zu sein. It was no secret that transport to the east meant death. But her D.P. camp was the largest in the American zone, and the Jewish population was swelling. Feter was thin as smoke, reading the camp newspaper printed in Yiddish when she found him. She had not shed a tear in so long. Not even when Eema was taken from her. Her tears had simply evaporated, but suddenly, at the sight of his emaciated face, tears surged from her like an ocean. It is said that believing that miracles occur is foolishness, but believing that miracles are not possible is blasphemy.

Feter Fritz is clasping her hands warmly and conducting her through the crowded room toward an empty chair, asking, "Are you hungry? No? Can I offer you a coffee? A deviled egg with paprika. No? Please, there must be *something*," he insists.

"No," she tells him. "No, nothing, Feter. Nothing, thank you." She doesn't want him spending a nickel on her, because how many nickels can he have? His fingernails are dirty, which makes Rachel sad. Her uncle was once immaculate in his grooming. But there is a fragility about him now. At home, she scrimps with her housekeeping money so she can slip him a few dollars when required. She buys her husband margarine at the store instead of butter. Instant coffee over ground. She defends her uncle against Aaron's suspicions and even against her own. All this she does in support of his pretenses, even though this morning he seems bent on proving that his poverty, his feeble impact on the world, has reduced his once-superior instincts for art and business to a shady caricature. A man with a head full of grimy intrigues and a shoebox of crumpled dollars.

Silverware clinks, and conversations rumble about them. An ancient waiter has appeared tableside. Gray hair thinning, features broadening with age, earlobes elongating. "So, for the gentleman. You want the lentil and bean soup," he says to Feter Fritz, not a question.

"Thank you, Alf. You always know."

Turning to Rachel. "And the little missus? A blintz."

"No. Thank you, Mr. Fishman, nothing."

The old schlepper can't credit this. In Yiddish, he asks her, "Nit afilu a moyl?" Not even a mouthful?

"Just a tea," says Rachel.

"She's artistic, Alfie," her uncle explains.

"So I know. But even Rembrandt ate a bagel, didn't he?" A fatalistic shrug. "Okay. One bowl of soup, one cup of tea. I'll see what I can coax from the kitchen."

Rachel breathes inwardly. Silently. The Miltown is doing its work. She is a candle flame balanced on the tip of a wick. "So, Feter," she begins. "Let's not beat about the bush, the two of us. Tell me, please. What is the reason you've asked me here?"

"The reason? Well, the reason is that you're my *family*, Rashka. Is that so hard to accept, I wonder? An uncle likes to *see* his niece on occasion."

"And so you *see* me, Feter," she says. "Here I am. Now what is the *other* reason?" she asks, though doesn't she already *know*? Moolah, bubala! Kies und Shotter! The old Berliner bywords: Ohne Moos, nix los! Without moss, nothing happens!

"Should I be stung by your tone, Rokhl?" her feter wonders with a careful smile. "Since when is my niece so cynical?"

A small shrug in reply. "You called me? I came."

"*Fine*," he says flatly, down to business. "I don't want to say a big word," the man confides with intimate restraint. "But I *believe*, Rashka," he tells her. "I *believe* that I have discovered one of your mother's lost masterpieces."

Rachel feels herself grow cold. Her fingers go numb as she gazes back at her uncle's face. She knows he is searching for some reaction. Perhaps he is hoping for even a small surge of surprise—or, dare it be imagined, a spark of *joy*. But this blunt dumbness that has struck her is all she can offer, forcing her uncle to ask the question directly. "Do you know what that will *mean*, Rokhl?"

"Mean?" Rachel repeats. Does it mean that there is some proof remaining of her eema's brilliance? Does it mean that her eema's reputation will be resurrected from the footnotes of art history texts? Does it mean that a part of Eema has survived beyond the quarrelsome specter that Rachel raises from the ashes? But all Feter's shrunken perspective and empty pockets can permit him to whisper is "It could be worth a tidy *fortune*."

"Which one *is it*?" This is really the only question that's important to her. Which painting has survived? Her mind races through an inventory of possibilities. The unfinished portrait of Rathenau interrupted by his assassins? The portrait of Harry von Kessler, le célèbre comte libéral, holding his dachshund on his lap? The bespectacled impressionist Ernst Oppler, painted the year before his death? Or could it be the actress Brigette Helm, armored from the neck down in her costume as the Maschinenmensch in *Metropolis*?

"You must *tell me*, Feter." She removes a cigarette from the packet of Camels from her coat. She often carries things like men do, in her pockets, but she must open her bag to find matches. "You need to tell me *which*," she insists, searching anxiously, her Miltown calm shredded and the cigarette dangling from her lips.

Feter Fritz, however, is circumspect. He seizes the opportunity to prevaricate by igniting her cigarette with the snap of a lighter that features a Pepsi-Cola bottle cap, part of the collection of accoutrements that underpin his frayed elegance. "Let's say for now," he suggests, "that all I can tell you is…it's one of her major works."

"So I will recognize it?"

"Oh, yes." He nods with smug certainty. "Oh, yes, you will quite definitely recognize it, tohkter," he tells her, adopting that oh-so-charming and yet quite irritating custom of old-world men, addressing young women as *daughter*. It's a term of "affection" but also intended to detract from Rachel's competence in this conversation by juvenilizing her. *All in good time, child*, it says. *It's a sticky matter for experts, not for les demoiselles*. For now, he's said all that he dares.

"So that is all I'm permitted to know?" she asks with a frown.

Well. Her uncle expels smoke with manly dignity. Perhaps there *is* one more thing he admits he should mention. And that's when it comes. The meat of the matter. "All I need is fifty," Feter informs her.

"Fifty?"

"Dollars, Rashka," her uncle clarifies gently, as if Rachel may be sweetly dense. And then to add a splatter of grease to the skillet, he declares that "the fool in possession has not a whiff." A shmegegi is how he describes this man. "He thinks the value is in the *frame*, a gilded monstrosity," Feter sneers cozily. "The poor shlub has no idea what he has."

"And who—" Rachel starts to press but silences herself when the ancient schlepper appears.

"One cup Visotskis Tey for the big eater," he announces dubiously as he delivers Rachel's tea on saucer. "Plus one bowl lentil bean for the regular. And don't worry," he adds, setting it down in front of Feter. "It's Wednesday. The cook never spits in the soup on Wednesday. It's bad luck."

Feter ejects an affected laugh at this, perfected over decades of charming waiters, hotel porters, and doormen. "Thank you, Alf. And my compliments to the chef, of course."

"Still nothing for the little missus?" the man inquires.

"Still nothing," Rachel tells him.

A shrug. If she says so. And he slumps away. Only then does Rachel bear down on her question. "And who *possesses* this masterpiece, Feter?" she pushes. "Who exactly?"

But once more, her uncle bats her question away. "A nobody," he declares. "A bedbug from a pawnshop. I could shout his name from a rooftop, and he'd still be anonymous."

"Is it the place on West Forty-Seventh Street? Where you lost your diamond stickpin?"

"Unimportant," he declares in between loud slurps of soup. His table manners disappeared at Auschwitz and never really returned. Rachel draws a breath deeply into her chest before releasing it. Her feter must sense a quickening resistance on her part, or at least a confusion of emotions, because he sets his spoon into the bowl and alters his tone sympathetically.

"I know I'm asking a great deal," he is willing to concede.

"Yes."

"Fifty dollars? It's a significant sum."

"Yes."

"Especially when money doesn't grow on trees," he agrees. "But, child. *Think* of it. A canvas painted by your mother's hand, *surviving*. A part of her legacy, undestroyed." And here he strategically allows his cuff line to expose the tip of the number tattooed onto his forearm. A reminder of his suffering that his niece was spared.

Rachel swallows a small rock. "Yes," she says, her eyes now gleaming with tears.

"You won't regret it, zeisele. Fifty dollars? In the long run, it will be nothing."

"But you must tell me, Feter," she insists, wiping her eyes. "You must tell me. Which one *is* it?" Vos moler iz ir geredt vegn? "Which one has survived?"

Suddenly, her feter looks hunted. A moment before, his expression was animated. His voice excited by desire and manipulation. But now his eyes darken, and she can read in them that he's calculating how to answer. How *not* to answer. So she is forced to read his mind. She knows he intends to keep her heartstrings thrumming. But he must be fearful too—what if he reveals too much? Will he frighten her off? *What if*, of all the paintings her eema ever produced, *what if* there is one so volatile in memory, so dangerous in its passion, that Rachel might bolt from her chair at the very mention of it and flee into the street? What if such a painting exists? And what if after all the decades, after all the blood and black smoke and burnt history, what if it has survived? Without realizing it, Rachel has clamped her hand over her own mouth as if to stop herself from uttering another word. She feels a breathtaking horror. An exhilarating, electrifying moment of panic.

Rachel's hand slips from her mouth to her throat. "It's *her*."

Her feter huffs out a breath to forestall a panic. "*Rashka*," he says.

But Rachel's eyes have gone oily black. "Tell me the *truth*, Feter. The painting. *It's her.*" Her breath shortens.

"She's *dead*, Rashka," Feter is compelled to remind her.

"That was never proven."

"*Yes*. It *was*. She committed suicide in Russian custody," her uncle insists. "Hanged herself in a Red Army cell. She can't hurt you any longer, Rashka. You must realize that."

Rashka is searching her bag and pulls out the bottle of Miltown.

"Now what's this?" A frown. "A potion pill? I thought you were over that, Ruchel."

"It's a *prescription*, Feter," Rachel answers firmly, swallowing a capsule dry. "From my doctor." She is suddenly sick of Feter Fritz. Sick of his opinions from the old country. Sick of his paternal posing and the devious nature of his affection. "I don't need your criticism."

"Rokhl," he says, speaking her name defensively.

"*Promise me* she is dead, Feter," she demands, her eyes swelling with tears. "*Promise me.*"

"Oh, my *child*." Feter sounds pained but also alarmed.

"Even if it's a lie, promise me," she begs. "Promise me she's *dead*."

"I promise you, Rokhl," her uncle swears, "that she can't hurt you any longer. *This* I can promise. Never again."

She is yanking a handkerchief from her coat pocket. Mopping herself up. "I'm sorry," she starts to repeat. "I'm sorry. I'm sorry."

"No. No apologies. No apologies," he tells her, his tone comforting but his expression distressed. "You should go home. You're overwrought. I'm sure it's these pills. Doctor and pills—they put a person on edge." He comforts her in an overbearing manner, makes excuses for her teary eruption, though at the same time, he is preparing to make his escape. A crying woman in a public place—vos farlegnheyt!

Rachel glares blankly at him. She feels shame like she feels anger—deep down in the middle of her heart.

"Perhaps your old uncle should be going in any case," Feter declares as he stands, abandoning his bowl of lentil bean. Setting his old roll-brim at its customary angle on his head, he slides his tweedy coat over his shoulders. "Consider my request, Rashka," he offers softly. "For what does money matter, compared to the chance to restore your mother's name to its proper standing? Imagine that, Rashka, within your grasp." And with that, Feter Fritz is sailing toward the door and the gritty traffic of East Broadway, leaving his niece with the bill.

3.

God Laughs

A PERSON PLANS AND GOD LAUGHS. THIS IS WHAT'S SAID. RACHEL is standing in a weak drizzle outside a shop window on 47th Street, her head covered by a rain scarf. The grimy glass is dotted with the same sprinkle of raindrops that she blinks away from her eyelashes. A display of once-coveted objects fills the window, objects traded for cash loans, now ticketed with price tags. Over the door, a sign features a troika of golden balls hanging from a bar. The ancient symbol of the pawnbroker.

A bell jangles as she pushes into the shop. The glassed-in counters are filled with more of the hocked treasures never collected: watches, rings, necklaces, silver plate, precious brooches, all the sad glitter. The rest of the shop resembles a cluttered attic filled with items slowly devolving into junk. Appliances, a dress dummy, musical instruments hung from nails, cameras, vacuum cleaners, a dragoon's saber, ugly prints in ugly frames, a stuffed bear's head mounted on the wall. The bear growls glass-eyed at eternity.

A man with a cigarette in his mouth appears, squinting one-eyed through the smoke. He wonders what he can do for her in a slack-jawed manner. His hair is in need of a trim or at least a shampoo. His chin is pimply. He's tall and slouches and wears a brown pullover, frayed at the cuffs, and a closed-collar shirt. This must be the bedbug. The anonymous little man of Feter's description.

"I'm looking for a painting," she tells him.

He sniffs, removes the cigarette from his lips, and taps ash into a dirty enamel ashtray. "Yeah? Okay. Paintings I've got. What're you looking for? Something for what? Like over the sofa? Over the mantel?"

Rachel swallows. She brushes her rain-damp hair away from her forehead. She looks up at the bear. "Is that real?"

"Oh, you mean Smokey Bear up there?" The bedbug smiles. "Yeah, he's real. Shot him myself when he tried to kick my campfire out," he offers. Rachel looks back at him without comprehension.

"It's a particular painting," she reveals. "A painting of a woman."

"Oh, so it's something you know we've *got*. Why didn't ya say so?" he asks. Rachel licks her lips. She finds it hard to describe, she tells him. But what she doesn't tell him is that she finds it hard to describe because finding it terrifies her. That it could have *survived*, indestructible. That it could have followed her *here* to America.

"It's a painting of a woman," she repeats. "A painting of a *girl*. She was only a girl back then. A teenager. Painted all in monochrome. All in red."

Oh, and *now* the bedbug *gets* it. "Ah, *red*. Sure! You mean the *nudie*," he announces with a touch of emphasis that is both lecherous and disdainful. "It's in the back," he tells her, parking his cigarette in the ashtray. "But I gotta warn you, sweetheart," he prepares her. "It ain't exactly cheap." Disappearing through a door marked PRIVATE, he leaves it standing open so he can still talk. "And I should also mention? I've already got an interested buyer on the hook for it. But here we go. Let's give it a look, because why not?"

Rachel feels a wave of panic strong enough to pull her under. She's not ready. Not ready to see that face again. Not in her mother's painting. A voice emerges from the past inside her head. A woman's voice. A purring, menacing voice:

Wo ist dein Stern, Liebchen?

Where is your star, little darling?

Rushing toward the door, Rachel pushes it open as the bell jangles and the damp air strikes her face. But she is stopped by the figure of her mother, blocking her exit, naked, a victim of the Konzentrationslager, her hair nothing but a cropped scrub of gray, her yellowed, pockmarked skin gloved tightly over her skeleton, and her eyes oily with death.

"Hey, where you goin'?" the bedbug wants to know. "You wanna see this thing or not?"

She stares starkly into the pit of her mother's gaze, then turns swiftly, eyes wet with fear. "I'll see it," she says. Rachel steps back into the shop, her breath a slow bellows in her chest. She approaches the counter with the reluctance of the condemned.

Her mother always favored large canvases. They made her feel at ease with her subject and with herself. Herr Lemberg, the Galician Jew who constructed her frames, also stretched her canvases, always according to la standard française for sizing. Eema insisted that painting on anything smaller than une toile de quarante gave her hand cramps.

The canvas that faces Rachel now is trapped in an ugly gilded salon frame. But it must be une toile de cinquante. A canvas of fifty. Converting to American measurement? An approximation would be called three feet by four feet, standing taller than little Rashka stood when it was first painted.

She hasn't set eyes upon this painting in nearly twenty years, but she remembers as vividly as she would remember a lightning strike.

Even as a child, she liked to watch her mother at work in her studio. Every canvas began simply with the application of an imprimatur of Dammar varnish and turpentine. Then a dry-brush underpainting of umber followed by what was then called la couche morte. The Dead Layer. An underpainting of grays. Once applied, the hidden palette of the work would lift the colors of her brushwork into the heavenly realms of translucence.

The figure before her throbs off the canvas.

A sensual inferno of red pigments. It both repulses Rachel and draws her in. The long, willowy body. The beatific face with the untamed eyes of a leopard. Persephone erupting from the Underworld. La muse du rouge. She glares at it as if staring straight into a furnace.

"So for a lousy fifty bucks, I wrap it up," the bedbug informs her. "And this little gem is all yours, hon. I'm sure it'll kill over your sofa."

Rachel blinks. Her eyes shoot to this skinny specimen with his buggy eyes.

He presses. "So what'll it be?"

Rachel's head is a tangle. She is desperate to flee, desperate to return to a world where her mother's work has been completely incinerated by the past. But knowing this piece has survived…this terrifying canvas. How will she live now without it?

"Fifty dollars," she repeats blankly back to the man. She has, perhaps, a dollar in her billfold, plus a quarter in her change purse and a couple of vending machine tokens. Fifty dollars, when they pay eighty-nine dollars a month for their apartment? How can she possibly lay hands on such a sum? She could try to what? Raid Aaron's wallet at night after he undresses, even though she knows he doesn't carry more than cab fare.

She could write a check. She thinks there's some money in their checking account, because Aaron was paid last Friday, but that would leave them too broke to cover their rent and monthly bills. The only possibility that remains is the twenty dollars her husband has stashed in his copy of the *Merriam-Webster Dictionary*. Only for emergencies. "Rainy-day cash" he calls it. Well, it is a day, and it is raining.

"Will you take less?" she probes.

The bedbug looks confused by the word. "Less?"

"I can give you twenty dollars. In cash."

"First off," he tells her, "I *only deal in cash* when I'm selling to women. Even the pretty ones, sorry to say. I've been screwed too many times by husbands canceling their wives' checks. And second, why should I accept *less*? For chrissake, the frame alone is worth more than twenty."

"How about thirty? If I can get your thirty dollars *in your hand?*"

Retrieving his cigarette from the ashtray, he spills ash onto the counter. "Sorry, baby. Fifty shekels. That's it."

"*This is my mother's painting*," Rachel hears herself announce.

The bedbug looks at her like maybe she's just lost her head in front of him.

"My mother. She *painted* this," she declares with greater purpose. "You *see*—that's her signature. Right at the bottom." She points at a series of parallel strokes. "*LML*. That's how she signed everything! Lavinia Morgenstern-Landau. Morgenstern, her husband's name, and Landau, her father's name!" Is she shouting?

The bedbug still looks confused and maybe a bit perturbed. "Okay, okay, just calm down for a sec, will you? No need to have a cow, lady."

A cow? Rachel shakes her head. "What does that *mean*?"

"It means give me a minute to think for cryin' out loud," he tells her and then snorts out a breath. "Okay, so look," he says, setting the painting down on a chair below the glass-eyed bear head. "Let me get this straight. You say this thing was your *mother's*?"

"Yes."

"That *she* painted it?"

"She did."

"And you can prove it?"

"Prove it? Prove *what*? That I am my mother's daughter?"

"*Yeah*, I guess. Just *that*," the bedbug confirms. "That Lavinia whoever. Husband's name, father's name, whatever. That it's *true*, ya' know? Show me a driver's license or something."

Rachel licks her lips. "I don't drive. Anyway, my name is different now."

He grins, catching on to the con. "Oh, *uh-huh*. I get it. *Different*."

"I'm *married*. I'm a U.S. citizen now. My name is *different*."

"So no proof," the bedbug concludes.

No proof. How *can* she have proof? All the proof of her life before was either stolen or incinerated. How can she prove a thing? She tries to speak, but no words are forthcoming. Only tears. And maybe the tears are enough to wipe the smirk from the bedbug's punim. Finally, maybe, he finds a drop or two of pity in his heart.

"Okay, okay," he is repeating. "No need for the waterworks. I get it. Things get emotional," he decides. "But you gotta understand, honey." And he says this almost pleadingly. "I'm running a business here."

Rachel sniffs, wipes her nose on her coat sleeve like a child. "What about forty?" she says and blinks. "What if I can get you forty dollars…"

"Forty?" The bedbug speaks the word like it pains him. But then he puffs out a breath, deflating. "H'okay. If you get me forty—*in cash*. Then I'll cut you some slack. *All right?*"

Rachel swallows. Sniffs again, tries to force out a small smile of gratitude. "All right," she agrees.

"But you better not take your time about it. Like I said, I got another buyer for this item. Farshteyn? I'd like to sell it to *you* over him, but if he walks in here with a fuftsik in his hand before you get back?" The bedbug shrugs. "Like I said. I'm running a business."

This time when the bell jangles in honor of her exit, the rain has quit and a pale sun peeks out from the clouds. Her belly is tight. She can understand her uncle Fritz's frustration. His desire foiled by money or the lack thereof. On the 42nd Street Shuttle, she makes her calculations. And good news, she finds that she has a five-dollar bill in her billfold! Five dollars! A New York miracle! Add that to the rainy-day twenty, and she's only fifteen dollars short. But fifteen dollars? That's nearly a week's worth of groceries. She could write a check at the bank and hope for another miracle to cover their bills. Or simply let them turn off the electricity for a month. Would that be so bad?

The D.P.W. is doing some kind of work on Delancey Street. A man with a jackhammer is pulverizing the pavement. It's deafening. Obliterating. Rachel can't think; she can only endure as the chatter of the pneumatic hammer pounds inside her skull. Down in the subway, the platform is sparsely populated. She sits alone on a bench, smoking, waiting on the Sixth Avenue Express. Her guilt is a secret weight she carries. She accrues it daily simply by breathing, because she will never be absolved of her crime. The crime committed by a Little Goat in a little café up the Friedrichstrasse.

⌐•=

January 1944, the fifth year of the war. The Tommies have attacked the so-called Gustav Line in Italy. The Red Army has breached the border of Poland, and it's only a matter of time before American and British forces invade the French coastline. The military situation is slowly disintegrating. Germany is losing the war to the Allies. But the war against the Jews? That war is still pursued with fervor. The rumor mills agree: transports to the east continue on schedule from Berlin's Grunewald Station.

The windows of the Café Bollenmüller are frosted over. The noise of the lunchtime service fills the air as steam rises from pots of coffee brewed from ground acorns. An accordionist plays a Berliner favorite, "Du, du, liegst mir im Herzen." A din of conversation from the crowd rises from the tables, but there is a certain tension in the room. Sharing the table with Rashka, Eema looks as exhausted and threadbare as everybody else but also hunted. And she *is* hunted in a literal sense. Like an animal set loose in the brush and pursued by hounds.

Rashka is sixteen now. She has grown into a thin adolescent, molded by the crushing routine of everyday terror. A terror that's only been amplified since Eema unstitched the stars from their clothing—that yellow, six-pointed Judenstern branding them as enemies of German blood. Eema always regarded the star as a badge of shame, an indignity, and shedding it, she assured Rashka, was a kind of victory. But Rashka is not so sure. Now that it is gone from their clothing, she feels naked. The Shield of David has been removed and she is unprotected, no longer under the pale of regulations. A Jew discovered without a star, after all, is a Jew on the road to a concentration camp.

Today they have come to the café so that Eema can negotiate some rationing coupons from a black marketeer known as "Dickes Dora." Fat Dora, a Berliner's joke, because the woman's thin as a shadow. They are here to spend money they can't afford to lose. When Fat Dora arrives, Eema girds herself for action. "Stay here, and don't *move*," she instructs her daughter. "*Understand?*" But when Rashka doesn't answer, her mother doesn't wait and leaves the girl sitting by herself.

From across the room, a redheaded woman is gazing at her. Why? Rashka does not know. She cannot guess, but she gazes back. A lit cigarette stained with lip rouge touches bright-red lips. She is quite handsomely dressed, this woman, not in the normal wartime drudgery but in real glamour rags. A sable-trimmed coat. A smart crimson day suit and a matching lady's Alpiner with a swooping brim. The black lace gloves are a most elegant touch, exquisitely delicate. Rashka knows she will never obtain such heights of beauty. That the best she will ever manage is a certain dark, peasant comeliness due her from the Landau side of the family. Pretty, maybe, with deep eyes, but she'll never be so exquisite as the redheaded Bathsheba who is now crossing the café and seating herself at Rashka's table with a scrape of a chair.

"Hallöchen, Liebling," the woman says with the smile of a hungry cat. "Did your mummy leave you all alone?"

A sharp jolt. Only now at this intimate degree of proximity does Rashka feel a burn of confusion as she recognizes the beautiful face. La muse du rouge, her eema once called her. Though she's famous now by another name given her by the Jews whom she hunts. Der Rote Engel she is called.

The Red Angel.

4.

The Episode

HER SHRINK'S OFFICE IS ON THE UPPER EAST SIDE JUST PAST THE planned site for the new Guggenheim Museum. The entrance is down a short flight of granite steps. An elegantly varnished door to a cellar office in a soapstone apartment house. A discreet brass plaque is fixed to the door. DAVID A. SOLOMON, MD, PsyD. Inside, the framed diplomas on his office wall confirm his degrees from Columbia and Harvard School of Medicine, a rare Ivy League accomplishment for a Jew of his generation. Also, a framed wartime certificate commissions "Lt. Col. David Albert Solomon" as a "Psychiatric Consultant of the First Service Command."

He is supposed to be part of the solution, Dr. Solomon. The blinds are drawn, filtering light. It's a well-appointed space. Built-in shelves crowded with books. Dr. Solomon is a balding, straight-backed mensch with a gentlemanly beard fringing his jawline. He sits with a notepad on his knee, a quiet, thoughtful presence, yet he wields a probing gaze. Always trying to exploit the cracks in her story. Always trying to bore into the holes in her heart. He has good eyes, though, behind those horn-rims. She does not dislike him, but of course neither does she trust him.

He maintains a calm posture. Nothing is ever rushed. Even his diagnosis sounds like a suggestion. Stress response syndrome. It's a new category usually reserved for men mustered out of the army, where it was called *battle fatigue* and *shell shock*. But stress response syndrome? That doesn't sound too terrible. "People have stress, and they *respond* to it" is what her husband has decided. "Who doesn't?" he'd added. "You put a burger on a burner? It cooks. Turn up the heat? It burns." She knows that this is how Aaron has learned to accept his bad luck at marrying a poor meshugana refugee from Berlin-Wilmersdorf instead of the good Jewish girl from Flatbush that his mother had certainly envisioned for him.

After the Episode at the department store, her confinement to the madhouse is a blur of unreality. A harrowing remembrance of being locked up between gray walls facing a gray steel door. Later she would be informed that it was for her own protection, that she had been tied into a straitjacket. The suffocating nature of such helplessness, of such intimate imprisonment, is what pains her most. Sleeves fastened behind her back, her arms wrapped tightly around her body without her consent. The claustrophobia of a cocoon.

The blinds are drawn as they are always drawn in the doctor's office. He fills the opposing leather club chair, but silence stands between them.

"So you have nothing to say today," Dr. Solomon deduces.

The painting, she thinks. She sees it in her mind's eye. The flush crimsons and scarlets of her mother's palette. The luminous female gaze from the canvas, drilling into her. "Must I," she wonders aloud, "*always* have something to say?"

"No. Not always." And then he asks, "Did something happen?"

"Such as what something?"

"Something that has upset you?"

In her mind, she hears the whisper. *Wo ist dein Stern, Liebchen?*

Rachel replies to the doctor, "Not a thing."

Dr. Solomon removes his horn-rims and must rub his eyes as if rubbing away her obfuscation. "Rachel," he says. He seldom speaks her name with such weight. "It seems to me that something has changed."

"Really? Changed how?"

"In our discussions. Since I suggested that you start painting again, you've become more…" What's the word he's going to choose? "Resistant," he tells her.

"No, Dr. Solomon. You're wrong," she says.

"Am I?" He slips his glasses back into place. "Still. I can't but feel that there is something you're avoiding. Something you're denying, even to yourself."

"That I'm crazy?"

"No. Sometimes I think you say things like that—use the word 'crazy'—not as a provocation but more as a diversion." And then he says, "There was a Dutch psychiatrist, after the war, named Eliazar de Wind. He'd been sent to a concentration camp by the Nazis, but he was one of the few who lived to be liberated. As a result of his experiences, he developed a theory that he called 'KZ syndrome,' describing the pathological aftereffects that often afflict those who endure such trauma."

"But I wasn't *in* a concentration camp, Doctor," Rachel is quick to point out. "That was my mother. That was my uncle."

"Regardless, I think my point applies. Think of your scrapbook of air disasters, Rachel. Think of your elevated levels of anxiety and depression. Your chronic nightmares. Your mood swings and loss of motivation. Even your breakdown at the department store. All these indicators suggest that you are suffering from what might be termed 'the guilt of the survivors.' Think of all those who died at the hands of the Nazis. Millions that we know of. Yet you did not. Why?"

For an instant, Rachel thinks he might be about to answer that question. *Why?* For an instant, Rachel believes he might be about to grant her some kind of absolution. Some psychological escape mechanism that will wipe the slate clean for her. But it turns out that all he has is the question itself. Why? A question to which she already knows the answer. Why? She survived because of her crime. The crime that saved her life.

No seats. Rachel is hanging again from a strap in the subway, her mind a jumble. Returning home, she is pursued by memories. Memories of

Berlin. Memories of war. The noise of the lunchtime service at the Café Bollenmüller off the Friedrich. The accordion player, squeezing out "Du, du, liegst mir im Herzen." Sitting with her mother, hoping for a roll and a cup of hot milk. The café is an enticement for Jews in hiding. U-boats they are called. Submarine Jews on the run, who have submerged beneath the surface of the city in a bid to escape the transports east.

The Bollenmüller is a place they come to bargain for needed hiding places, black-market rationing coupons, falsified identity papers. All such items are on the menu here, in addition to ersatz coffee and pastries baked from potato dough. But the U-boats come also to escape the arduous life on the streets. To discreetly trade in gossip or simply settle quietly for a few precious moments and pretend. Pretend that they are still who they once were. Pretend that they can reinhabit their vanished lives just long enough to enjoy a fleeting respite from reality over a taste of Baumkuchen. But Eema is too anxious for that. And there is no money to waste on hot milk or a roll for her daughter.

Pulling into the 59th Street station, a seat opens up, and Rachel takes it. Beside her, a pair of well-dressed middle-aged women chat lightly. Their white-gloved hands grip the handles of their shopping bags, each decorated by a spray of Bonwit Teller violets. Rachel inhales a wisp of Essence of Lilac, one of the favorite house scents at the perfume counter. On the morning of the Episode, she had spritzed herself with the same scent at home, the bottle an anniversary gift from Aaron that she'd picked out for herself. But she had been a tad too exuberant with it, and she smelled it on herself all day. All day and then all night, locked up in the bin like a dangerous animal, stinking of sweat and Essence of Lilac.

Even after a year, Rachel can relive the trauma of the event at will. She can call every moment into a fever of the present tense.

On the morning of the Episode, she is looking into the mirror above her vanity and asks Aaron about a scarf. It is a zebra print, this scarf, like the one she has seen Audrey Hepburn wearing in *Vogue*, and she has it loosely wrapped around her neck. But maybe it is too much for the sales floor at Bonwit Teller? They are supposed to be stylishly dressed, but not so stylish that they detract from the merchandise. So she asks her husband: Is it too much? He looks at her, his eyebrows raised in appraisal as he buttons his shirt cuffs, but all he has to offer is, "I dunno, honey. It's a *scarf*. Looks fine to me."

"You are such a fat help," she declares crossly, whipping the scarf from her neck.

"A *big* help," he corrects.

"What?"

"I'm such a *big* help."

"*No*," she says. "You are *not*."

Riding the train into work, Rachel is still incensed that Aaron is so poorly equipped to live life with a woman. Displaying herself like a mannequin modeling the scarf, she had been willing to submit herself to his judgment, *and yet* he had carelessly shrugged her off. Simply tossed the opportunity into the trash like he was tossing the wadded remains of the mail into the wastebasket.

The front entrance of Bonwit Teller is a spacious, modern portico under a limestone deco facade that rises austerely twelve stories above the sidewalk. Flashing glass doors revolve like cylinders of light in the bright sunshine. But that's for customers. Employees enter through a featureless door on 56th Street. The corridor is vivid with the sterile glow from the overhead fluorescents.

Rachel waits with the women queuing for their turn to punch in, listening to the mechanical *ka-thunk* of the time-clock stamp repeating itself in an assembly-line rhythm. *Ka-thunk*, stop, *ka-thunk*, stop, *ka-thunk*.

From the Fifth Avenue entrance, the grand dames themselves arrive to cruise the richly carpeted interior boulevards of the store. These are not the wily shoppers come to wrangle tooth and nail over bargains in

Klein's on Union Square. These are the ladies who have come to rack up towering charges to their accounts at the gleaming glass carousels of first floor fine jewelry and the perfume counters under the luminosity of ornamental chandeliers. These are the ladies who have come to lunch on watercress sandwiches in the Caffe Orsini, second floor, sip coffee from Italian demi-cups as a pageant of shapely young models, their daughters' age, parade the best-selling creations of the Bonwit label for their perusal, fourth floor collections. These are the ladies who have come to consider their reflections in queenly mirrors, swathed in mink stoles and sable coats, second floor, West 57th Street wing.

On the sales floor, Rachel is covering for Suzy Quinlan—seventh floor, Miss Bonwit Jr.: junior dresses, junior sportswear, junior coats and accessories. Normally, Rachel works a different department: La Boutique, third floor bed and bath shop. But today, since they are so shorthanded with Gladys Mulberry down with a cold and Nancy Kirk having quit after her engagement, the floor walker, Mr. Bishop, has assigned Rachel to cover the section while Suzy catches a quick bite down in the store commissary. Rachel is busy refolding a white knit cardigan embroidered with pink and red roses. Such a sweet little sweater for a damsel in first bloom. Assez jolie. She feels the first pinch of heartbreak at this point yet ignores it.

When a customer appears, trailing a light mist of Yardley, she quickly summons her smile. The lady is obviously a regular by her air of imperial familiarity. She asks for Suzy by name but must settle for Rachel. She's a slim specimen creeping toward the autumn of her life, wearing an azure silk blazer with snow-white gloves. She's looking for a little something as a gift. Just a little something for "my *granddaughter*, aged twelve," the lady whispers, obviously unprepared for the news to leak that she could have reached such a grandmaternal age. She displays waxy bright lips that crinkle when she smiles. Hair expensively dyed, eyebrows erased and replaced by perfect penciled-in arches. Obviously, a woman denying her age.

Rachel maintains her smile for the lady as she has coached herself to do. Even if she's not on commission like the full-time staff, she has learned to take satisfaction in the act of the transaction. Providing for customers' desires permits her a feeling of utility that she seldom experiences otherwise. Certainly not when she opens her sketch pad or—it shouldn't happen!—she is confronted by a blank canvas from the rack at Lee's Art Shop.

So Rachel is happy to oblige, ready to suggest the freshly folded embroidered cardigan. An adorable choice, she calls it. Perfect for la jeune fille about to enter her première rougeur de féminité. The lady compliments her French. Votre français est très naturel, she tells Rachel. But the lady has a roving eye. Something else has caught her attention. "*Oh*, I like *this*," she declares softly with an elevated chin, as if announcing the news to herself alone. It's a beret. A simple thing. The lady has lifted it from the padded display stand and is modeling it for herself, boosting it aloft on her white-gloved fingertips. She coos appreciatively. "Just darling. She'll look si parisien, tu ne trouves pas? Tout à fait chérie!"

Yes, Rachel nods. Très charmante, such a thing. A burgundy beret. Eine burgunderrote Baskenmütze. Such a darling little thing. So stylish. So Parisian. And so vulnerable, a girl at that age. So very vulnerable to the world. So easily victimized. So easily extinguished.

Rachel doesn't really remember what happens beyond that moment, once the Episode begins. The darkness floods her consciousness and scalds her heart. And then she sees the face. The innocent caramel-brown eyes. The brunette braid and the burgundy beret. For so many years, she has kept the memory of this face submerged. Suppressed. Locked in an iron vault. Yet suddenly the past confronts her on the seventh floor of Bonwit Teller. The schoolgirl is there before her, conjured from the past, her velvety eyes staring out from death. Rachel feels the world turn on its ear. She hears the sound of shattering glass. Hears a scream that might be her own or might not be. Hears the lady shouting frantically. There's blood splattering and a trembling pain shooting through her hand. That's the last thing she remembers.

"Do you love your husbands, ladies?" This is the question posed by a sweetly smug voice on the radio. "If you do, then you should serve him only the finest of instant coffees, Imperial Blend. It's freeze-dried for a richer coffee taste!"

Gray light hangs outside the wrought-iron fire escape over West 22nd Street like dingy, overbleached sheets clothespinned to a line. In honor of the reappearance of her mother's work, Rachel has decided it's best to destroy her own. Eema had always talked about her daughter's God-given talent, but again and again, the real lesson to be learned was that there was only room for one superior artist in the space between them, and it was never going to be Rashka. So Rachel has just set her latest shmittshik afire, lighting it from the stove burner and washing the remains down the sink. It made her feel good to burn it. A satisfying pain to see her own face turned to char. Eingeäschert is the word in German. Reduced to ashes.

Now she lights a cigarette to mask the smell of the burned paper as she hears the sound of Aaron's key in the door.

"I got you the vegetable lo mein," he announces as he enters, crossing to the kitchen table with the paper sack smelling of hot fish oils. He is wearing his Brooks Brothers overcoat and a felt Alpiner with the silk headband and a tufted feather. A narrow maroon necktie divides the crisp white of his shirt, and he's smoking a cigarette. But his face is blotchy and tired. The end of the day, dealing with the Wednesday matinee crowd, dealing with Leo's craziness, dealing with the help. The grindstone. The salt mines. The calamity before curtain time. That's his joke. "You said to surprise you, right? So surprise." His voice is drained. He removes his cigarette from his lips as he bends down to kiss her.

"Yuck," she says.

"Yuck to the kiss or yuck to the lo mein?"

"The kiss. My husband tastes like an ashtray."

"What a coincidence," he says, screwing out his Lucky in the ashtray. "So does my wife." He sets the paper sack on the kitchen table and starts to unload it. "Do we need plates?" he wonders. Sniffs at one of the cartons.

"*Yes.*" Rachel has opened the cabinet in the kitchen galley that stores plates and cups. "I hate eating from the containers. They drip." She clunks the plates down on the table.

Aaron's mother gave them this china as a wedding present. Eight place settings of Syracuse China dinnerware, the Edmonton Blue Old Ivory pattern, plus one sugar bowl and one creamer, the handle of which Rachel has already had to reglue. Nice, but nothing too fancy, and good enough for every day. "I've had the same set for fourteen years, and there's hardly a chip," her mother-in-law had assured her confidentially, as if Aaron would not possibly understand such intimately household matters, which was absolutely correct.

Rachel can recall an evening as a child in Berlin when a young scion of a poor but ennobled Viennese family was dining at their home. The young man had insulted Eema with his impertinence by turning over his dinner plate to examine the backstamp, as if he could hardly be expected to eat his dinner off any dish that did not bear a crown mark. Fortunately for all concerned, Eema's porcelainware was Berlin KPM. Le Cabinet Hohenzollern.

"What did *you* get?" Rachel asks Aaron.

"The kung pao shrimp." He's opened his container and picks out a shrimp with his fingers, popping it into his mouth.

Setting down forks and paper napkins, she says, "So then you'll be up half the night with a sour belly."

"You know, my mother didn't eat a single shrimp until she was thirty-two years old," Aaron announces. "And it wasn't 'cause she kept kosher, either, 'cause *she didn't*. She just grew up in Flatbush." He pops another shrimp in mouth. "Who served shrimp on Utica Avenue?"

"And what if your mother saw her only son eating with dirty fingers? *Go*," she shoos him lightly. "Wash."

"Yes, ma'am."

Rachel removes a pair of water glasses from the shelf and plants them on the table. She is clinging to normal routine. Her normal paths of dialogue with Aaron. The jolting discovery of her mother's painting knocked her off course. Home after the pawnshop, she had taken another two tablets of Miltown, off schedule. But instead of feeling balanced, she feels brittle. Vulnerable. The painting's unwelcome incursion into the present has made her defenseless against the intrusion of her own past. It has ignited her memory of green eyes raw with feline hunger. The fiery red tresses. The monstrous beauty of a murderess.

Eema called her la muse du rouge.

A red-haired feline, who possessed both la beauté de Vénus and le feu de Feronia. But her name was not divine. It was Rosen. Angelika Rosen. A pretty Jewish girl from the crooked streets of the Scheunenviertel, scarcely nineteen when she first stood posing on the dais in Eema's studio, more slum-born than foam-born. And now the painting has emerged. That terrifying, mesmerizing portrait in oils on canvas, which until that morning had been lost to the bonfires of history. But now? Resurrected from its ashes. A phoenix in an ugly frame, held captive in a pawnbroker's prison between Fifth and Sixth Avenues.

Yet how can Rachel possibly ransom it? Fifteen dollars short. Fifteen dollars! And even if somehow dollars fall from heaven like manna and the painting drops into her lap, what then will she *do* with it? She can't give it to Feter Fritz, because he'll sell it to God knows who for either a minor fortune or a bag of subway tokens, depending upon the madness of his moment. But how can she herself dare keep it? Where will it go? In her closet? Under the bed? And then what? It stays there until the eyes slowly burn through the bedsprings and mattress and the bed goes up in flames? Rashka had been a dusky little five-year-old when it was painted. Dark-eyed and dark-haired. But even as a child, she had been captivated by those wavy red tresses and jealous of them. Jealous, too, of the intensity this maidel drew from her eema's gaze. It's easy to see the proof of that intensity in the painting, even after twenty-some-odd years. Maybe she can convince Aaron that she bought it from the Goodwill in the Village for twenty cents. Or better yet, found it abandoned on the sidewalk beside the trash.

Of course there is another solution. She can hear her own rage whisper from deep inside her, urging her to destroy it. It's a whisper that wants to see it burnt. Reduced to ashes or torn to pieces. A whisper that presses her to slash it into ribbons with the butcher knife from the kitchen drawer. Wouldn't that be justice? Though, for now, her guilt is stronger than this whisper. Her guilty devotion to her mother. Her guilty terror of the dead.

Aaron lathers his hands in the kitchen sink with the sliver of Ivory Soap while, for the umpteenth time, the radio is playing "The Ballad of Davy Crockett," prompting Aaron to break into song. "'Day-vee—Day-vee Crockett—Took a dump on the wild frontier.' I'm sorry I gotta turn this off," he says. Snapping off the volume, he wipes his hands on a dish towel. "Any mail?"

Rachel plops the cardboard takeout containers on the plates. "A bill from the electric company and a bill from the telephone company."

"The two biggest crooks in town."

Rachel opens the refrigerator. The old Kelvinator often emits a dull, mechanical drone like it's thinking too hard. "Will you have a beer?"

By now, Aaron has collapsed into his chair at the table. "Sure, why not?"

She snatches two Ballantine Ales from the back of the fridge with a light clink of bottles and brings them to the table, where she sits and uses the wood-handled opener to pop the caps. She tries to settle herself into the streamlined mood that Miltown offers, but even after another eight hundred milligrams, the painting has stirred her. She feels her blood churn too recklessly, so she tries to center herself using

Aaron as a touchstone, as she so often does. The regular guy, her husband, a boychik from Brooklyn, steady as a heartbeat. His face has filled out since they married. He's lost the boyish leanness of his cheeks he possessed in pictures while he was in the service. Sometimes she spies on him as he checks his hair for threads of silver in the bathroom sink. It makes him so human and so vulnerable.

But does she love him? Does she love her husband, ladies? Yes. Or at least she loves much about him. The quietly invested way he reads the newspaper. That thick disorder of his curls right after he wakes. Yes, she loves those curls. The strength of his hands opening the unopenable jar of Vlasic Kosher Dill Spears. And she depends on him too. She knows this. She depends on his eccentricities. His tastes for salty and sour write her shopping list. His restaurant hours underpin her nights and days. She depends on his punchy wit, their snappy to-and-fro, and even their ongoing arguments to give her structure that helps her breathe evenly on a daily basis. She can imagine herself continuing to depend on him for the rest of her life, though there are times when she suddenly goes dead to his touch. When darkness overtakes her, and she knows that they will always be separate, regardless of how long they are together. It makes her want to flee. To escape it all. Aaron, the apartment, their furniture, the impossibly slow drain in the kitchen sink. Herself.

Yes. If she can just keep running, perhaps she can escape herself as well. Is such a thing possible?

"*So,*" Aaron says, busying himself opening the mail, ripping open the envelopes with his fingers. "You got to your whatchamacallit today, right?"

Spooning out a large helping of rice for Aaron, Rachel raps the spoon against his plate. "I don't know. What is the whatchamacallit?"

"You know. Your appointment," he says and frowns at a bill. He doesn't like to speak the word *psychiatrist* aloud.

Spooning out a small helping of rice for herself with only a light tap of the spoon against her plate, she says, "You mean my appointment with the shrink?"

"Do you have to call it that?"

"What do you want me to call it?"

"I dunno. Call it whatever. I'm just asking is all."

"Yes. I went," she says. "I told you I would."

"Okay, just checking up. If I'm gonna be laying out all this dough for him…"

She spoons kung pao shrimp onto Aaron's plate. "Yes. You must get your money's worth."

Rachel spoons out her lo mein. "Do you want to use the chopsticks?"

Aaron waves them off with a shake of his head and uses his fork. Rachel decides on the cheap takeout chopsticks and stirs her food absently.

"So what happened with your uncle?" her husband wonders out loud.

Rachel sniffs, frowns lightly at her plate.

"I mean, you saw him for a coffee someplace this morning, didn't ya?"

"Yes," she answers as if confessing.

"So how'd it go?"

She clips a bite of the lo mein with her chopsticks and lifts it from the plate. "He doesn't look so well," she announces, causing a crease in her brow. "I'm not sure how he's been eating." She chews, swallows, not tasting.

Aaron sighs. "H'boy."

"What?"

"Nothing," he says and shovels in his food. "It's only that I know what *that* means. How much is it gonna cost me this time?"

"That's an ugly thing to say. Must you make him sound like a beggar?" Rachel despairs. "He's the only family I still have."

"Except for a husband and a whole mishpocha of in-laws," Aaron points out but then relents at the pained expression that strikes Rachel's face. "Okay, okay. Sorry. Not the same thing, I know. Sorry I brought it up."

"It's *not* the same thing," she confirms.

"All right, please," he begs, frowning over the bill from Con Edison. "Let's just have dinner, can we?" he says, chewing, then loudly tsks. "Aw, now will ya look at *this?*" he complains. "Four dollars and twenty-two cents for what? Turning on a light bulb."

But Rachel isn't ready to relinquish the topic. "You didn't have a single person from *your* family poisoned in a gas chamber."

"I said I *surrender*, okay?" Aaron reminds her, his face blanching. "I know. I'm just the big American dope who doesn't understand a thing. I get it. I spent the entire war in Culver City, while the rest of the world was going insane, and all I got to show for it is the Good Conduct Medal. So what do I know anyhow? I'm just a Jew from Flatbush."

"Don't say that. I hate it when you say that."

"Well, it's the *truth*," he says, getting steamed. "Sorry to tell you." Then he frowns down at his kung pao shrimp. "Don't believe me? You can look at my birth certificate."

Rachel's eyes dampen, and she stirs her rice with the chopsticks absently. The oil gleams on the lo mein. "You don't understand."

"*Yes*, I think we've *established that*. Of course. The idiot husband doesn't understand *because you never tell him anything*. It's all some unspeakable thing, and anytime I dare mention a word about it, all I get is 'You don't understand.'"

"Because you don't. You can't."

"And this is exactly what I mean! You shut me out. You say you hate when I say that I'm just a Jew from Flatbush, but that's how you make me feel. Like some fucking schlemiel from the neighborhood."

Rachel freezes up, glaring at the table. Aaron returns to his plate, scowling, sticking his fork into the rice, but she remains tightly contained.

"It's the space heater," she says.

Chewing. "What?"

"I get cold, so I bought the space heater. That's why the electric bill is high."

Aaron slumps, but his voice is charged. "Rachel, forget about the farkakteh electric bill, will you?"

"*I'm sorry*. I'm sorry I'm so much trouble! I'm sorry I'm not somebody better. I'm sorry I'm only me. Only a worthless Stück!" she cries.

"And now you're angry with me for no reason! I don't know what I did or said or didn't say to set you off, and I don't even know what you're talking about. Whattaya mean by 'stuck' anyway? I got no idea. It's like this morning when I asked about your birthday, and suddenly *ka-boom*."

"It's too much." Rachel feels herself falling apart. "*Too much*," she repeats. Ein Stück! A *piece*, the Germans called them. Less than a human. "Who cares about my birthday? You have to make a big tsimmis because a person turns another year older? There are plenty who didn't, *who never will*. Who cares if *I* do?"

"Who cares? *I* care," Aaron informs her. "I'm your husband, for god's sake. And I think that your birthday *should be* a big tsimmis. Please. All I want to do is something nice for you. Why is that so frigging impossible?"

"You never wanted me to paint," she suddenly declares, a full-bore accusation that leaves Aaron looking confused, maybe constipated.

"I never *what*?"

She repeats the accusation but more slowly this time, so the Jew from Flatbush can understand. "You *never* wanted me to paint. You didn't approve. You didn't want a wife who was an artist. It was embarrassing for you," she decides. "You wanted a wife like your mother was a wife, to cook and clean and be a hausfrau."

A half cough at the shock. And then an angry expression screws up his face. "Well, if that's *true*, I certainly didn't *get* one, did I?"

"You see? That's an admission."

"No, it's… I don't know what it is. Where do these things *come* from? We're sitting here at dinner and suddenly *bang*. I'm the guy who stopped you from painting."

"But isn't it true, Aaron?" she says, adopting a tone as if she wishes he could just confess it. Could just get it off his chest.

"*No*," he answers firmly, fixing the word in place. "It is *not* true. I thought it was great that you were painting. I was sorry when you stopped, 'cause I knew how important it was to you."

"I stopped because I went insane," Rachel declares.

Aaron surrenders. "H'boy. I dunno how to answer when you say things like that."

But Rachel has shut down.

Aaron huffs and shakes his head as he returns to the mail. Paper rustles over the silence. "Oh, for cryin' out loud," he whispers to the air. "Three dollars and twenty cents for that fucking toll call when Ma was down in St. Pete for Uncle Al's funeral." He pops another shrimp into his mouth with his fingers, sulking. "Crazy," he pronounces glumly.

"I found one of my mother's canvases," Rachel quietly admits.

Aaron looks confused, as if she's started speaking gibberish.

"You found who's what?"

"One of my mother's canvases. One of her paintings. Well, it wasn't *me* who found it," she corrects. "It was Feter Fritz. At a pawnbroker's shop."

Still, Aaron looks baffled, his expression squished. "Honey, whatever you're saying, I'm just not following. Your uncle was at a pawnshop?"

"Yes. On West Forty-Seventh Street."

"Uh-huh." His expression is still compressed. Ready to judge such a ludicrous story. "And so *there*? There on West Forty-Seventh Street, in the middle of New York City, he discovers a *painting* that your mother did *how many years ago* back in Germany? Decades ago? Is that the gist of it?"

"Yes."

"Just like that. There it is. Boom."

"Boom, yes."

"A painting. Your mother's painting—*that everybody thinks was destroyed*—reappears outta nowhere. And your *uncle Fritz*," he says, as if the very name is greasy with larceny. "Your uncle Fritz *happens* to find it in a hock shop in Midtown."

"Correct."

"So how can that happen?" is what Aaron is trying to say. "How can that be true?"

"Because it *is* true," she tells him. "I know it is because I saw it too."

There's a touch of the clucking chicken head tuck in the motion of Aaron's chin jerk. It comes whenever he disapproves of what he's just heard. "*So*," he says, just to get this straight, "you were in this hock shop *together*?"

"No. Not together. I went afterward," Rachel tells him and tries to enlarge her side of the feud. "It could be worth a minor fortune, Aaron."

"Oh, *really*," he replies, unconvinced. " A *minor* fortune. Not a *major* fortune, but a minor one."

"Feter Fritz knows of these things," she defends. "He knows from what he speaks," she tells him, thinking: especially when it comes to *this* painting. Especially when it comes to the portrait of Angelika Rosen. How Eema and he had sparred over the girl, the desired but unpossessable treasure. Even after decades, her uncle's voice was still ripe with covetous greed. Not even five months in an Auschwitz barracks block quelled it. Astonishing, Rachel thinks. To still feel so deeply. To desire so feverishly.

"*Ohhh*," her husband begins roundly. "I get it now. Feter *Fritz* says it's worth a minor fortune. Oh, *well* then, it must be true, because God knows Feter Fritz is *the* trustworthy authority."

"When it comes to *art*? Yes," Rachel insists, but she knows she is losing this battle. "*He is*. He was one of the most sought-after art dealers in Berlin. You know this!"

Aaron shakes his head. His voice softens, becomes conciliatory in a paternal fashion. "Honey, look. I know you're fond of the old guy. *More than fond.* And I know he was a big shot once, a long time ago. I know," he assures her. "But times," he points out, "have changed. Can you argue with that fact?"

Rachel keeps her mouth closed.

"No. I didn't think so. Anyhow, considering all that, I don't know what you want me to do here," he says.

And then the phone rings. It rings and rings again. Rachel does not move.

"So I guess we're letting it ring?" Aaron observes. "Never mind. I'll get it. It's probably Abe telling me Leo took a whiz in the deep fryer." He is up and crossing the room. She listens to him snap up the phone.

"Hello! *Abe, for cryin' out loud,* I just got home!"

Rachel wipes a tear from her face covertly.

"Okay, okay," Aaron is telling the receiver. "Okay, I get it. Tell Mr. Big Shot to keep his goddamn shirt on, will ya? I'm coming." And hangs up heavily before he speaks the same sentence that he always speaks when called back to work, back to the grind, back to the salt mines: "So guess where *I* gotta go?" It's a rhetorical question that he no doubt learned from his father, the late and long-suffering Arthur Perlman, may his name be a blessing. The original Jew from Flatbush.

5.

Therapy for the Shell-Shocked

WHENEVER RASHKA NEEDED A NEW FROCK OR NEW SHOES OR a new coat, her nanny took her to Karstadt's department store in the Hermannplatz. It was a gargantuan temple of merchandise the size of a zeppelin. It had lifts and escalators. Escalators! Slightly terrifying—would she trip and be accidentally shredded by the moving steps? But also marvelously fun, like a carnival ride, going up, up, up! It was an adventure. An expedition to the top floors! But it was always a nanny who took her. Fräulein This or Fräulein That. Her mother employed and then dismissed them with regularity. But never did Eema bother to lead the expedition herself. Shopping for Rashka was too trivial a matter to gain her attention; she had her work to consider.

So when Eema returned that afternoon from the Hermannplatz, trailing a porter loaded down with haberdashery boxes and ribboned dress boxes, it was a shock. Especially when Rashka saw that Eema was arm in arm with the red-haired fräulein. Obviously, Eema had taken the girl shopping! Rashka was wounded. They were laughing, the two women. Touching each other on the arm, the shoulder, even the face! And the new outfit that the girl was wearing! The beaded frock, the fur-collared cloak. The snug little hat with the long feather tucked into the band. The leather gloves the color of wine. Was Eema going to paint her with clothes on now?

That night at supper, Rashka refused to eat. She kicked the empty chair beside her under the table. But it was only the nanny who bore the

brunt of her anger. Eema was out for supper. Not even there for Rashka
to lash out against.

Rashka was a still a young child. But not so young that she couldn't
feel pain. Not so young that she couldn't feel envy. No so young that she
couldn't feel abandoned.

⌐•⌐

"Have you considered my suggestion further, Rachel?" Dr. Solomon
wonders. "That you return to painting?"

A pause before she lies. "I've considered it."

The doctor shifts in his chair, always a sign that he is about to
mount an effort to overcome her obstacles. "Have I ever mentioned the
name Mary Huntoon to you?" he asks and doesn't wait for an answer.
"At the end of the war, there was a woman I worked with briefly. An
artist," the doctor tells her, "named Mary Huntoon. She had an art
studio for patients at the Winter General Army Hospital in Topeka,
Kansas. Her idea was to use art as a therapeutic treatment for veterans
damaged by combat neuroses."

Aha. "So. Therapy for the shell-shocked meydl, Dr. Solomon?"

"Is that how you'd like me to put it?" he asks.

"You know, my mother told me that every artist is cursed at birth."
And now Eema appears in order to chime in. *Your imagination again. I
never said any such thing.* "My mother thought that it would be smarter
for me to become one of the 'sheep' as she called them. A simple sheep
who finds an ordinary man and makes an ordinary marriage."

And you see? That was true.

"Though men, she said, were also a curse."

Also, true, her mother agrees. *Men and children both.*

Leaving his office, Rachel is pursued by his suggestion. Narishkeyt!
Folly! Returning to painting? Dangerous even to consider! Her heart
is thumping.

But on the way home, she tries to calm herself with a Miltown. It planes down the rough edge of her panic, allowing her to at least *consider* such a thing as picking up a paintbrush again without sobbing or puking or losing her mind. A night in Bellevue cured her of the painting disease. All thought of such oily, messy endeavors had screamed to a halt after the Episode. It was as if the memory of holding a brush was fully erased from the muscles of her hand. She was sure that if she tried to employ a brush after Bellevue, her fingers would lose their strength, and she would simply drop it to the floor. And even if she did manage to find the temerity to slap paint onto a canvas, who knows what misshapen demon she might release into the world?

Still. She feels her eyes tear up.

She tries to imagine, as the downtown train bores through the tunnel, what might have happened if she had not been ruined. If she had not had her future torn from her and shredded. Might she be standing right now at an easel? She thinks of the paintings she has not produced in the same way as she thinks of the children she has not borne. The empty spaces of a life she is not living.

And then there is this young girl. This specter seated across the aisle between a woman with a shopping bag on her lap and a man dozing off over his newspaper. The schoolgirl with her brunette braid and burgundy beret, interloping across time. Do the dead also wonder about the lives they did not live?

Rachel closes her eyes.

Look for *yourself* in the crowd. Those were her instructions. *You* are who we're hunting, Bissel. This is what the woman always called her. Bissel. Little morsel, A bite to swallow.

If one were to travel back in time, one needed simply to eavesdrop on any whispered conversation of contraband Jews huddled in a Berlin café to hear the woman's name spoken in hushed tones. Pry into the nightmares of those huddled Jews, and one will see the woman's face. She is well known to the U-boats. Angelika Rosen. The ginger-haired beauty in the service of the Gestapo, the huntress of jüdischen Illegalen. Rashka's mother's *la muse du rouge* now notorious under a different name. She is the Red Angel in the service of malakh ha-mavet, the angel of death.

At home in the bedroom, Rachel sits propped up on a pillow, shoes off. Of course, she has never spoken a word aloud about the angel, not to her husband, not to her shrink.

Eema, on the other hand, simply can't shut up about her.

You were nothing to her, tsigele, her eema scoffs. *She wanted a mirror held up to herself, and you served that purpose. You were nothing more to her than a moment's vanity.*

Is this truth or jealousy?

The German language loves abbreviations, so the unwieldy designation of Konzentrationslager was reduced to "KL" or "KZ" or simply to "ein Lager." There were two major Auschwitz camps in the marshlands of German-occupied Poland: KL Auschwitz I and KL Auschwitz II. KL Auschwitz I had been an abandoned Polish cavalry barracks when the SS arrived to rebuild it for forced labor and mass murder. This is where Feter Fritz received the number tattooed on his arm, passing under the infamous gate that promised, "Arbeit Macht Frei." Work Makes Freedom. But really it remained a small-scale operation compared to its sprawling brother camp a kilometer and a half down the road. That was Auschwitz II, also known as Birkenau. Birkenau was vast, with acres and acres of stone and wooden barracks housing the misery of its inhabitants as the chimneys of *five* Krematorien stood smoking sacred human soot into the sky. It was a camp for slave labor, yes, but mostly it was devoted to the murder process on an industrial scale. This is where Eema had been sent, and this is where her ashes lie still, at the bottom of a pit.

That night, Rachel sits on the couch with a cigarette smoldering, alone but for Kibbitz, purring like a motor as she absently strokes his furry stripes. But when she feels a chill, she is not surprised that the cat's head darts up, and he leaps from nesting on her lap. Her eema has occupied the opposite side of the sofa, her head shaved to the skull, as it would have been on her arrival at Lager Birkenau, her eyes deeply set, and her emaciated body hung with her filthy camp rags. Rachel had seen the newsreels of Auschwitz-Birkenau at the D.P. camp when her name was still Rashka. British Pathé had screened the Red Army's footage. The pits crammed with decaying bodies. The piles of shorn hair. The tangled heaps of eyeglasses and gaping dentures. The mountains of discarded clothing, sleeves and skirts flapping disembodied in the breeze like a pile of ghosts. She had forced herself to watch every second of them. Kept her eyes pried open, an unblinking witness.

Do you remember, tsigele, when I taught you how to properly clean your brushes?

Rachel says nothing, but her mother does not seem to notice. She is smiling at her memory with rotting teeth. *How I taught you to use the wire brush to comb the paint from the bristles? How to soak them in the mineral spirits before blotting them? And then to squeeze the spirits from the brushes with your finger?* The decaying smile remains. *How you made such a mess, poor thing. Do you remember?*

Rachel's eyes brim. "Yes, Eema. I remember."

And then her mother's eyes grow raw. The skin of her face is drawn so tautly, she cannot produce tears. But a desolate longing burns her gaze. *Don't let me be forgotten, Rashka.* Her voice is a command, a dreadful plea. *It's a daughter's duty to keep her mother's memory alive. Don't let me be forgotten.*

The next morning delivers a white sky as a portent of the coming winter. Rachel is making coffee, scooping spoonfuls of instant into the percolator. The floor is cold as she pads across it in her socks to find her husband dressed for work. The drain in the kitchen sink is now so slow that water stands in the sink. "You should call the super," Aaron tells her, filling a glass with tap water and then drinking it without a breath.

"The super," Rachel repeats darkly.

"Yep. That's the guy," Aaron confirms. Then he gives her a business-like smack on the cheek. "It's his job to unclog that which is clogged," he tells her. "Uh, no coffee for me this morning. No time. I gotta get moving. The lunch crowd's gonna be murder today. Special matinee of *The Vamp* at the Winter Garden with Carol Channing."

This means nothing to her. "No coffee, no breakfast?"

"Don't worry. I'll have somebody scramble me a coupla eggs at the restaurant and stick 'em on a roll." It's obvious to Rachel that he has securely stowed yesterday's dispute in the drawer in his head marked WIFE TROUBLES: ONE OF MANY. Though it's also obvious that he's skipping breakfast because maybe it's wiser not to hang around. He does, however, insert a tentative question. "So you okay?"

She glances into his eyes. "Hunky-dory," she replies. That seems to be good enough.

"Look, I gotta close tonight," he tells her, breaking away, heading toward the door. "'Cause Solly's still in Miami."

"I thought you said he was back."

"No, I said he was *supposed* to be back, but then his mother broke a hip or a leg, or I dunno, she broke some damn thing. So it's double shifts for me," he tells her, grabbing his coat and hat off the branches of the hall tree. "*Do something today*," he commands thoughtfully on his way out. "Call Naomi. Go see a movie or something. Just don't hang around in your bathrobe like a mope."

"Are you saying I mope?"

"I'm saying some fresh air wouldn't kill you. Don't wait up."

When she hears him descending the stairs, Rachel goes straight to the bottom shelf of the magazine table by the sofa, loaded with her copies of *ARTnews* and *American Artist*. But it's also the spot where Aaron keeps the *Merriam-Webster's Dictionary* stowed for his occasional battles with the paper's Sunday crossword puzzle. It's a dog-eared copy from his school days, this dictionary, in which can still be found his covert schoolboy doodles of naked breasts and such. Opening the pages, she flips through till she finds what she's looking for. The rainy-day twenty. Once it's in her billfold, she considers hunting around the apartment for some small treasure. If she had anything of real value, she could put it into hock, but what does she have? Nothing. A bundle of everyday items. Household appliances. Costume jewelry. Nothing that would command a price of more than a dollar or two. Here! A can opener! Please take it on account! Think of the many cans of soup you can open at home with such a prize!

No, all she can hope for is that he'll take pity on her. The bedbug. That he'll take her measly twenty-five as a down payment maybe. She can skimp for a while, promise to pay him a few dollars per month. He'll understand paying over time. Even a businessman can take pity, can't he? Can't he take pity? That word that she both dreads and covets.

Outside, the air is indeed fresh, briskly scrubbed by yesterday's rain, as she heads for the uptown subway.

She can still so easily return to her mother's studio. The pleasing sharpness of the spirits in her nostrils. And the oily aromas of the paint on the palette. Her eema used only a certain brand of hand-mixed Belgian oil paints famous for their vivid colors. Rachel can remember the smell of sulfur in the cadmiums was so strong it was like the smell of a match head as it ignites. Even in the pawnbroker's shop, had she somehow expected to detect the sulfur emanating from the canvas after so many decades? In her mind's eye, she can see it. The canvas seated firmly on Eema's massive easel. The figure of a girl rendered in fiery colors. The pungent perfume of the cadmium red. Folklore warns that the smell of sulfur is a sign of the presence of demons. In this case, perhaps true. She can summon the image of the girl seated on the dais at rest, lazily smoking a cigarette, wearing a gauzy robe that exposed the color of her flesh. Hair red as a blaze.

Rachel was just a child. Still Rashka. She had come to her eema's studio with her nanny. Eema, of course, was too busy with the nanny, dispensing directions, to pay much notice to her daughter, but that was bearable. Certainly not unusual. Really she had been hoping to pet the cat who lived there. A big tawny beast who often snoozed in the light that poured through the loft's windows.

But then there was this girl. The subject of the painting that was still glossy with freshly applied paint. Rashka inhaled the telltale whiff of sulfur. It was this girl who had the cat under her spell. With Rashka, the beast was impatient. Too big for her handle. Easily provoked into scratching. But in this girl's arms, he was tamed. Purring loudly with contentment. Rashka was jealous. Not just of the girl's capture of the cat's affection but of the affection itself. She was mesmerized. It was easy to fall under this girl's spell just like the cat had. A wink and an intimate smile were all it took. She imagined what it must feel like to absorb such tender attention. She pictured herself as the cat in the girl's arms.

<hr />

The bell jangles above her upon entry. But when the curtains divide, it isn't the bedbug at all who greets her from the back room, it's a gray old man. Tall and slouched like the bedbug, but with one gold tooth in a row of brown and a belly hung over his belt. "Can I help?" he asks her, digging at the old tobacco baked into the bowl of a pipe with a penknife. His voice is throaty and rough. She can smell the sweet stench of smoke on him.

"I'm…" she starts to say. But what? She's what? The gray man lifts a pair of wiry eyebrows. "I'm looking," she says. "There was a gentleman here yesterday."

Maybe the gray man thinks this is funny. A joke. "A *gentleman*, was he? Well. Won't his mother be proud to hear?"

"He showed me a painting," Rachel tells the man. "Is he *here*?" she asks with a certain polite impatience. "I was hoping to talk with him."

"Not here. Not today. But tell me again." The man scrunches his brow together. "He was showing you what?"

"A painting," she repeats. "It's monochrome," she says.

"Oh, *yeah*, is *that* what it was?" he replies, still sounding grayly amused.

"It's a painting of a girl done all in red," she says.

"*Ah*." The man's expression lifts. "Sure." He grins. "The *nudie!*"

Rachel breathes in.

"Sorry," the man tells her, "but *that one*? That one's gone," he explains.

Her heart thumps a single stroke against her rib cage. "Gone." She says this as if she suddenly may not understand the meaning of the word.

"Yep. That's what I said." The gray man sniffs, banging the pipe bowl against the rim of the black enamel ashtray, loaded with crushed cigarette butts. "I sold it this morning first thing."

"*Sold?*" This can't be. "To whom? Who *bought* it?" Rachel hears herself demand. She realizes that she has gripped the ledge of the counter. "Was it a man?" she wants to know. "Old? Silver in his hair? Slim? A pointed beard?"

But the gray man only shrugs. "Sweetness," he tells her. "You *know* I can't say. I'm running a business. There are rules," he explains. "A customer bought it. That's all."

Michnik Brothers Tobacconist on Rivington Street feels like a dusty mausoleum when she enters. Dark wooden shelving. The air infused with an ancient odor of tobacco. She was hoping to find her uncle behind the counter at the far end, where the most expensive cigars are displayed in their boxes, but instead it's the owner, Mr. Michnik, gazing at her through the thick lenses of his eyeglasses. He looks glumly disappointed to see her, but then doesn't he always look a little disappointed?

She doesn't take it personally. "I was hoping to find my uncle," Rachel tells him. "Is he working this week?"

Mr. Michnik appears pained by this question. He's a hunched old fellow. Also a refugee, but one who left Poland twenty years before the war. Business was good here in America. He opened this shop with his brother. They sent money back to the mishpocha in Warsaw. And then he blinked, and all were gone. An entire family reduced to ashes. Then his brother passed a year after the war's end. Heart attack, said the doctors, but who knows about the power of grief? Anyhow, he keeps the place going. She knows that he's seen the number tattooed on her uncle's arm. She knows he employs him more out of a sense of charity than of business. A part-time clerk to work the cash register. Shelve the stock here and again and maybe pick up a broom. What's the harm? Especially when he thinks of all those who perished.

But now he's shaking his head. "I'm sorry. I just couldn't keep him on any longer. Sometimes he wouldn't show for his shift. Or I'd come in and find him in the back room smoking instead of working the counter. And *then*," Mr. Michnik says before he sighs. He doesn't want to say it. He doesn't want to, but he must. "Stock went missing," he confides. "Not much. A box or three of Phillies Panatellas." He shrugs. "A nine-cent cigar. Not so expensive. But when it happened more than once, how long could I ignore? Add to that the miscounts on the cash drawer, and I'm sorry," the old man repeats. "I had to let him go."

Rachel feels her cheeks burn. Shame. Shame and pity. Pity and guilt. Which is worse?

She searches Feter's downtown haunts. Not only the café where they'd met the previous day but also the coffeehouses and cafeterias, the delicatessens and dairy restaurants along Delancey, and that place on Essex Street that serves everything pickled. She searches any and all of the corners below Houston where her uncle has been known to perch, but all to no avail. She finds the old snowy owl, Mr. Smushkevich, the chess maven, contemplating his board alone, trying to crack the code of some obscure gambit from les jours de tsar as he nurses his tepid tea. He shows her the ancient smile as he offers his regrets. "Ikh hob nisht leygn an aoyg aoyf im, liebling." Haven't laid an eye on him.

At the counter of the I.G.K.P. she finds Mr. Katzenelson and Mr. Pollak, two former theater critics in exile, still arguing over the premiere of *The Rite of Spring* at the Théâtre des Champs-Élysées forty years ago. But nothing from them. Only shrugs. They care like cats care, which is to say they don't. It's Thursday, so maybe check that Milkhiger restaurant on Rivington Street. She finds one of Feter's cronies, the socialist writer Mr. Garfinkel, known for his story from thirty years ago, *Hurrah for Schmeul the Waiter!*—still available by mail as a pamphlet through the Yiddish Publishing Company. He sits with his dairy noodles, proudly wearing his I.W.W. union button pinned to his collar, but is of no help.

Nor are there any clues forthcoming from the place on Broome Street that serves milk from a ladle and has the sink installed outside the toilet for Hasidic customers. Mr. Rubinstein is a Zionist who's never put a foot in the Promised Land but who keeps a white-and-blue tin for donations to Israel on the table with his black coffee. Also no help. "Sorry to disappoint, Kallehniu," he tells her and gives the tin a tap, so that costs her a dime for the Promised Land.

She walks. It's only a block away, but she saves it for last, because really why would she want to go back to such a place if she doesn't have to? She has managed for five years not to take a step back inside. Now, against her own desire, she confronts a sooty, terra-cotta brick tenement house on Orchard Street. One among many around Seward Park, where shabby canyons of flat-faced brick and wooden rental barracks stand. Jews have lived here for decades, filling up the cramped apartments and spilling out onto the stoops and into the streets and markets. More since the war's end, but not from the shtetlakh this time. Instead of all those little villages dotting Eastern Europe, this time the deluge has come from the displaced persons camps.

Rachel stands on the sidewalk facing the building's wood-frame entrance with its peeling varnish. Above, a latticed ironwork of fire escapes zigzags down the facade. A couple of teenaged girls burst from the door and come clattering down the steps in saddle shoes, gabbling in a language from the old country. A Baltic dialect maybe. They ignore Rachel. Ascending into the tenement's upper floors, where the light of the stairwell thickens to soup, she hears a radio blaring Yiddish from somewhere and the yap of a dog. Mounting the stairs, she notes that the tattered step runners she remembers have been replaced by rubberized treads. The ancient smells linger, however. They're in the woodwork, the sweat and cook pots of generations of poor immigrant Jews, boiling kraut and pickling beets, breaking their backs for a few American coins to jangle in their pockets.

On the third floor, she stops in front of the door of a flat. She wonders… If she presses an ear against it, would she hear the echo of her own voice, that skinny D.P. girl who once lived there? She had spent her days then waiting on her uncle like a servant. Preparing the food as best she could, washing clothes, sweeping the floor. She thought it was her duty to tend to her elder, and he did not disabuse her of that idea. He could still pretend that he was the master of the house.

She didn't care. What else was there for her to do? She had no friends and no desire for them. She was content with her ghosts, who understood her pain. Understood her guilt. At night, while Feter snored to high heaven, she would lie on a lumpy mattress plopped on the floor and try to sleep—though night was when the muscularity of her fear and shame threatened to strangle her. This was her life back then, until she met Aaron. Barely a life at all.

A tarnished tin mezuzah is tacked onto the doorframe. *And thou*

shalt write them upon the doorposts of thy house, and upon thy gates. So says
the Mishneh Torah. The mezuzah had been left behind by the previous tenant who died of pneumonia in a hospital bed, may his name be
a blessing, whatever it was. How many times had she touched it and
brought the touch to her lips? *Shema Yisrael. The Lord is our God, the Lord
is one.* She had been teetering then on the cusp of changing from Rokhl
to Rachel. She takes a half step forward as if to touch the mezuzah now,
as if she is stepping into the fringe of a dream, but a sharp crack of the
floorboard under her feet wakes her up. Reminds her she is not here for
memories; she is here for her answers. How could Feter have possibly
raised the money? He begs her one day for charity, then the next yanks
such cash from his pockets that he drops fifty dollars on the pawnshop
counter in a blink? *How?* What pile of straw had he spun into gold?

Rachel presses the buzzer. "Feter?" she calls urgently. "Feter Fritz?
Will you open the door?" she asks him in Yiddish.

Nothing, until a voice that isn't her uncle's surprises her. She turns,
gripping her shoulder bag as if she might need to repel an attacker. A
squat old lady is slowly descending from the upper floors. "You'll have
no luck finding *that* one at home," she tells Rachel. "I know, I've been
knocking all morning." The lady's hair has gone gray like steel wool
fashioned into a bun. Her high cheekbones are swollen now and her
eyes pouched darkly. Yes, the lady has aged since Rachel saw her on the
day she moved out to marry Aaron. As she descends the steps, Rachel
notes that the woman's hobble appears to have worsened. The lady
stops, gripping the stair rail, huffing lightly over the exertion of living
life. "Up and down these steps, it's torture, you know, for an old widow."

"Mrs. Appelbaum," Rachel says.

"That's *me*," the lady answers, peering more closely through the
thick lenses of her eyeglasses. "But who are *you*, little treasure?"

"I'm Rachel Perlman, Mrs. Appelbaum. Though when you knew
me, my name was Morgenstern. I used to live here."

The lady frowns, but maybe she can recall. "Ohh." She nods,

peering. "I might remember a certain girl. A skinny little thing with big calf eyes. Was that you?"

"That was me. But I'm married now. My husband and I live in Chelsea," she says as if it is an accomplishment. "On West Twenty-Second Street."

"Ah, well. Mazel tov," the lady wishes her.

"Thank you. B'karov etzlech."

"It's a wonderful thing to be happily married."

"Yes," Rachel says and nods.

"For forty-six years, I was happily married to Mr. Appelbaum, may his name be a blessing."

"That's a long time."

A shrug. "Time passes. But I'll tell you what my problem is *now*, child. Your poppa, is he?" she asks, pointing at the door.

"Meyn feter," Rachel corrects.

"Ah. Your *uncle* then," the lady confirms. "He's got a bad memory. He forgets to pay for his rent."

Rachel feels a sting of embarrassment. "How much does he owe?"

"Two months. Two months and not a penny offered. I've told him: 'Mr. Landau,' I said, 'I'm only the concierge, but I have a legal responsibility to the landlord.' I told him if I don't see some rent soon, I'll have to call for the authorities."

Appearing behind Mrs. Appelbaum, Rachel's eema has commentary to offer. *Ah, Fritzl,* she laments. *He could always make his money. That he had the gift for. But to keep it?*

Rachel is already digging into her purse. "How much?"

"How much?" says Mrs. Appelbaum. She frowns in her accounting, eyebrows raised as she observes Rachel's billfold. "For two months? Twenty-four dollars," the lady answers. "Twenty-four dollars and forty cents."

Cracking open her billfold, Rachel produces the five and the rainy-day twenty, handing it over. "Now he's paid up."

Mrs. Appelbaum looks surprised and frowns but not unhappily. "*Well*," she says. "Who could say no? A sheynem dank," she thanks Rachel formally, folding the money into the pocket of her house dress.

"Ni't do kein farvos," Rachel answers her tightly. Her eema has disappeared from the steps.

"I'll write out the receipt and slip it under his door," Mrs. Appelbaum assures her. "Rent paid in full with sixty cents in credit." She is smiling now like a contented bubbe. "Such a thoughtful person you've grown into, mammele," the lady observes, calling her "little mother." An endearment reserved for obedient, well-behaved daughters. "And so pretty too. Your uncle? He should know how lucky he is to have such a devoted niece," she says and then looks up at the creak of footsteps on the stairs. "And here we *are*," she announces with the brightness of a hostess greeting her guest. "Speak of its wings and the angel appears."

For an instant, Rachel feels her nerves tingle at the mention of an angel, but when she turns about, she sees it is only Feter Fritz, a wary expression hung on his face that he is attempting to mold into a smile.

"Look who's come for a visit, Mr. Landau," the old lady sings. "Your little plimenitse, a married lady now, pretty as the moon!"

Smiling very cautiously. "So I see, Mrs. Appelbaum."

"And with such a pretty head! You must be proud!" the old woman declares as she continues her laborious journey downward, gripping the rail. "I'll leave you two to your own company. Be healthy!"

Feter Fritz inspects Rachel with eyes that are pleasantly suspicious. "So this is a surprise," he points out.

Inside? The apartment is no different than when Rachel left it five years before. No different, only dustier without someone to sweep. Only dirtier without someone to clean. Only with a coat of downtown grime dulling the window glass. And the smell? Maybe it smelled this way even when she lived here fresh off the boat back in '49 and '50. The upholstery and rugs polluted by the stale reek of her uncle's smoking habit and the interior stink of ancient plumbing. Maybe it smelled back then too, and her nose was blind to it. But now it hits her as if she's walked into a wall. Her uncle, though, is obviously inured to the stench as he busies himself clearing a spot on the horsehair settee that's dribbling its stuffing. "Sit! Sit!" he is commanding graciously. "I'll make some tea."

But instead of sitting, Rachel surveys her surroundings. A few bleach-stained shirts hang on metal hangers from a nail tacked into the wall. Yellowing editions of *Forverts, Dos Eydishe Aoyg,* and the *New York Post* clutter the same wobbly old table where she and Feter Fritz used to take their meals and play their games of cribbage and backgammon. Also there is an open box of Phillies Panatellas, empty of cigars but now a receptacle for loose change, vending machine slugs, and train tokens.

"I'm sorry that I'm out of coffee at the moment," he apologizes, setting an aluminum kettle on his old hot plate. "But there's some very decent tea from Zabar's."

"Tea is good," she assures him.

"I'll see about some sugar," he buzzes, maintaining his industrious tone till Rachel puts an end to it.

"So where do you have it hidden?"

"Hidden? You mean the sugar?" He really is a perfect liar. Vos a talant!

"No," Rachel tells him. "I mean Eema's painting."

Her uncle is frozen for an instant in the act of holding open the door of the cabinet above the sink. Then he turns, looking painfully mystified. "Her painting? Here I was hoping you'd changed your mind about the fifty dollars. But instead you think *I* have her painting now?"

"I went to the pawnbroker, Feter," Rachel says in a tone that declares the jig is up. "The one on Forty-Seventh Street. I had money. Not fifty. Perhaps not enough, but I was hoping to strike a bargain. Yet when I arrived there, it was already gone. So," she asks again. "Where is it hidden? Behind a cabinet, perhaps? Or under your bed?"

Oddly, her feter is not chastened but bleakly amused at such an idea. He pulls down a half-empty sack of sugar from the cabinet, the paper at the top crimped closed. "I sleep on the same Murphy bed, Rokhl, don't you recall? I pull it down from the wall every night, so hiding secret contraband underneath would prove futile."

"Then *where*, Feter?"

"What on earth makes you *imagine*, Rashka dear, that after *begging* my dear niece for a few dollars the day before, it was *I*, your poor Feter Fritz, who this morning waltzed in and purchased it?" He smiles grimly at his surroundings. "With all my riches abounding?" He actually picks up the cigar box and shakes it, rattling the change to prove his point. "You think I collected enough pennies from the gutter, do you? Or perhaps you think I bought it with a smile?"

A blink. It's now Rachel herself who feels chastened. She looks down at her shoes. The penny loafers she bought with her Bonwit Teller employee's discount.

"Ziskeit!" he calls her with a dry laugh. Sweetness!

"I thought you must have found the money somewhere," she says. "You are usually so talented at such work, Feter, when it's essential for you. But if it was not my uncle, then *who* could it have *been*? Who else would have known its true value but you?"

A shrug over the serendipity of life. "We had our chance, my dear. Our chance," he says, "to rescue your eema's name from obscurity. But it was not to be. Fate is impatient; it doesn't wait on the indecisive. So now it's gone. To where? Who knows? Perhaps it went to some nish-tikeit with a new sofa looking for a picture to hang above it. I have no idea, Rashka. I'm just a poor Jew trying to eke through his final years before the grave."

"Don't say that."

He switches on the hot plate, no longer smiling. "Everyone dies, Ruchel," he reminds her.

"But not yet." She feels her eyes go damp. "You still have a long life to live."

"Do I?" he wonders. And now when he smiles, it is with no more than a hint of paternal condescension softening his eyes. "If you say so, child. From your lips to God's ear."

Rachel breathes in and then makes her admission. Her admission that proves her devotion to him, though why does it sound like a crime she's confessing? "I paid your rent."

"Say again?" A crooked expression of confusion. "You did what?" He has removed a package of Wissotzky Tea from the shelf above the hot plate, the coil now glowing red.

"Mrs. Appelbaum told me that you were two months in arrears."

A flash of embarrassed anger streaks across his eyes. "Oh, she *did*? She thought that was news for the front page?"

"She remembered me. From when we both lived here."

"And so you decided to what? Empty your bank account as a remedy for an old man's financial dilemma?"

"It was an impulse," Rachel attempts to offer as an explanation. Now that his theatrics are done, she knows that she must suffer through her uncle's genuine embarrassment over money, even though yesterday he was, as he'd reminded her, *begging* her for it. But money for a painting? That was a deal. Paying his overdue rent? That's charity. C'est une insulte!

Feter Fritz turns his back on her, busy filling a small mesh tea ball. "An impulse," he says. "One of which *I'm sure* your good husband will disapprove."

"I was trying to help. I was looking for you at the cigar store, and I talked to Mr. Michnik."

"Michnik." Feter repeats the name sourly. "A true racketeer if ever one was born. The markup on those loathsome cigars of his? He's a swindler and a cheat, and I'm well out of his employ."

"I didn't mean to offend you, Feter. Please understand. I was trying to be helpful."

"Yes, yes. Of course, Rokhl. Le vieil homme comprend, ma chère," he says, still showing her his back. "I'm a broken old bum living in a trash dump."

The kettle begins to gurgle on the hot plate; steam dances from its spout. But her uncle does not touch it. His shoulders square, and he does not move even as the gurgle becomes a shrill squeal. Finally, it's Rachel who crosses the room and turns off the burner.

"I am *not* in possession of your mother's painting. I wish I *was* hiding it under a bed I do not have. But I am not," he tells her.

At this point, all she can do is wipe the tears from her eyes with the back of her wrist.

"I'm sorry that we could not protect her work from the hands of some anonymous philistine," he says. "But if it is gone, it is gone. It pains me deeply, yes, but God has His plan, and who can argue? What is worse for me? What is *truly* painful? It's seeing the effect of this on *you*, Rashka dear. How deeply it has disturbed you. You inherited your eema's mistrustful nature, this much I know, but now? To doubt *me* to the point where you've concocted a fantasy? A fantasy that even your old uncle is deceiving you? Stealing your mother's legacy from you? Honestly, Rokhl, I regret having involved you at all. It was thoughtless of me. In my excitement, I forgot how fragile you remain. It would have been better, perhaps, had your eema's painting simply appeared and then disappeared in the same breath, without you ever having known. But now?" he says. "Now, all we can do is share the loss."

6.

Doughnut Paradise

RACHEL'S LIFE WITH AARON BEGINS IN JANUARY OF 1950, WHEN, still fairly fresh off the boat, she has some trouble with a desk attendant at the Seward Park Library. A young balding fellow with a brown mole on his cheek gets sharp with her. "*Hey.* Whattaya you think you're *doing?*" this fellow demands to know, though the answer is really quite obvious. Air France Flight 009, flying from Paris to New York, has crashed into a mountain in the Azores, dispatching all aboard, and Rachel is busy tearing the article from the branch's copy of the *Daily News*.

Stopping in midtear, she blinks blankly at the fellow with the mole. "I beg your pardon?" Her accent is on display.

"That is *library property*, hon. Know what that means? Other people get to read it *too*. You can't just start ripping it apart."

Her spine straightens. A beat of panic stabs her heart. It simply hadn't occurred to her that she might be committing a library crime. She lets go of the paper and balls her fists as if she may be forced to defend herself, but before she speaks another word, her eyes attach to the man who will, within months, become her American husband, Aaron Samuel Perlman. A solid young mensch, dressed in a black wool jacket, with a soldierly haircut growing out into curls and hooded eyes of manganese blue. He's come to the Seward Park branch, she will later discover, to return an overdue copy of a book called *Battle Cry*, but now he goes to battle for her.

"Hey, can we give the young lady a break?" he suggests with some force to the offended attendant, stepping into the scene in a help-fully assertive manner. "You can hear that she's obviously new to our country, am I right? And who knows? Maybe this is how they do things back in Odessa. I mean, *come on*," he insists. "Here's a dime," he says, slapping a coin on the desk. "Really. I'll cover the cost of a new copy so none of your very important customers miss out on the news of the day. Or maybe they can just read the *Post* instead. Whattaya think?"

Of course, she isn't from Odessa. She is from Berlin, that pulverized city on the Spree, which is what she tells him over the lunch he buys her at Katz's Delicatessen. KATZ'S, THAT'S ALL! reads the ancient maroon sign on East Houston. *How-sten* Street, he teaches her to say. Entering the restaurant, Rachel is light-headed. She hears Yiddish ringing off the walls, yes, but she's also dizzied by how expansively *American* the place is in its size, its veracious noisiness, and its overwhelming plenty. Not just the luxurious aromas of Jewish cooking but the towers of stacked pastrami and corned beef. The platters of plump, orangey-pink lox. The golden loaves of rye and challah crowding the racks. The bagels and bialys. The monstrous dills in monstrous jars. Abundance like this can make her nauseous.

"So. Why *were* you tearing up the newspaper?" this boy with the curls has to ask. But that's when the harried, slightly surly waiter arrives at their table, and the boy orders for them. A Reuben with extra Russian for him, a sweet-potato knish for her. And two egg creams.

She avoids the question of newspapers. "And what," she wonders, "what is this egg cream?"

"It's a drink. Like a, uh, like a chocolate milk only with a spritz of seltzer. Very sweet, very fizzy."

"Where is the egg?"

"There is no egg."

"And the cream?"

"There is no cream, but don't worry. You'll love it."

"There were no such drinks where I grew up," she tells him. "When I was a child, we had only a 'Schlammbowle' at parties," she says, producing a ten-cent packet of cigarettes. "In English, you would say, I think, a 'Mud Bowl.'"

"Yes. I *would* say that. I would definitely say that," the boy assures her, eyes bright.

"So. Into this bowl go the fruit juice, the tangerines, the peaches and, uh—die ananasscheiben. How is it called? The *pineapple slices*. From a tin. All with the ice cream," she says, almost tasting its sweet flavor. She is not accustomed to the taste of happy memories. "Of course this was for the children. The adults? They must add schnapsen. *Booze*," she translates with fervor and laughs.

The boy is producing a shiny Zippo lighter. "Sounds scrumptious," he says earnestly, flicking open a tear of flame. She leans forward to accept the light, touching his hand. Just a small touch, but she can tell it has its effect because his pupils dilate.

"I collect the stories of the aeroplane crashes," she confesses. "This is why I tore the paper."

The Zippo snaps closed. "Hmm. Interesting," Aaron decides. "Only airplanes?"

She exhales smoke. "Nur," she tells him. Only.

"Not trains or cars or anything? Why is that?"

"Must I know? I hardly know why I do many things I do. Do *you*?"

He smiles, baffled. "Yeah, pretty much," he says with a lightly comic note of lament. "I pretty much *always* know why I do the things I do."

This boy lifts her heart. His name is Aaron. He is funny and lithe and interested in talk. Perhaps Rachel catches a glimpse of a destination in his eyes. He is teasing her over reading the dictionary, which she does in order to learn new words.

"I won't give away the ending," he tells her, "but it has something to do with zoos."

She does not understand.

"Because Z is the last letter in the alphabet," he must explain. "Never mind. Things just come outta my mouth. I dunno. You get used to it after a while."

His smile is so unpretentious. So very down-to-earth American.

"Okay, so—dictionary or not, you speak pretty great English. How'd you learn?"

"Languages were important to my mother," she says. "So she hired different tutors for my education. One for the English, one for the French, even the student from the Hildesheimer Akademie für das hebräisch. Though my Hebrew is very light."

"Wow," says the boy. "Wow. I hear this and I'm like… Holy mackerel."

Rachel does not know what this means, of course, but can tell from his expression that she is drawing him in, just like the sweet taste of the egg cream from the straw.

"I mean, I had some Spanish in high school. Erasmus Hall High on Flatbush Av'—so public school kid all the way here. I can still maybe remember how to ask where the bathroom is, I think. Dónde es? Dónde está el bañoá? Or something like that." He shrugs and chuckles. "But Hebrew? Hebrew and I pretty well parted company after my bar mitzvah." Saying this, he chomps into his sandwich. The Reuben with extra Russian. Chewing and swallowing in a hurry, so he can ask, "How's your knish?"

"Oh, it is *good*," she says, nodding. "So big." She cuts off another small forkful and slips it into her mouth. Many times with strangers, she cannot eat in front of them. But she finds that with this boy, she has an appetite.

"Yeah, ya can't beat Katz's." He nods sagely. "That's all I gotta say." When he leaves a spot of dressing on the corner of his lips, she reaches over and wipes it away with her thumb. His eyes widen at the touch, and he confesses the truth. "I gotta tell you. I am just—what? *Gobsmacked*.

That's it. That's what I am. I am just absolutely *gobsmacked* by you, Rachel Morgenstern."

Incomprehensible. "This is good?" she asks with hope.

"You can't get better than gobsmacked, my friend. It's the top of the line."

Top of the line? Also incomprehensible. But she smiles at his beaming expression.

"So," he says and hunches forward. "Are you a skater?"

She blinks. "Skater?"

"Ya know. On the ice. An ice-skater."

"Oh. *Yes*," she answers. "Ha! Very long ago. There was the Rousseau-Insel—uh, which is the *island* in the Tiergarten. I would go there with friends to skate on Sundays in the wintertime. *But*"— she expels a breath—"then the Nazis came, and Jews were no longer permitted."

Immediately, she feels the conversation wobble. Immediately, she tastes regret. Is she *stupid*? Why did she *speak* so?

"Ah," says the boy in response. His face grows dim, and she can feel him recede from her. She thinks he has a strong male face, and she finds that she has a desire to weave her fingers through his mop of impossibly curly hair. But the space has clouded between them. She has opened up a divide. It's only that she has lived so long under the laws against this or against that, they became rather commonplace to her. Words slip out because she *forgets* that not everyone's daily existence was stamped by the Nürnberger Laws.

"I'm sorry," Rachel tells him. "I shouldn't be speaking of this. It is not so polite, I think."

"No, no," he answers quickly, his voice gaining a higher pitch. "It's fine. It's fine," he repeats. But is it? She cannot tell. He catches a breath but seems somewhat bewildered over how to proceed. So it's Rachel who decides to lean forward this time. If she has opened a divide, then she must find a way for them to leap it. Elbows folded on the tabletop under her breasts, she bends her shoulders toward him, closing the gap. "May I have a taste of your pickle?" she asks and watches him blush.

The first time the boy meets with her for a rendezvous, it is called "a date." They go to the ice-skating rink in Radio City. She does not own a pair of skates, and the ones available for rent hurt her feet. Such high arches, her mother always said. She grimaces as she stands on the skate blades and wobbles.

"Whatssa matter?" the boy wants to know. And when she tells him, he knows immediately what the problem is. The problem is that they aren't laced properly. "Sit," he says. "I'll do it for you."

And to her surprise, he is right. "Can you feel your toes?" he asks after he yanks the laces taut.

Is this a test? What is the correct answer? "No," she says. "I cannot."

"*Good*. That means they're nice and tight."

She is relieved. She has given the correct answer! She can also tell that he is not wrong. Even while she's sitting there on the bench, the skates feel comfortably snug instead of painful. The fact that this boy knows better how to lace her skates than her? Does it also irritate her slightly? A bit perhaps. She does not like to be bested at anything, even the art of skate lacing. But at the same time, he is so very competent. She realizes she wants to touch him. She holds on to his shoulder as she stands to test her balance, even though she does not need to do so.

"How's it feel?" he asks.

"Good," says she, then pushes up on the blades and kisses him on the lips. Just a small kiss. A peck, not much more. Just a Küsschen. But when he smiles at her in surprise, she is surprised that she is smiling back.

"Well. *Thanks*," he says in a pleasantly awkward way.

"You are welcomed," Rachel replies.

The boy blinks. Swallows. Then suddenly bends forward and returns the kiss she'd given him.

"That was nice," he informs her with a certain profundity weighting his voice as their lips part. "That was a nice kiss."

Out in the rink, music is playing over the loudspeaker. Calliope music. Carousel music, with a gusty melody that turns its own circles. Rachel is happy to feel her muscles moving as she pushes off onto the ice, holding on to Aaron's arm. Happy to feel the fresh chill on her face, and soon enough, she feels the swift balance of her body as they whoosh around the inner lane, letting the momentum carry them. The boy grips her hand in his, and they let themselves float into the long straightaway.

⌐•⌐

That night, on the Lower East Side as Rachel tries to sleep, she feels a strange energy vibrating through her body. As if her body is waking up. Returning to life. Returning to something she feared was lost. Her desire to create. The next day, she introduces something new into the flat she shares with her uncle. A piece of Masonite board. Not very large. Nowhere near the size for big ideas or a giant talent. But big enough to receive paint. Odd shapes emerge. Ghostly fumes. Nothing living, but the colors—blues, purples, thin grays—rise up like chimney smoke. When her uncle sees what she is doing, he frowns thoughtfully. "Is this a painting?" he asks. She, however, is not prepared to answer that question.

Three weeks later—or was it only two?—Aaron takes her to a theater on Broadway. There's singing and laughter in the play. The audience laughs, Aaron laughs, so Rachel laughs too, timing her laughter to match his, even though she doesn't really follow what's happening onstage. Still, the laughter makes her feel light.

Later, they go to a homey, all-night doughnut shop on the corner of 14th Street and Seventh. The coffee is overheated and bitter, and the doughnuts are greasy with sugar. But it's a busy concern even after midnight, and Rachel and Aaron share the counter with other night owls. Aaron is taking the opportunity to instruct Rachel on the proper dunking technique, using a plain brown old-fashioned.

"*See*," he instructs, dunking the doughnut into his coffee cup, "now this is a regulation dunking. Grasp the doughnut with two fingers positioned on the forward area, and the third finger to the rear in a support role. Then lower the doughnut at a steady *but moderate* pace into the coffee. And here's the essential part," he stresses. "*Two dunks*, no more, for maximum exposure to the coffee flavorfulness without endangering the all-important doughnut integrity. Remove doughnut from coffee, followed by one single lightly applied tap on the rim of the cup to prevent dripping, then raise doughnut to mouth and…" He demonstrates by biting firmly into the doughnut and chewing with gusto. "*Mmmmm*" is what he has to say about this sort of perfection. "The result? Doughnut paradise."

Rachel has been smiling throughout his technical demonstration, but now she pounces, attacking the doughnut in Aaron's fingers with passionate appetite.

Chuckling, he tells her, "Hey, hey, leave some fingers, will you?"

She chews the doughnut with exaggerated hunger. "*No*, I will leave nothing. I will devour you entirely." And she falls on his neck, devouring him next, making hungry noises. He fends off the attack in a maybe kind of embarrassed-in-public-but-still-pleasurable sort of way. "H'okay, h'okay, h'okay." He's laughing.

The night owl beside them lifts his eyebrows in late-night surprise. Or is it appreciation? Aaron can only speak the truth. "What can I say? She's a tigress." The night owl lifts his coffee cup in salute. Rachel laughs.

Outside, the snow is coming down, piling up, but she is safe inside a doughnut shop. Not huddling inside a cold cellar or walking the ice-slick streets. That is how Eema and she had lived as U-boats until the day of their arrest. But now she is *warm*. Warm in her wool stockings. Her wool pullover. Warm with this boy. In the doughnut shop, she holds the cheap white china mug with both hands, stealing from its heat. He, though, has set his coffee aside with quiet intention. Then planting the jeweler's box between them, he squares his elbows on the tabletop and gazes at her in a clear, affectionately businesslike manner. "So? What do you think?" is his proposal.

She stares back at him, still gripping the china mug. "What is *this*?"

"What is it? What's it look like?"

Another swift stare at the small black velveteen box.

"Aren't you going to open it?" he asks.

"You wish me to?"

The curve of his smile deepens. "*Yes*, I wish you to. Of course. What else?"

A swallow. Then her fingers move, opening the box with a quick movement and a soft pop of the box's hinge. Her eyes settle on the contents, but her expression remains controlled. The pinpoint gleam of the precious stone makes her uncomfortable. She has the urge to snap the box shut and squirrel it away, as if it is a chunk of bread that she will hoard.

"*So*," Aaron repeats. "Whattaya think?"

"You wish…" she begins, then stops and starts again. "You wish to *marry* me?" She asks this because she just wants to be *sure*. To be clear about the proposal being made. She fears, for an instant, that he might answer her with sarcasm or impatience. Or with the knowing irony he often adopts. But instead, his face loses all its calculation and grows soft.

"Yes," he says. "Yes, I wish you to marry me, Rachel," he assures her, his voice gentle and without hesitation. "Rachel Morgenstern, I wish you to marry me and become my wife. Will you?"

"What does your mother say?"

"My mother?"

"What does your sister say?"

"My mother says a lot of things. My sister says a lot of things, but *I'm* asking *you* to marry me, not them."

"But how do they feel about adding a poor refugee to their family?"

"We're Jewish. We were all refugees at some point in history. Besides, my sister's crazy about you. She likes you more than she does me."

"And your mother?"

"My mother? Whatever makes me happy makes her happy. This is what she says to me."

"And I make you happy?"

"Yes," he says. And it sounds so true that when he removes the ring from its velvet box, she permits him to slip it onto her finger, a tiny sparkle of light.

That night, they make love for the first time in his dingy downtown efficiency, with the flaking wall paint and wheezing plumbing, and she takes him inside her as if she is taking him completely. It hurts for only a moment. A curt cleaving. She is making him *happy*. She, Rashka Morgenstern, has the *power* to make him happy.

In six weeks' time, only how many weeks after they first met— ten maybe? Something like that. They are both so primed for change, so primed to escape their oppressive lives, how long should it take? So three weeks after doughnut paradise, Rachel Morgenstern enters the Office of the City Clerk, Brooklyn Municipal Building. There, in the dingy, pillared edifice across from Borough Hall, she is married to Aaron Samuel Perlman by the power invested in a notary of the Marriage Bureau by the State of New York and Kings County. *Blessed are You, Lord, our God, Master of the Universe, who creates joy and gladness, groom and bride, mirth, song, delight, and rejoicing, love and harmony, and peace and companionship. B'aruch ata Adonai, m'sameiach chatan im hakalah.*

Aymen.

For their first year, they live on East Tenth Street. A one-bedroom on the top floor of a sandstone apartment block across from Tompkins Square Park. Rachel likes to walk through the park sometimes in the afternoon or sit and smoke on a bench where the old men read their newspapers in Yiddish, though Aaron forbids her to enter the park after dusk. Too dangerous for a woman alone, he insists. The reason? Hopheads. Hopheads, dope peddlers, and beatniks, a ghastly array of interlopers in her husband's mind. The neighborhood was going to hell, he complains, and they should find a place uptown. Somewhere on the Upper West Side maybe. But really Rachel doesn't mind the peeling paint, the unswept gutters and dilapidated streets. Even in the face of Aaron's hopheads, dope peddlers, and beatniks, who are waiting to plunder any woman who steps too close, she feels free there.

She strolls down to the coffee shops, to Washington Square. She can go sit in the park or eat a pierogi at the Ukrainian luncheonette on Ninth Street. Reconnoitering the Book Row on Fourth Avenue, she finds she has a taste for mystery novels. Whodunits, especially Nancy Drew. She sits in the Reggio all afternoon reading *The Ghost of Blackwood Hall* or *The Clue of the Velvet Mask.* The Upper West Side may have Murray's Sturgeon Shop to recommend it, but really, who wants to live in the Eighties as a slave to the Seventh Avenue Local?

Then certain phone calls are made.

When Aaron's cousin Ezra mentions that a one-bedroom is opening up in the building where he rents with his wife and brood just above the fur district? *Well.* Wheels are set in motion. *Ezra's* mother calls *Aaron's* mother, and anyway, the rest is history. The Perlmans move into a new home in a five-story walk-up, not in the Upper East Side but on West 22nd Street between Ninth and Tenth Avenues in Chelsea. A prewar red brick with black-iron fire-escape scaffolding bolted to the facade. Aaron refers to it as a shitty little one-bedroom while talking to Ezra, because he certainly doesn't want his cousin to get a big head about it, but honestly it's not so shitty at all.

Rachel finds it rather roomy. Inside there is the salon, or should she say the living room? There is a sofa flanked by matching lamp tables, but not matching lamps. Then comes a galley kitchen with a linoleum floor and a narrow apartment stove from Welbilt, the bedroom with a double bed and foam mattress, the bath with a claw-foot enameled tub and a showerhead. A hall tree by the front door, opposite a closet. A few other sticks of furniture here and there, and that's it. Basic digs. Not a luxury penthouse maybe, but not a dump either.

She misses their old place at times, maybe not the drippy faucet or the noisy steam radiators, but the park? The homely old neighborhood?

Those she misses, she thinks. Though what does that really mean to her, *misses*? Things, neighborhoods, homes? They have no real hold over her. She knows if she must, if she has to save herself, she can walk away from any address. Any home. Any possession. Perhaps even any person. She can slip away like a shadow. Though at night, she often lies awake listening to the dark rumble of the trains traveling the elevated West Side line and fights an urge to crawl beneath the bed. She fears trains. Fears their power. Once you're on a train, you can't always simply decide to get off at your stop. Sometimes your stop is decided by the train.

Night. Rachel lies in bed, her eyes open and gazing upward. She is examining her eema's painting in her mind. Shining an inner light on the brushstrokes. Seeing it in the rubbish heap of the pawnbroker's shop, even dulled by a film of dust, it shocked her how Eema's brush-strokes were still as fiery and challenging as they were when paint first touched canvas. The moody crimson of the background eclipsed by la muse's figure, a thick rush of color overtaking the foreground. A brightly alluring female shape. Flesh on exhibition. Eema painted la muse like an icon. The sacred red harlot, the intimacies of her feelings revealed on the canvas by the impassioned attention of Eema's technique. Rachel can still recall how the canvas stood on Eema's easel in the blaze of a sunset. Transcendent.

Will she ever create something so stunning? She's heard that if a thousand monkeys are set before a thousand typewriters with a thousand reams of paper, they'll eventually hammer out the works of Shakespeare. Could that work for her as well? If she slings enough paint across enough canvases, will she eventually create a masterpiece? She once wanted to believe this could happen. But she knows better now. She knows that she'll never create anything of value until she has freed herself from her ghosts. Freed herself from her guilt. Freed herself from her crime. Angelika Rosen made murder easy. Easy enough for anyone to commit. Even a little morsel. Was that God's plan as well? And if it was, what's His plan now? Why has this painting reappeared one moment only to disappear the next? Is it bait? A lure to her entrapment or a path for her deliverance? Salvation or damnation?

The front door opens in the next room and then quietly shuts. Rachel pushes herself up on her elbows and switches on the bedside lamp. Aaron appears, still dressed in his shirtsleeves, his collar open and tie unknotted, home from another double shift managing the restaurant that isn't even his. The business in which he owns no equity beyond the equity of sweat.

"I woke you," he observes, unbuttoning his shirt.

"I wasn't really asleep," she tells him and lights a cigarette from her half-empty pack of filter tips, feeling the smoke biting the back of her throat.

He sits on the mattress beside her with a scrunch of bedsprings. Steals a drag. "So I'm sorry about last night. It's been bothering me, getting so bent out of shape about everything. I mean, what do I really care about the electric bill in the big scheme of things? So it's a little higher than normal if it means you stay warm?"

She gently brushes a few stray curls from his forehead. He smiles dimly.

"I just thought this year on your birthday, we'd *make it* a tsimmis. Not a big tsimmis, but a small tsimmis, that's all. Have a nice meal at the restaurant and then take in a show. Like for instance, I dunno, *orchestra* seats for *The Pajama Game*?" He says this as if he's revealing a prize. The cat trots in and hops up on the bed, but Aaron scoops him up one-handed and drops him back on the floor. "They got a big hit going at the Saint James. Supposed to be gangbusters. Sold-out crowds. But I've got a guy who can swing tickets."

"Who is a guy?"

"Just a regular at the bar. A guy named Chernik. He's a booking agent. Knows all the big fish on Broadway. Very funny, always cracking everybody up." He waits for a beat. "So whattaya think?"

Rachel gazes at him. She understands how important it is to him. How important it is to him to be able take her out someplace nice and remove her from her own intimate insanity. To *rescue* her, just like he did at the library that first day, only now he is trying to rescue her from herself. She knows that his identity is still tied to playing his wife's hero even after years of marriage. She can hear it in the boyish buoyancy of his voice—to be the big shot himself for once and get the Broadway show tickets.

"Okay." She surrenders. She can swallow her shame at surviving, can't she? At having been spared the smoking ovens that consumed the millions? At least for an evening. "You win," she whispers. "We'll have a tsimmis."

But across the room, standing by the sofa, is her mother. Head shaven, eyes like pits. Rachel knows why she's come. It's the painting. Eema cannot permit her work to be so easily lost again, like a pair of gloves left behind on a café table. She cannot permit her painting to be so simply forgotten. Forgetting the artist's work is no different from forgetting the artist.

7.

A Heartbreaker!

WHEN SHE IS SIX YEARS OLD, RACHEL LEARNS THE TRUTH about the world. About the world of a Jew in Berlin. The American stock exchange has failed, tipping the world into ruinous depression. Economies have collapsed, and Germany's fledgling democracy is losing its tenuous foothold. The Communist Party surges in parliamentary elections, as does the so-called National Socialist German Workers Party. Political mayhem bloodies the streets once more, as it had a decade earlier during the runaway inflation.

In the face of chaos and fearing revolution from the left, the ancient fossil, Herr Reichspräsident General-Feldmarschall Paul von Beneckendorff und Hindenburg, the Hero of Tannenberg, once more evokes Article 48 of the Constitution to rule by emergency decree. On the first of January 1933, he uses his powers to appoint a former army corporal named Adolf Hitler to the most powerful post in the land, chancellor of the German Reich. The monarchists agree. Put this upstart Bohemian paperhanger in charge to eradicate the Marxist threat and then control his excesses. They think they've hired him for their show.

But this upsets Rashka's mother greatly, and anything that upsets Eema also upsets Rashka—though, at six, she does not understand so much the reasons why. She only knows that when she hears this man's voice on the wireless, her mother's face darkens, and Rashka feels a knot of painful confusion tighten in her belly.

The wireless booms: "It is my sacred mission to purge all German art of the intentionally disruptive modern jargon created by Jews and social perverts," the newly minted Reichskanzler bellows over the airwaves. "So-called works of art that are grotesque, unmanly, and deliberately perplexing shall now be recognized as the insulting inventions of deranged minds!"

Rashka is drawing. She is safe, she believes, at home in the salon of her mother's Gründerzeit villa in the Fasanenstrasse, not so far from the Elephant Gate of the Zoologischer Garten. The walls are hung with Eema's work. Her mother's bright, savagely colorful gouache and inks. The oils on hefty canvases. Figures, faces, ugly, beautiful, human. Little Rashka is on the soft floral carpet drawing in her pad, and her eema is seated in her favorite upholstered chair, the Viennese wingback, but she is frowning at the voice from the radio bawling into the empty space of the room. Her eema's face is a mask of tension as she smokes a cigarette screwed into her amber holder.

"It will be my eternal vow that such Jew-inspired perversion will be forever thwarted in its attempt to poison the artistic soul of our German Volk!"

Rashka is trying to concentrate on her drawing, but the wireless broadcast is distracting her, confusing her. And when the speech concludes with a storm of Heils, Eema tersely switches off the dial.

Rashka suspends her drawing and looks up. "He is a paskudnyak!" she reports, a child trying out a grown-up's insult she'd overheard, but her mother reacts with unexpected force.

"*Never call him that*, Rashka. Not in *public*," Eema warns, eyebrows arched. It's a command underpainted with a stain of fear. "Where did you *hear* such a thing?"

Rashka swallows. Ehrenberg's Konditorei is a pastry shop on the Lindenstrasse that she frequents with the housemaid, Manka. Was it Frau Ehrenberg who spoke this word? She decides it was. "Frau Ehrenberg. I heard her say it."

"That woman is a fool with a loose mouth, and so is her husband," Eema declares. "The both of them. Fools! Manka shouldn't take you there. It will get us all into trouble."

This is a disappointment, and Rashka complains. "But, *Eema*, they have the Mohnkuchen there!"

"Never mind Mohnkuchen. Just watch your tongue. And *never* call that man such a name again."

But then Rashka remembers: "Feter Fritz has called him so too." This time, however, Rashka is surprised when her mother bites off a short, bitter laugh.

"Ha! Your Feter Fritz thinks he's the cat with nine lives. But *you*, Rashka? *You* are *not*. Out beyond our doors? Be a good little goat and keep your mouth closed. This man Hitler may indeed be the worst kind of paskudnyak. But he is no longer any kind of a joke."

Rashka breathes this in. Not a cat but a goat. "But *why*?" she must ask. "Why is he so angry with Jews?"

"Because he hates us," Eema informs her, smothering her cigarette in the red sandstone cendrier. The sentence is spoken curtly with the weight of common fact. But Rashka is really rather startled. Certainly, that can't be completely true.

"Not *all* of us," she says, as if perhaps her mother is mistaken.

Her eema, however, remains rigid. "Yes. All of us."

"You, Eema?"

"Yes."

"Feter Fritz?"

"Yes."

"And me *too*?"

Her mother's glare is merciless. "Especially you, Daughter," she declares. "He hates you because you, Rashka, are the future."

Rashka is mortified at the thought of such hatred. She has never imagined that anyone could hate her. Her, personally. Rokhl Morgenstern.

"What are you scribbling there?" her eema suddenly demands. "Show me."

Rashka dutifully stands, pulls the page from her sketchbook, and presents her mother with it for inspection. "It's *me*," she says. "I drew myself." Rashka is really quite pleased with it and hopes for her mother's approval. But Eema scowls and rips the drawing in half, causing Rashka to burst immediately into tears.

"*Eema!* Why did you *do* that?"

"Because you can do better. And because loss is part of life, tsigele," her mother explains. "You should learn that now." Eema stands and drops the torn drawing into the fire that's crackling in the hearth, leaving Rashka crying and bewildered.

<hr>

She had left the house this morning with intention. Her sister-in-law, Naomi, is something of a bohemian type but is also something of a clotheshorse. Rachel is hoping that she might have something she can borrow for the Big Tsimmis, because really, who should be spending money on a new dress for one night? Also, since the Episode, Rachel avoids department stores.

She has relieved the crowded medicine cabinet at home of the bottle of Miltown and started carrying it in her bag. On the subway, she opens the bottle and downs two, even though it's hours away from her normal schedule. But she takes two now, and by the time she is exiting the Lexington Avenue train at West Fourth, the Miltown has done its work. She feels as if she's walking a straight line. Following the trajectory of a quiet arrow.

All manner of craziness can find a home in the Village. Aaron speaks of it as if it's a kind of neighborhood mental asylum between Broadway and the North River, but it's where his sister has chosen to live, in a redbrick walk-up at the intersection of MacDougal and Minetta Lane. A stately old Italian ristorante sits across the street and farther down a neighborhood joint called Kettle of Fish.

Up the building's stoop, Rachel finds the door unlocked as always and wanders through it, heading up the stairs. She can smell the ancient cigarette smoke, generations old, that clings to the carpet runners. But on the third floor, she catches the aroma of chemical developer. A record player is spinning the Platters hit, "Only You." When she knocks, she calls through the door, "Naomi?"

A scratch as the record player quits and the door flings open. Answering the door is a breezy young woman in a peasant blouse over red toreador pants with bare feet. "Hey, it's *you*," her sister-in-law declares with a startling happy grin.

"It is me," Rachel admits and accepts the big smack Naomi plants on her cheek.

"Well, get in here, you. I'll break out the booze!" This is Aaron's kid sister, though really, she is no longer a kid at all. Naomi Beatrice Perlman, known universally by the members of the Flatbush tribe as Naomi-rhymes-with-Foamy. A troublemaker, a subversive, at least compared to her brother Mr. Don't-Make-Waves. She likes to stir the pot. Chestnut hair in a ponytail and velvety brown eyes. Pretty in a careless, go-screw-yourself kind of way. A real meydl mit a veyndl.

Inside, the place is its usual casual mess, and the smell of the developing fluids is stronger. Rachel lights a cigarette against it. She stares back at the faces assessing her from the walls. Naomi works for a commercial agency on East 70th to pay the rent, photographing Sara Lee's all butter yellow cake for magazine advertisements, but her walls at home are papered with looming photographic prints of the quirky hardscrabble denizens of the Village. Battered, scarred, suspicious, or confrontational faces glaring in black-and-white. Close up. Intentionally ugly and beautiful at the same time. Camera equipment and paraphernalia are scattered everywhere. A Kodalite Midget Flash Holder sits beside a carton of GE Surefire flashbulbs, like a carton of eggs with several eggs missing. A yellow tin of Kodak Microdol-X Developer is ready to roll off the top of the bookshelf with the next bump. All around, there's an air of post-explosion, as if a minor rupture of chaos in the cosmos has scattered everything everywhere.

Naomi is quick to uncork the half bottle she has in her humming fridge. Maybe it's only noon, but this is the Village, so she sloshes Chianti into mismatched glasses from her shelf. The wine is over-chilled and tastes like it's about to turn, but what the heck? They drink it anyway, seated on the sofa where Naomi has cleared away errant bits of clothing and photo magazines.

"Your brother is taking me to a Broadway show," Rachel announces.

"Oh, so the shtoomer finally stuck a crowbar in his wallet, did he?"

"A crow?"

"A crowbar. You know." Naomi makes a prying motion. "For prying shit open."

"Oh. Yes." Incomprehensible. "He has a friend in the ticket business."

"*Of course.* Always a friend somewhere. Always looking to squeeze out a few pennies." Naomi drinks. "He gets that from Pop. The man who bought his coffin from Sherman Brothers ten years before he died so he could get the discount."

There's this goulash of family turmoil with the Perlmans of Flatbush, always roiling just under the surface, which *all of them* so nonchalantly stir. It confuses Rachel. She understands bitterness and envy, anger and resentment; God knows she understands all that. But it's so casual here in America. In Berlin, accusations were formal and heavy as bludgeons. Here it's all a sport of stinging anecdotes dis-guised as humor. It baffles her, and when she tries to imitate and play along, the words come out like cold poison. "Well, *my* mother, you know, was the worst kind of public egoist with a stone for a heart. She once abandoned me in the Karstadt department store because she had forgotten I was with her and had gone instead for supper at the Adlon. But I was forced to love her anyway." Only a clumsy silence follows that.

"So I have no clothes to wear," Rachel says. "Nothing glamorous.

Aaron says I should *buy* something, but…" She lets that sentence finish itself.

"No worries. Naomi's got you covered," her sister-in-law assures her and begins to disgorge the clothes from her closet. And not just any old rags, but the stylish velvets, silks, satins, and gabardines. Where does such a closet come from? "Try the pencil dress," Naomi tells her. "Black always does the trick."

Rachel no longer retains a sense of modesty when it comes to undressing. That was driven from her in hiding. She strips off her blouse and pants and slips into the dress, completing it with black satin three-quarter-length opera gloves. The wine is working a happy magic through her. Posing in front of the closet mirror, she shares the dress's reflection with Naomi.

"*Perfect,*" Naomi decides. "With a string of pearls? You're Audrey Hepburn."

Rachel is pleased with her reflection in this flattering mirror. She feels as buoyed by it as she does by the Chianti. "It's not too much?" she asks just as a test.

"Nope."

"Not too phony? Your brother doesn't like phoniness," she says, causing Naomi to pull a face.

"Oh, my *brother,*" she replies and blows a raspberry. Then picks up her Leica from the sofa and advances the film. "Screw him and his opinions. He *has* no opinions that he didn't inherit. Mostly from the materfamilias, by the way, if you haven't noticed by now. He may *sound* like Pop? But scratch an inch underneath and it's the Iron Hausfrau of Webster Av'. Mind if I take a few shots?" she asks but doesn't wait for an answer and starts snapping pictures. Winged by the wine, lightened by the Miltown, Rachel plays along for a bit, posing this way and that way. This sort of attention is rare for her.

Naomi gives a laugh and shakes her head in delectable admiration. "Christ, you're a heartbreaker!" she declares. "The camera fuckin' loves you."

8.

The Big Tsimmis

THE EVENING COMES. THE EVENING OF THE BIG TSIMMIS masquerading as a Small Tsimmis. In the bedroom, Aaron is gabbing away from the bathroom as he finishes his shave. "By the way. My mom called. 'Mazel tov' she says for your birthday."

"That's nice." Rachel has just taken a dose of Miltown to level herself. To allow herself to participate in normal life. A normal wife.

"Not to ruin the surprise of this year's present," Aaron is telling her, "but it's gonna be pot holders."

"Pot holders," she says. This fits. Usually gifts from her mother-in-law are meant to fill some deficiency that the lady has noted. A kitchen whisk. (Now maybe you won't need a *fork* to beat an egg every time.) A set of eight Lucite coasters. (No more rings on your furniture!) Tupperware measuring cups. (Now you won't have to guess!)

"*Crocheted* pot holders," Aaron informs her. "It's what you get for burning your fingers on the casserole dish that time she was over."

"Two years ago and she still remembers."

"What can I say? The woman never forgets."

"Is that *all* she said?"

"Like what else?"

"I don't know. Like anything."

"Nope. Just pot holders," Aaron answers. But she must wonder if that's true. After how many years of marriage with no kids, his mother has stopped asking directly. But there's usually *something* said. (Maybe it's a blessing after all that you don't have kids. They just break your heart.)

"Okay. I'll send her a very enthusiastic thank-you note," Rachel assures him. She stands in front of the vanity's mirror, a glass that *by name* is designed to flatter, and examines herself in Naomi's black pencil dress, adjusting the satin opera gloves. Her lips are Pure Red from Elizabeth Arden, her face is powdered, her cheeks lightly rouged, her eyelashes thickened with mascara, her eyebrows shaped and defined by a brow pencil. The dress fits her in spots where she seldom notices the fit of clothing. Aaron steps up behind her in the dinner jacket he usually reserves for New Year's Eve, knotting his bow tie. "Okay, now here's a meydl mit a kleydl," he says appreciatively.

"Zip me up, please, sir," she whispers.

"Yes, ma'am." Aaron obeys, cheerfully solicitous.

She eyes herself as he zips. "Now the pearls."

Aaron connects her necklace at the back of her neck. "Yowza," he proclaims.

"Yowza?"

"Yowza. Caramba. As in, holy mackerel, I've got Audrey Hepburn for a wife. Where'd the dress come from anyhow?"

"Your sister lent it. I was worried you'd think it was too much."

Frowning his appreciation. "Nope. For once, the screwy kid got it right." He slides his arms around her from behind and kisses her on the neck.

Rachel gazes back at their mirror image. Tonight she is content with this counterfeit image of herself. This *beautiful* counterfeit image. "I'm glad we're doing this," she informs him. "Really. It's a good idea."

"Yeah?" He is pleased.

"A perfect idea."

"Well, I have them from time to time," he can only admit. "So happy birthday, Mrs. Perlman." He nuzzles her neck lightly. She reaches back to sift through his hair with her fingers. "Hey. You smell good."

"I wonder why," she replies. His gift that morning at the breakfast table had been a bottle of perfume. Moonlight Mist from Gourielli, though she suspects Naomi's involvement in the choice, since her husband so often likes to compare perfume scents to paint thinner. One bottle smells like the next to him. "You have the tickets?" she asks softly.

Still nuzzling. "All taken care of by my dear friend Mr. Chernik," he starts to say.

"Do you even know his first name?"

"I do, but it happens to be Rumpelstiltskin, and he's very sensitive. As I was saying, my dear friend Chernik—"

"Rumpelstiltskin Chernik."

"Is going to meet us at the restaurant with tickets in hand. Air-conditioned orchestra seating, no less. It's all under control."

In the cab, Aaron makes a small deal of lighting her cigarette for her. Something he very seldom bothers with any longer. She smiles. Puffs a bit of smoke back at him in a playful way. He smiles too, pretends a cough as a joke—but then cracks the window. He's happy but anxious. Anxious for things to go well. She can tell by the slightly pained but eager tone of his voice that he's looking for distraction by suddenly devoting his attention to the cabbie, instructing him how and when to turn to avoid Midtown traffic. Rachel cracks her own window as well, and the smoke slips away into the night.

Her feter had telephoned her that afternoon when she had just stepped out of the shower and had to stand there, dripping, wrapped in a towel, as he'd sung an old Hebrew song for her birthday with a fair number of Yiddish colloquialisms intruding. *Mazel Tov!* he'd told her. *Mit mazel zolstu zikh yern!* Your new year should bring you luck! Though was his sudden ability to recall the date of her birth strategic? His tenor had been nothing but upbeat. The caring uncle! The last of her living blood relatives, and who knows for how long he can keep holding on, but never mind. *Mazel tov, ziskeit!* And then the show was over, and he'd hung up. It was as if nothing had happened, as if no painting in a ugly frame had appeared and then disappeared.

A truck horn beeps. "So okay," she hears Aaron instructing the cabbie. "One right turn, and you'll hit Broadway."

Fine Dining Before Curtain Time. That's what the matchbooks advertise. Charades on Broadway, across from the Winter Garden. A deco masonry facade with a scribble of neon sketching its name in the gathering dusk, punctuated by flashing masks of comedy and tragedy. Aaron makes a show of discreetly tipping the liveried doorman who holds the door of the cab for them, calling him Smitty. "Thanks, Smitty, my friend. You're a mensch," he says.

"Thank *you*, Mr. Perlman," says Smitty in a raspy voice. Though Rachel cannot help but notice a hint of something in the aged brown eyes above the man's smile. Pain? Resentment? Something older. Something stronger.

"A new guy," Aaron explains out of Smitty's earshot.

"What happened to Mr. Rubenstein?"

"Made tracks for Florida. Leo decided to hire a colored guy to replace him, like it's *Gone with the Wind* or something. I dunno. He thinks it's snazzier. Also cheaper."

Inside, it's faux Corinthian columns, marble-tile floors with carpet runners, and Moroccan leather booths the color of cognac. Inside, the faces are white. It may be otherwise in the kitchen with the Puerto Rican guys hired as dishwashers, but out front is a sea of whiteness because, here in New York at least, even the Jews are considered white. The only person who isn't included in that description is the snowy-haired gentleman at the piano, dabbling on the ivories. Rachel doesn't know what his real name is because everybody calls him Professor. He nods as he always nods, with a smile at Rachel whenever she appears, but it's a blind smile, the same smile he offers to all who bother to notice him at the piano bench. His expression alters attentively when Aaron leans over to him, slipping him a little appreciation, saying, "Gimme some of the sweet stuff, Professor. Ya know what I mean?"

"Oh, I do *know*, Mr. Perlman." The Professor grins. "I do know *precisely*," he says as if they're sharing a moment of deep understanding of the arc of the universe. But when the man seeks out a tingle-tangle melody on the piano keys, to Rachel's ear, it's really no different from the tingle-tangle melody he was playing a moment before.

Her husband, on the other hand, appears brightly satisfied. "*That's* what I'm talkin' about," he declares.

When Abe, the great golem-sized majordomo, looms toward them in his tuxedo, Aaron gives him a comradely slap on the shoulder. "*Evening*, my friend," says Aaron.

"Evening, Mr. P.," Abe replies. "And happy *birthday*, Mrs. P."

"Thank you, Mr. Goldman."

"So we ready to *go* here?" Aaron inquires, rubbing his palms together in a lightly greedy fashion. "Table twenty like I said?"

Abe confirms. "Best table in the house as ordered, ready and waiting."

But on the journey to the Best Table in the House, Rachel feels Aaron physically clench. "H'boy, here we go," he whispers to himself, and then she sees why.

It's Leo. Leo Blume, the owner, silver-haired and sleek as a seal in his immaculate white dinner jacket. A Jew who came from nothing. The Baxter Street side of the Bend. "Bottle Alley," Leo says. "The gutter." That's the story he tells. Now Hedda Hopper should be so lucky as to get a table during his dinner rush. He holds court at Table 27, one of the brass-studded, crescent-shaped booths in the main dining room. A premium table, as Aaron has explained it to her: not too near the service corridors, so there's no noise from the kitchen, near enough to the piano dais to hear "Stardust" without straining, but not so close that a person can't have a conversation. And Leo always takes the outside spot on the left-hand side, just in case he has to launch himself into the aisle in the event that a customer has a heart attack, or the waiter drops a lighted baked Alaska, or Red bombers have been spotted over Rockaway, or Oscar Hammerstein walks into the bar with his wife, Dot, for a midnight Bloody Mary.

Smoking his thick Montecristo B, Leo is busy gabbing away on the jade-green telephone, but spotting their approach, he cuts short his call, his voice full of gravel. "Milty, I gotta call ya back," he says into the green receiver, then frowns, apparently dissatisfied with Milty's response. "So I'll call ya *back*," he insists and hangs up, muttering. "My shmegegi brother, God love 'im." And then he shows Rachel his trademarked smile. Charming as a barracuda. "Ketsl, you're *gorgeous* tonight, sweetheart," he tells her, standing to exchange a peck on the cheek with her. "Like starshine."

Aaron smiles stupidly. "Am I married to Audrey Hepburn or what?"

"So look, I won't horn in," he tells them. "'Cause I know you two got an evening planned. I just wanted to say that dinner tonight is on me, got it? Soup to nuts."

The smile has stiffened on Aaron's face. "No. Leo. Please. Not necessary."

But Leo only shrugs. "It's nothing. A gesture on your beautiful wife's birthday, that's all. So go. Enjoy. And happy birthday, ketsl," he adds. "Mit mazl zolstu zikh yern."

"A sheinem dank, Leo," she replies.

"*Ha!* I love that this girl speaks Yiddish! Ir zent a sheyn shtern," he tells her, calling her a shining star before he motions to Abe. "Abe. Take this lovely lady and her husband to their table, will ya? And remember. My party tonight."

Abe's been on the staff since Leo opened the place after Prohibition and is as much a fixture at Charades as the Comedy & Tragedy ashtrays that everybody steals. As much a fixture as the Moroccan leather booths or the Tiffany chandeliers. His belly's as big as a barrel now, his forehead is livid with liver spots, and his earlobes have flattened and elongated like an elephant's. But even after twenty years of *Sure, Mr. Blume* and *Whatever you say, Mr. Blume*, he still sounds genial and pleased to serve. "Sure thing, Mr. Blume," says Abe with a smile. "Whatever you say."

The Best Table in the House features snow-white linen, gleaming silverware, and Comedy & Tragedy dinner plates rimmed in gold leaf. A flame flickers in a red Venetian lowboy candle lamp. Izzie is one of the middle-aged waiters schlepping hash here since Roosevelt's first term. He is resplendent as a grand duke in a crimson Eton jacket with epaulettes and golden aiguillette as he oversees the delivery of their highballs by a young runner, also in livery but without the tinsel. Aaron, however, is disconnected. He looks slightly petulant, so Rachel is smiling for both of them.

"A vodka gimlet for the lady," Izzie is announcing, "and for the gentleman, a whiskey sour."

"Yeah, thanks, Iz," Aaron replies dully. "We'll start off with a couple of the marinated herrings."

"Yes, sir. Perfect choice."

"So what's the tuna tonight? Off the trucks or off the docks?"

"Tonight? The trucks," Izzie regrets to report.

"Forget it then," Aaron instructs. "We'll do the poached salmon with the eggplant. And make sure Monsieur Bouillabaisse in the kitchen goes easy on the fennel, okay? You tell him that comes from *me*, okay?" he adds.

"Absolutely, Mr. P. Be back in a jiff with your appetizers." Izzie and the runner exit, but Aaron only huffs and lights a Lucky with a snap of his Zippo.

"What's the matter?" Rachel finally asks.

Deadpan. "Nothing."

"That is untrue."

"Nothing is the matter," Aaron insists. "It's only why did he have to *do* that?" he wants to know, followed by his gravel-voiced impression of Leo. "'It's my pawty—soup t'nuts.' Like I can't pay for my own dinner."

"He's being generous."

"Oh, *sure*. Mr. Generosity, that's Leo Blume all right. The big man's gotta make everybody else look small. Always looking for the lever," he says, yanking on the imaginary lever. "Always looking for the upper hand."

Rachel filches one of his Lucky Strikes, and a runner appears out of nowhere to light it. "Oh, thank you," she says with a smile, but then the smile departs as she returns to her husband. "So are we going to enjoy our evening," she wonders, "or are you going to sulk through it?"

He gives her a sideway glance like maybe he's *considering* coming around. "Haven't decided yet. Honestly, it could go either way."

Rachel breathes in, tries to remain calm. Glances around the restaurant. "Where's your chum Rumpelstiltskin with our tickets? I thought he was supposed to meet us here."

Izzie suddenly appears at tableside and clears his throat. "Pardon, Mr. P., but Pauli says you got a call up at the bar. A gentleman by the name of Chernik?"

Aaron turns to Rachel, vindicated. "Ah. *Ya' see now?* There he is. My *pal*."

"You want I should have the kid bring you a phone?" Izzie inquires, but Aaron waves the suggestion off as ludicrous.

"Nah, I'm not a big shot, Izzie, like you-know-who. I can get up and walk to the phone like the rest of us peasants do." He pats his wife on her shoulder reassuringly. "Be right back."

Rachel swallows. Alone at the table, her mind wanders toward shadow.

He's not so bad, your husband, I suppose. Not so bad.

She looks over to find her mother seated across the table from her in Aaron's spot, dressed in her furs and finery, a woman at the height of her renown. *At least the poor man is trying to make you happy,* Eema reminds her. *He's making an attempt. Of course we both realize, I'm sure, that the boy is neither milchidik nor flaishidik*—neither dairy nor meat—*but that's not necessarily bad. As men go? You could do worse.*

"Were *you* ever happy, Eema?"

Was I?

"With my father?"

Eema considers. *At times. At times I was. And when he died, I grieved. I did. But I was also relieved. At last to have my life back in my own hands.*

"And what about *her*?" Rachel asks.

Her? Who is her? Eema pretends not to know.

"You know very well *who is her*," Rachel insists. "Did *she* make you happy?"

Her mother shrugs slightly, expels smoke from her cigarette in the amber holder. *When a person sticks a dagger in your heart, can that person make you happy?* she wonders. An unanswered question.

At that moment, Aaron replaces her mother as he slides into the booth looking abashed. "Uh, honey?" he says and swallows something jagged. "There's been a bit of a wrinkle in the plan."

The atmosphere in the rear of a checkered taxi is chilly as they head west on 48th. Rachel glares through the window glass blindly. The only sounds are the passing traffic and the occasional snort of static on the cabbie's dispatch radio. Between wife and husband, there is only silence, until Aaron finally speaks.

"*What?*"

But all he gets is nothing.

"I'm sorry," he says, "but it was the only show he could get seats for that weren't up in the rear mezzanines with the cobwebs."

More silence.

"It's supposed to be incredible," he offers with hope. "All the reviews…"

Nothing.

"So whattaya wanna do? Turn around?" he asks. "Go home and play Scrabble? We can do that," he offers. A real offer.

Rachel breathes out and finally answers, looking down at her satin-gloved hands. "No." She sighs in a small way. "No, too late. It's only that you promised *The Pajama Game.* I was looking forward to comedy."

A moment more of nothing between them, until Aaron proffers his only defense: "I hear there are some funny parts…"

The Cort Theatre on West 48th. As the taxi slows, the marquee blazes.

THE DIARY OF ANNE FRANK

She sits beside her husband in the crowded auditorium. But she is unaware of him. Unaware of the audience surrounding her. She can only see the people onstage; she can only absorb what she hears from the performers acting their parts under the claustrophobic lighting. Her nerves are needles. Her muscles clenched. Her throat too thickened to emit the slightest whimper. She has made it thus far, as one act gave way to the next, navigating the desperation of Jews in hiding onstage, through the cloying scenes of fear and fearlessness, of joy and ennui, of petty squabbles, of soaring hopes, and of doomed dreams. Doomed, doomed, doomed by the coming betrayal. The evil blot of human betrayal. Glaring at the stage with sharp grief gleaming in her eyes, she hears the line spoken by the young girl standing center.

It remains her opinion, she informs the crowd, *that in spite of all evidence to the contrary, people in their hearts are still good.*

And that's it.

Rachel is up, shoving past annoyed patrons. She can hear Aaron whispering frantically after her, calling her name, but she ignores him. She must flee. She must flee. She must flee.

"My fault," Aaron is admitting. Breaking the silence in the rear of their cab heading down Ninth Avenue. Heading home.

"My fault," he repeats. "This is my fault. I should have said *screw it* the second that yutz Chernik called."

Silence.

Rachel's eyes are raw. She glares at the lights of the street as they stream past the taxi's window.

"*Diary of Anne Frank,*" her husband concludes. "Bad idea."

But Rachel does not speak a word. Up in the front, beside the driver, sits a schoolgirl. Her hair woven into a single braid, a wine-colored beret on her head. Her strong, beautiful face betrays patches of decay. The simple beauty of her eyes is hardly diminished by the rot of death; their humanity is still very clear.

"*Stop!*" Rachel hears herself shout aloud. "*Stop!*" But too late. By the time the cabbie stamps on the brakes, she has puked the dinner that Leo had treated them to into her husband's lap.

She does not sleep that night. Hunched over the toilet on her knees, she cannot stop the upheaval, even though she must be ruining Naomi's dress. Aaron kneels beside her, holding her hair, stroking her head in between heaves. He blames the salmon, and she does not attempt to correct him. She must have gotten a bad piece of fish is his explanation, though she has already heaved up appetizers, entrée, dessert, soup to nuts, and at this point is simply sputtering bile into the white porcelain bowl.

A schoolgirl is watching with melancholy. Brunette hair plaited into a single braid. A burgundy beret tugged at an angle. She dares to offer Rashka a tentative smile in the recesses of her memory, while the black pencil dress is flecked with her regurgitation. Rachel is sweating and shivering. She cannot stop. She must vomit up her life.

Her past. Herself.

9.

Things Went Amiss

THE NIGHT PASSES. DRESSED IN HER PINK CHENILLE BATHROBE, hair uncombed, she stares at her warped reflection in the toaster's aluminum. She had learned from the radio show *Alka-Seltzer Time* how to defend herself against a sour belly and drinks a glass of water in which she has dropped two tablets of antacids that are fizzing as they dissolve. It leaves a sour tang on her tongue, like a lime slice in seltzer, although more chemical.

Aaron appears, giving her his husbandly peck on the cheek but with an extra squeeze, bunching up her shoulders against his chest. "You need something in your stomach," he determines. "Some dry toast, maybe a little burnt around the edges," he tells her and actually opens the sack of rye bread to stick two slices into the toaster. Aaron the cook! "That's what Ma always gave us when we were sick as kids. Dry toast, a little burnt around the edges," he repeats, describing the miracle cure.

Rachel nods. "Thank you."

"Look," he says. "Again. I'm really sorry for what happened. Subjecting you to that play."

"It's okay," Rachel tells him.

"We should have," he says. "We should have gone to Naomi's like you wanted in the first place."

"It's okay," Rachel repeats. "You needn't keep apologizing. Really. You were trying to be the good husband," she says to let him off the hook, because she does not know how many more apologies she can suffer. "You were trying to do something nice."

He nods lightly. This is *true*, after all. He pours a glass of water from the kitchen faucet and downs it. "So you want me to call the super? The drain's still slow."

Rachel swallows. "No. I'll call him," she lies.

"Okay," he agrees. No more pressure. "You're sure you're gonna be all right if I head in to work?" he inquires.

"*Yes*," Rachel replies and tucks a renegade strand of her hair behind an ear. "I'm going to be fine."

"I mean I could call Abe. Go in a few hours late."

"Aaron. I will be fine," she tells him.

"Okay," he says, stroking her head. "And don't worry," he assures her with certain conviction. He will put a boot up somebody's ass today for poisoning his wife with a piece of bad fish. Oh yes, he will kick some tuchus, all right. You bet he will. Though he offers this information gently, as if it's comforting. But really her husband's voice is just a drone in her ears. A few minutes later, the apartment door opens and then closes. Rachel locks it behind him and leans her back against it, staring into the interior of their apartment.

The paint on the wall is eggshell white. When they first moved in, their landlord paid to paint the place every year, but that custom has fallen by the wayside, and the walls are getting dingy. They betray an underpainting of gray in the light. And the floorboards squeak at every step. Still, sometimes it feels like a palace, even though it's just the shitty one-bedroom. As U-boats hiding in Berlin, she and Eema would have happily settled for a fraction of the space she has here.

A thin wisp of smoke rises from the toaster, and she winces as the toast suddenly pops up, burnt black. Eema, in fact, is at the kitchen table, once more the KaZetnik in clogs and rags. One of the dead of Auschwitz-Birkenau, reconstituted from the ash pits and now smelling up a Chelsea apartment.

"So tell me this, Eema," Rachel says. "Do you think Feter is lying?"

Always a clear possibility.

"You think he knows who holds your painting?"

Perhaps or perhaps not. But I do think, without doubt, my brother knows more than he says. It's the diktat of his personality.

Rachel is quiet for a moment. "It is still a beautiful work," she tells her mother. A sheyn kunst verk.

Eema draws a breath and exhales a burnt stench. But her bloodshot eyes have gone soft. Even in death, she has longings. *She was a beautiful subject. So beautiful.*

"They say she hanged herself, you know. After the war as a prisoner of the Russians." But her mother has no further comment. She is gone, and Rachel is alone.

Days pass. She wakes up confused. Where is she? The chaos of her sleep has infiltrated her waking mind. For a moment, she thinks she is on the floor in Grosse Hamburger Strasse camp, a prisoner awaiting transport to the east. When she shouts out in fear, Aaron sticks his head out of the bathroom, interrupted while brushing his teeth.

"You okay?" he wonders.

"Yes," she lies. "Yes. Just a bad dream."

She is on the move, heading out into the street. She is convinced that her eema is right. That Feter Fritz knows more than he is willing to divulge. He's always had his secrets. Even as a Jew under the Gestapo's roof, he considered secrets a form of currency.

It's Friday, so it's easy enough to find him stationed at a table in the Garden Cafeteria. A plate of latkes with applesauce sits on the table in front of him, accompanied by a cup of coffee and a glass of seltzer as he is writing in his little dog-eared notebook. The notebook is a habit of his from decades before. The secret reminders and intimate scraps of information recorded. Who knows when a person will need to remember something? A date, a name, a transaction? The exchange rate on the pound sterling? Where to purchase the best Italian leathers? That was then. These days, he usually scribbles with a nubby pencil snatched from the library, and God knows *what* he's jotting down. Tips on playing cribbage for cash? Where to buy the cheapest shoelaces? How to trick a vending machine with a slug? Rachel can only imagine.

Feter pretends to be happy at her arrival, but she can tell that he is actually not so happy. After so many years, she has learned to see through the masks he wears. She sits beside him so she can whisper, so that no gossips of Feter's acquaintance can overhear. He wonders to what does he owe the pleasure of her visit.

"Isn't it possible, Feter," she begins, "that you know something that you're not telling me?"

In response, her feter appears more confused than wounded by the question. And maybe even a bit amused. "*Ah*, so the mother comes out in the child. The result of the rich diet of mistrust your eema weaned you on, I fear," he says and laces together his fingers on the table. "What *precisely*—if I may ask—what *precisely* am I supposed to know that I am pretending not to know?"

"Eema's painting," Rachel answers.

"*Ah!*" He should have known!

"I feel as if it was stolen from me."

"Stolen?" And her feter is the thief? Again, not hurt but merely amused. "Her poor feter? This is what she thinks?" he asks the air. "My own flesh and blood, and yet to her, I am the swindler?"

"I didn't say that," Rachel insists.

"Didn't you?" he wonders aloud. Then his voice dips. He adopts a forgiving tone, an understanding tone. "Ruchel. Ziskeit," he says. "I swear to you. God in heaven, I did not steal your mother's painting from you."

"I said I *feel* as if it has been stolen. I didn't say by whom. I only wonder what you know. That's all."

"What I *know*, Daughter, is that you suffered too much. Too much, Rokhl, at such a tender age. It's made you…*suspicious*," he decides to call it. Perfectly understandable, he tells her. A child with such a history? How could she not be fearful of her own shadow? He opens up his old leather-bound cigar case, lighting up with the matchbook advertising a fancy kosher steakhouse in Murray Hill. Rachel also notes the band on the cigar. H. Upmann, Habana. "Am I hurt?" he asks. "Who wouldn't be hurt? After all, didn't I come to you first? Ask for your help? A few dollars, Rashka, and we would have had your mother's painting in our hands. *But.* That was not to be. Things went amiss, and I know my niece. I know that for all that goes amiss, she must find someone to blame."

Someone laughs sharply from across the room. A truck grinds its gears in the street.

"So here's a question for you, Feter. When did you start eating steak at Yosef Levi's?"

Feter smiles in an interior way. As if perhaps this is a joke he is missing. "I beg your pardon?"

"The matchbook, Feter," she explains. "And when did you start smoking cigars from Havana?"

So now he must laugh lightly at her presumption. "Rokhl, the matchbook came from somewhere, who knows? I picked it up." A shrug. "And the cigars? An old man treats himself in his waning years. That's a crime?"

"I don't know. Is it?"

Feter's smile turns leaden. "Rashka. Ziskeit. What are you driving at?" This he asks her in English.

Driving at? Rachel catches a breath. "Nothing, Feter," she tells him, dropping eye contact. "I don't mean to accuse you of anything or to imply." She glances submissively at her hands to put him off the scent that she is onto him. Not her mother's hands, not the accomplished hands with the slender fingers, so expressive. Not those hands, but hands of the competent peasant. Her father's hands, she's been told. The hands of the missing man left behind for her at her birth. "I've been easily upset it seems. Perhaps I'm not thinking clearly."

Feter appears to accept this as an apology, a confession, and even as a statement of fact. He clasps her hands in his and gives them a consoling pat. "I understand, Daughter," he promises. The edge of his cuff has inched upward, revealing the tail of the number tattooed above his wrist. "I understand," he tells her.

A perfect touch. The small reminder of his tattoo. Of his suffering. Of course she shouldn't be surprised. She knows that her feter is a master of extemporaneous solutions, a talented ad-lib performer. This is how he has survived. This is why he is still alive.

On the way home, she thinks about the painting itself as the subway barrels through the tunnel. Of all her mother's works, it was the only portrait with a living heartbeat. Perhaps that is why the sight of it was so frightening. To be confronted by a demon in the flesh brought back from death. The angel resurrected. Terrifying. It makes her reach for the comfort of Miltown. She should be relieved, shouldn't she, that it vanished again? She should be *thankful* that it haunts the walls of some unsuspecting shlimazel with fifty dollars, who thought it matched the drapes.

Back at the apartment, she changes into her robe and sits on the bed, trying to distract herself until the Miltown can level her out. They have plans this evening, though nothing to look forward to. Dinner with Ezra and Daniela, oy gevalt, at Daniela's favorite kosher place. So Rachel is smoking a cigarette before she has to change into a dress and paging through an art magazine from last month. If she can concentrate on normal things, then she can *be* normal. Or at least imitate normal. Isn't that how it works?

She hears the front door open. "Halloo," Aaron is calling. "King of the castle's home."

"I'm in the bedroom," she calls back. According to *ARTnews*, David Glass, the princely scion of the House of Glass on Fifth Avenue, has brought Berlin to New York in a retrospective of Käthe Kollwitz.

We never cared for each other personally, her mother informs her.

Kollwitz and myself. But I respected her work and she respected mine. This is said with stately certainty. *She had hallucinations as a child, you know. She would see a house cat, apparently, but to her, it was the size of a panther. Or her mother would appear the size of a doll, poor woman.* Eema is sporting a fashionable sable-trimmed cloak but vanishes as footsteps approach. Aaron enters, tie loose, collar open, home after another day in the salt mines.

"So here's the lady of leisure," he declares pleasantly. "Scooch over," he tells her and sits on the edge of the bed her mother had occupied a moment before. Yanking off his shoes, he tosses them with a breath of relief. Florsheim Imperials, walnut-brown leather wing tips. $14.98 at Falk's Sports Wear on Delancey. You Save Dollars! We Make Pennies! "Scooch over, will you," Aaron repeats. "I own one side the bed, if you recall. It was in the fine print of the marriage contract."

Stubbing out her cigarette in the bedside ashtray, she discards her magazine and scooches. "This isn't Budapest," she says. "We don't have a marriage contract."

But Aaron has already left the joke behind. Satisfied with his space, her husband unknots his tie and drops it. "Man, am I bushed," he tells her. "Whattaya say we just dig in here tonight and relax? Order some Chinese or something."

"Because we can't."

"No?" He has rolled his weight against her and begun to nuzzle her neck. "You sure?"

"I am. We have dinner with your cousin."

Aaron groans. "Ah, jeez. Tell me that's not really tonight, is it?"

"It is."

"I thought it was *next* week."

"No, this week. Tonight. So go. Get ready," she instructs and interrupts his nuzzling by giving him a loud peck on the cheek before removing herself from the bed. "I need to change, and you could use a shower."

10.

The Shield of David

A S THE WAR DRAGS INTO ANOTHER YEAR, THE JEWS OF BERLIN
are considered aliens in their own land. Since the police decree
regarding the identifying emblem for Jews was issued last September,
all Jews over the age of six *must*, by law, wear the Judenstern. The
details were published in the SS-controlled mouthpiece, the *Jüdisches
Nachrichtenblatt*. "The Jewish Star," it declared, "is a six-pointed star,
drawn in black lines made of yellow fabric, the size of the palm of
a hand." At the center, the word *Juden* is machine-stitched in black,
mock-Hebraic lettering. Jews must display the star "visibly" on the left
over the heart. No pinning of the star either. What a slippery Jewish
trick that is! Slipping it on and off as it suits them? No! It must be sewn
securely! The police will check.

And of course, everyone has had to *pay* for the stars that mark them
as outcasts and pariahs. Ten pfennigs apiece. Rashka pricked her finger
sewing one of them onto the ragged, oversized coat she wears. It's a
coat for a boy, but she wears it because it still has a heavy flannel lining
intact. She pricked her fingers and left a drop of blood on the star,
marking it hers. Rashka's Star. Claimed by bloodshed.

Years before, when she was six years old, the Nazis had staged a boycott of Jewish businesses. They were new to power then, and their effort
fizzled after a few days, but Rashka can starkly recall standing inside
Ehrenberg's Konditorei in the Lindenstrasse, staring out through the
glass while a giant storm trooper in his dung-brown Sturmabteilung
uniform painted a sloppy Magen David across the shop's window.

Her eema used paintbrushes too. Sometimes Rashka was even permitted to play with the old ones that had been retired from work. She liked smearing paint on a scrap of canvas in the shape of a hare or maybe a pony with a bristly mane. She liked the feeling of the brush in her hand. She liked the smooth application of the paint, just as she liked the broom of color, thinning into cartwheels as she smashed the brush's head into a starburst. But to watch this behemoth storm trooper with his fat belly hung over his belt, using a *paintbrush* to mock the Jews? Terrifying. To single out Jews for ridicule! It was a stunning affront. A frightening theft of the power of a paintbrush.

Frau Ehrenberg was in tears behind the bakery counter, muttering "Eine Kulturschande" over and over. A culture shame!

But Eema was dry-eyed. "Don't be frightened, child," she had commanded Rashka at the time, gripping her hand tightly. "Don't be frightened." But it was obvious that even Eema was swallowing fear. And Rashka? She was only a small girl, but it both enraged and horrified her down to her soul as she watched the paint dribble down the glass.

A thump of her heart wakes Rachel to the present. She finds herself in the rear of a taxi with Aaron, pulling up in front of Gluckstern's on Delancey Street for dinner with the Weinstocks. The Barry Sisters sing the jingle over the radio: *Let's all sing! Let our voices ring! It's East Side Gluckstern's Restaurant and Caterers!*

It's just past twilight, when the city takes on the darkness from the ground up. Aaron puffs out his cheeks and straightens his tie as the cab pulls over to the curb. "Okay, so here we are," he tells Rachel grimly. "Let's get this fucking ordeal over with." He had a few beers while they were getting ready. A few beers that nudged him into a surliness that he barely pretends to hide. Frowning, he leans his head forward to the cabbie. "So, buddy?" he asks, yanking out his wallet. "What's this gonna set me back?"

Inside, the place is full and loud. An undercurrent of thunder thrums through the air as they're seated at a four-top, the two couples—the

Perlmans, Rachel and Aaron, and the Weinstocks, Cousin Ezra and wife, Daniela. Like many of the old kosher eateries, the place has a reputation for prickly service, as well as its corned beef and cabbage. There's an old joke about a waiter circling through the tables of some neighborhood kosher restaurant asking, "Who wanted the clean glass?" But tonight, their waiter is a middle-aged mensch who seems cheerful, even delighted to have them seated in his section. "H'boy," Aaron grumbles. "Smiley the waiter. He must have us sized up for big tippers" is her husband's explanation.

"So thank you for putting up with the menu here," Daniela says. Daniela Weinstock is the mother of a brood of little Weinstocks and seems to Rachel to have spent the last several years vershtuft. Pregnant. Though *vershtuft* is not a very nice way to describe it. Blocked! You would think of someone constipated! How many times has Daniela been pregnant since Rachel's known her? But Rachel never offers congratulations. That would invite misfortune. Umglik! Better to say b'sha'ah tovah. At a good hour. All should proceed at the right time: the pregnancy should be smooth, the baby should be healthy, and the birth should be without complication. All that comes at a good hour— wishes for the future rather than blessings for the past.

Daniella is as sweet as can be. A good Jewish girl from Queens. Always patient with her little Weinstocks, never a harsh word, she is always ready to help out or lend a listening ear. And if she's not exactly anybody's idea of an intellectual, then so what? She has a talent for calming stormy waters. And she has wonderful hands. Competent and unhurried in her movements. Rachel is calmed just watching her fold laundry. She is currently pregnant with their fourth Weinstock child, and there is something so captivatingly, even biblically voluptuous about Daniela that Rachel often has to remind herself not to stare. Eyes like dark wine. The sensual nose. Her belly is round and low, and in her eighth month, her breasts are swollen tight. Just the sight of her makes Rachel feel underfed, flat, and empty. "I know you two don't exactly keep kosher," Daniela says with a soft smile.

"Hey, no problem at all," Aaron replies. "How can you not love stuffed cow spleen, really?"

Daniela maintains her smile. "Well, if you're tired of spleen, I think I can recommend the schmaltz herring." And now everybody else is smiling too at the joke. But Rachel can see that underneath, Aaron is not really smiling at all. He is preparing to join battle in his never-ending duel with Ezra. Who did more in the war? Who is the better Jew? Who is living the better life?

"You know, I love Gluckstern's," Aaron declares and then sings a verse of the radio jingle while glaring at the menu. *Come on, Jews! Choose satisfaction, because it's good, good, good!* "Uncle Al use to take us here when Naomi and I were kids," he says. "Pack us into the tiny back seat of his old Studebaker."

"And which was Uncle Al?" Rachel must ask. "I get them confused."

"Uncle Al. Chief garment cutter for D. L. Horowitz, twenty-six years," Aaron says. "Never married, but once a month, he'd bring us kids here for a meal."

Daniela sounds pleasantly surprised. "*Really?* He was observant, Uncle Al?"

Aaron shrugs. "Well, nothing much got past him, if that's what you mean."

Another joke. But Ezra snorts disdainfully.

And here it comes. "You got a problem there, cuz?" Aaron wonders aloud.

Ezra Weinstock. The goodnik, or maybe a *too*-goodnik as far as Aaron is concerned. "The Fucknik" works better for her husband, as in, "God, but do I have to spend another evening listening to the Fucknik lecture?" Always carping on the responsibilities of the Jew, as if Aaron doesn't have enough to deal with already! A large, physically imposing man, with thinning hair and cloudless eyes, Ezra is given to wearing socks with sandals. In the war, he was awarded a medal for driving a Sherman tank in North Africa. "The holy Bronze Star," Aaron calls it,

as if it was some kind of big, combustive Magen David bulging through
the firmament above Ezra's head. And maybe it is. While Aaron was
in charge of the logistics for the U.S.O. camp shows, busy pissing off
Hollywood caterers in California, Sergeant Ezra Weinstock was chewing up Nazis in his tank treads.

"Problem? No." Ezra shrugs back. "Who could have a problem with
Uncle Al? Everybody's pal, Uncle Al."

Daniela offers a quiet correction by speaking her husband's name.
"Ezra."

Aaron frowns at the menu. "Nothing wrong with the man as far as
the Perlman household was ever concerned. He always did good by us."

"That's 'cause he knew your pop was an easy tap," Ezra tells him.

And now the anger shows. "Hey, *genius*. My pop was a *generous
man*. Fault him for that if you want, but at least he didn't burn down his
own goddamn business for the insurance."

Rachel spits out a not-so-quiet correction. "*Aaron*."

Their waiter returns. "You folks ready to order?" he wonders
pleasantly.

Aaron jumps in, obviously making an ugly joke. "Uh, yes, how does
the chef prepare the jellied calf's feet?"

Rachel says, "He'll have the Romanian cutlet with a fruit cup."

Aaron says, "And she'll have the lungen and milz stew with the
chopped herring."

Rachel goes about collecting everyone's menus. "Don't listen to
him," she tells the waiter, handing over the menu stack. "I'll have the
kasha varnishkes, please. Thank you."

"And you, Mrs. Weinstock?" asks the waiter.

"The usual for us, Mr. Katz."

"Wonderful. And how are we doing on the Almonetta?"

"I think we're fine, Oskar," Ezra decides, but Aaron is past accept-
ing anything his cousin has to say about anything.

"Hey, hey, speak for yourself, Sarge," he says as he empties the bottle into his glass. "Some of us have a taste for fine wine. Let's uncork another bottle of 'Man-oh-Man-ischewitz.'"

The waiter gives him a suspect glance, but what's he supposed to do? Argue?

"Sure. If that's what you want, I'll have the steward bring it out," he says and leaves silence in his wake.

Leaning over to her husband, Rachel asks, "What are you doing?"

Aaron frowns to himself. "Nothing, nothing." Then he turns to Ezra. "Look, I apologize, okay? That was a lousy thing to say about your old man."

"No, no. You're right," Ezra admits. "Everybody knows my pop had the place torched. He practically admitted to it himself. But he was desperate. Ma, thank God for her recovery, was still in the sanatorium with the T.B., he had three kids to feed, and his business was in the toilet. It was wrong, no question. But maybe at least a little forgivable."

The silence that follows is clumsy.

"I think I'm going to have the chocolate rugelach for dessert," Daniela decides aloud. "It was so good the last time."

"Well, actually, I'm not sure we will have the time for dessert," Rachel decides to say in an apologetic voice.

"Oh, *no*?" Daniela sounds disappointed.

"Aaron has his fish market tomorrow, don't you, Husband?"

"Yep," Aaron responds, tight-lipped.

"So he has to be up early. Very, very early."

"Aw, well, that's too bad," Daniela concedes sympathetically. But then here comes Ezra wading in up to his hips.

"You know, cuz," he says to Aaron. "You really are lucky you *don't* have kids. They keep you up all night, the little stinkers."

Aaron blinks. "And who was talking about having kids?" he wants to know. "Was that a topic I missed?"

Ezra only shrugs. "I'm just saying. You're lucky. That's all. So *what* that your mom's going gray waiting on her share of grandkids," he says.

A little joke, that's all. A little poke as he's picking a roll to butter from the basket.

Aaron fails, however, to see the humor. "Hey! Knucklehead!" he objects, face reddening. "My mother's doing just fine!" he declares, poking a finger into the air at his cousin.

"Sure. I'm sure she's good, cousin," Ezra says to Aaron. "I'm sure she's just great."

"*Ezra.*" Daniela speaks her husband's name as if it's a command. "Stop. There are *two* people in every marriage making decisions," she reminds him. "And what they decide is none of our business."

Ezra nods and raises his hands in surrender, holding a roll in one hand and a butter knife in the other. "Right. You're right," he agrees, expending a breath of regret. "I'm sorry. My wife is correct as always. None of my business, and I shouldn't have brought it up. Okay, Sergeant Perlman?"

"I just don't get why you feel like you can shoot your mouth off anytime you please."

"Well, I won't talk about the kettle or who's calling it black," Ezra says. Finishing his buttering, he sets down the roll. "But *okay*. Point taken," he announces. "Mea culpa," the man adds with the softened tone of any good public apology.

"*And* I think you should apologize to Rachel too," Daniela points out.

The attention of the table shifts, and Rachel feels a sting of panic. Through all this, she has felt herself shrinking. Growing smaller and smaller until she feels like no more than a gnat flitting about the table.

Ezra is only too happy to concede. "Apologies, dear lady," he says, making praying hands as he makes one last stab at a joke. "It must be tough enough to be married to this guy without me kibbitzing in."

"Oh great." Aaron nods, frowning. "That's a great apology. Just terrific. You should carve that one in stone." He lights up a cigarette and blows out smoke that settles with the silence over the table until he says, "You know, I think I *will have* the stuffed cow spleen after all. I mean, why not? I've already got heartburn thanks to the nudnik here," he says, shrugging his head toward Ezra. "So what the hell?"

In the taxicab on the way home, Aaron and Ezra with Rachel in between are all squashed into the rear seat in imitation of ten pounds of baloney in a five-pound sack, while pregnant Daniela sits up front in the passenger seat. Not a word passes between them. In the hallway of their building, the women exchange brief farewells, but the men remain silent. Ezra is already trotting up the stairs to the fifth floor, Aaron already digging his key into the door lock of their apartment.

Sorry, Daniela mouths with a sad little smile and touches Rachel's arm.

Inside the gray light of the apartment, Rachel slips off her coat one arm at a time. "I don't understand," she is saying. "Why must you compete so?"

"Because he's an overly competitive dope," Aaron answers, tossing away his hat and roughly scratching his head of curls.

"*He* is?" says Rachel, closing the door behind them.

"Hey. People *compete* in this country, Rachel," Aaron says, yanking off his coat. "It's the American way," he declares, aggressively hooking his coat on the hall tree and flipping on the light switch. "It's why America is America. It's why we're the richest country in the world and have never lost a war."

"All I'm asking is this: what do you hope to gain by this war between the two of *you*? He's not an enemy. He's your *cousin*."

"Twice removed," he corrects.

"And what does this mean, 'twice removed'?"

"Twice removed from the list of people I can stand to socialize with. At *least* twice I removed him, probably ten times, and yet he keeps coming back. Honey, the man is a judgmental dope, even when he's 'apologizing.' My mother's always said that Ezra's a first-class tumler, just like his old man, and she's always been right."

"Tumler or not," Rachel says, picking up the cat who comes meow-ing toward her. "He's still your family. And this is how you treat him? You should be glad you *have* family."

"H'boy, here we go."

Rachel turns, hugging Kibbitz in her arms. "Here we go *what?*"

Aaron loosens his tie, lights a cigarette from a leftover pack on the coffee table. "Nothing. I know. I'm lucky to have family left."

"That's right. *You are*," she says and shifts the cat's weight onto her shoulder. "So don't *you* be the judgmental dope."

In the bedroom, discussion continues as they prepare for bed. Aaron sits slouched on the bedspread, jacket gone, collar opened, tie pulled apart and hanging from his neck, cigarette smoldering in the bedside ashtray. He sighs as he tugs off each shoe and tosses it. "H'okay, h'okay," he surrenders. "I get it. Family is family. He just gets under my skin is all. Always acting like the almighty goodnik. 'My responsibility as an American Jew,' with his big bronze star gleaming." Kibbitz is mewing on the bed. Aaron picks him up and plops him on the floor. "Like he single-handedly routed the whole friggin' Nazi war machine."

Rachel turns her back to Aaron, lifting her hair so he can unzip the back of her dress for her. "Maybe he takes being a Jew seriously."

Reaching up and *zip* he's done. "And you're saying *I* don't?"

"I'm saying that maybe you think you don't. And that's why he gets under your skin." She slips her shoulders free. "And *by the way*, it cer-tainly was *not* Ezra Weinstock routing the Nazi war machine." Rachel steps out of the dress. "It was the Red Army doing that."

Aaron yanks off a sock, tosses it. "Yeah? Well, tell him that, why don't you?" Yanks off the other sock. "No, on second thought, don't. In fact, don't tell anybody that, okay? The last thing I need is a Commie lover in my bed." Suddenly he seizes her and pulls her onto the bed on top of him. She yelps, but then her eyes go wide when he kisses her.

"I *know*," Aaron admits, an intimacy entering his voice. "Even though it's not easy to believe, considering the tribe from Webster Avenue. I *know* that I am lucky to have family. But luckier to have you."

A second kiss goes deeper.

She could ruin her life quite easily, or at least her madness could. It wouldn't take much to drive her entire existence on West 22nd Street over a cliff. She could light a match and drop it on the sofa upholstery and sit back. The simplicity of it both terrifies her and entices her. She knows that it's her guilt that pushes her to mad thoughts. But her desire for a just atonement is strong. Biblical, even.

Do not let guilt for the blood of the innocent remain among Your people, Israel.

Both wife and husband lie together naked under the covers. Comfortable in their marriage bed, Rachel allows herself to drop her guard enough to feel the heat of their intimacy. That is, the intimacy that she is so desperate to maintain and so tempted to ruin. Without Aaron, without her marriage, what is she? A refugee. A mental case, as they put it in Flatbush. A resident nut of the booby hatch. She needs to be Mrs. Aaron Perlman, even when she resents the need. It's the shelter she has built for herself against the storms of her own mad guilt. So she loves him. She does. She loves him, she puts up with him, she serves his humble husbandly requirements—answering the telephone, shopping the grocery, making the coffee, washing dishes—when she must. Wifely chores. Yet she is compelled to thwart him in his greatest desire.

She has, once again, taken measures to block his ability to deliver a belly, as is said. She has performed a certain operation with a rubberized insert that will permit him to be satisfied but prevent her from absorbing his deposit. And this time, even with all this argument about who has given whom grandkids, Aaron doesn't complain. He seems to have grown stoic about her measures. Perhaps because, like her, he's simply happy to have the connection. The escape. The release. Now he begins snoring dully. But Rachel stares into the darkness of the room above, searching out the ceiling crack, listening to the train cars of the West Side elevated line as they pass.

⌐•⌐

By the end of February 1943, there are very few things Jews are still permitted to do. Starving is one of them, but at least for now, so is eating. If one can call it eating, that is, what they're forced to consume! Jews are not permitted meat or milk. No white bread, chocolate, tea or coffee, or most anything that would make up a normal Berliner diet. No fish, eggs, or butter, only black bread and gruel and stews made from rotting vegetables are on the menu. Yet even on the diet of scrapings and stale loaves, Rashka is changing physically. Her body maturing from a stick to a shape. She's growing up. Her eema says so. "Rokhl, you're growing up," her mother tells her as if it's perhaps not a crime but probably an unavoidable liability. Rashka employs the reflecting glass of passing shop windows as mirrors, and these mirrors agree: time is busy transforming her into a young woman passing the glass with the yellow Shield of David sewn to her breast.

They have long ago lost the villa in Wilmersdorf, auctioned off from under their feet after the laws stripped Jews of most of their property rights. Since then, they have been forced to inhabit various ramshackle flats in various ramshackle locations. The villa feels like a distant dream of her childhood. Rashka has learned to live with leaking roofs and drafty windows, polluted plumbing, bedbugs, and the skittering rats from the gutters. But she can see how this daily squalor is paring down her mother. Whittling her body to bony poverty, carving her face into an ax blade.

Eema's eyes now are brutal black buttons, and she no longer paints. Of course she doesn't. Her palettes and brushes were stolen from her and thrown onto the rubbish heap. But she seems to have lost the will, the desire to paint as well. God has robbed her of her gift, Eema declares. "Living now is by the minute only," she explains to her daughter. "To think an hour ahead is impossible." Though, in fact, it seems to Rashka that Eema never *stops* thinking about the next hour. Where they can lay hands on a few scraps of food, some bread, another blanket, a pair of shoes, paper for the toilet, matches for a candle. Meanwhile, God has taken her gift. For safekeeping perhaps? This is a theory Rashka wishes she could propose, but she is too fearful. What if it turns out that God is just a little bit vengeful? What then? Maybe He's punishing Eema for some sin she has committed. Some secret transgression. And if so, what might He do to Eema's little goat?

The latest of their residences is a so-called Judenhaus. An officially designated house for Jews located on the corner of the Duisburger Strasse and the Konstanzer Strasse. Jews are still permitted bus passes if the distance to an assigned workplace is seven kilometers away or more, but the distance, west to east, from the house to the factory where they must work is only six kilometers, so they walk. And in their travels to and fro in the cold, they are often jeered at, spat upon, struck, or otherwise assaulted due to the stars they wear. Once, a shopkeeper suddenly shoved a broom at them and demanded that they sweep the sidewalk of his shop.

Inside the house, it's overcrowded squalor from corner to corner. Everyone is hungry, everyone is sick, everyone is afraid because of the rumor mill that says that Berliner Jews are being shipped like cattle to a ghetto in Occupied Poland called Litzmannstadt. Trains leave on a weekly basis from Bahnhof Grunewald, the rumors inform them. "Transports" they are called.

Uncle Fritz, meanwhile, has excelled at becoming a privileged Jew. Two years before, he had wangled membership on the board of the Jewish association organized under the control of the Gestapo's Jewish Desk, Referat IV B4.

"We're trying to save what we can," Feter Fritz explains in a serious tone to his sister.

"You're trying to save yourself, Fritz," his sister counters.

"Well, that's a rather vile thing to say to one's own flesh and blood, Lavinia. Even for you."

"Vile it may be," she shrugs. But true.

"There are many good men. Important men. *Courageous* men. Good, solid, salt-of-the-earth menschen who have taken on the thankless responsibility of representing our communities to the SS. Do you doubt that?"

"It's *you* I doubt, Fritzl," she says. "*You.*"

Now, on a cold February night, Feter Fritz stands on the steps of the interior stairwell of the Judenhaus. He is here to prove his worth. Eema and Rashka stand with him. Rashka is silent, her hand in her mother's grasp. Her uncle's chin is poorly shaven. His once immaculately manicured fingernails are dirty and ragged. His hair is greasy, and his clothing hangs on him like he's dressed in a bag of rags. But the most alarming element of his appearance is not what he's wearing. It's what he's *not* wearing.

"Friedel, you're not wearing the star," her eema is saying, her voice low, concerned for him, yes, but also with a note of panic. But Feter's mouth is set. His eyes are dark with determination. He speaks closely to them.

"You must listen to me now," he instructs. "Are you *listening*, Lavinia? I need you to listen to me."

"I'm *listening*. Yes, for God's sake." Her eema's eyes are wide. Her expression raw.

"Tomorrow morning," Feter Fritz begins, "before you leave for work, I want you to pack whatever you have of value and take it with you."

"What do we have of value any longer?"

"*Listen*, Lavinia," he scolds her impatiently. "Don't talk. *Anything* of value. Any food you can carry without drawing attention. Fill your pockets. Sew what you can into the linings of your clothes. Whatever money. Whatever jewelry. Anything of value that you can lay hands on. But do it covertly. You don't want to encourage questions from anyone."

"And *why* am I doing this?"

"Because tomorrow morning, you are not going to work," he informs them, followed by the unconscious tic of the German glance— his eyes darting from side to side to safeguard against eavesdroppers. "The Gestapo," he whispers grimly. "They're planning an aktion. In the factories." An aktion on a scale that dwarves everything that's past, he says. Raids all over town. Gestapo and Kripo men. Companies of Waffen-SS troops dispatched with empty lorries to fill with Jews. "Are you understanding me, Vinni?" He so seldom calls her by this name from their childhood.

Eema, however, appears confused, maybe a bit incensed. "But. But that's nonsense," she insists. Her grip on Rashka's hand is steadily tightening. "We are doing their *labor*. For the *war*, Fritzl. Why would they take us from this? It's meshugaas!"

"Meshugaas, perhaps, but it's happening none the less. Listen to me. I can't stay much longer. The story is that Goebbels is champing at the bit to declare Berlin 'Jew-free.' So he doesn't care if you and Rashka are vital labor for the war. He simply wants you *out*. And you should know *this* too—the SS have quit sending people to the ghettos. Now they are shipping them straight through to camps in Bohemia and Poland. This is not what you want for your daughter, Lavinia," he assures her. "Fortunately, your little brother has a plan. We are diving under."

"Under?"

"Submerging, Vinni, beneath the surface. As of tomorrow morning," Uncle Fritz announces with a spark of his old playful confidence, the Macher, the maven of deals who gets things done with a gleam in his eye. "As of tomorrow morning, we are U-boats."

11.

The Clog

RACHEL AWAKENS WITH A BOLT OF LIGHTNING SHOOTING through her. For an instant, she is still in Berlin on the morning she and Eema step out into the street without their stars. She remembers those first steps, the scuff of her ill-fitting shoes on the slate pavement, and feeling as if a thousand eyes were spying from every window. She must catch her breath, return to the present, to the traffic noise from the windows reminding her that she is in her bedroom on West 22nd Street, not Berlin.

In the kitchen, murky water stands in the sink. And then a plunger appears. A plunger being plunged at an even, measured pace before it's removed. Water gushes in from the faucet for a moment before it's shut off. Small drips. But the sink does not drain.

"So the drain is clogged," Aaron announces.

"What?"

"The drain in the kitchen sink. It's now officially clogged."

"Are you *sure*?"

"Pretty sure, yeah. Three inches of standing water, not draining even a little. Makes me suspect."

"Can't you just try the plunger?"

"You didn't notice? I just *tried* the plunger. Got me nowhere."

"Try it again."

"Did you call the super like you said you would?"

"Did I what?"

Aaron expels a slow breath, sticking the plunger back under the sink.

"Rachel. Honey," he says with a note of strained husbandly patience. "He's just the super," he assures her. "*That's all.*"

"That's not all."

"I know. I know. He's a kraut. But his name is Bauer, honey, not Bormann."

"You don't know *who* he is, Aaron. Mr. Klinghoffer said he came here *after* the war. He could be anybody. How do you know he's so innocent?"

"I know that Klinghoffer hired him as the super. And when the drain clogs, it's the super's job to unclog it. This is what I know. Now, I gotta go. *No Time for Sergeants* just opened at the Alvin with what's-his-name. The hillbilly guy, so the matinee crowd's gonna be a ball-buster, and we're down a waiter. G'bye. *Call 'im.* You'll be fine. G'bye."

Door opens, then closes.

A beat.

A clattering noise and then suddenly here comes the plunger again, but this time splashing furiously into the standing water, thumping hard before it's yanked out.

A beat.

Nothing.

Nothing until here it comes again—the plunger smacking the water, thumping manically before it is yanked out.

Water settles.

No change.

Still clogged.

"*Scheisse!*" Rachel swears.

Bauer the super. He's held this position since last year, inhabiting the cellar apartment opposite the boiler room. Rachel used to go down there when friendly Mr. Fitzroy was the occupant. Old Mr. Ruddy-Faced Fitzroy, who sang loudly and lyrically while he fixed your plumbing or rewired your doorbell. But they found him on the floor two days after Christmas, dead of heart failure, and since then, their landlord, Mr. Klinghoffer, has replaced him with this—this *Hun*. Whenever she travels down to the cellar to put the trash in the bins, Rachel stares at the door, picturing a charnel house behind it stacked with bones that the German shovels into the furnace to heat the apartment after Aaron jacks up the thermostat.

Now, this tubby Boche is half under the kitchen galley sink in their apartment. Dull-faced with greasy hair going gray, though only his big white belly and dirty work pants are visible to Rachel as he clunks about with his wrenches. Smoke from his cigarette drifts upward from the pipes.

She sits, nursing a lit filter tip in a kitchen chair, dressed in a brown cardigan and a pair of Sanforized denim pants. Her hair's tied up with a kerchief. Her arms are wrapped around her knees. She is caged by her own posture, glaring suspiciously at the interloper, when the cat suddenly leaps up onto the table and yowls loudly. Rachel seizes him as if he's set off an alarm, drawing him into her cage as if she fears he will give her away.

There was a thuggish Waffen-SS trooper in the Grosse Hamburger Strasse Lager known as Di Shtivl—The Boot—because of his reputation for kicking the prisoners—men, women, but especially children. Put a few pounds on him and gray his hair a touch, she thinks, and this could be him. Him or some other assassin of the Jews.

Kibbitz complains about Rachel's ever-tightening grip, and he slips from her embrace, nipping her arm lightly, not to hurt, just to send a message, then bronking with frustration as he hits the floor and padding away. Rachel rubs the skin of her arm. The chair where her eema sat is now empty. To the super, she says stridently, "Excuse me. This will take *how much* longer?"

A squeak of a wrench. "The trap is clogged, Missus Perlman," he tells her in his ugly, filthy Nazi Boche accent and sits up. His face is blotchy and pasty from all the steins of beer he must lift. Unshaven. A cigarette clenched between his lips. "It can be cleaned, but it also needs replacement."

"And this will take how long?"

The super blows out smoke. "To *clean?*" he shrugs. "A minute, no more. But for the replacement, I must go to the hardware store." He says this as if the hardware store is the highest authority on the matter. The Kommandantur of plumbing to which he must report. Rachel is incredulous at the ramifications of this pronouncement.

"So. You mean you must come *back?*"

"You feel hatred toward the Germans?" Dr. Solomon asks her.

"Don't *you?*"

"We're not here to discuss me, Rachel."

"Yes. I feel 'hatred' as you say."

"Toward all Germans? Even those who might be innocent of crimes?"

"If they aren't guilty of the crimes, then they are guilty of knowing of the crimes and doing nothing. There is no such being in my opinion, Dr. Solomon, as an 'innocent' German."

"I see," says the doctor and makes a note.

"Did I say something shocking? Something to reveal myself? What have you just made note of?"

But the doctor is deaf to the question and switches topics. "I don't mean to press you too firmly on this point, Rachel, but have you given any more thought to my suggestion about painting?" Dr. Solomon wonders.

"I've been busy," she answers. Surly and flat. She hasn't been sleeping well. Last night, she awoke convinced there was someone in the apartment. Aaron had to check out every corner, open every closet and cabinet door, before she was forced to admit she had been dreaming. But was she dreaming? Since the day she was confronted by her eema's

painting, she has been feeling watched by hidden eyes. A growing feeling that there was something terrible waiting for her concealed in the
darkness. She expels smoke from her cigarette. "I think I should be
going, Doctor," she decides and begins to assembles herself.

The doctor is surprised. "But there's still time left in the hour," he
points out.

"Nevertheless. You cannot help me any further today, Dr. Solomon.
Who can? I have a sickness that cannot be cured."

But on the subway, the brunette schoolgirl with the burgundy beret
returns, sitting across the aisle, the manifestation of Rachel's guilt.
Sitting in the café up the Friedrichstrasse, hearing a voice: You're not
here on a holiday, Bissel. You must earn your keep.

The schoolgirl gazes back at her. She never appears accusatory.
Never. Merely confused. Merely saddened by the lies Rachel lives by.

Pulling a half pound of frozen hamburger out of the icebox freezer, a
frosty brick of meat wrapped in cellophane, she sticks it in the sink and
turns on the hot water to defrost it when she hears someone knocking
politely on the door.

"Missus Perlman?" the German is calling. "Hallo? Missus Perlman.
It's Bauer the super. I have come from the store with the new sink trap."
He rings the bell once, twice, then knocks again.

The cat, alerted by the buzz of the bell, meows. Thumps down onto
the floor from his spot on the sill and pads over to the apartment door
to investigate. He meows at the noise, but Rachel has shut off the water
and become motionless. She is still an expert at silences.

The next morning, she makes coffee and drops two slices of bread into
the toaster. Aaron walks over to the kitchen sink in his wrinkled flannel
pajamas over his undershirt. Carpet slippers flopping.

"Shall I cut a grapefruit?" she asks him.

"Sure," he says, stepping up to the sink beside her. He turns on the tap water and lets it gush into a glass. He drinks, draining the glass as the faucet still runs. Thirst quenched, he releases a satisfied *Ahhhh*. Then frowns down at the sink. "Hey. I thought the super fixed this."

Rachel slices a fat yellow grapefruit into halves. "You what?"

He shuts off the tap. "I said, I thought the super had fixed this drain. Didn't he come by?"

Rachel hesitates, but only for an instant. "He came by."

"And?"

The toast pops. "*And* he cleaned it out, but then said there was something else wrong. He must get a part from a store."

"And so when is that supposed to happen?"

Rachel only shrugs. Starts spreading margarine on toast.

"Well, that stinks," her husband announces. "Just what we need. A drain that doesn't drain. And for this we pay *how much a month* for this place?"

"Ninety-eight dollars," Rachel answers.

"No, honey, I *know* how much we pay. I'm just saying." He sets the emptied glass in the sink. "I guess I'll have to talk him."

Rachel sets the toast on her husband's plate. "I guess you will."

"So there's coffee?" he wonders.

"In the pot on the table."

Aaron nods. Pads to the table and manages to pour himself a cup on his own, then snaps on the radio. Drags out a chair where he sits and ignites a cigarette with a click of his Zippo. Opens his newspaper as Rachel nestles the two grapefruit halves in their bowls. She is not speaking another word on the subject. The super came, the super went. That's all. The song on the radio makes a defiant statement: *I hear you knockin', but you can't come in!*

12.

La Muse du Rouge

I WANT A CIGARETTE."

"Too bad."

The studio is a high-ceilinged space bathed in daylight on the top floor of the villa. The year is 1932. No one knows it yet, but the German Republic is staggering through its final months of existence. Meanwhile, Angelika Rosen, aged nineteen years, poses in the nude for nine marks an hour. Straight-backed, a hand combed into the thick red mane of hair that cascades over her shoulders, this is the first time she has been naked in front of a woman whom she does not know. This is the first time she has been naked and on display. An artist's model.

It felt daring in the beginning, answering an advertisement in the newspaper. *Life model sought.* It felt good to hurt Tatte and Mamme, *especially* Tatte, in this way by putting his daughter's body on display, even if they were completely unaware of what she was doing. *She* knew that she was hurting them, and that was enough. But after the initial exhilaration, the hours passed, and the excitement drained. She began to feel stiff from keeping to a single position, and her mind began to wander into a void. "I'm bored," she announces.

"You are paid to pose, not talk," the artist tells her.

A moment passes.

"How much longer?"

"Until I say."

Another moment. But it's too much. "I'm *dying* for a cigarette," she groans.

"Contemplate the suffering of women," says the artist. The artist, whose name is Morgenstern. Frau Lavinia Morgenstern-Landau. Aged thirty or more. Hair bobbed. Her painter's gaze dark-eyed and concentrated. She stands at her easel working on a very tall canvas. Her fingers are paint-stained; her smock is paint-stained. She paints from a warm palette. Cadmium red, alizarin crimson, cadmium orange, yellow ochre, burnt umber. A tall bank of windows keeps the room awash with light. A table is cluttered with the paraphernalia of the painterly craft, and a fat yellow cat lies dozing at the artist's feet as she studies her model, then puts her brush to work.

There's something mysterious that Lavinia is searching for in her painting of this girl. This little Jewish meydl from the Prenzlauer Berg. Cette belle créature rouge. Perhaps it's the essence of human beauty? Could she be searching for such a thing as that? Or perhaps it's simply the mystery of her own art. Her quest to capture that which cannot be captured. The flatheaded brush roughs up the edge of a shadow that outlines the warmth of the painted flesh.

There's a noise of a door from behind, and a confident baritone voice bursts in the air like a cannon shell. "Shalom! My brilliant sister!"

She frowns but does not turn even as she listens to her brother's footsteps approach. "And so, he arrives," she replies. "Shalom, little brother."

Fritz steps up behind the artist at work, a stylish bamboo cane in hand, and kisses her cheerfully on the temple. As usual, he is impeccably clothed and coiffed. Dressed in a coal-black Rudolf Hertzog suit and a diamond stickpin in his cravat. He scrutinizes his sister's canvas with interest and, as is his custom, offers his opinion unsolicited. "Stunning but disturbing. Just what I want to see," he announces.

Lavinia still dabs at the canvas. "Tell Herr Möller you have a painting for him. All he must do is spend a king's ransom to obtain it."

"That's what I *always* tell him, Lavinia. He'll pay, don't worry. He's entranced by your work."

A laugh or a grunt. It's hard to tell which. "Yes. 'Stunning but disturbing,'" she confirms.

"And speaking of both. Won't you introduce me?"

Lavinia looks up and frowns as she sees her brother drowsily eyeing her model. "Fräulein Rosen. My brother, Fritz Landau. Who is *married*," she reminds.

Now Angelika has regained an interest in posing. Aware of the power of her beauty, she unblushingly casts a smoky-eyed look at this man. Fritz is obviously captivated.

"*Enchantée*," he offers.

"If you're going to stay, then allow the girl to put on some clothes," the artist suggests, but Fritz certainly doesn't wish to interrupt.

"*No, no*, I won't stay," he insists, his gaze hanging languidly. "The last thing I'd wish is to disrupt the artistic process."

In response, the girl draws a long, lazy breath that causes her breast to heave slowly before she expels it. "I would murder for a cigarette, Herr Landau," she announces.

Fritz grins, but he defers to his sister. "Lavinia? May I be permitted?"

Lavinia, however, is a wall. "She can smoke when I'm finished with her," she decrees.

"Then I should be going. I only wanted to confirm that you'll be in Wannsee tomorrow."

"Wannsee?"

"The Lieberman villa? The Akademie luncheon?"

"Is that really tomorrow?" Lavinia asks.

"It is. And, Sister, you must be there."

"The only woman in the room."

"I thought you considered that an honor."

"I consider it a travesty. But fine. I'll be there."

"One o'clock," says her brother with a smile. A smile he then raises to Lavinia's model. "So very pleased to meet you, child. Lavinia, what did you say is this charming young woman's name again?"

"Rosen, I said. Fräulein Rosen."

The girl jumps in. "*Angelika*," she declares.

"Of course," Fritz agrees, still smiling. "A name for an angel."

Afterward, when Fritz has taken his leave and Lavinia is soaking her brushes in glass jars of spirits, Angelika glares frowningly at the tarp covering the canvas. "Why can't I see it?"

"It's not finished, that's why. Here," Lavinia tells her. "Have your reward." She lifts the copper lid of a box stained with fingerprints of paint. It's filled with cigarettes. And when Angelika grabs one to smoke, Lavinia lights it for her with an equally paint-stained table lighter. "I wish you wouldn't do that," the artist tells her.

Expelling smoke. Eyes languid. "Do what?"

"Flirt with my brother."

Angelika raises her eyebrows. "Was that what I was doing?" she asks. A question that ratchets up a sudden tension between them. It's a certain magnetic force that has been powering their connection. An intimacy between artist and model? Or something more? Angelika does not move. She permits the tension to build, and then she breaks away. Scooping up the lazy yellow cat, she waltzes it across the room, calling it her precious treasure.

The Adlon. Berlin's premier hotel. Let those nationalist thugs and Hitlerites pollute the dining room of the Kaiserhof if they must, the Adlon wouldn't have them in to sweep the rugs. The Brandenburg Gate looms immensely through the windows as the liveried doorman and bellhops busy themselves with the arrivals of their guests from a stream of taxicabs rolling up to the granite curb. Only the top cut of people, of course, come to enjoy a final vestige of Kaiserliche glory that the Adlon proffers within its imperial walls. Fritz owns a garden villa in the Grunewald but keeps a suite here as a matter of course. The hanging chandeliers, the fine linen, the cathedral windows of the dining room provide the luxury that he feels comfortable with. A spot where the great and near-great sit for luncheon. A string ensemble in tailcoats plays Mozart, the Quartet in D minor, as if they are spinning threads of gold.

Angelika's hair is plaited in a crown, ladylike, and she is dressed in what's obviously the best dress available to a girl from the inner courtyards of the Wilhelmine Ring. Their waiter is a stiff-necked old soldier of the hotel, dressed in black cutaway and crisply pleated bib. "A brandy for the honored gentleman," the Herr Ober announces as he serves the cognac. "*And*," he adds with a certain spring to his tone, "a brandy for the gnädige Fräulein." Even a staunch Adlon Prussian is not invulnerable to the desire she generates.

She touches Fritz's hand as he ignites her cigarette with a gold lighter bearing a shell cameo. "What a pretty bauble," she says.

"Alfred Dunhill," Fritz reports.

"Is it valuable?"

He shrugs. Valuable? "Value is relative, I've learned." He ignites his own cigarette screwed into a short black onyx holder. "You strike me as a person who *appreciates* value," he observes. "Is that so?"

"My father runs a wholesale business in the Prenzlauer Berg. He sells buttons to garment makers. It costs him one pfennig to sell a button for two pfennigs. That's all I understand about value, Herr Landau." She says this and takes a sip from her snifter of cognac. "Besides, that isn't really what you want to talk about. Is it?"

Fritz lifts his eyebrows. "Isn't it?"

The girl shrugs but does not alter her gaze.

"You're different now," he observes.

"Am I really?"

"You're better dressed. This lovely frock you're wearing. The lovely pearl earrings."

"Money buys things. Your sister paid me well to pose for her."

"Nine marks an hour is what my sister pays when she uses a model," he contradicts. "And in any case," Fritz points out, "you're no longer *posing* for my sister."

A small smile but without pleasure. That's all she offers.

"What happened?" he wants to know.

A shrug, inhaling smoke. "You should ask *her*."

"I did," Fritz assures her.

"And?"

"And she said it was none of my business."

"Ha," says Angelika.

"But she's wrong. It *is* my business. *She* is my business, in a quite literal sense. So I'm going to ask you again, Angelika. What happened between the two of you?"

The girl takes a gulp of cognac and frowns. "She broke her promise."

"Promise?"

"She said she would send me to Feige-Strassburger. To study fashion."

"*Did she really?* Well, that's a surprise."

"I'm not lying."

"I didn't say you were. But then she changed her mind?" Fritz wonders.

"She broke her promise," the girl repeats. "She was jealous."

A sip of cognac. "That's interesting to hear. Can you explain what you mean?"

The girl snorts a laugh. "Do I *need* to explain?" She can't believe that she does. So all she says, with a crooked smile, is "She wanted me all to herself."

Fritz sets down his glass and strokes the point of his Vandyke, as if to make a study of this woman in front of him. He may not be as artistically gifted as his sister, but he has a certain artistic instinct about people. He can recognize a true work of art. "What do you *want*?" he wonders aloud.

Angelika raises her eyebrows. "Want?"

"Yes. What does Fräulein Rosen *want*? From today?" Fritz asks. "From tomorrow? From life?"

"Oh. That's simple," she tells him. "I want freedom. Freedom to do whatever I please. Freedom to be whomever I choose. Freedom to be *with* whomever I choose," she says. And then: "Your sister. She made a point of announcing that you are married."

"I am," he admits in an uncomplicated tone. "My wife lives in Frankfurt."

"That's far away for a wife."

"She keeps her own home, and I keep mine. I send her a gift on her birthday. I believe last year it was a set of crystal sconces."

"So this is a sport for you, then? Schtupping pretty girls who aren't ashamed to take off their clothes for—as you reminded me—nine marks an hour."

Fritz considers. "Is that what I'm doing, you think?" he asks. "Having sport?"

For a heavy moment, both hold the gaze of the other. Then comes an unwelcomed burst of noise from the street. A lorry roars across the Pariser Platz, bristling with hooked-cross flags and hung with a banner exhorting Berliners to "Vote List 2!" Brownshirted storm troopers bellow their narrative through megaphones. "Germany Awake! Jews Perish!" they bawl, tossing armloads of hooked-cross confetti into the wind.

But inside the Adlon's dining room, the Schubert quintet continues without the musicians skipping a note, as Fritz and Angelika gaze grimly at the storm of tiny Hitlerite crosses blowing past the window in the lorry's wake.

"Should we be frightened of them?" Angelika wonders aloud.

Fritz frowns at the window glass. "You mean as good Germans?" he asks. "Or as Jews?"

A certain tension defines Angelika's silence. She waits for him to answer himself.

"We'd be foolish not to be cautious," Fritz says. "But what can they do *really* other than act the bully? Von Hindenburg, that old fossil. He'll never agree to the Viennese tramp as the Reich's chancellor. It's impossible. He despises the little paskudnyak."

"I heard that he wanted to be an artist."

"Who?"

"The paskudnyak. I heard he wanted to be a painter, but the academies wouldn't have him."

Fritz tosses a shrug. "I had heard he was a former paperhanger. But if he had *artistic* aspirations? Well. Too bad for him. And too bad for us if the impossible happens. Because it's been my experience that there is no more embittered creature on the face of the earth than a failed artist." He says this and then offers her a light smile. "Shall I order another brandy, Fräulein Rosen," he suggests, "and we can put politics aside?"

The beautiful face changes again. She fastens her eyes on him. "She'll be angry with me, if we do this. And she'll be angry with you too."

Fritz is reassuring. "Liebling, she'll never need know."

Morning arrives. The drapes are open in the bedroom of Fritz's suite. Angelika stirs groggily. She blinks at the sunlight that stings her eyes. Then suddenly realizes she is not alone. There's another presence filling the space at the end of the bed, and it's not Fritz Landau. It's a little girl. A little dark thing stationed at the foot of the bed gazing at her in silence.

"And who are you, Bissel?" Angelika wonders.

But the child's answer is silence. She only stares.

Then footsteps arrive, but they don't belong to Fritz Landau either.

"Rashka? Where have you gotten to?" a woman calls out in a voice that Angelika recognizes all too quickly.

"Shit," she breathes. "You should go to your mummy now," Angelika instructs the child urgently, scrambling to gather the satin bedclothes around her to cover her nakedness. "She's calling for you."

But little Rashka ignores Angelika's instruction just as she ignores her mother's call.

"Damn me, but you're a stubborn one," Angelika whispers. "Go on. *Shoo.*"

Too late, though, too late. The bedroom door creaks, and there she is. The artist. Rashka's mummy, Lavinia Morgenstern-Landau. "Rashka, what have you—" the woman is in the middle of asking when she halts in her tracks at the sight of Angelika ensconced in her brother's bed, obviously without a stitch under the sheets.

Angelika can only stare back at her.

At this point, Fritz manages to make his appearance. "Hello? Who's here leaving my door standing open?" he's calling as Lavinia seizes Rashka by the hand and drags her from the bedroom. Angelika can hear the short melodrama that follows.

"*Lavinia*? You simply disregard my privacy now? Appear uninvited without notice?"

"You must have it *all*, mustn't you, Fritz! You must sully everything with your licentious appetites."

"I beg your pardon? My *what*?"

"Is there nothing you won't take from me? Nothing you won't *steal*?"

"Well, that's an interesting way to put it, chère sœur. What exactly have I *stolen* from you?"

Angelika exhales a breath. Selects a cigarette from the lovely teakwood box by the bedside and ignites it using the shiny sterling table lighter. The smoke from her cigarette balloons into the air. Beyond the bedroom, angry words are supplanted by angry footsteps in retreat, followed by the slam of a door. Angelika waits till Fritz reappears and leans against the threshold.

"Well, that was unfortunate," he concludes.

Angelika draws in smoke and exhales it through her nostrils. "She looked wounded."

Fritz only shrugs. "Of course she did. You're her muse, Liebchen."

"Her *muse?*" Why does it hurt her to hear this?

"Oh, yes," Fritz assures her and gathers up the blankets covering her until flesh is exposed. "You," he says, "are her muse du rouge."

Two days pass. The artist at her easel, pursuing her work on the canvas. She's attempting to finish the painting even though the dais is empty. Even though the subject is no longer posing. There is a certain leaden pain in her heart as she works, though it is a pain she has resigned herself to carrying. Since when is pain something new to the artist?

Frowning, she hears a door open behind her. "Rashka. I told you. You must leave Eema alone," she calls to her daughter. But she does not turn until the fat yellow cat at her feet stands and runs to the intruder. Angelika scoops him up, slowly scratching the scuff of his neck as he begins to purr like a drill bit boring into wood.

"Am I your muse?" Angelika asks her. She is wearing hand-stitched Ferragamo heels and a fashionably cut frock from Paul Kuhnen. Proof that Fritz Landau maintains his accounts in all the best shops and with all the best designers.

The artist does not speak a word at first, but her expression is a complex mixture of pain, shock, and relief. "You've cut your hair."

"Yes." Her long red tresses have been bobbed.

"Was that my *brother's* suggestion?"

"No. Don't be cross. I did it for you. I thought you might like me more modern." The girl touches the straight line of bangs that frames the arch of her eyebrows. "Do you approve?"

Lavinia stares. "What choice have you given me?"

Angelika approaches the easel, cradling the cat in her arms, as she gazes with deep fascination at the painting. "*Look,*" she tells the feline. "I have been transformed. Little Gelika from the Kastanienallee has become a goddess," she says with a quiet astonishment.

Lavinia pets the feline's head. "She speaks like a slum girl," she informs her cat. Is it possible to say this affectionately? Only then does the artist raise her head to meet the muse's eyes, and there she lets them settle for a deep moment before returning her brush to the canvas. "Hurry," she says. "Shed those glamour rags you're wearing and take up your pose. Before I lose the light completely."

13.

The Infinite Air

Aaron is still asleep after a late-night closing, the blanket drawn tightly over his shoulder. His face scrunched up as if he's dreaming of walking on nails. Staying quiet is easy for Rachel, of course. Living life as a U-boat, she learned to walk as quietly as a cat. At the kitchen table, she turns down the ankles of her socks and slips on her pair of saddle shoes. She lights a cigarette and sticks the rest of the pack in her sweater pocket. She's on the way to pick up Naomi's dress from the dry cleaner's on West 23rd, slipping on the kid leather gloves with the silk lining from Gimbels.

From out in the hall, she hears children, overlaid by a firm but lyrically maternal voice, and when she opens the door, she finds that it's Daniela Weinstock, who else? Maneuvering her hugely pregnant belly down the stairs with her three-year-old twins, one boy, one girl, and a toddler in a red metal stroller. The toddler, also a girl, is playing with the stroller's ring of wooden beads. The twins gaze up at Rachel with their mother's deep, dark eyes.

"Well, look who it *is*," Daniela announces to her children in a sweetly prompting manner. "It's Mrs. Perlman. Say *hello*."

"*Hello!*" the boy repeats loudly, grinningly, with a wave of his small hand, happy to participate. But the girl remains silent.

"Hello, Josh," Rachel replies to the boy, smiling, positioning her cigarette away from the child so that the smoke drifts up toward the ceiling. She cups her hand around the crown of Josh's silky hair. Josh has his father's myopically squinted expression—he'll be wearing glasses by the time he's five—but unlike his poppa, he is always full of joyful hellos, full of dimpled smiles and inquiries. *Mommy, why is your hair black? Mommy, why are there cats?* The fullness of life sings in his voice, innocent in his bustling joy.

Rachel cupped his head because maybe she hoped to snatch some of that from him. Is that a crime? No, he has so much he could hardly miss it. A small bit of childish joy stuffed in her pocket, who would know? But perhaps it's that covetousness that Daniela detects and instinctually guards against as she absently presses the boy to her side in Rachel's presence. The girl, Leah, on the other hand? She's always unsettled Rachel. Those watching eyes, as if the child can look through skin and see the interior schemes of a skeleton at work.

"So how are you doing? How are things?" Daniela is asking. "Haven't seen you in a bit."

"I've been busy," Rachel explains. "Things are crazy."

"Really?" Daniela lifts her eyebrows with interest. "Crazy how?"

Rachel swallows. She thought she had learned by now to field these hallway chitchat questions. And *crazy* is one of her preferred American words, because it's a cover-all word, like a big crazy blanket. *Crazy.* Work is crazy. Our schedule is crazy. Things are *crazy.* No one is supposed to ask *why.* "Well, the restaurant's the usual nuthouse for Aaron." She has learned *nuthouse* the hard way.

Daniela's brows knit. "Oh, I'm sorry to hear that." She sympathizes.

"And how are things with all of *you?*"

"Fine. Except Ezra's caught a cold," Daniela reports.

"Oh?" Rachel asks, sounding concerned.

"Yes. It's going around his office. I just hope he hasn't brought it home. The last thing I need is for *these three* munchkins to come down with runny noses." And then, "Wouldn't that be too bad?" she asks her children, inserting them oddly into the conversation. "Wouldn't that be too bad if Daddy spreads his sniffles? We don't want that, do we?" She does this often, Rachel notices: addresses her "munchkins" in this manner, even though she's talking with an adult, as if she cannot help but include the children in her every breath. But the children aren't paying attention, so to Rachel, she says, "He thinks it's all the fumes. The car exhaust, the bus exhaust in the streets." And then, her voice drops, grows more confidential. "By the way, I just want to say again how sorry I am that Ezra wasn't himself at dinner the other night."

"Oh, don't worry," Rachel assures her quickly.

"He must have been on the verge of getting sick. Also, he's just been under so much *pressure*. The workload is terrible at the P.D.'s office. Almost unbearable. He's always trying to juggle clients and cases, and of course there's no money for public defenders. So he can be grouchy," she chooses to say, "when he shouldn't be."

"I understand," Rachel assures her. "Aaron too. Exactly the same way." Once more. Two wives apologizing for their husbands' poor conduct.

"You know they'll be back to normal with each other in no time."

"Well, wasn't it sort of *normal* for them anyway?" Rachel asks. It's a gamble. It's a joke that could go wrong. But to her relief, Daniela laughs aloud.

"Yes," she happily concedes, "I suppose it is. Men can be such children," she confides, as if this is such a big secret.

Going down the stairs, of course, Rachel volunteers to help with the stroller, though it's awkward, and the Taylor Tot contraption is not exactly light. Picking it up from the front, she must carry it while walking backward down each flight to the foyer, while Daniela grips the handle from above, the weight of the toddler in between. Step down, step down, pause. Step down, step down, pause. And all the while, the little child gazes deeply as if Rachel is a foreign object. Until the girl starts banging loudly on the stroller's metal tray with a frown darkening her little face. Can children, in their innocence, perceive her crime against innocence? She's honestly feared this now for years.

"Okay!" Daniella announces brightly. "I can take it from here, I think," she tells Rachel as they reach the foyer. "The stoop steps are easy. Just bump, bump, bump."

Rachel opens the front door and holds it for the caravan of mother and children to pass.

"Thank you! Thank you!" Daniela repeats buoyantly and prompts her twins. "Say 'thank you' to Mrs. Perlman!" Daniella never probes. She never probes. Rachel's past is an undisturbed country, though she must wonder, mustn't she? And Rachel wonders too. What does this young mother from Astoria think late at night? What is her conception of the murder factories that polluted the skies with death? Does she ever dare let it touch her? Does she ever lie awake, while Ezra snores beside her, imagining herself on the final march to the smoking chimneys, gripping her crying toddler so tightly in her arms, instructing the twins to hold each other's hands? Hold your sister's hand, Joshua. Be Mommy's good soldier. Be Mommy's darling little soldier.

Rachel knocks on the door of Naomi's apartment. A pause, then a dead bolt slides, and the door opens, revealing Naomi in her chemical-stained work clothes, hair in the usual ponytail. "Oh my God. *It's you*," she declares as a greeting.

"I'm sorry. I should have called," Rachel apologizes. "I brought back your dress."

"Oh, jeez, you didn't have to take it to the cleaner's."

"Actually? I did," Rachel replies, handing it over by the wire hanger, still in the clear plastic bag. "So I don't want to interrupt. You must be in the midst?"

"No, no, I'm not. Just fucking around with some stupid pix I took over the weekend. They're not even very good. *Come in*," she invites. Inside, the apartment is in the same basic disarray as always. Naomi snatches up a blouse from the sofa and tosses it onto a chair. "You look like you could use a pick-me-up," she decides, dropping the dress in its dry cleaner's sheath over the ladder-back chair. "What's your poison?" Liquor bottles clink as she sorts through her inventory.

Rachel has crept in carefully behind her, reconnoitering the scene. "Whatever you have," she answers. "What are the pictures about? From the weekend."

"Oh. *Nothing.* A bunch of the alter kockers on the benches when I was up in Tompkins Square. But they turned out—I don't know—kinda boring." She says this while examining a bottle of gin. "I'm a little low on provisions. No more vodka, and no more decent scotch. But I've got some Gordon's and some Lejon extra-dry vermouth. I could make us martinis if you don't mind drinking them without olives. *Oh! Wait!*" She spots it. "There's that bottle of Four Roses you and your *huzz-band* brought over last month." She never misses a chance to razz Aaron, even when he' s not there to score against.

Rachel sits carefully on the sofa. "I remember it. That was the night Aaron got his elbow caught in the subway door."

Naomi laughs as she unstops the bottle of bourbon. "And kvetched about it the whole fucking time if I recall." She pours out two measures neat and ferries them over. "So! Tell me all about the big night! How was the show?" Naomi wants to know. "Was it hilarious? I read it was hilarious."

"Ah. Um. We ended up seeing something else. Something that was *not* the *Pajama Game.* And it wasn't very funny."

"Oh? Well, *that's* too bad. Did the shtoomer fuck things up? Forget to bring the tickets or something? He must have," she insists.

Rachel changes the topic. "I'm sorry it took me so long to return your dress," she tells her sister-in-law.

"Forget it. Nobody's taking *me* to a Broadway show anytime soon," Naomi says and swallows whiskey.

"Really? I thought… Isn't there the law student?"

"Y-y-yeah," Naomi answers evasively, "but jazz clubs are more his speed. Which reminds me. Are you and Aaron…" she starts to say but then stops and starts the sentence again. For an instant, Rachel fears that she's going to ask, *Are you and Aaron having trouble?* But what she says is "Are you two still planning on coming over on Saturday night?"

"Saturday?" Has she forgotten something again? Plans she agreed to inadvertently, while not really listening? It happens. It's how she once ended up suffering through a matinee of *The Girl in Pink Tights* with Leo Blume's first wife, Muriel. "I suppose we *are*," Rachel replies too tentatively.

"Oh, so Aaron didn't mention it?"

"I don't know. Maybe he did. It's been a very exhausting week. He's been closing at the restaurant almost every night."

"Well, then. Just in case Mr. Big got *too busy* to remember. You and he are invited for dinner this Saturday night for the new specialty of the house: chicken Kiev and asparagus in remoulade sauce."

"*Okay*. Well. That sounds wonderful," Rachel tells her, because it *does*. But there's something behind her sister-in-law's voice. Something hidden.

Naomi kills her whiskey. "So, darling, you wanna see what I was working on when you knocked?"

"You mean in your darkroom?" Rachel asks. She is slightly surprised. Her sister-in-law has always been resistant to opening her darkroom to those she deems "civilians."

"Why the hell not? I could use an artist's eyeball for a change. Just don't get your hopes up," she warns. "'Cause great art it's not."

Printmaking in the red glow of the darkroom is a cramped business. "I'm trying to put together a new portfolio," Naomi is explaining. "Something other than shots of Swanson's frozen dinners, and I'm bored with most of my old Village stuff."

Images emerge on Kodak paper soaked in a bath of developing fluid. From a white surface to a gray ghost, to a sharp contrast of light and shadow. It's a shot of a park bench lined with Naomi's alter kockers. Old men dotting the benches.

"It's magic," Rachel says. "A blank sheet, and then out of nowhere, a picture."

"It *is* magic. You're right," Naomi agrees. "It still feels like that even to me."

She removes the print by the corners, wearing a pair of rubber gloves, then rinses it in a tray and pins it onto the line where it hangs drying with a number of others. Paper curls on the line. The old men smoke, drowse over Yiddish newspapers, some just sitting in the sun or in the shade because that's their life now.

"These are wonderful, Naomi."

"You think so? I'm not so sure. Old farts on park benches? Pretty kitschy."

Rachel disagrees. "No, no. Not these. You can—you can *feel* the weight of the years they're carrying." She smiles. Is it nostalgia? "I can recall the Orthodox men with their long beards gathering outside the cafés in the Grenadier Strasse. This was in Berlin. The Scheunenviertel, uh—the 'Barn Quarter' I should say. It was called so because long before, it was used as sheds for cows. But the men? I was only a child, but they looked so ancient." So strange and exotic, she explains, with their dangling side curls and their great fur hats. The Ostjuden from the shtetlakh. "Most were destitute. As poor as the dirt under their feet. I remember the very sour aroma of salted fish perfuming the streets."

The horse dung, the musty smell of browning cabbages and damp potatoes piled high in the carts of the vegetable stands. The Ostjuden orthodoxy in their beaver-skin hats and airless black kaftans, sweating into their beards. Dangling payot, fringed tallitot. They were the first to feel the brunt of the anti-Semitic pogrom, years even before the Nazis arrived, and the first to be stripped of German citizenship under Hitler.

"Most Jews in Berlin?" says Rachel. "They regarded the quarter as a kind of plague town and the inhabitants as the sweepings of the

Pale of Settlement. Certainly my mother did. It was they who were to blame for the ugly, hooked-nose caricatures in *Der Stürmer*. That was the common thinking. But *I* thought they were beautiful," says Rachel. "Such faces. As if God had modeled them from the original clay."

There's a beat of soft silence before Naomi speaks, sounding quietly surprised. "I've never heard you talk about..." What shall she call it? "About your *past*," she says.

Rachel shrugs it away. "What is the point? The city I was born to is gone. Ground to dust. And the Ostjuden? The crematoria took them. They're all at the bottom of the ash pits now." Eingeäschert. And now the silence in the tiny darkroom has gone morose. It's the trap of her past. "I'm sorry," Rachel apologizes. "I shouldn't have said that. It was morbid." She wipes the dampness from her eyes.

"No, no, it's all right. *Really*," her sister-in-law insists. "There's so much I don't know." This sounds like a small confession on Naomi's part. An American Jew with blank spots on the map of Europe where the Jews once lived and died. But Rachel isn't interested in teaching history. She offers a flimsy smile.

"You can be glad over that," she says. "Knowing too much is not so pleasant. So. *Show me*. What else?" Pushing up a smile, nodding her chin to the developing bins.

"Oh. Okay, sure," her sister-in-law agrees, probably just as happy to be changing the subject. "There're a couple more."

The rectangles of light-sensitive paper are submerged, and images float to the top. Thickening shadows evolve into more alter kockers. More pigeons, more mothers pushing prams down the sidewalk, kids trailing.

And then truth emerges.

A sleek young man maintains a certain élégance d'attitude even as he is seated on the weathered park bench among the pigeons and hopping squirrels.

"That's David Glass," Rachel declares, a note of trouble in her voice.

"Who?" Naomi asks, but Rachel does not answer.

The young Mr. Glass sits politely attentive as any wolf of the steppes, listening to an old scarecrow of a man beside him. Friedrich Landau was the name once engraved on his calling card in Berlin. Though Rachel has always known him simply as Feter Fritz.

"Is something wrong?" she hears Naomi inquiring, with a light note of concern, and shakes herself free of the photo.

"No," she says, bringing up a flat smile. "No. Just a headache. It must be the whiskey. I hardly ever touch it."

"Could be inhaling the emulsion fluid too. We should get you out of here. Sometimes the silver nitrate gives people headaches."

"Yes," Rachel agrees, feeling gutted. "Yes, that could be it too."

On her way back to the subway, she stops at a pay phone and rings up Feter Fritz. Le conspirateur. The pay phone rings until one of the other tenants picks it up. A man. Has he seen Mr. Landau today? No? No, not all morning, sorry. She hangs up. She thinks she could get on the train and head for the Lower East Side. She could track him down, her feter. Grill him. Isn't that what it's called in the detective movies? Give him the third degree. What scheme were you hatching? What bargain were you sealing? Talk!

But does she forget? He is the master of prevarication, Feter Fritz. The maven of obfuscation, of half-truths and full lies.

Was I sitting on a park bench conspiring with the likes of David Glass? Oh, yes. And later on, I had coffee and a bun with Albert Einstein.

She would never get a straight story from him. Ever. So she will wait.

Sitting at home on the windowsill. She has shoved up the sash to free Kibbitz from the apartment, but now she sits there, the chilly air washing over her, smoking a juju, a parting gift from her sister-in-law. "Dope!" Naomi calls it. Better than aspirin! Better than Miltown! Smoking a little reefer. That's Naomi's prescription. It smells to Rachel like the sour weed from a poor man's pipe.

Sitting on the edge of the window like she's sitting on the edge of the world, Rachel feels a lift. She will not worry. She will wait. She will wait and be watchful for the truth of her uncle's subterfuge to emerge. She knows that if Feter Fritz has a fatal flaw, it is that his ego will not permit him to keep silent. Eventually, he will confess his intrigues in order to boast of them.

She takes another puff, and her thoughts follow the smoke out into the infinite air.

PART TWO

The Good Hour

14.

The Grosse Hamburger Strasse

NOVEMBER 1943. AFTER FOUR YEARS, THE WEIGHT OF THE WAR is depressing daily life in Berlin. Ersatz tobacco and greasy margarines are commonplace, as are meat shortages and leather shortages, while chemical substitutes of every ilk abound. Long lines lead to short tempers. Everyone's patching and mending and re-mending, and everyone smells stale. The newsreels and headlines are still shrill about ultimate victory, but even the Propaganda Ministry cannot fully camouflage the truth. Hamburg has been incinerated by the British Royal Air Force. And while huge flak towers have been erected around Berlin, bristling with antiaircraft guns, the city remains a regular target for bombers.

In the darkened cinema mezzanine, Angelika listens to a fanfare of trumpets. An iron eagle perched on a wreathed hooked cross is silhouetted by a sunburst as the newsreel title unspools: "Die Deutsche Wochenschau." Angelika gazes up at the images and listens to the newsreel's narrator's bombastic tone. On the screen, at least, the Wehrmacht advances! Victory is still inevitable even in defeat.

She is bundled up against the cold in clothes that are ill fitting and patched. Ten years before, modeling for Lavinia, she'd been dressed in silks from the finest designers. She walked Berlin in the most fashionable shoes. Tuition had been paid for her classes at a well-known fashion school. She thought she was finally free of the scrimping life. The miserly life of the Barn Quarter. Counting pennies, counting buttons. But then everything was stolen from her, step by step, year by year, until she had nothing left but her looks. Nothing but the green of her eyes and the flame of her hair.

Now she is scrounging her clothing from street markets and rubbish bins because at least these clothes do not include "the yellow ornament" as her father calls it. The Judenstern. She had tried to design stylish cloaks and dresses that could absorb the star into their color combinations, that could truly transform the badge into an ornament of fashion. But ration coupons for material were beyond her grasp. And then? Deportation orders had arrived for her and for her mother. Her mamme was frightened. She didn't want to go underground, she wanted to obey the authorities, she wanted to report as commanded, but Angelika's father had refused to allow this. Tatte did not believe the propaganda. At least Angelika can be grateful to him for that. Jewish resettlement camps with work, but also food and warm clothing? What Nazi potentate would invest in that? Think! What was more likely? There were already terrible stories circulating of mass executions and special camps for gassing. No, they would not report. He had stashed away a bit of money. They must go into hiding, Tatte insisted.

Now, up in the mezzanine of a cinema, Angelika's mother is sunk in beside her daughter. She is also bundled in frayed clothes. Mamme was once a stunning beauty, as she likes to remind anyone who will listen. She could have married a banker's son. Oh yes. He was interested, and he was a smart man too. He would have seen it all coming. She's sure of this. Now she could have been living in safety and comfort in Cuba or perhaps South America, in a big house with servants, but instead she picked love like a fool. Her looks are all gone now. Worn away. She looks half-starved and exhausted. There is something jittery, high-strung, and childlike about her. With an edgy whisper, she clutches her daughter's arm. "*Something must have happened.*"

Nothing is said.

"He should have been here by now."

Still, no words spoken by her daughter.

"*Something must have happened.* Gelika. Are you listening to me?"

Nothing.

"I said, 'Are you *listening* to me?'"

"I heard what you said, Mamme," Angelika tells her. "Please be quiet."

Silence between them. Then, "Where has he *gotten* to?"

"Mamme, please. He's coming. Just stay calm." Angelika returns to gazing at the newsreel, but her mother is clearly not comforted.

"Something must have happened."

But then *there he is*, thank God for that, if there is a God to thank. Angelika's father is squeezing into the chair beside her mother. He is still a handsome man, Tatte, with a silvering beard, though poorly barbered. His face is terribly careworn and his eyes heavy like lead. He wears a hat that's lost its shape and an oversized coat, and he grips a kraft-paper envelope, pressing it tightly against him.

Her mother gushes with raw relief. "Oh, blessed is the name, Tatte, you're *here*. But you're so *late*."

"It took time, Mamme," he says. "It's not a simple business."

"Well, never mind," his wife says dismissively. "At least we can be thankful now it's *over*."

"Not quite."

His words take a moment to sink in.

"*What?*" his wife wants to know. "Gelika, what is Tatte saying?" This is an irksome habit of her mother's, asking Angelika to translate her father's meaning. But it's Tatte who answers.

"There was a *complication*," he says in Yiddish, pretending to watch the newsreel. Es iz geven a kamplakeyshan. "The man wanted more money."

"But…" Mamme swallows. "But that's all the money we have. There is no more money. Didn't you tell him this?"

"*Of course*, I told him, what do you think? Am I an idiot? The man doesn't care about our problems, Mamme. He wanted *more money*." Finally, he confesses at the end of the story. "All I could afford was one."

Again, a blank terror hushes Mamme's voice. "One?"

Tatte does not respond to her. He relinquishes the envelope quickly, reaching across his wife and forcing it into his daughter's hands. "For *you*, Angelika," he declares. "Put it away quickly."

Angelika blinks at the envelope, stupefied.

Her mother is asking, "Why only one, Tatte? Why only *hers*?"

"Because she is our only child, Mamme. She is the only one who matters to the future." Then he frowns at Angelika. "*Put it away*, I said."

"But what are *we* to do, Tatte?" Mamme wants to know. "You and I? Gelika, what is your father *saying*?"

But Angelika understands that her mother has been erased from the conversation.

"You should go. *Now*," her father commands. "I think I may have been followed."

The fear rises in Mamme's voice. "Followed? Followed by whom?"

Again, to Angelika he speaks. "*Go*. Your mamme and I will look after ourselves. Go. *You must*."

Mamme is whispering frantically. "I don't understand. I don't understand... What is *happening*?" But her daughter understands perfectly, and she is on the move. She kisses her parents quickly. Deflects her mamme's beseeching voice.

"Goodbye, Mamme. Goodbye, Tatte." That's all she says. What else can she say but goodbye? Vacating the mezzanine, she forces the image of her parents into the background of her mind as the martial sweep of the newsreel anthem reaches its crescendo.

The sound of the film is muted as Angelika descends the stairs to the lobby, hurried but measured. Excusing herself, she shoves past a slower-moving patron, who squawks a mild complaint as he's forced to clear the way, causing him to bump into two men in leather trench coats who are ascending the steps to the mezzanine. The leather coats and snap-brim hats are the standard uniform of the Gestapo, so it's the patron who's apologizing now. Angelika makes it past without a whiff of Stapo interest.

Cutting through the lobby crowd, she's almost at the doors to the street. Almost free! When a hand seizes her by the wrist.

"Not so fast," she hears the man instruct. She doesn't call out, just tenses for confrontation. The hand belongs to a slyly handsome young man with flaxen blond hair and eyes like gray smoke. He wears a snap-brim hat and an expensive cashmere coat, but there is something of the working-class scavenger about him. A handsome fox from the proletariat. Drawing her in closer, he has a question for her. "So. Where is your star, Liebchen?"

He gives her a piece of advice. He, the man with the flaxen hair. Make yourself *useful* to them. These are the words he speaks as she and her parents are loaded into the rear of a green police lorry along with other captured U-boats. One of the Gestapo trench coats calls over to him with a certain camaraderie. "Not a bad haul. A good day's work!" The blond fox grins, showing teeth, but then squeezes Angelika's arm and whispers into her ear. His lips close. His breath heated. "Make yourself *useful* to them," he instructs. Nützlich is the word he chooses for her. Helpful. Beneficial. Valuable.

The stones in the oldest Jewish cemetery in Berlin have been desecrated. Workers have used pickaxes, spades, and sledgehammers to smash tombstones and to dig a zigzagged air-raid trench through the burial ground. Fractured gravestones bear the Magen David and epitaphs in Hebrew. Bones have been cleared like roots. This is Grosse Hamburger Strasse. Across the street from the cemetery stands what was once the Jewish Community Home for the Aged, but the elderly inhabitants have long since been evacuated eastward. Now the building is the Grosse Hamburger Strasse Sammellager, a collection camp for Berlin Jews. An assembly camp run by the Gestapo for filling deportation quotas set by the SS Jewish Bureau, Referat IV B4.

Inside, Angelika is shivering alone, confined to a dark portion of the building's cellar. She had been beaten and bloodied for two days in a Gestapo cellar in the Burgstrasse before being trucked over to this place and dumped. It was not the first time in her life she had been struck. As a child, her mother would slap her or come after her with a wooden kitchen paddle, and after a certain age, after certain changes in her body, her father would slap her too. Once after she was caught kissing that goyische boy from the bottle factory, her tatte struck her so hard with a closed fist that she saw stars in the middle of the day.

But never before had she been subjected to a sustained beating as she had been in the Burgstrasse cellar. It was a pounding, administered by a Gestapo brute in his shirtsleeves, who had "interrogated" her while she was manacled to a chair. He struck her face and split her lip. Tore her bloodstained blouse and struck her shoulders with a cudgel, punched her in the stomach so that she vomited bile. Twice he jammed the muzzle of a pistol against her forehead and threatened to fire. And all the while repeating the same demand. *Talk.* Yet she had nothing to say. She did not *know* anything. She was not privy to names or locations of black marketeers. She knew nothing of the forger who had produced the false identity card she had been arrested carrying.

Tatte had always handled all the logistics. Their contacts for food. For a roof over their heads. She never knew the names of their hiders and seldom even recognized where they were. Somewhere in Little Wedding? Somewhere in Berlin-Kreuzberg? They traveled during blackout hours. No lights beyond an electric torch with colored tissue over the lens. But this brute didn't really seem interested in her explanations. He didn't really seem interested in answers at all. His entire justification for existence was to beat. To strike. To hurt. This continued until she lost all track of time. Until she felt each blow like a numbing vibration thrumming through her body, until she wondered if the dim light of the cellar would be the last light she would ever see.

But a day later, her lip scabbed, her eyes blackened, she was transferred here. To the Grosse Hamburger assembly camp. Deposited alone in another cellar, where she now assumes she is waiting for death. She assumes that the beatings will begin again and that when the next brute finally grows weary of dispensing the blows, she will actually get the bullet. Since she met Audi Goldstein when she was fourteen and he took her in the rear of his glossy Invicta, since then she has learned many things about men and their desires. Men and their weaknesses. Men and their brutalities.

A slash of light cuts across her face as a key clanks in the lock and the door thuds open. A uniformed SS warder steps in. "On your feet, Jewess," he tells her, already bored with the process of her death. She is taken to a room abovestairs. A harshly lit room, where she is seated at an oaken table. Can this be the room where she will be shot? It seems a bit too neat. And would they really bother to seat her in a chair to shoot her? There are no manacles here as there were in Burgstrasse. A photo of the SS chief, Herr Reichsführer Himmler, hangs above the head of the table, gazing into the air, as if she is too insignificant for him to notice. The same bored SS man who brought her in now stands by as the door creaks open, and in comes a man dressed in a tailored, double-breasted suit and a silk tie, sporting a party badge on his lapel. He seems harried as he strides into the room, all business, and plops himself into the chair facing Angelika. Opens a sheath of papers and scowls at them.

"You are the Jewess Angelika Sara Rosen?" he asks, though it doesn't sound like a question as much as a dreary accusation. His eyes flick upward in response to her silence. "Answer, please," he tells her. A small moment of instruction.

"Yes." Angelika obeys.

"I am Kriminal-Kommissar Dirkweiler. But you will address me as Herr Kommandant," he informs her.

She repeats the lesson. "Yes. Herr Kommandant."

"You were found in possession of illegal identification documents," says he. This time, all he needs do is flick his eyes upward to prompt her reply.

"Yes. *Yes*, Herr Kommandant."

"*Forged* documents."

She swallows. "May I ask, Herr Kommandant? Where are my parents?"

The man frowns absently. "Your parents? They are in the room above us. What we call the Ost Zimmer. Tomorrow you will join them on the train that will transport you to the east. Unless…"

She stares. Opens her mouth, but her voice has deserted her. All she can manage is a weak gasp for air. The east. It is well known among the U-boats what this means. Regardless of the promises of propaganda, regardless of the lies told about resettlement of Jewish war labor, by now the truth is known. The east is death.

"Unless"—the Herr Kommandant repeats himself—"you decide to confess to your crime."

"It's true." Angelika's eyes go damp with tears. "It's true, Herr Kommandant. The documents were forged. It's true."

"It's *true*, you say. And yet according to the report from Untersturmführer Dr. Kraus of the Stapoleitstelle Burgstrasse, you have refused to divulge the name of the criminal who supplied you with these forged documents. The forger himself."

Tears burn her eyes. "I cannot, Herr Kommandant," she says. "I cannot divulge what I do not know."

"So you purchased forged documents from a man with no name?"

"I have no idea, Herr Kommandant. About any name. I never saw the man."

"Is that so? Very strange," he says. "For according to the confession of the Jew…" He must consult his paperwork for the name. "The Jew Ernst Israel Rosen." He raises his face to her. "That is your father, is it not?" he asks but does not wait for a reply. "According to his confession, it was *you*—his daughter—who organized illegal transactions."

Angelika is stunned. Devastated. "My father?" She cannot. She *cannot* believe this. "My *father* said this?"

"Are you telling me he lied?" Dirkweiler wonders.

But Angelika is too shocked to utter another word in response.

"Must I repeat my question? Are you *telling* me that your father has *lied*?"

Angelika stares. Her eyes are bright with tears. Her brain is steaming. She is trying to work out the puzzle. There is a strong answer and a weak answer, but which is which? Whom does she incriminate? Her tatte who just betrayed her? Or herself? And then she thinks of the blond Jew's instruction. Nützlich! Make yourself *useful* to them. "No, Herr Kommandant," she answers. "My father does not lie."

"No? Then you will confess to your crime, please, and give me the name of the damned forger!"

"Yes, Herr Kommandant," she answers. Her tears are like acid. "I do confess. And I will give you the name. But first, I beg you. Allow me to see my parents."

Again the smirk. "You are a very attractive specimen," the Herr Kommandant decides, but she senses no physical desire behind his words. Only a statement of fact. Then he is up from the chair. "The name of the forger in one hour," he demands, his voice dull now, devoid of interest. "Either provide it for me, or you and your parents will be on the train tomorrow."

It's true what the Herr Kommandant told her about the room abovestairs. In the Grosse Hamburger Strasse Lager, the most unfortunate of the Jewish prisoners are housed on the top floor. The so-called Ost Zimmer. The East Room. Women, men, children, some U-boats, some with the Judenstern still sewn to their clothing, all packed together on dirty straw mattresses. Some cry in the Ost Zimmer. Some pray. Some sing to their children. All fear desperately. Angelika is crouched in front of her tatte and mamme. Her bruises still sting. Her rage is an oven. But she contains it all. No screaming. No hysterics. All the pain, all the anger is distilled into the cold of her eyes.

Tatte is beseeching her. "Please, Angele. Forgive me. I had *no idea*. I thought, with *a female*, they would be lenient."

"Look at my face, Tatte. Does it *look* as if they were *lenient*?"

"I'm sorry. I'm sorry." Tearfully he reaches out to cradle his daughter's face. "My child," he says, as if perhaps a father's touch alone can heal the bruises. She winces but does not draw herself away.

"Do you know why we are here, Tatte? *Here*. Up on the top floor? It's because…" she starts to say but stops. Removes her father's hand and gives a quick glance around them. Her voice drops. "It's because tomorrow, everyone here will be loaded onto the train."

Mamme is confused, which only amplifies her fear. "The *train*? *What* train? Train to *where*?"

"*Mamme*, keep your voice down," Angelika orders and then turns to her father to answer the question. "The train to the east."

A fearful whisper from Mamme. "*The east?* Tatte, what does that mean, *the east*?"

"Shoosh, Mamme. Quiet," is all her husband has to say to her. He has not broken eye contact with his Angelika. "Is there something?" he says very carefully. "Something you can *do*, Daughter? Perhaps if one of these officials… If they *notice* you."

His daughter stares back at him.

The door opens at the opposite end of the room, causing a rustle of panicky voices. A pair of men from the Jewish orderly squad appear. They wear the yellow star, but they have adopted a bully's swagger in their dung-gray coveralls. Of the two, the stocky ordner with the facial scar seems to be the man in charge, since he carries the list, while the other carries the placards.

"Everyone listen clearly!" the stocky one shouts. "If your name is called, you will raise your hand and keep it raised until you have received a placard. You are to wear the placard at all times hung from around your neck until tomorrow when you are boarded onto the train. If you have infants or children under the age of six, they will travel with you but do not require a placard. Is this understood?" He does not wait for the answer that is not forthcoming anyway but goes straight into his list. "Grünberg, Moses. Grünberg, Silva. Hirsch, Otto. Hirsch, Shira. Hirsch, Eva!" And so it goes. As the ordner continues to shout out names—"Blume, Alfred. Blume, Gottfried!"—the prisoners dutifully raise their hands, even the children, and the second ordner distributes small placards on strings bearing the letter T.

T for Transport.

"Rosen, Karlotte. Rosen, Ernst. Rosen, Angelika!"

"Must we raise our hands, Tatte?" Mamme wants to know.

He replies with his eyes still locked into Angelika's stare. "Yes, Mamme. We must raise our hands." And so he does. Mamme anxiously follows. But Angelika's hand remains unraised, and her face is coolly decisive.

"Give me the name," Angelika says.

"The *name*?" her father repeats.

"The name of the forger," she tells him.

He swallows. "Angelika. That's a death sentence for the man."

"You want me to do something, Tatte?" she asks him. "Then I must give something. *Speak.*"

Angelika is seated again at the battered table but with the T placard around her neck. The same Waffen-SS man stands by when the door creaks again sharply, and in comes Kommandant Dirkweiler, now in a necktie and his shirtsleeves. He is no sooner in the room when Angelika blurts it out.

"Heinz Zollinger!"

The man stops dead.

"You asked for a name, Herr Kommandant. I have given you a name," she says. "Heinz Zollinger. He is a printer's apprentice in the Warschauer Strasse, Horst-Wessel-Stadt. *He* is your forger."

The Herr Kommandant slumps slightly at the shoulders. He looks satisfied, perhaps even slightly entertained. "Well. That wasn't so difficult, was it? To be a little useful after all to the Reich?" he asks. "To me?"

Angelika raises her eyes level with his, those eyes that can cut a man to shreds. "No, Herr Kommandant. Not so difficult. All I ask is for a small amount of mercy. For me," she says, touching the placard. "For my parents."

"Fine," he answers in quite an offhanded manner, waving the matter off, like swatting away a buzzing insect. "You and your parents are off the list." An inconsequential matter when there are so many Jews in his custody to replace them. "I will see to it that you and they can turn in your necklaces," he says, indicating the card hung from her neck.

Angelika breathes. "*Thank you*, Herr Kommandant."

"But perhaps you are unaware?" he says, frowning.

She is confused.

"Unaware of the special privileges available to some in this lager. There are Jews here who I *keep*," he explains. He seems quite intent on apprising her of this. "Certain choice specimens who work in my service."

His service? "Herr Kommandant. I don't understand." Does he mean as a concubine? She's heard rumors of such arrangements with lecherous types in the party or the SS. Men who keep a Jewish girlfriend for fun. "*How*—in your service?"

Dirkweiler smiles briefly, a spasm. "By catching up with your fellow Jews still out on the streets. Your fellow Israelites on the run," he clarifies, obviously proud of his clever operation. "The Jew Cronenberg, for instance, who brought you in. He's one of my top hounds, and he seems to think that you are worth my consideration," the Herr Kommandant informs her. "I'm beginning to believe he might be correct."

15.

Rewards for Those Who Work

Der Suchdienst is what it's called. The Search Service in the employ of Kommandant Dirkweiler. Search Service Jews are allotted special permits typed on green card stock that authorize their travel to anywhere in the city where they prowl the cafés, the cinemas, the street corners. They patrol the parks and the air raid shelters looking to net Jewish U-boats. They are known as "Greiferen." Grabbers. Catchers. They are given extraordinary privileges inside the Grosse Hamburger Lager. A share in the loot. Nice clothing that's free of the Judenstern. Jewelry, liquor, and money to pocket. The best are issued their own pistols. They travel with Gestapo handlers, or sometimes they work without supervision in pairs, surveilling the U-Bahn stations, the S-Bahn routes, the parks, the foreign embassies of neutral countries. They are Jews who hunt Jews.

Inside the lager building, they are separated from the population who are headed for the trains. Some are even assigned rooms with a door that they are authorized to close. They are permitted a bed, a chair, and lamps, a table to place a phonograph upon. Emil selects a record for the turntable and lightly drops the needle. A well-known chanteuse warbles. *Sing, Nachtigall, sing.*

Emil Cronenberg. Tall, slim, handsome as a wolf, but most importantly blond like any Aryan. He is always happy to explain his ancestral history. A Mischling grandmother and an Aryan grandpa, or was it the other way around? Every time he reviews his family tree, the good German branches tend to change. The tree is never the same twice.

But this much Angelika is sure of. He comes from nothing. The factory slums. And even with his fancy leather trench coat and snap-brim fedora, he holds himself like a prole, hunched against the world. He sounds like a prole. It only takes a few shots of Gilka and he reveals himself as an Urberliner from Neukölln. "Ick gloob' meen Schwein pfeift!" he shouts in disbelief. I think my pig is whistling!

But there's a boyishness to him, underneath the leather trench. A defensive posture. It's obvious to her in his obsession over the phonograph. So proud of it is he. She thinks it means more to him than the glossy blue French Citroën that Dirkweiler has authorized for his use in touring the town on the hunt. The phonograph's dark mahogany case, the polished brass trumpet. A little slum boy with this elegant possession. It is touching. Having that phonograph, she supposes, is proof that he is *someone* now. Like all men, he wants to see himself as a force to be reckoned with. And in many ways, he is. A charming force. A brutal force too.

There are other catchers in the Grosse Hamburger Strasse. She works briefly beside a true killer, a man called Grizmek, but he stabs his Stapo handler on a train and vanishes. Why does she not do the same? Why would she? How can life as an underground Jew possibly compare? When Dirkweiler pairs her with Emil, it is a successful match. They grab four U-boats on their first outing together.

Emil is driving the Citroën up the Friedrichstrasse, a blond forelock hanging out from under the brim of his hat, a cigarette dangling from his lips. He likes the Bulgarian brand. Makedon Perfekt. They are rough smoking, just like he is. Angelika can hear her own voice, edging toward seduction. "Emil Cronenberg... Who is this Emil Cronenberg?"

But really, even as she asks, she wonders: Who will ever know the answer to such a question? That night, they have intercourse on Emil's bed while the phonograph plays. Rosita Serrano's chilly "Roter Mohn." Red Poppy.

Colder weather for Berlin at this time of year. The windows of the Café Bollenmüller are steam-clouded. The noise of the café's lunchtime service is subdued. The accordionist is taking a break for a smoke. Angelika and Emil share a table. She wears a long, trimly cut black woolen coat with Bakelite pinwheel buttons and a thick lambswool collar. A black felt hat with a wide, dipping brim and a single pheasant feather tucked into the velvet band. She knows where they came from, these clothes. They came from those who will no longer need such glamour rags.

A shabbily clad girl, skinny as a pike, enters the café and stands anxiously alone by the bar, rubbing her fingers for warmth.

"There's one," Emil says. "You see her? The skinny broom that just walked in."

Angelika looks closer. She wants to learn. He says she has the gift. All she needs is to learn the tricks. "What gives her away?" she asks.

"You tell me. Does she look Jewish?" he asks her.

Angelika squints. This question feels like a trap. "I don't know. Do *you* look Jewish? Do *I*?"

"Pay attention," Emil instructs.

A pause as she studies the prey. Smoke drifts across her line of sight from Emil's cigarette.

"She's frightened." Angelika can see that.

"Yes, but more. What else?"

"Her clothes are patched," Angelika offers.

Emil shrugs as he taps a bit of ash into the tin ashtray. "Many people patch their clothes. It's rationing. But you're close," he tells her. "What else?"

Another pause. Her eyes go deeper. Deeper. Then it strikes her like a match struck to a flame. "Her *shoes*."

Emil shows her an approving smile. "Good. You have it. She's a U-boat. She walks everywhere, day and night, searching for a place to hide, so her shoes are falling off her feet."

A dark-headed youth in an old winter coat enters and touches the skinny girl's arm. She is startled but then relieved. They confer quietly, and the youth guides her to a table.

"Now, *he* looks Jewish," Angelika decides.

But Emil is shaking his head. "No," he tells her. "Never trust that. Never trust the propaganda. Hooked noses, Jewish earlobes. It's rubbish. See beyond it. You *can*. You have the hunter's instinct."

Another young woman appears at the café's entrance with a limp. She is alert. Well-dressed. Olive skin and a thick bush of dark hair.

"Oh no," Angelika hears herself whisper.

"What is it?"

The girl with the limp searches the room, eyes darting, until she spies the two young people at the table and, with an uneven gait, hurries over to join them. Sitting closely beside the dark-headed youth. She looks happy. Happy to see them. Happy to be sitting next to this boy.

"I know that girl. The girl with the limp."

"You *know* her?"

"We were in the art school," Angelika says. "Years ago when I was a student at Feige-Strassburger. Her hair was shorter then, but I remember that goose's waddle."

Emil sounds pleased. "Well," he says, "sometimes the manna simply falls from heaven." Crushing out his cigarette, he slips on his snap-brim hat and stands, removing a Walther PPK automatic pistol from his coat pocket. "So are you with me," he asks her, "or am I working alone?"

The Grosse Hamburger Strasse Lager. Inside the dreary room, her father jumps to his feet as if to rush to embrace her under the gaze of Himmler's portrait. "*Angelika*," he cries aloud, but then he stops dead, stands like he's nailed to the floorboards. She closes the door behind her, gazes back at his fearful, hopeful eyes.

No embrace is offered. "Sit down, Tatte," she instructs. But he remains on his feet.

"Your mother," he says. "She is still abovestairs."

"Yes," Angelika tells him. "I didn't want to deal with her hysterics," she explains bluntly. "I wanted to speak to you alone. Now, *sit*." This time, it's fully a command. A command he follows, sitting slowly. Carefully.

"You've done well, Gclika," he tells her with a cautious touch of pride. "Managing yourself. Look how beautiful in such clothes. Like a page from a magazine." Angelika says nothing.

"So?" he asks. "Are we to be released soon?" he wants to know. In other words, has she done her work? Has she done what is necessary— *whatever is necessary*—to rescue them?

"Released?" She swallows the word with a stroke of anger. "No. Not released, Tatte. But you'll be seen to."

And now her tatte looks wary. "Seen to? What does this mean, Daughter?"

"It means you'll both be given work," she tells him. "There's a factory in Kreuzberg. It manufactures buttons. You know buttons, Tatte. You and Mamme will be taken there in the morning and brought back here at the close of the day," she says.

"Buttons?" Her father is trying to smile. "To sell them I know. But to make them?"

"You'll both learn what is required," Angelika assures him. "There'll be food. You'll be safe from transport. But you'll—*both of you*—remain on the camp rolls." At this point, she removes two yellow cloth stars from the pocket of her coat and places them on the table. Yellow cloth edged in black, the dimensions officially proscribed. "Tell Mamme she must sew these to your clothing. Tell her to trade some bread for a needle and thread. If you don't wear them," she says, "if you're seen without the stars, you'll be put on the next transport and shipped east, and no one will be able to save you from that. Not me, not anyone."

Her father suddenly has nothing to say. He appears dumbstruck. Blinks at her in pained confusion.

"This is the best I could do, Tatte," Angelika informs him. Her eyes are suddenly hot with tears, which makes her even angrier. "This is the only deal I could strike."

"And *you?*" her tatte asks, looking closely at her now, as if he is only now seeing her. Really seeing her. "What will become of my Angelika? I notice *she* wears no star."

Angelika can feel her face harden. "She has her own work to do."

Herr Kommandant Dirkweiler is also an Obersturmführer in the SS. Forty-two years of age. Father of four girls. Twenty years in the police services. A middle-ranked detective with the Kriminalpolizei before transferring to the Gestapo when the war began. Athletic once, obviously, but aging into his body with a certain sag. Fingers stained from too much nicotine as he types at his desk, then yanks the rectangle of green card stock from the rubber roller with a flourish.

A signature is scribbled with his fountain pen before he employs the franking stamp, blots it in a businesslike fashion. GEHEIME STAATSPOLIZEI BERLIN the stamp reads in a circle around the Reich's eagle. And the name he has typed on the card? Angelika Sara Rosen. When he hands it over, he says, "Now you're one of us," as a joke.

Angelika accepts the gift, gazing at it with a kind of covert exhilaration. Even as a prisoner, she feels truly free for the first time in her life.

So she and Emil share a comfortable ersatz existence. They share a room, share a table, share the bed. They share like a married couple, Emil likes to joke, but in fact, Herr Kommandant Dirkweiler has pressed them to marry. Really! As if all those bürgerlich morals and strictures still mean something. He likes to keep his world tidy and in order, the Herr Kommandant. He like to keep his command in order too, likes to keep the moral niceties in place, though sluicing doesn't bother him. Sluicing meaning a routine of theft. Using his whip on a prisoner's back doesn't bother him either. Shipping people to their death? That doesn't qualify as a matter of morality; it's a matter of following orders. The Führer commands, I obey! But permitting Angelika and Emil to remain shacked up under the roof of his police lager? This offends his sense of propriety.

But for now she is sharing a sweaty bed out of wedlock. She lies there in her satin slip, listening to the tinny sound of Emil's phonograph. Heinz Müller singing an upbeat hit, "So Schön Wie Heut!" As Beautiful as Today! The bedsprings creak as Emil stands and starts dressing. His body is lean, as lean as his face. There is something detached about the way he approaches intercourse with her. Something lonely. As men go, he is skilled at touching her. She has no objections there. And they are vigorous together. But she is given the feeling that he is searching for something in the process that has nothing at all to do with her. Searching for something lost. It's baffling, his lack of animal passion for her. Sometimes she feels rejected, even insulted. Could it be that she is losing her allure? Men have always been frantic for her. She's learned to count on that as fact.

"Light me a cigarette," she commands him. A small power play.

He glances at her distantly. But then sits down on the bed beside her, his shirt still unbuttoned, and removes a cigarette from his case. Tapping it, then igniting it and passing it along. She accepts. It both annoys and charms her that he has answered her command in such a way as to quietly rob her of any power over him. Inhaling, she expels smoke in a plume aimed at the ceiling. "So what do you think?" she asks him. "Shall we resolve the Herr Kommandant's moral quandary for him?"

He snorts a short breath. Lights his own cigarette and breathes the smoke toward his feet. "Is that what you want?"

Angelika lies back. "It wouldn't kill me, I suppose. To be married. To be Frau Cronenberg," she says. "I mean, don't you ever think about the future? About our life after this war is done?"

And now Emil smiles. Not in a happy way but as if he's smiling at the stone on his own grave. "You really think we'll have a life after this war?"

An uncomfortable shrug. "Why not?"

Emil doesn't answer her. He simply smiles again and buttons his shirt, when there's a knock at the door.

"*Angelika?*" she hears a familiar voice inquire.

But Emil answers the voice, buckling his belt. "Who is it?"

A pause, and then the answer comes: "It's Fritz Landau. I'm here for Fräulein Rosen."

Emil glances back to her with a questioning expression. She shrugs. Blows smoke. Doesn't bother to cover herself. When Emil answers the door, she sees Fritz's posture stiffen. He's aged over the years since they parted, and he looks like an old rubbish collector in his orderly's coveralls. All his glamour whittled away. It was a shock when she first spotted him in the camp, dressed as an ordner with his red armband. A shock and not a shock. He may be a prisoner, but he still retains his cunning for accumulating power, shred by shred, doesn't he? Even as a Jew in an SS prison camp. They've spoken—briefly. She's aware of his position as the deputy to the Jewish lager manager and honestly has been expecting this visit sooner or later. So here he is, frowning from the threshold at her casual half-dressed insolence.

"How may I serve you, Herr Landau?" she wonders in a languidly vicious tone.

"I thought you should know," Fritz informs her. "Your parents are on the list."

She bursts into Dirkweiler's office, pushing past the outraged objections of his secretary, that ugly SS bitch. The door bangs open. She finds him standing behind his desk in his shirtsleeves. "Take them off the list!" she shouts into his face. "You *promised* me they would be safe! Take them off the list!"

His face reddens, and his response is simple. He strikes her hard across the face with the back of his hand. She staggers, grabs for the chair to keep from falling, but pulls it over when her knees buckle and tumbles to the floor.

"See what happens when you forget yourself!" he roars at her, a vein popping at his temple. "You filthy Jewish sow, you think you are some kind of *queen* here? You are Jewish trash! And Jewish trash does not give me orders. *Do you understand that, you filthy slut?*"

She is still trembling from the blow, her head ringing. She paws at the chair.

Dirkweiler huffs heavily. Dismisses his secretary who had followed the chaos into the office and tells her to shut the door behind her. The anger in his voice has slackened as quickly as it rose. "Get up, get up," he tells Angelika, now sounding more put-out than incensed. "Oh, for Christ's sake, *get up*," he commands, righting the chair. Angelika feels herself wrenched to her feet and plunked into the chair's seat. Her fingers shake as she touches her face. It throbs.

Dirkweiler steps back behind his desk and plops into his own chair as if deflating. He ignites a cigarette and hands it over to her. "Here. Take it."

She does, drawing in smoke as her hands tremble.

"You see, *this* is what happens," Dirkweiler explains. "I'm a reasonable man, but I will not be disrespected."

She nods. Nods quickly, spewing the smoke. "Yes. Yes, Herr Kommandant. I apologize...apologize for my outburst. You were right to strike me."

This appears to mollify the man. He frowns and lights his own cigarette, huffing smoke into the air. "So. This is about the list, yes?" he surmises. "This is the problem?"

"Yes, Herr Kommandant," she confirms. Meekly now.

"You're agitated because I put your parents on the list for Poland."

She cannot answer this. Her words forsake her. She can only keep her eyes down, staring blankly at the desktop cluttered with files.

"You must understand," he explains, "that it's really for your own good."

Her heart thumps heavily, but she does not look up.

"They are an impediment to you," the man assures her. "Can't you see? They are an anchor around your neck. You must know it's true," he says. "To do your work, you must be *free*. You must free yourself of them. Of their old mentality. I'm sure you know this. I'm sure you know *exactly* this."

And now her eyes rise.

"Now, I know that even Jews have feelings in such cases," the Herr Kommandant is willing to admit. "One's parents," he says. "But you must be strong. You must be like steel."

She blinks downward. "Would it… Would it be possible, Herr Kommandant… Could they be sent instead on the train to Theresienstadt?" she asks. "Not to Poland."

Theresienstadt. The so-called Paradise Camp in the Protectorate of Bohemia and Moravia. A showpiece for visitors from the International Committee of the Red Cross. But this request causes the Herr Kommandant to sigh. He taps his cigarette against the edge of a brimming ashtray, frowning again. "*Well*," he replies. "I have my quota from headquarters to consider. The pencil pushers in the Kurfürstenstrasse demand their numbers be met, and I have a train to fill. Besides, you're missing the *point*," he tells her, leaning forward. "You must free yourself from them completely. Even from their memory. You must take this opportunity to wipe them from your mind. Be truthful with yourself. Are you *truly* venturing into the streets every day to protect two old Jews? That's a distraction. A falsehood. You are out there to do your job. And to do it exceedingly well."

When she leaves Dirkweiler's office, Fritz Landau is waiting. He takes in her face. The mark of Dirkweiler's knuckles. But all he asks her is, "Do you want to see them? Before they go?"

She blinks. Then shakes her head. What good would that do? To see them? She couldn't possibly keep the truth from them. "Let them keep their hope" is all she says.

Fritz nods. He is a man, after all, who can understand the cruelty of truth and the merciful utilities of lies.

A week later, after a day during which she had personally dragged a middle-aged woman from the toilet in the Café Trumpf, she is called into the Kommandant's office. It is morning. A crisp Berlin day outside. The birds enjoy the greenery of the cemetery across the way. A pair of mourning doves have taken up residence in the trees, and she can hear their cooing. When she enters the office, she finds Dirkweiler hunched over the telephone. He frowns, snapping his fingers and signaling that she should step forward and shut the door behind her, though he is still mumbling into the receiver. She closes the door and waits, standing like a department store mannequin. There is, she notes, a striped dress box with a ribbon sitting on one of the chairs in front of the man's desk. Still frowning over his conversation, Dirkweiler breaks free of it long enough to order her to open it.

She hesitates but then does so. She recognizes the box. It's a famous design, those stripes, from a noted Berlin modiste in the Ku'damm. She unties the ribbon, slips off the top, and draws a delicate breath inward. For an instant, she forgets herself and touches the dress's fabric intimately. Soft as a cloud. Good Saxon merino wool. Berlin blue, dark as midnight, with scarlet tulle-covered satin-weave charmeuse buttons, handmade. Beautiful. But her fingers snap away from it when Dirkweiler's chair squeaks.

His hand is over the mouthpiece again. "Take it out," he tells her.

She feels a lift under her heart. Such a lovely creation. She slips it from the box and automatically holds it up against herself to size it, knee lifted and toe pointed, a hand pressed to the waistline. Long fitted sleeves, with a shoulder wedge silhouette and a standing collar. It breaks perfectly below her knees.

Again comes the squeak of the chair. "There are rewards for those who work," he tells her, then waves her away and returns to his call.

16.

The Empty Canvas

MACY'S THANKSGIVING DAY PARADE IS STILL WEEKS AWAY, BUT Christmas shoppers are starting to crowd the sidewalks and jam the trains. Women labor to manage packages. On the Eighth Avenue Local, Rachel gives up her spot to an overloaded middle-aged lady, because men seldom surrender their seats unless the woman is pregnant or struggling with an infant. An armload of shopping bags from B. Altman's, they seem to agree, she brought upon herself. Rachel stands staring at a poster of a well-barbered husband embracing his smiling wife who sports a polka-dot apron and holds a feather duster.

So the harder a wife works, the cuter she looks! the husband proclaims.

Growing up in Berlin, Rashka had compared all advertisements designed to attract women to her mother. How would that dress look on her eema? How would that perfume smell compared to the smell of oil paints? But in America, Rachel has often relied on advertisements to construct her own makeshift identity. Ads offer lessons on how to shop, how to behave, how to fit in, and she has tried to learn from them. She has tried! If she buys Heinz condensed cream of tomato soup, her husband won't yawn over her cooking. Even a woman can open Alcoa Aluminum's bottle caps—without a knife blade, a bottle opener, or a husband! The most important quality in coffee is how much it will please your man.

Out of the subway, the sky is white above the city. The café radiators hiss with steam. She has finally tracked down her Feter Fritz. He is still dressed in his secondhand suit, but there is a certain zippiness about him. She notes that he acquired a bamboo cane as if he'd plucked it out from the past, when such a thing was required by every metropolitan gentleman. "How is your blintz?" he inquires, and Rachel realizes she is actually *tasting* the blintz delivered by Alf, their ancient waiter. Its sweetness.

"It's good," she is pleased to report, nodding. Her uncle has a gossipy tongue this morning. Artists he's known and their fated decline from their zenith back in Berlin. Wolfgang Schnyder, Paul Genz, George Grosz. "Grosz left Germany to teach here in New York City at the Art Students League but now lives upstate. It seems he's given up the old chaos of his canvases for the tranquility of Hudson River landscapes. But can one blame him? Who could maintain Dada for three decades and remain sane?"

But then Feter, as he inevitably does, gets down to business. "So, ziskeit," he begins, smiling to himself. "I have something for you."

She feels a perk of interest, foolishly, childishly. "Something?"

"Yes," says her feter, removing a kraft-paper envelope from his jacket and placing it on the table beside her plate.

Rachel frowns at it, confused. Chews slowly and swallows. "What is this?"

"This is the money you paid to Mrs. Appelbaum for my rent," he tell her brightly.

But Rachel still frowns.

"It's what I owed you," her uncle says. "For your kindness," he must explain, his brightness dimming.

"But where did it come from?"

"Where does money usually come from?" A slightly insulted smile. "It came from hard work. Your feter is not a man without ingenuity, Rokhl. I don't make a habit of living on other people's charity. Go on," he bids her gladly. "Take it."

She lifts her eyebrows at the yellowed envelope. Taking money from Feter Fritz feels irregular. On the other hand? She can stop worrying about Aaron's reaction if she can replace the rainy-day twenty in the *Merriam-Webster* before he notices it's missing. She fingers the envelope. Thank God her husband has not been moved to solve a crossword puzzle lately.

"Have I said? I'm moving out of our old rat hole."

Rachel looks up. "You call it a rat hole?"

"I call it what it is, zeisele. I've found, uh, a much more *suitable* place," he decides to describe it, spooning the kasha into his mouth. He's been to the barber, she notices. His fingernails have been groomed. "Nothing palatial, of course. A bachelor efficiency in a building on 42nd Street. And should I mention? It has a doorman."

"So. You're leaving the Lower East Side?"

Her feter raises his eyes from his bowl to give her a closer look. "That distresses you, Daughter?"

"No. It's just that you've been there so long."

Feter only shrugs, then frowns at the envelope, still in her hands. "Your blintz. Eat. You don't want to offend Alf, do you?" Which means don't insult me. Put the money in your pocket. Yet she leaves the envelope in its place on the table and takes a bite of the blintz.

Her feter holds his frown, but then, as if he has plucked a thought from a passing cloud, he wonders aloud, "When was the last time you held a paintbrush in your hand, Ruchel?"

The sweet taste in her mouth turns to mud. She shakes her head. "Feter."

"Think of the art you once produced, Rokhl. Only a year ago, you had the beginnings of a career. People were taking an interest in your art. You were starting to sell. Have you forgotten?"

And now she feels the darkness up close. "I haven't forgotten my own life, Feter," she answers.

"Then what is it? Why have you stopped?"

"You know why."

"Because of what happened. Such a small thing."

"A night in Bellevue was not a small thing, Feter."

"No? So you think what? That's you're crazy now, Daughter? Ha!"

he laughs. "Perhaps you haven't noticed, but *everyone* is crazy. We have bombs that could burn continents into cinders. Who is *not* crazy?"

"That's a different craziness."

"Meshuga iz meshuga. How is it different?"

"It's *different*," she insists. "I shouldn't have to explain."

"You know, Rashka, sometimes I think," her uncle tells her, "sometimes I think that you'd rather *deny* what happened. To us. To the Jews."

Rachel glares, eyes like flint. "I don't deny anything."

"No?" he asks, raising the spoon to his mouth. "That's good to hear. Because people should *know*. It's *important* that people should know."

"What people want to *know* is exactly *nothing*."

"Then *force* them to know. Don't be so courteous and give them the choice. Make them open their eyes. Teach the world with your paintbrush. All I'm telling you is this: You are gifted. But think how many gifted Jews," he says, "are no longer with us."

Rachel gazes back, her eyes gone wet.

"You think the world doesn't care? *Make it care.* You think the world doesn't remember? *Make it remember.* This what I'm telling you," says Feter. "Put your gift to work."

Rachel wipes at her eyes and retains her silence.

Feter leans farther forward, adding a confidential note to the urgency of his voice. "There's a man. David Glass."

The name casts her mind backward to Naomi's photograph. Feter and the man Glass on the bench. The two conspirators at work in Tompkins Square Park. She has been waiting for her uncle to reveal himself. To reveal the fox's scheme. And now that moment has come.

"You must know from him," Feter tells her. "He a very influential art dealer."

"Of course I know from him, Feter. Everyone knows from David Glass. Who *doesn't* know?"

"Exactly. Who doesn't?" her uncle agrees. Almost eagerly, he agrees, as if this is exactly what he wants to hear. "But what you may *not* know,

Ruchel," he is saying, "is that he is always on the hunt for talent. Like *yours*, my dear."

Rachel frowns. Uncertain. "Oh, so you think so, do you, Feter?"

"After all," he observes, "are you not the daughter of Lavinia Morgenstern-Landau? So for the sake of her memory, I encourage you. Open up your paint box, set a canvas on an easel, and begin the great labor."

Rachel does not smile. "Begin the labor. Open my paint box," she says grimly. "I understand." She nods darkly. "Eema is gone, so you want to take *me* to market as the *calf* of a prize cow."

He is stung! "Rashka!"

"It's true, isn't it, Feter. S'iz ams!"

"No, it is untrue." Her uncle is adamant. "Es iz nit ams. I'm thinking of *you*, Rokhl. Nor du!"

"Nor ich? *Nor du*, Feter! You're thinking of yourself, as you always have. It makes me wonder what else you're keeping hidden from view. Eema always said this too."

At this, Feter becomes obviously angry. Not just at having his *generosity* rebuffed but now this insult from his sister. "Child, you have no idea what my bond with your mother was about. You knew her for no more than what? A few years past a decade? *I*, on the other hand, knew her since the day of my birth. We were often competitive, the two of us. That's true. Highly so. We argued sometimes over means. But we always, *always* saw the world through the same eyes. So don't you dare lecture *me*, Rokhl, about my sister. Everything I did was to protect her. To protect *you*. I can only grieve that she isn't alive today to testify to this truth, but she is not.

"For her, in the end, I failed. But for *you*, Rokhl, the gem of her heart—for *you* I have given everything I have. My sweat and blood and my soul. And *this* is how you respond to me? To so cruelly suspect my intentions? To spit on my sacrifices? I am struck. Cut to the bone, Ruchel." His face is reddened, his eyes steaming darkly. He grinds his teeth and straightens his spine imperiously.

"So there is an envelope. Take it up or leave it behind, I don't care which," he tells her, flapping his coat over his shoulders. "It'll be a welcome gratuity for Alf, I'm sure." Standing, he slaps on his fedora at a rakish angle. "I think perhaps we should enjoy a bit of distance from one another for a time. And since I am such a disreputable character, I'm sure you won't miss me."

"I know there is something you are hiding from me, Feter!" she shouts out. "You who are stuffed with money." These words she speaks with contempt. "It's falling out of your pockets for your haircuts and manicures. For your steak dinners and your ridiculous cane! You think you are the sophisticate again, Feter? Rachel is on her feet. "The cosmopolitan man? You are not. You are a relic. A fossil."

Her uncle's face has gone bloodless.

"You sold Eema's painting, Feter! *Somehow* you laid your hands on it and sold it to David Glass for your own profit!" she shouts, her eyes a welter of tears. "And you think that now *what*? You can sell me *next*?"

"How dare you, child?" he wants to know. "How dare you think I've ever done *anything* but look after your welfare? I stayed alive in Auschwitz with the thought of *you*! Of you and your eema, that's how I lived! So to hear you hurling such hurtful claims? It's an insult to life!"

The ancient waiter has arrived, hoping to quell the commotion. "Say, folks. Can maybe we try to calm ourselves down a little?" he wonders. "People are trying to eat here."

"Not to worry, Alf," Feter assures the waiter with brisk righteousness. "I think we've said all there is to say," he decrees. "You can give the check to my niece!" And then he is gone. Whirling out of the door, leaving a void of silence in the midst of the room.

She walks, crying. Walks aimlessly. She is so angry and so hurt and so frightened and so shamed. On the subway, she never imagined that she would be one of those women who cries alone in her seat, yet here she is. Returning home, she seizes the cat tearfully, but Kibbitz is in no mood for comfort, so she allows him to escape out the window.

By the time darkness rises, she has finally cried her eyes dry, lying on the bed, empty. Traffic noise filters dimly up from the street. She thinks of the painting. That it could be reduced to nothing more than "the nudie!" Seeing her mother's canvas in such disreputable circumstances, on the counter of a shabby pawnbroker's shop. A shame and a disgrace! It was nicked in spots. The paint scratched here and there. The colors dirtied by insensitive handling. Two decades of careless journeys had left their mark, but even beneath the thin coat of grime, the painting still projected fire.

The first time she saw it, even as a child, she was entranced by its bright beauty. Standing on her mother's easel, the oils freshly gleaming, the painting glowed like rubies in the sunlight. She could not remove her eyes from it. Until she heard a voice.

Hallo, Bissel...

Berlin was a sunny city that day. Feter Fritz had promised Rashka an outing as a treat, but first they had to stop at the loft where Eema painted. Rashka was looking forward to the cakes at the Hotel Adlon afterward. The chocolate cream torte. But then Feter and Eema had set to arguing again, out in the hallway, having quickly forgotten Rashka's presence. So she'd slipped into Eema's studio. She liked the studio. The light that poured in through the glass ceiling. She liked the smell of the paints and bottles of oils. She liked the collection of brushes, flat, thick, long, and thin as needles, and would often pick them out of their jars to pretend to paint a picture on the air—but only if Eema wasn't there to catch her. Today, though, she was mostly hoping to cuddle with Gilgamesh, her eema's fluffy, tawny-furred studio cat.

The feline, however, had been abducted. There was a girl sitting on a stool. The same girl who had been lying in Feter's bed. She was barely covered by a gauzy robe, this girl, and smoking a cigarette as Gilgamesh purred in her lap and she stroked the beast's head. Rashka blinked. She felt paralyzed by the sight. This girl was as entrancing as her eema's painting. Red hair turned fiery under the sun that beamed down on her from the skylit windows above. Her beauty made Rashka feel the same way she did when she watched Eema comb her glossy black hair in the gilded mirror. Both filled and emptied. It was a face that called for the most beautiful of descriptions. She was azoy sheyn vi di zibn veltn. Beautiful even as the seven worlds.

"Hallo, Bissel. Shall I call you that? Little morsel? You look like you could be gobbled up in a single bite." There was a teasing quality to the girl's voice, but Rashka felt a pinch of fear. That she might be swallowed in a single bite? But before such a thing happened, in came Eema, her voice still heated by her dispute with Feter Fritz. "Rashka! Come!" her mother demanded. "Time for you to go. Your feter's taking you to the Adlon to rot your teeth!"

"But I wanted to pet Gilgamesh," Rashka complained, trying to gain time, trying to maintain herself in the girl's presence a little longer. Just a little longer.

Eema, though, was not having it. She snatched Rashka's hand and gave it a yank. "Come, I said!"

Rashka had no other choice but to obey. She glanced backward as Eema hauled her out of the studio. The girl, she saw, had returned to petting the cat as if Rashka had never existed.

～•━

The subway is packed. Rachel ignores the bumps and gropes of the crowd. Switching to the uptown I.R.T., she hops off at Columbus Circle, breathing in the open air, and walks down to West 57th, where she finds Lee's Art Shop waiting for her.

Stretched canvases are neatly stacked by size in large sets or wooden racks. She slides out a 24 x 36-inch. Considers it with a frown. Slides it back in. Slides out a 36 x 48 instead. She needs the space. A great breadth of clean, unpainted canvas.

Returning on the Broadway Express, she stands with the large canvas wrapped in paper in front of her. But it is so big that it's hard not to keep bumping the knees of the other passengers, who shoot her irritated looks. She pretends to see none of them and instead focuses on the advertisement of a contented husband holding a steaming coffee cup.

Now, even a man can make perfect coffee in just seconds!

Back at the apartment, she has placed the canvas on a chair stolen from the kitchen table so she can stare at its white emptiness from the sofa. It stares back at her with a vacant canvas face. A key turns in a lock. The apartment door opens without further warning, and Aaron steps in, his Alpiner shoved back on his head and his coat flopped over his arm.

"Halloo. Guess who's home early?" he calls.

She is caught out—her private exchange with this canvas interrupted by the intrusion—but what can she do? "The king of the castle?" she guesses.

"None other," he concedes and thusly bestows a hello kiss on her cheek before he stands back and surveys this new unexpected wrinkle. "So what's this?" he wonders.

With Aaron home, it turns out that two's company but three's a crowd, especially if the three includes an empty canvas as tall as the coffee table is long.

"So you're painting again? Is that it?"

"Is *what* it?"

"This gigantic thing on the kitchen chair."

"I don't know what you're talking about. What gigantic thing?"

"H'okay. I surrender."

She feels exposed, vulnerable, naked in her desires. Here is a husband from Flatbush chomping on the corned beef sandwich he's brought home from some stupid deli, wiping his greasy fingers and mouth with a paper napkin, when all she wants to do is sit with her canvas. And his tone confirms just how betrayed he still feels. By her. By her Episode. How suspicious he is of any uncertain development now. Once, he was happy to see her painting. And if he wasn't happy, at least he wasn't watching her like she was a bomb with a lit fuse. As if any deviation from normal was a threat. The anger settles in between them, her anger, his anger. And finally some comment he makes strikes Rachel wrong, or maybe it's when he does that awful imitation of the woman on the subway making her sound like a nitwit, because doesn't he really think all women are nitwits? Suddenly they are shouting.

In the morning, she remembers throwing her glass of Gomberg Seltzer at the floor.

Pulling herself from bed, she finds it cleaned up. She finds her husband sitting at the kitchen table in his shirtsleeves and with his necktie loose at his open collar. Smoking over a cup of coffee with sleepless, burdened eyes. The cat goes prancing before her as she enters, but Aaron ignores him, looking up at Rachel.

"Good morning," he says blankly.

She is dressed in her pj's as she pads in sock feet over to the stove and ignites the burner under the kettle with a match. "You made yourself coffee," she observes.

"Just that instant stuff," Aaron says. No big deal.

Now, even a man can make perfect coffee in just seconds!

Rachel feeds the mewing cat, Little Friskies poured into his bowl. She sets it down, then fills up a bowl for the cat's water from the tap. Sets it down as all the while, she can feel Aaron watching her from his chair. Feels his eyes follow her as she passes him again and crosses to the sofa where she picks up the pillow and wrinkled sheet upon which her husband slept.

"You cleaned up the broken glass," she says without making eye contact.

"How many years in the restaurant business?" She can hear the shrug in his voice. "You think I've never picked up after somebody makes a mess?"

"I'm sorry," she offers, concentrating on shaking the pillow from its case. "I'm sorry you had to sleep on the sofa."

"It wasn't too bad. Better than the army."

Rachel stops. Hugs the pillow against herself. Gazes back at her husband with large eyes. "I know I'm a terrible wife."

"Oh. You're not so bad," Aaron tells her, exhaling a breath. Then he checks his wristwatch. Stubs out his cigarette. Standing, he leaves his coffee cup behind. "I gotta go."

"You're opening today?"

He sighs, slipping on his suit jacket. "Opening *and* closing. So God knows, as usual, when I'll be home." He crosses the room, stopping to give his wife a soft kiss on the cheek, which she absorbs in silence. "Look, I get it. Being artistic? Not so easy. I shoulda been more—I dunno—more *something* when I saw you'd brought this thing home," he says, measuring the immensity of the canvas by wagging his hand up and down like an elevator gone crazy. He crosses behind her, removes his hat and coat from the hall tree. "So *paint*, why don't you?" he suggests. "Who knows? It could be fun."

Rachel lifts her eyes to the canvas still on the chair in front of the sofa. In another minute, the door to the hallway opens and shuts, leaving Rachel staring at the blank expanse of unpainted universe. The fear is so crippling. If she dares to pick up a brush and touch it to her palette, is she willing to risk her sanity? Her soul? Is there another straitjacket waiting for her the moment she releases the madness in her onto the canvas?

In Washington Square, people are strolling under the arch, milling about pavement under the bright-white sun. It's breezy, hold-on-to-your-hat weather. The fountain's been shut down since the end of summer, but there's a klatch of beatnik kids perched around the basin, one curly-headed boy strumming on his guitar, though his singing is caught by the wind and blown away.

"Are you sure we won't get arrested?" Rachel asks.

Naomi is beside her on one of the green park benches, lighting up a juju. "For what? This is the Village. Everything's legal." She draws in a hit and hands it over to Rachel. Was it really so very long ago in her life when a Jew sitting on a public bench was committing a criminal offense? Yellow benches only for Jews in Berlin! Nur für Juden! And now here she is on a regular bench, breaking the law by choice! C'est étonnant! Carefully she draws in the smoke, but then coughs it back up harshly. Her face goes flush.

"Sorry." Naomi half grins. "I should have warned you it's strong as fuck." Naomi retrieves the juju for another drag. Holding it in, she speaks in a stifled voice. "It grows freely." She releases the breath with only a light waft of smoke. "Freely as weeds. Right here in the city in vacant lots and shit. You can pick it like dandelions if you know what to look for."

"Is that what you did?"

Naomi laughs. "Nah. This I bought," she says. "This stuff is Mexican. Much more heavy duty that what you had last time. There's a guy who's good for it in my building. But really, these days? You can buy it pretty much anywhere around here. There's probably half a dozen guys selling it right here in the Square." She offers to share again, and Rachel accepts. Draws in smoke and holds it until she can't any longer. But this time, the cough is easier to manage.

"So. You had a row again?" Naomi asks. "You and the shtoomer?"

Rachel is wiping her eyes. "It wasn't really"—she huffs out a breath—"really a *row*." Shakes her head and hands back the juju. "I don't know what it was," she confesses.

"Not a row, but he's sleeping on the couch."

"He was last night. Tonight, I'm not sure. He usually does his double shift on Wednesday, so I'm already asleep by the time he gets home."

"Just like Pop, the poor dope," Naomi laments, but without much sympathy. "Slaving away for the sake of a buck."

Almost in a whisper, Rachel asks the question. "Do you think I'm wrong?"

"*Wrong?*"

"Is it so unreasonable for a man to want children from his wife?"

Naomi pulls a face over that one. "Is *that* what this is about?"

Rachel shrugs like a child.

"Well. Who the fuck knows what's 'reasonable'?" Naomi decides. "It means *shit*. Nothing's 'reasonable.'"

"But isn't it," Rachel says, "isn't it part of the *deal*? When people marry. Isn't it part of the contract?"

Naomi shakes this off. Contract schmontract. "It's not like you signed an agreement to pump out a bunch of brats by a certain date," Naomi tells her. She takes another draw, holds it, then releases it. "And it's not like *he's* gonna carry a kid in his belly for nine months. It's *your* body, not his. *You* should decide." And then she asks, "So you want another toke?"

"Toke?"

"Another drag?" says Naomi.

Rachel breathes in but takes the offered toke, drawing in deeply, tasting the sour smoke as she accepts it into her body. Holding, then exhaling. Her head lightens. Her body lightens. Different from the Miltown. Miltown is pedestrian. A mood dampener. This feels as if part of her brain is unmoored and on its own course.

Naomi drops back her head, eyes closed, to soak up the chilly sunlight. "God, I love sunshine," she declares with a sweet tranquility. And then? Still with her eyes closed to the sunlight, "Can I ask you a question? I mean, it's kind of a personal thing."

This should have warned Rachel off, but maybe with the juju, her guard is down. "Sure," she replies. Honestly, she thinks it's going to be a question about Aaron or maybe about some sisterly element of feminine biology. Menstrual cycles or tampons. A personal question.

But what Naomi asks her is "Why did you stop painting?"

"Why did I *stop*?" Perhaps, if she repeats the question aloud, she can stall for time. Because she's afraid that if she's not careful, she might actually give a truthful answer. Naomi is unaware of details of the Episode. Aaron passed it off to his family as an anemic attack. Iron-poor blood. Maybe Naomi believes this and maybe she doesn't, but either way, it was a lie that Rachel has maintained, even though it has created a gap between Naomi and her. A small unspoken thing as painfully annoying as a pebble in a shoe.

"You were so good," her sister-in-law assures her. "Those ghosts or spirits or whatever. They were scary in a way," she says, "but really moving too. And then you just stopped."

"I was sick," Rachel answers.

"Yeah. I know. The anemia thing. But you didn't go back. So I've always kinda wondered why."

Rachel has to suddenly concentrate on keeping herself in check. No tears. No tears.

"I'm sorry," Naomi offers. "I'm upsetting you." She can see that. "Never mind. Forget I asked."

"I stopped," Rachel declares. "Because I was afraid to continue," she confesses. "I was afraid that if I continued? Something *terrible* would come out of me. Something," she says, "unforgivable."

Night. Alone in the bed. The racket of the elevated West Side freight passes, rattling the bedroom's window glass. Rachel absorbs the blunt thunder of the tracks completely. Then speaks quietly to the air. "Tell me the story again, Eema."

The mattress creaks softly.

Which story?

"The story of the drowned kittens."

Eema is a silhouette, shrouded by the room's darkness, but she has brought the perfume of the Krematorium to her daughter's bedroom. *Ah. Well. My mother. Your grandmother of blessed memory. You never knew her, I know. But she taught me a lesson when I was very small, which I would never forget.*

Rachel smokes in silence, her eyes gleaming with the ruby ember of her cigarette.

A terrible thing had happened, her eema tells her. *A frightening thing. I had seen a man drown a bag full of kittens by dropping them over the side of the Weidendammer Brücke. I could hear them, their panicky little meows from inside his burlap sack. And when he tossed them over into the river, he listened for a moment for the sound of the splash. When he heard it, he simply walked off as if he had done nothing. As if he was an innocent man.*

I was so—so shocked. So overwhelmed that I lost my voice. It's true, she says. *Your eema didn't speak for days. I was so utterly racked by guilt. Guilt that I should have stopped him, this criminal. That somehow, I should have rescued those little kittens from their fate. And I felt the remorse of the world on my heart like a heavy stone,* she says. *Until my mother came into my bedroom one night, just like this, while I was lying in the dark. And she said to me, "Vina. You cannot rescue what cannot be rescued. You cannot save what cannot be saved."*

A beat.

Laughter floats up from the street. Rachel's eyes are chilled by tears. "And me," she asks quietly. "What about your little goat, Eema? Can I be rescued still?"

A police siren whines sharply past, and a sudden red light invades the room from the window, exposing her eema as she must have looked on the day of her final Selektion before the ovens took her. A corpse stripped naked, skeletal, her hair nothing but a wiry scrub. Eyes bottomless. Arm imprinted with her number. *Rescued? Only by your own hands,* she says.

The siren and flashing red fade, but as the room passes back into darkness, Rachel is alone. Until she hears the front door opening, then closing. A beat of silence is followed by the noise of Aaron clearing his throat. A gleam of light as a floor lamp in the living room is switched on. "Aaron?" she calls out to him.

The lamplight invades as he opens the bedroom door and enters in his shirtsleeves, sitting on the edge of their bed with a chirrup of springs. He loosens his necktie with a hook of two fingers. When he speaks, he sounds utterly spent. "You know, I think you're right. I *don't* understand. I really don't." He pauses. The glow from the living room lamp paints his eyes. "I don't understand what those people did. To you," he says. "To your family. I *try*, I honestly do. I watched the news-reels when I was still in the army. Battalion ran screenings. A.P.S. foot-age from, ya' know, from liberated camps. There were grown men who couldn't stand it. Some were vomiting. Sick with sobbing. *Soldiers* doing this, you understand," he stresses. "Trained men. Some of these guys had seen combat, yet they just couldn't stomach what they were seeing on the screen. But me? I stayed. I watched them all. I had no choice. As a Jew, I felt I couldn't just look away. But then whattaya do? What's a person supposed to do after seeing all that?" he asks.

"To me, I guess, there was only one answer. It seemed so simple really. Hitler murdered six million Jews? So we make *more*. Shouldn't that be what we're doing? I mean, shouldn't that be our *job*?" he asks his wife but does not appear to expect a reply. "I keep thinking: It's just her fear. Just her fear, and all I gotta do is be patient. But down deep, I have to admit that—to me—Buchenwald, Dachau, Auschwitz? They're all just words. Just the names of places that might as well be on the moon. Maybe I saw the newsreels, but I have no idea, *not the slightest actual idea*, what they really mean to you."

His words drift away.

Rachel wipes tears from her face. "It's not your fault," she tells him.

Aaron expels a sigh. Rachel sits up to guide them both back down to the bed, where they spoon together, Aaron still dressed and in his shoes.

But when she closes her eyes, feeling him nuzzling into the back of her neck, all she sees is a gust of blinding snow, obscuring the outline of the white mountain that is rising to meet her.

17.

A Jew from Flatbush

HE INSPECTS THE NOSE-HAIR SITUATION BY EXAMINING THE reflection of his inner nostrils. Funny how he can remember his pop doing the same thing. He sees the old man there in the mirror, staring back at him from his own reflection.

"Com'ere," he hears Pop command, in that flat summoning tone that always signals trouble, motioning him over to the cash register. He can tell what's coming next, the whack on the side of the head, but he obeys anyway and absorbs the whack when it comes. The whack that's not supposed to *punish* him but just knock some sense into his kop. "Look at this," his father instructs. "How many times I gotta tell you, huh? You don't mix the *ten*-dollar bills in with the *twenties*, okay? How many *times?*" he wants to know. "It makes you look like you're stealing."

This shocks Aaron. *Stealing?* "How, Pop?"

"Never mind. *It does* is all," his father assures him firmly, placing the ten in its proper spot in the cash drawer. "I'm trying to *teach* you something, Aaron," he explains with a frown. His face is set in a serious affect, trying to get through to this domkop son of his. Trying as hard as he can. "I'm trying to *teach* you something," he repeats. "There are two kinds of people in the world. Are you listening to me?"

"Yes, I'm listening to you, Pop."

"There are two kinds of people in the world," his father explains. "Those people who don't *care* if they do it wrong and those who work *hard* to do it right. Now which kind should a man be?" he asks, his voice muted but demanding.

Now, two decades later, Aaron stands in front of the bathroom mirror. He has never veered from his answer. The man who works hard is the man who does it right. It's the man he will be. *Must* be. That much is chiseled in goddamned stone. But sometimes he wonders why. Sometimes he wonders what's the point, ya' know? To work and to die and to leave what behind? His pop left *him* behind when the old man's heart burst an artery.

Standing behind the counter punching the keys on that holy cash register he was so damned proud about. The R.P.P.C. Cash Register from Burl & Kenny on Atlantic Avenue. Leased, not owned! But that was top secret information. God, how Pop worshipped that thing. It was his tabernacle. Not because he gave a shit about money, 'cause, really, everybody knew that money was like water running through his fingers. He never learned how to hold on to it. Mr. Generosity. Mr. Soft Touch to the whole fucking neighborhood. But that machine was a sacred talisman of menschenschaft. The orderly cash drawer was the sign of the orderly mind. The orderly soul. The *ethical* soul. It showed that he was *somebody*. A man who ran a cash register out of his own business, made his own buck, was a cut above.

But after he died, the guys from Burl & Kenny came and carted it off, and what was left? So they buried another mensch in Washington Cemetery off the Bay Parkway. So what? What was left of Pop? Only his children? A son, a daughter. A blessed memory to his wife. What else? Nothing else. *I'm trying to teach you something, Aaron.* So when it's Aaron's time to be planted in the ground, what will *he* be leaving behind? A shadow? Shadows don't last, but maybe that'll be it. Maybe a shadow on the ground, on a wall, on a door is the only mark he's ever gonna make.

On his first day back in New York after the army, he'd stepped out into the cathedral concourse of Grand Central and felt the buzzing crowds sucking him in. Like he could step into the throng of people zigzagging though the station and be borne anywhere. Swept up into a vast, bustling chaos, and God knows where he would end up! Over the moon maybe. He's spent the prime of his life in the service. And now he was twenty-three years old, standing there with his duffel bag beside him, kitted out in his khaki service dress. Technical Sergeant Aaron S. Perlman, Serial No. 47 412 997. Tie tucked into his uniform blouse, garrison cap at a slight angle on his head.

He'd been shipped from California to Fort Sam Houston in Texas to be mustered out after serving the standard duration plus six. Like a million other schmoes, he'd been drafted in '43, but lucky him, he's never seen a minute of combat. A lot of the men from basic ended up in some desert death trap in North Africa, but Aaron had spent the war as a quartermaster sergeant battling U.S.O. caterers in Culver City.

Now he was back home. Back home to New York, standing on the precipice of the Greatest Fucking City in the World. He lights one of his issue Lucky Strikes. Even the smoke is sucked into the swirling, gorgeous pandemonium of destinations.

But in this giant world, where is he going next? To the most constricting address in the world is his answer: 360 Webster Avenue in Flatbush.

Home.

1950

The year they marry at Brooklyn City Hall is the year that the Knesset passes a resolution that Jerusalem is the capital of the State of Israel. It is the year that Alger Hiss is sentenced to prison for perjury and that a senator named McCarthy announces that the State Department is home to 205 Communists. Not 204, not 206. It is the year that the Kingdom of Jordan annexes the West Bank, that President Truman sends American troops to defend South Korea from the North. A gallon of gas costs about twenty-seven cents and three cans of Campbell's pork and beans costs a quarter. They honeymoon for six days in the Poconos at the Paradise Resort Hotel, where Aaron steps in poison ivy and blows up with toxins. It is also in this momentous year that Aaron takes his bride, the *younger* Mrs. Perlman, to the home of his mother, the *elder* Mrs. Perlman, to celebrate their first Seder together as wife and husband. Husband and wife.

It's an hour's trip on the bustling Sixth Avenue Local. Crossing under the river, the train thumps through the tunnel's heat, and Rachel lets herself be bobbled by its rhythm. Finally, at Eighteenth Avenue, they get out and walk ten minutes. It's not the first time Rachel has visited the house on Webster Avenue where Aaron spent his childhood. There have been suppers, there have been drop-bys on their way back from Coney Island on the B.M.T., smelling of sea salt and suntan oil. (Well, look who got some color!) Drop-ins to pick up this or that item for "setting up housekeeping" as his mother always calls it. The old vacuum cleaner from the synagogue. (It still works! Why buy a new one?) The oscillating electric fan and the brass floor lamp. The kitchen gadgets that Aaron bought for Mother's Day but that his mother never bothers with. (You should just take them, dear. Make them useful.)

But this is their first holiday gathering. The house is one in a row of functional, well-kept, two-story brick or wood-frame dwellings with shingled porches and small grassy patches of yard that form a fringe against the sidewalk. Trees shade the street at uneven intervals, but otherwise the sun brightens the springtime greening and shrinks the shadows under the porch roofs.

"God knows she's been cleaning like a maniac since Purim," Aaron advises Rachel. Still outside as they are heading for the front door. "You won't find a particle of schmutz for fifty miles in any direction," he says, "so mention how spotless the house looks, and you'll be in like Flynn."

At the door, a mezuzah. Nothing too fancy. A functional little brass casket inscribed with the holy seal of God. Aaron performs his usual tap-and-kiss routine and doesn't notice that his wife breaches the barrier without any such gesture. He is already busy announcing their arrival in his favorite singsongy Yiddish bubbe's voice, thick with diphthongs. "Halloo! Cherished mishpocha peoples! Guess who it is come from the big city!"

Inside, the sun's bright edge fades as it's filtered through the drapes. A homey, murky veil of daylight hues color the living room. The house is small on the inside but appears content with its crowd of bulky furnishings. The armchairs and living room couch are comfortably padded but not voluptuously so. The bureaus and tables are thick, dark mahogany. The rugs on the floor vacuumed half to death. The air pungent with the deeply simmering aroma of chicken soup and matzah balls.

"So, Ma, I see you took the slipcover off the sofa," Aaron calls to his mother in the kitchen, then turns to Rachel and takes her jacket. "You must be very special," he says. "She never does that. I'm serious. The Prophet Elijah could actually walk through the front door, and she wouldn't take the slipcovers off the sofa for him."

"What a fresh-mouthed boy I've raised," his mother declares as she walks in from the kitchen, wiping her hands on her apron. She is a thin, diminutive woman dressed in a pale-green sweater and black hostess skirt. The green of the sweater is obviously chosen to highlight the green in her eyes. She is a woman who must have been beautiful in her youth and has become handsome with middle age. Her hair is a dark chestnut like her daughter's with threads of silver. "Hello, troublemaker," she says affectionately to her son.

"Hi, Ma," he answers with a boyish smugness and gives his mother a confident peck, still his mother's boy who gets away with the moon and the stars.

"And *hello, darling*," she says to Rachel and plants a motherly kiss on her cheek.

"Hello, Mrs. Perlman," Rachel replies.

"*Please*, so formal. Call me Miriam. I keep telling her, Aaron," she complains with a smile. "We're family now," she says, and there's only a small hint of *like it or don't* in her voice as she says it.

"Miriam," Rachel repeats. "Your house is so nice and so well kept."

Miriam glances around the room, just to confirm that this is true. "Well, thank you, dear." She lifts her eyebrows with approval to Aaron. "Such a courteous thing," she commends him. "Now if only your sister could learn how to be so polite. But of course, her father, may he rest, took care of that. There was nothing I could do," she confides wearily to Rachel. "She was always her poppa's pet, and he let her get away with bloody murder."

"Why, *thank you*, Mother," Naomi announces as she enters from the kitchen, without an apron but with a goblet of wine. "I see you don't waste any time, do you?"

"Oh, Gawd, Naomi," the woman squawks. "I see *you* don't waste any time either. You're into the wine *already*?"

"Relax, Ma," Aaron injects magnanimously. "We've all gotta drink four cups, right? Don't have a stroke."

"*Thank you*, shtoomer," Naomi replies with acidic gratitude. Then gives Rachel a sisterly smack. "Poor girl. To think you're *married* to him now."

"Will you lay off, please?" Aaron instructs his sister amiably enough. "Rachel's not like you. She doesn't have the hide of a rhinoceros. And speaking of rhinoceri, where's the *boyfriend*, Mr. Hockey Player?" he asks.

"His name is Roger, as I'm sure you're aware, and he couldn't come. It's his weekend with his kids for the month."

Miriam huffs out a thick sigh of disapproval the size of a billboard.

"*What*, Ma?"

"Nothing. I just still can't believe, Chella, that my daughter is seeing a divorced man."

"And don't forget, Ma," Aaron chimes in helpfully. "He's also a goy."

"Don't get me started." His mother frowns.

"*Ma*. This isn't Budapest," Naomi points out. "Things are different in America."

"Well, I was born in America *too*, Missy, and I have news for *you*. If I had *ever* stepped out with a man who'd left his wife of twenty-two years to futz around with me, I would have been shipped off to Budapest on the next boat!"

"I *told* you, Ma, Roger's marriage was over before we even *met*."

"Never mind. I don't want to hear it," Miriam commands. "I'm only glad your father didn't live to see the day. It would have killed him." The doorbell rings and punctures the argument. "Go. Answer the door like a person, will you?" Miriam commands her daughter. "It's probably Bubbe and Zaydi."

"Oh God," Naomi groans dully, but she trudges off in the direction of the door. "If Bubbe pinches my cheek, I'm gonna lose it, Ma. *I swear it.*"

"Mind your manners!" her mother instructs her in a loud, routine scold, then turns to Rachel, eyebrows arched over her cat's eyes. "Rachel, honey," Miriam says. "How about you come into the kitchen to help me finish up?"

"Of course," Rachel agrees.

In the kitchen, a table knife in Rachel's hand, she scrapes butter across the brittle unleavened surface of the matzah crackers. The bread of slavery, the bread of freedom. Miriam likes them buttered and stacked on the plate catty-corner so that they form the angles of the Magen David. Meanwhile, the woman is peeling her hard-boiled eggs. "So you'd tell me, right?" she asks.

A half glance. "Tell you?"

"Yeah. You'd tell me. If there was any news."

Rachel scrapes the knife. "I'm sorry, I don't know what you mean. News of what?"

"*News*," Miriam repeats with a bit of added force. Maybe it's that her daughter-in-law is simpleminded. "I mean you and Aaron have been married for how long now?"

"Seven months."

"Okay. Well, I was just *asking*, ya know?" She rolls the egg against the cutting board, fracturing it, then peels the shell away from the glossy egg meat. "I thought you might have some *news*."

Finally, Rachel gets it. She breathes in and then out as she butters. "Oh. No. No news."

"Well," Miriam says with a smidge of a frown. "I suppose things are different today," she says. "Nobody's in a hurry."

The table is set with her mother-in-law's finest. The Paragon china with floral sprays. The Royal Danish sterling and Lenox crystal. The delicate lace table linen that was a wedding gift from Miriam's mother, may her memory be a blessing. And beside every neatly arranged place setting is a thin yellow-and-burgundy paper booklet from the grocery store with pages numbered back to front.

Her husband and sister-in-law refer to them with wry affection as the Maxwell House Haggadahs. A publication available to every Jewish housewife for free at the Foster Avenue grocery and every other grocery across the land that stocks matzah and gefilte fish. Rachel's is pristine. Picked up new for the occasion of her introduction to the family Seder table. A hammered steel emblem is printed on the cover. *Deluxe Edition Passover Haggadah in English and Hebrew, Compliments of the Coffees of Maxwell House, Kosher for Passover.* But the other copies have obviously been exhausted by the years. Dog-eared and stained, both Naomi's and Aaron's are mottled with childhood wine spills and have been thumbed halfway to rags. "Ma, do ya think you might pick up a couple of new ones for *us* at some point?" Aaron says. "The pages are falling out." But Rachel can tell that he's not really complaining.

"New? These are the ones with history," his mother insists. "Your whole childhood is in them practically. You want new? Go to the Ornsteins. They got everything new there. Okay! Calling all cars," she broadcasts from the kitchen. "Everybody who hasn't should go wash up so we can sit down."

The table could stand to be a little longer. What with Bubbe and Zaydi Perlman, Great Uncle Meyer with his enormous belly, Aunt Deenah and her husband, Walt, who owns the bakery on Ditmas Avenue, neither of whom anyone could mistake for thin, Uncle Hyram grown fat in the scrap iron business, plus the cousins from Parsippany, whose names Rachel has forgotten, their twin boys, whom Naomi calls Leopold and Loeb, their sullen teenaged girl who must be the tallest girl in her class, and the chair reserved for the Prophet Elijah, remembered for good. With the entire balibt mishpocha seated, *they're a little crowded*, so it's just as well that Naomi's goy stayed on the Upper East Side with his kids. Otherwise, they would have had to suspend him from the glass bowl chandelier. This is the joke Aaron must make, because he's the funny one.

Rachel feels, she must admit, a little hemmed in. A little trapped. Once she and Eema hid out from the Gestapo in a closet in Moabit after an SS crackdown during the race to call Berlin "Judenfrei." She could see the Stapo men's shadows pass by in the line of light from under the door. Hear the creak of the floorboards under their shoes. When she and Eema survived that ordeal, it felt like such a miracle. The Finger of God! They celebrated the Seder for the first time in years. Also for the last time. The two of them together in an attic of a bomb-damaged building with a rabbi's son, creating their Seder out of nothing. A precious egg. A bit of horseradish and green onion. A scrap of chicken bone. A bottle of kosher wine gone sour.

Then, it had felt like a victory. The Nazis thought they were winning their war against the Jews? They thought they were obliterating all things Jewish? They wanted to declare Berlin "Jew-free," but how wrong they were, because here were three Jews at the Seder table!

Reciting the ancient blessings, singing the verses of history, alive, still keeping faith, still remembering the struggle against bondage as the angel of death stalked Pharaoh's streets.

But now, at the table on Webster Avenue in Flatbush, Rachel feels like a stranger. If Elijah stepped through the open door with his scrolls and mantle, would he politely inquire exactly what she was doing here, sweetness? Rachel thinks of her eema's blessing over the candles as she lit them in that bomb-wrecked hiding place, her recitation of the Shehecheyanu, how practiced and poised. Bubbe Perlman's blessing isn't exactly as graceful, but she spits out her Hebrew without hesitation as she lights the candles, like some ancient gristle she's been chewing for years. Bubbe Perlman, hands gnarled and purple, her spine bent. Her glasses are as thick as cake icing, but the golden tears of flame dancing on the candle wicks shine in her lenses.

The Seder plate is the antique pewter that Miriam's great-grandmother bundled across the Atlantic from the old country. Rachel's mother-in-law places it in front of Aaron, who's standing with stiff authority at the head of the table, wearing a black silk yar-mulke. It's so odd for Rachel to see him like this as he pours the wine from the silver pitcher, Aaron assuming his father's presence. The white sleeves, the narrow black necktie. The stern concentration as he recites the Kiddush, the brightly polished chalice raised a careful nine inches from the table.

Her mother had a chalice that came from her husband's side of the family, the artistry of a Berlin silversmith dating back to Bismarck. A gleaming relief of the ancient city of Jerusalem, the Temple of Solomon at its pinnacle. Gone now, of course. Lost. Temple and chalice melted down in the furnace of history.

Rachel breathes in and stares at her husband. Where did Aaron's yarmulke come from? Was it the same one he wore for his bar mitzvah? Has Miriam kept it in a drawer ever since, along with a lock of his baby curls? Rachel is nearly positive that Aaron doesn't have one at home.

She puts his socks and boxer shorts away and has never come across anything of the kind.

She licks her lips and craves a cigarette. What would her own mother think of the people of Aaron's family? Would she think them gauche? Vulgar? Gemeinbürgerlich? Or what would Eema's beloved grandfather think? An observant man, Eema's saba, come from a world of solemn worship, ritual baths, the separation of the women from the men. Come from generations of those who would not round the corners of their heads and who actively mourned the destruction of the Temple. Those who listened to the tinkling bells of the Torah crowns and yearned for the Messiah.

Would he, if he were to stand up from his grave, even recognize these Americans as Jews? Could he identify Cousin Sheila, who's training as a beautician in Long Island, or her husband who sells refrigerators and washer-dryers, as members of God's Chosen? Does Uncle Hyram study the Holy Book at night after he comes home from the scrap-yard office, or does he light a cigar and turn on *People Are Funny*? But then, speaking of judgment, how would she explain *herself*? Or her eema for that matter? *Artists*, Saba. We are *artists*. You see? With the paint? With the canvas? Nit! It's not debauchery. It's art! Kunst, Saba! Azoy zeyer sheyn!

As the basin is passed for the Urchatz on Webster Avenue, Rachel notes that her eema has slipped into Elijah's chair in her camp rags and is dunking her filthy fingers into the water, leaving it oily with death. But the daughter says nothing, keeping her mother's secret. The truth is she's happy to see her. The truth is she's envious of all the cranks and colorful oddballs of Aaron's family. The quarreling and long-standing bickering, chiseling away at everybody's nerves. The despair that the people you love will never understand you. The bitter root, the sacrifice and mourning, the bondage of family. The hard edges and soft tugs, the ugly bigotries, and the sudden flares of laughter. She envies all this. The shared history of family blood. The unspoken knowledge of the family heart. A togetherness that is more than a simple congregation around a table. It walks you home. It tangles your dreams as you sleep. It glues you into one piece.

She knows that they are doing their best, their very best to treat the little refugee from cindered Europa like a member of the clan. Bubbe Perlman worries over her, clucking tearfully through the agenda of tragedy that tags along with Rachel as she hugs Rachel's shoulder to her old bony body. Zaydi Perlman offers her the nice chair, bowing to the sheyne kleyne khlh. The lovely little bride. Even Uncle Lou, who can only grouse over those goddamned Puerto Rican kids soaping his windshield and how the Internal Revenue Service is robbing him god-damned blind—even he wants to know how married life is treating her. But her sense of family has been shattered. She can only press her nose against the glass and peer through. She is a specimen from a blackened planet. Alone at this table, except for the shadows that cling to her.

After it's over, after the candles have been extinguished and the plates cleared, Rachel is in the kitchen with her mother-in-law, helping with the dishes. Miriam washes, Rachel dries as in comes Aaron searching for a bottle of Ballantine in the fridge. "Scusi, scusi," he announces with a fake Italian accent.

"So who's that one for?" his mother wants to know, keeping track.

"Uncle Meyer," he answers, popping off the cap with the opener hanging from a hook.

"I see," says Miriam. "So if it's for Uncle Meyer, why is it my *son* who's drinking it?"

Aaron belches casually after swallowing the slug of beer and leans against the refrigerator door. "'Cause I'm his beer taster, Ma. You know how upset he gets if his beer's too hoppy. So did she *tell* you?"

A glance. "Tell me what, smart aleck?"

"There's this woman who sold a painting."

Rachel feels a furious burn rise in her cheeks. "*Aaron.*"

"What? Nobody should know?" Aaron shrugs. "Somebody buys your painting? It's good news, isn't it? She had like an exhibition at this gallery," he announces. "It was even in the newspaper."

"The newspaper?" Miriam echoes.

"Yeah. Didn't you send Ma the clipping?" he's asking Rachel but then turns back to his mother. "I told her to send you the clipping."

"I must have forgotten," Rachel decides. "Besides, it was only the *Post.*"

"Hey. A newspaper's a newspaper," Aaron assures her, but all Rachel can hear him say is, *Look what my wife can do! Such tricks she can perform!*

"It wasn't even much of a gallery," she says. "Just a place on Tenth Street where for five dollars, you can pay for a little space on a wall."

"Hey. It was a good enough gallery to sell a painting, okay?"

Miriam slants a glance at her son, not Rachel. "So what's the painting, dear?" her mother-in-law asks her.

Aaron answers for her, helpfully. "Well, it's a kind of—*you* know." Another shrug, turning to his wife. "I don't know, honey. How would you describe it?"

"How?"

"Yeah, uh. It's kinda like. I don't know. Kinda spooky looking."

"I painted a ghost," Rachel admits.

"Really? A ghost? Of *whom*?" Miriam wonders. "Like a special ghost? What's the name of that ghost in the story for Christmas?"

"Just a ghost," Rachel lies.

"A hundred bucks she's made so far," Aaron injects eagerly. "And that just for the first one. The guy from the gallery's interested in more."

"A hundred dollars?" Miriam says. Impressed or skeptical? "For a picture of a ghost."

"People pay money for art, Ma. That how the art business works," Aaron says as if he needs to explain it so his mother will understand.

"The buyer's making an *investment*. He pays a hundred bucks now, but in *ten years* or whatever, who *knows* what it'll be worth."

"I get it," his mother tells him.

"Like when Pop bought those Liberty Head silver dollars."

"I said *I get it*, Aaron," his mother informs him with quiet menace.

Aaron blanches slightly and must steal another swig of his uncle's beer. "Okay. So now you know. Great. I was just saying."

"Well," the woman says to Rachel, "that must be some kind of thing, sweetheart."

Rachel dries another dish with the hand towel and places it atop the stack on the counter. A pause. A clink of a dish as it's soaped.

"It was my mother," Rachel suddenly announces.

Another pause as this sinks in.

"The ghost. It was my mother as I imagined her after she went to the gas."

When Rachel looks up, she sees that both Aaron and his mother appear deflated. Quite literally as if the air has been let out of them. Miriam gazes at her with those blank cat eyes for a moment. And then when she speaks, all the scold, all the challenge, all the archness has been displaced from her voice. Instead, she sounds uncomfortably per- plexed. "And that's something you want people to *see*, hon?" she has to wonder.

At which point Naomi enters the kitchen.

"So what's going on?" she asks, eyes flicking from face to face.

Aaron blinks, sounds vaguely defensive. "Whattaya mean, what's going on?"

"Well, what I *mean* is you went to get Uncle Meyer a beer like a year and a half ago and never came back."

"I got carried away by little green men," Aaron answers bleakly. "Here," he says, going into the fridge for another Ballantine. "Give him this one."

"Too late for that," says Naomi, grabbing the opener and snapping off the cap for herself. "He's already conked out on the couch, snoring like a pardon-my-French freight train."

On the way home, sitting on the subway, Aaron finally says it: "You never said before. About the painting. I mean, about who the ghost thing was supposed to be or the other stuff." By this, he means the gas chamber. His voice is neutral, but she can tell that underneath, there is a tint of irritation that he was ambushed by her pronouncement in his mother's kitchen. That he was embarrassed for her and for him both.

"I never said because you never asked," she replies.

"Never asked? Well, of course I never asked. I'm a Jew from Flatbush. What the hell do I know about art? You painted a picture, so I figured, *okay*—maybe it looks a little creepy but it's supposed to, right? You said it was a *ghost*."

"Did I offend her? Your mother?" Rachel wants to know.

"Offend her? No. Terrify her? Kinda sort of."

"I should keep my mouth shut," says Rachel.

"*No*," her husband disagrees. But only kinda sort of. "You don't need to do that. Just…I dunno. Prepare a person for what's coming maybe."

Rachel nods. "I should keep my mouth shut," she says.

18.

Safe 'n' Sound in Brooklyn

AFTER THE EPISODE AT BONWIT TELLER, RACHEL WENT TO THE museums every day for weeks. At the Frick, she was consoled by the simple humanity and the quietly troubled beauty of Whistler's portraits. She would gaze at the reverence of Sassetta's *The Virgin of Humility Crowned by Two Angels*, gleaming with gold leaf. Maybe she was Jewish, but the worship of the Mother was something she could understand. At the Whitney, she loved the warmth of color played against the ascetic solitary geometry of Hopper's work, but once, while lost in Pollock's *Number 27, 1950*, her body absorbed so much of the stunning chaos that she had to run to the toilet to vomit. And the Metropolitan? She felt she could travel its galleries forever, happily vanished into its universe of beauty.

But did she ever imagine during a single moment of fantasy that her own work could be hanging on a wall at some future point? No. *Her eema* was the famous artist, not her. That much had been drilled into her kop. Finally, Aaron started gently complaining about her poor housekeeping again, and so her museum visits diminished. He had only so much patience with sickness and recovery. Especially in the world of mental instability. Isn't that what it's called these days? Not insanity. Anyway, it's no secret that his measure of a well-ordered marriage is a well-kept house. If the apartment is clean, then all is in order.

Dr. Solomon believes that her arguments with Aaron about housework are never about housework. That they are indicative of feelings of neglect or stress or unfulfilled desire. Of unrealized dreams or something else entirely unrelated to unwashed dishes or dirty floors. Feelings of jealousy or a struggle for control in an uncontrollable world. If this is the case, then perhaps the resurgence of the housecleaning complaint was Aaron's signal. Enough with the craziness. Shouldn't she be recovered by this point? Shouldn't she, after how long, be getting back to normal? But what is normal?

Rachel lights a cigarette. "I'm not his mother," she tells Dr. Solomon.

"You think that's what he wants in a wife? Another mother?"

"Isn't that what all men want, Doctor?" she answers. "But it makes no difference." She feels a terrible weight in her belly, because the truth is always heavy. "God made me to be *me*," she answers. "Not to be a mother. Not be *anyone's* mother."

The Metropolitan is a sanctuary. A refuge. At the Met, Rachel settles down in front of a Vermeer. The magician of light. Seated on a leather cushioned bench, before her is *Young Woman with a Water Pitcher*. She gazes into the painting as if gazing through an open window into a quiet home. The purity of the light descending. The purity of the silence. This woman on display, her privacy exposed without her knowledge. Bathed in Vermeer's tranquil balance of colors. Yellow, red, blue defining the fall of light on the woman's stillness. Rachel longs to experience that same stillness.

She thinks of her uncle. She has been angered by Feter's talk of advancing her work, not merely because it made her feel used but because it was so ludicrous! So impossible to believe! *As if* she could possibly be of curiosity to the House of Glass. An absurdity among absurdities! But even if it *could* be true, which it can't be. Even if it *might* be true in the realm of some dreamworld where her talent is valued? Sought after? Even if this *could be* possible, it's too false. Too dishonest an aspiration to accommodate. Of course, she is incensed with Feter. How selfish of him to flatter! How cruel of him to tempt her with potential. The scene she precipitated with him? If nothing else, she was simply defending herself from the obscenity of hope.

She stares into Vermeer's painting on the wall. She would like to step into it. She would like to enter all that quiet light and take shelter in it.

<hr>

In May 1933, the National Socialists are still new to power, still blustering like amateurs when the book burnings commence. At night, the Hitler Youth join nationalist fraternities in building a bonfire in the Franz-Josef Platz across from the university. A fire to rid Germany of all un-German spirit. The newly anointed minister of public enlightenment and propaganda makes an appearance, speaking to youth. "The old past lies in flames; the new times will arise from the flame that burns in our hearts. Wherever we stand together," he shouts into the microphone, "wherever we march together, we want to dedicate ourselves to the Reich and its future!"

The newsreels record it all for the cinemas. Rashka sits beside Eema, shrinking into her seat in the newsreel house in the Ku'damm, bombarded by the singing and salutes as books are heaved into the flames. The hooked-cross banners borne by the S.A. men and the fraternity youths poke into the night. "We join together in the vow that we so often promised to the nightly sky," the Herr Reichsminister crows. "Illuminated by many flames, let it be an oath! The Reich and the nation and our Führer Adolf Hitler! Heil!"

Artwork is included along with the books. Eema has heard that two of her paintings were consigned to the pyre as well. The portrait of Rathenau that had hung unfinished as a kind of memorial in the Jüdische Bibliothek and the portrait of Fritz Elsas filched from the Red Town Hall. The first to be reduced to ashes.

<hr>

Campbell's tomato soup, thirty-three cents for three cans, still cheaper than a single tin of SPAM. Aaron likes a bowl of soup for lunch before a Wednesday matinee shift at the restaurant. A bowl of soup with two slices of buttered bread and a glass of milk. At the moment, Rachel can hear him in the bathroom, clunking about. Flushing. Playing with the squeaky taps. She has lit a cigarette but is letting it burn away, the smoke rising into the air and arcing. When Aaron arrives dressed in his slacks and shirtsleeves, he tucks into the table in a businesslike fashion, buttoning his cuffs. "So how's it going with the thing, anyhow?" he asks, picking up his soup spoon.

She butters two slices from the sack of Silvercup bread on the bread board and cuts both in half on the diagonal. "What thing?"

"You know," he tells her as if she's being willfully dense. Slurps soup lightly. "The *thing*. The doctor. What's-his-name."

She pours his glass of milk from the bottle. "Solomon."

"Yeah. Him." Slurp. "How's it going? What's he think?"

A small shrug. He thinks what he thinks.

"He still got you on the pills?" She knows that Aaron is ambivalent about his wife on tranquilizers. He doesn't like to be the guy at the drugstore who has to have the pharmacist fill an order of crazy pills for his missus. *But*. Neither does he want any repeat of the Episode. So.

"I take them, yes," she tells him.

"Because they're *helping*?"

"*Yes*. Because they're *helping*," she repeats, then adds, "*Why else?*"

And now maybe he's getting a little steamed. "I don't *know*, Rach. I guess that's the only *reason*. I'm just *asking* 'cause you're very closed-mouth about it, ya' know?" Slurp. "Very closed-mouth." The spoon pauses before his lips. "I don't hear a word." Slurp.

She ferries the glass of milk and the plate of bread to the table. "I'm seeing him this afternoon."

"Okay. Great. But that still doesn't answer my question. What's he *think?*"

"He thinks I should be shipped to the nearest insane asylum because I'm nuts."

Aaron plunks down his spoon and puffs out a woeful sigh. "I just don't get it. Why do you *talk like that*?"

"Why are you yelling?"

"I'm *not* yelling! I just don't understand why we're paying this gonif a ton and a half of money if he's not *helping* you. *That's* what's nuts!"

This is the end of the discussion. When it's a ton of money under discussion, Rachel knows it's best to shut up and just let Aaron stew. In the following silence, he calms down, slurps at the soup, then stands. "Look, I gotta go."

"But you've hardly touched your lunch."

"You eat it. You're getting too skinny," he says and crosses the room to the hall tree. She watches him lug on his coat. "I just want you to get better," he tells her wearily. "Ya know? That's all. I just want you to get better and feel happy once in a while."

"Like normal people," Rachel answers to sting him. Not because she's angry but because she's ashamed of her "mental illness." That's what it's called now, isn't it? An *illness*. But it still feels like a *shameful* illness. Not like a decent disease. A well-adjusted disease that a person can suffer under heroically. Like cancer or polio—diseases that no one could confuse with wallowing in self-pity.

She pours the soup into a Tupperware container and swathes the bread slices in Saran Wrap. The milk she pours back into the bottle, except for the portion she donates to the cat's bowl for Kibbitz to lap up. The garbage pail is starting to smell, but she decides not to bother with it now, because she too is on her way out the door. As noted, she has an appointment with her shrink. She sets Aaron's dishes in the sink and ties a wool scarf on her head before she slips into her coat. She is happy to be free of the apartment if nothing else. Free from the little chores that define the life of a wife. Also? Free from the demands of the empty canvas, that snow-blinding cliffside sitting on the chair waiting for her to crash into it. But on her way out, she bumps into Daniela with the twins in the hallway. Daniela is moving slowly, her swollen belly leading the way, but she smiles warmly at Rachel as usual. "So how's your work these days?" the woman wonders aloud.

"My work?"

"Yes. You know—your artwork? Are you doing anything?" She sounds hopeful with this question. It surprises Rachel.

"Well, um. I'm thinking about it," Rachel is willing to concede.

"Mmm." Daniela nods. "I don't know how a person does it. You *artists*," she says. "Sitting down in front of a blank canvas and then having to fill it up with a picture out of your own head? I could never even imagine. It makes me jealous." She smiles, making that sound like the sweetest compliment. "I could never draw a straight line." The little girl is tugging on her mother's hand.

"Mommy, I'm bored."

"Leah, be patient please, darling. We've talked about how to be patient."

"So." Rachel looks up from the child, changing the subject. "Where are you off to? The playground?"

"The zoo," Daniela answers, smiling down at her children, as if one of *them* had asked the question.

"*The zoo!*" Josh repeats victoriously.

"The little one picked up her daddy's sniffles, so I thought it was better to call up Mrs. Bethel from downstairs and let her nap." Instinctually Daniela seems to know never to bother Rachel with such a request. Watch my child while she naps? No. "So where are *you* off to?" Daniela asks her.

"Oh, nowhere. Nothing important. I've got an appointment with my shrink," Rachel says. She doesn't know why she admits to this so bluntly. So casually. So *needlessly*. How hard would it have been to say she was off to the store for a quart of milk? She's certainly quite aware that it's not the sort of thing Aaron likes her to broadcast, and yet? It comes out of her mouth. The tiniest flash of dismay brightens Daniela's eyes, though she quickly blinks it away and digests the information with a gentle curiosity.

"Hmm," she says. "You know I've always wondered. Why do they call psychiatrists shrinks?"

Rachel stands there, trapped now by this question. "I don't know," she admits. "Maybe I should ask."

And that's it. That's the end of words for both of them. They were in short supply to begin with. Daniela begins to cluck sweetly at the Kinder, and Rachel pretends to have forgotten her subway tokens in the apartment so that she can avoid accompanying Daniela and children down three flights of steps.

Sitting in the chair in Dr. Solomon's office, Rachel announces, "My husband says you're a quack."

A small blink behind the doctor's horn-rimmed glasses. "I beg your pardon?"

"He called you a gonif."

For an instant, the blank, fixed stare, and then with mild interest: "*Did* he?"

"Why is he paying you if I'm still insane?" she says. Then she asks the question: "So *am* I insane?"

"No," the doctor answers matter-of-factly. "'Insane' is not a diagnosis."

This briefly heartens her. She looks up from the cigarette she is igniting, then snaps open the brass table lighter and inhales smoke. "Then what *am* I?"

"Clinically? You're depressed," he informs her, pad balanced on his knee. "So have you been doing any artwork?"

Why is everybody so suddenly fucking interested in the answer to this question? "Why do they call psychiatrists shrinks?" she asks instead of answering.

"Why do?" Dr. Solomon cocks his head to one side.

"Why," Rachel repeats, "are psychiatrists called *shrinks*?" She pronounces it, *see*-ky-a-trists. "My neighbor wanted to know."

"Why?" The doctor is cooperative. He tries to answer these questions of culture when they arise for Rachel. Such as the difference between Pepsi-Cola and Coca-Cola. Why "Go jump in a lake" is not an inducement to suicide. (Ah! As in "Gai kaken oifen yam!" Go shit in the ocean!)

"Well," he offers, "I suppose the term 'shrink' comes from the headhunters."

Without comprehension. "Headhunters?"

"Yes. You know, in the jungle? Borneo, I think? Headhunters shrink heads."

Her gaze clouds. "They *shrink* them."

"It's a type of *custom*, as I understand it. A type of ritual."

"So are you trying to shrink *my* head? Is that it?"

The doctor surrenders. "Never mind. I really don't know the answer to that question, Rachel. It's a colloquialism of the language. Let's leave it at that, shall we?" the doctor suggests. "Is that why you're here today? To ask me this question? Would your neighbor like to know why an egg cream has no egg in it?"

Rachel takes in smoke from her cigarette. She feels it circulate in the emptiness inside. "I feel such shame, Dr. Solomon."

The doctor settles quietly across the room. Patient. Waiting.

"Such shame," Rachel repeats. "You say I'm depressed. That's my diagnosis? But it's the shame I feel. I feel it like a disease. I know," she says and then must stop. Her voice thickens and her eyes welter. "I know that I am a bad person," she says. "That's the truth of me. Oh, I can *fool* people. I've learned how to do that and blind them with a facade. But under everything, I have a diseased soul."

Solomon shrugs delicately at the weight of the air in the room. "Children," he says. "Children who are…who are made to feel rejected at a very early age. Even in infancy. They are often vulnerable to deep feelings of shame as an adult. Feelings that attach themselves to the moments of their daily lives. It is quite easy, psychologically speaking, for such a child," he says, "*such a person*, to have assumed responsibility for consequences that were actually far beyond any personal control."

Rachel does not speak.

In the subway, she sobs, the train clacking through the tunnels. No one pays her any heed, beyond a few troubled or curious glances. Another nutcase on the train? What else is new? She doesn't care. She is beyond caring. The tears are her reward for defending her own shame against the shrink! That's how it feels.

When she gets home, the building stairwell creaks. Entering the apartment, she is met by the sight of her husband on the telephone, scrunched into the gossip bench with the phone's receiver tucked under his chin. "Yeah, well, of course you think that's funny," he is saying into the phone as he looks up and gives her a perfunctory wave. She looks back at him as she shuts the door. He's talking to a woman, Rachel can tell. The cozy charm in his voice. For an instant, she feels a bright bite of jealousy.

"Well, of course you think that's funny," he repeats. "You're twice as much of a klutz as I ever was. Ask your mother."

And then she knows that it's only Naomi on the other end of the line, which modifies her twinge of jealousy but doesn't eliminate it. They are so easy together, sister and brother. Siblings, so connected by an intimate language of family that Rachel does not speak.

"*Yeah*, and what if I get hit by a *bus*, huh?" he is asking the receiver with a grin in his voice. "What then? What if I get hit by a fuckin' cross-town bus? She'll be all *yours*, baby. All yours! *Naomi, for Gawd's sake,*" he scolds, mimicking their mother's smoky, mezzo soprano, "*if you're gonna use your brother's urn as an ashtray, then at least set it on the coffee table like a person. I just took the cover off the sofa!*"

Rachel breathes in and breathes out.

"And who'll be laughing *then*, huh?" Aaron wants to know, now openly grinning into the mouthpiece. "I mean, who gets the last laugh then?" Rachel hangs up her coat, listens as the jokey familiarity in her husband's voice gives way to the business end of their conversation, now that Rachel has intruded. "Okay, okay, yeah. We'll be there," he assures her. "*What?* Yes. Because I said we *would*, Red. Look, I gotta go," he declares next.

His voice turns clipped and efficient. Tech Sergeant Perlman managing the logistics. "We'll bring a bottle of something," he says. "I don't *know*. We'll bring a bottle of *both*, so that way we're covered." And then, "Yeah, I gotta go," he repeats. "Your sister-in-law just walked in and is wondering what the hell I'm doing home on a matinee shift." Then, with a quick "G'bye," he clamps the phone's receiver firmly into the cradle. "That was Naomi," he announces.

"Yes," says Rachel.

"She wants us at her place Saturday at seven thirty. I told her we'd bring the wine."

"And did you suss out her agenda?" Rachel inquires.

It is Aaron's belief that Naomi always has an agenda. Especially when dealing with him. He sniffs and rakes a bit of phlegm from his throat. "As I anticipated," he declares in a voice that is both grudgingly resigned and self-congratulatory. "A new goy in the boyfriend department."

Rachel nods. "Ah" is all she says in response. This is an ongoing family controversy for the Perlman clan. Naomi's obsession with gentile beaus. But Rachel has no wish to engage with it. "So what in hell *are* you doing home on a matinee shift?" she asks instead.

"Water main busted on West Fiftieth," he reports happily. "Con Ed's got the whole block shut down. So I get the rest of the night off," he says and claps his hands together. "Zo!" he begins, adopting the alter kocker's accent that he finds so amusing. "What's fur supper, bubba doll? You want maybe I should put on some pants and go down to the Chinese for takeout?"

Rachel strikes another match to life and inhales the puff of sulfur before lighting a burner on the stove. "I thought I might cook something," she answers.

"Really?" says Aaron skeptically but at least dropping the irritating accent. "Well, that ought to be interesting."

Spaghetti. She's learned how long to boil it so it doesn't stick together by adding a few drops of Wesson oil. And she can heat up the sauce from a can she bought at the market. The label on the can assures her that *Every meal's a masterpiece, when Chef Boy-ar-dee makes the sauce!* The choice was sauce with meat with a red label or simple marinara with a yellow label, but she always picks the meat sauce and then douses the steaming spaghetti with it as soon as she drains it from the boiling water, serving it with a slice of buttered white bread. Aaron eats without much complaint and seems to take some satisfaction in demonstrating the best way to twist the spaghetti onto the fork by pressing it against a spoon. The things a Jew from Flatbush learns, he observes.

"So I ran into Daniela Weinstock in the hallway today," she mentions. "With her twins."

Without interest. "Yeah, ya did?"

"They were going to the zoo."

He sniffs. Clears his throat. Stabs a small orange meatball with his fork. "Okay."

"I told her I was on my way to my shrink."

Silence. Then Aaron sucks in air and sets the fork down.

"You told Ezra Weinstock's wife that you're *seeing a shrink*," he says. Then he drops his head back and shakes it with disbelief. "Oy fucking gevalt," he declares with utter desolation, as if he's echoing the last words God spoke to Abraham. "My *wife*."

"It just came out."

"*It just came out?* Honey! Do you *know*… Can you *conceive*, for just a moment, with what lightning speed that bit of news is now going to flash across Brooklyn to my mother? Like the speed of a rocket. Like breaking the sound barrier, with the big boom at the end included."

"I think," she says, "you're overreacting."

"Oh, *do you*?"

"Plenty of people have see-chiatrists these days. It's not a stigma."

"Trust me, in Flatbush, it's plenty stigma enough. And by the way—it's *not see*-ky-a-trist, it's *sigh*-ky-a-trist." He says this with such force that the impact is too much for Rachel. She does what she hates doing in front of him during an argument. She bursts into tears.

Aaron drops his utensils and releases a plummeting sigh. "Okay, I'm sorry," he says. Pushing back his chair, he's on his feet, wrapping his arms around her shoulders for comfort. "You're right. Everybody needs a shrink these days," he tells her and kisses her on the neck. "I'm making too big a thing. Ma likes you anyway. If she hears?" he decides. "She hears."

The next day, as Rachel comes into the house, the telephone is ringing. She yanks off a clip-on earring to answer. "Perlman residence, hello?"

"Hello, honey, it's Miriam Perlman. How you doin'?"

"Hello, *Miriam*," Rachel replies, eternally uncomfortable calling her mother-in-law by her given name. "I'm fine, thank you."

"*Good!*" Does she sound surprised at this? "Glad to hear it."

"I'm sorry, but Aaron isn't home. He went in early today."

"Of course." The woman sighs. "Just like his father. But that's okay, sweetheart. It's really *you* I want to talk to."

"Me?"

"How're you feeling? Good, you say?"

"I'm fine, yes. Fine."

"'Cause I heard that maybe you were having some difficulties." Rachel breathes in.

"Hello? You still with me, sweetheart?"

"I'm seeing a psychiatrist, Miriam," Rachel declares. She even pronounces the word correctly.

"Yeah, that's the thing I heard," her mother-in-law confirms. "And so I'm wondering what's going on? Is my son driving you crazy?"

Is this a joke? "Aaron. Uh, *no*," Rachel manages to reply. "No."

"Just kiddin', honey," Miriam explains. "But I'm wondering what this guy has to say…this psychiatrist, I mean. What's his verdict?"

"Well, he doesn't give a 'verdict,' really."

"No? So he can't figure it out?"

"*It?*"

"The problem, sweetheart," Miriam explains. "If you're seeing a doctor, there must be a problem, right? I mean, far be it from me to stick my nose into things, but you're my daughter-in-law. I'm concerned."

"Yes," Rachel says.

"Is it—you know—like an *intimate* thing, if you'll excuse me for asking?"

"I don't know what you mean, Miriam."

"What I mean," she says, "is there maybe something wrong in the bedroom department between you and the boy? I only ask 'cause I'm trying to be helpful."

"Oh. *No*. No, nothing like that." She realizes that she is gripping her earring so tightly that the clip is digging into her palm.

"Okay, so not that, good. Then what?" Her mother-in-law tempers her tone as she asks the next question. Her voice recedes self-consciously, almost sheepishly. "Is it," she wonders, "is it what those dirty shtunks did to Jews back in the war?"

This is the most direct question she thinks her mother-in-law has ever asked her on the subject. Yet Rachel says nothing.

A painful sigh from the other end of the line. "I saw the newsreels, honey. After the war was over, they played them at the Waldorf over in Rugby Village." A pause. She must be replaying them in her head. "I just can't *imagine*. I mean, how *evil* does a person have to be to treat human *beings* like that?" she asks. "It made me feel *horrible*," Miriam admits. "And so guilty? I mean, here I was safe 'n sound in Brooklyn, while millions—*millions*—who can even conceive of such numbers? While all those millions of other Jews were being… You know…"

Miriam can't find the word to finish her sentence, but Rachel can.

"Exterminated," she says.

There's a deep pause. And then Miriam tells her, "I'm gonna talk to Aaron." She declares this stridently as if she's hit upon a solution. "I am. I'm gonna talk to that boy and make sure he doesn't give you a hard time about your feelings, okay?"

"Oh. No, Miriam."

"I mean *of course* you need to see a doctor. Who wouldn't? I'm gonna make sure he understands, that's all. That he treats you *thoughtfully*. That's all I'm saying, honey. I'm just gonna make sure that he *gets* it. I mean we both know that boychik can be a teensy bit self-centered at times, to say the least."

Rachel releases a breath.

"All right, sweetheart. You take care now," her mother-in-law commands. "Okay?"

"Okay," says Rachel.

"Okay. G'bye then. Be well," Miriam adds, and that's it. Until evening, when the phone rings just as Aaron is walking in the door, so he actually picks it up, though it's obvious he immediately regrets the impulse. Much later, he is dead bushed from the earful he's still getting, planted on the gossip bench, still in his overcoat and hat, with his elbows on his knees. "Yes, Ma. I saw them *too*. We *all* saw them," he's saying.

And then, "Okay. Okay, Ma, *I get it*. Yes, I *get it*," he keeps repeating before he's finally allowed to say goodbye. Hanging up with an exhausted clamp of the receiver, he heaves out his last breath. "H'oy!" he declares, sending it up to the ceiling. Rachel has been observing him from the safety of the kitchen table with a purring cat hostage on her lap.

"So guess what?" he begins. "Apparently? Whatever happens? It's all my fault."

19.

Naomi's Soirée

THE NEXT DAY, THE LATE-AFTERNOON SUN GRAYS THE APART-
ment. Rachel stands in the shower, allowing the water to pour
over her. Staring at the empty white of the canvas has exhausted her.
Emptied her. All that flat whiteness, and not a crack to pry it open. It
remains the opaque blizzard the instant before the plane punches into
the mountain, a solid storm of white.

Aaron appears at home an hour before his usual time.

"You're here," Rachel tells him, still dressing from the shower.

"I am," he agrees.

"And it's not even six o'clock."

"Well, I was instructed by my darling wife to be home early," Aaron
replies, tossing his hat and coat onto the sofa. "Don't you remember? I
think your exact words were, 'Please be home before six, because I will
be forcing you to have dinner with your sister and her latest whatever.'"

"Those were not my exact words," Rachel says. Her skin is damp
and she is in her slip in the living room, a towel tied in a turban around
her hair as she pours Little Friskies into the cat's bowl.

"Whatever story makes you comfortable," he says. Passing by her,
he plants a kiss on a damp bare shoulder.

"Did you bring the wine?"

"Nope. Forgot."

She puts back the Little Friskies on the shelf as Kibbitz crouches
on his forepaws and burrows his nose into the bowl. "So go back out
and get it. That place down the street is open till ten."

"I don't like the guy in that place. He always calls me 'sweetheart.'"

"Calls you sweetheart?"

"I buy a six-pack, and it's: 'That'll be a buck ten, sweetheart.' I dunno, it gives me the creeps."

"Well, you have to go somewhere. We need wine."

"So we'll pick it up on the way," he says, heading in the direction of the refrigerator. "Is there beer?"

"There's *root* beer."

"Okay, well, I guess that'll have to do."

"Do for what?"

"Do for I gotta fortify myself, don't I?" is all Aaron says on the subject. "Hey, did ya know? You can buy Coke in a can now instead of a bottle. An aluminum can. Crazy," he says. Then snaps off the cap of a bottle of A&W with the opener and takes a fortifying slug. "So how's it going?" he wonders, frowning over in the direction of the canvas. "Looks like the canvas is still winning the staring match."

She lights a Camel from a matchbook. "Don't pressure me, please," she says pleasantly enough.

"Who's pressuring? I was just making an observation," he says and glugs down root beer. "Hey, so whatever happened to those paintings you did when we first got married?"

Rachel says nothing.

"You know, the guy had one of 'em in his gallery for a while?"

"It was hardly any kind of a 'gallery,'" she says dismissively. "It was in a tiny place on Tenth Street." She cannot bring herself to speak the truth, which is that she left them on the subway or on the street. Just abandoned them, one at time. "I gave them to the Salvation Army," she lies instead. An answer so preposterous that Aaron doesn't bother to press further.

He emits a soft belch from downing the root beer.

"You know, I'm not wearing a tie to this little tête-à-tête," he warns her.

"So who asked you to?" Rachel answers. "Besides, le tête-à-tête is a face-to-face, a private talk. What we will be attending, Monsieur le mari, is une soirée or une petite fête." She says this, walking over and poaching a swallow of root beer from his bottle. Then she poaches another kiss, a kiss deep enough that she leaves him hard in the trousers. "But you should change your shirt," she tells him. "You smell fishy."

"Hey, that's black beluga caviar you're smelling," he corrects. "Thirty bucks an ounce."

Naomi answers the door dressed for a fancy affair in black capri pants and an elegant off-the-shoulders top that accentuates all those natural curves of hers. She also wears a look of happy surprise. That's natural too. Rachel has always marveled at her sister-in-law's ability to keep her smile so genuinely fresh. "Oh, *hello*, gorgeous," Naomi announces gleefully and gives Rachel a loud smack on the cheek. When she turns to her brother, her expression makes allowances. "And hello to you, shtoomer," she says affectionately in a tone that lightly teases the sourness of Aaron's expectations for the evening.

"Look, let's just get this little nosh-up over with, okay, Red Riding Hood?" Aaron grumbles glumly. But he's still brought a nice bottle of sauvignon blanc, along with a bottle of that particular Chianti that he knows Naomi loves. "Here," he says, squeezing out a frown and handing over the sack. "Open 'em up early," he instructs. "I gotta feeling I'm gonna be drinking heavily."

Naomi shakes her head lightly. "Whatta ma-*roon*," she says. "How lucky you are to have snapped him up, Rach."

Inside, Naomi tells them to make themselves at home as she pries the cork from the Chianti, pouring it out into three goblets that actually match. Rachel leaves her pumps by the door and sits stocking-footed on the sofa, removing her cigarettes from her purse. She's amazed at how clean the place looks. All the mess is stored in closets maybe, but

still the surfaces are free of the standard clutter. The rug's been vacuumed. And Naomi's small dining table is set for a crowded four. There's
a large, elegantly shaped pottery ashtray with a red-gold glaze on the
coffee table that Rachel's never seen before, and she tugs it closer as she
lights up. Aaron, on the other hand, is still the wandering Jew, roving
the boundaries of his sister's apartment. He's so antsy that he can't sit,
so he paces without destination, hands still stuffed in his pockets. "So
where is he?" he wants to know.

"Tyrell?" Naomi says, raising her eyebrows as she hands her brother
a glass. "He'll be here soon," she assures him.

"Tyrell, Tyrell," Aaron repeats, jingling the change in his pockets as
if he's talking to himself. "What kind of name is 'Tyrell' anyhow?"

With a glance, Rachel spots a glimmer in Naomi's lake-deep eyes
and the slight up-curve at the corner of her mouth. "It's a name" is all
she says as she delivers Rachel's goblet to her. But there's definitely
something she's *not* saying. An agenda.

"Sounds Irish," Aaron says after a hefty swallow of wine. "Is he an
Irishman, this one? Should I brush up on my faith 'n begorrah?"

But Naomi is busy uncorking the white. "Aaron, can you just take a
pill or something?"

"Oh, I can do *many* things," Aaron answers with mildly menacing
assurance. "Many things."

Naomi snorts, and then the oven dings pertly. "Ah! That's my cue!"
She grins, delighted again, and returns to the stove with a pair of heat-
stained oven mitts.

Rachel drinks. The taste of the Chianti mixes with the taste of
tobacco in her mouth. Actually, she misses the clutter and chaos of
the place, and she's happy to see that at least the bookcase retains it. A
frantic old-time mess. Books shoved this way and that, stacked atop
each other, dust jackets ripped and tattered from the friction and over-
use. She envies Naomi these shelves. She herself can never hold on to
books. Books, letters, gloves, fountain pens, checkbooks, one earring

out of the set, cigarette lighters, they simply slip through her fingers and are gone.

"Ten more minutes for the chicken!" Naomi sings out. Returning from the stove, she seats herself on the blanketed sofa beside Rachel with her wine goblet and lights up a cigarette, blowing smoke. "Hey, shtoomer. Can you *quit your pacing*, please?" she demands of her brother. "You're wearing a hole in my rug."

"Yeah, yeah, like I haven't heard *that* before," he says and falls into his impression of their mother. "*'Quit your pacing and sit. You're wearin' a hole in my rug, for heaven's sake.'*" He says this, dumping himself down on the sofa and puffing out a long breath. "So speaking of the crazy lady, does she know about your latest? Mister Faith 'n Begorrah?"

"Maybe." Naomi shrugs.

"Which means *no*."

"I don't believe I need my mother's approval," she explains to Rachel. "Unlike some people."

"Oh, yeah? Tell that to the woman who bore you, why don't you?"

"I believe that we live in a world of individual freedoms, where people are responsible to themselves alone," Naomi declares.

"Sure, well, that's because Ma dropped you on your head when you were a baby."

"*Aaron.*" Rachel scolds him with a slap on his leg.

"What? Ouch. It's *true*. I get assaulted for the truth now."

"It is true," Naomi admits with a sigh. "She tripped over a throw rug in the bedroom and ker-*plop*."

"Yeah, and ever after, it was 'I hate that rug. It's a cursed rug,'" he says, mimicking their mother again.

"Cursed," says Naomi, "but she never got rid of it."

"*Get rid of it?*" Aaron's mimic rises in pitch. "I should get rid of a rug while it's still perfectly *good*?"

"So instead, for nearly thirty years, she walks *around* it."

"Right," Aaron agrees. "Like it's a land mine or something." He half laughs at the thought of this. The homey exchange with his sister at their mother's expense has blunted his edge. The shared memory. The shared ridicule even. Then there's a knock on the door. A confident knock. Not overly polite and not overly aggressive, but solid in its intention. The knock of a person who knocks on a door with self-assurance, whether the door opens or not.

"That's Tyrell," Naomi announces, a swift excitement lighting her face. She sets down her wine and cigarette and eagerly crosses the floor.

Aaron stands in an obligatory manner. "Faith 'n begorrah," he grumbles into the bowl of his goblet, taking a deeper swallow, but then quite literally, he begins to choke on his own words.

His sister must thrust herself up on her tiptoes to kiss the man now standing in the threshold of the apartment. "Hello, darling." She smiles at him. The man smiles back at her and then smiles half blankly into the room. "This," Naomi announces, looping her arm around his, "is Tyrell Williams."

"How do you do," the man says. His voice is deep, and he is over six feet tall. Must be over six feet tall. Dressed in a handsomely fitted gabardine suit. His features are striking. Powerful. Sculpted, one might call them. His hair is perfectly barbered. And he is Black.

Rachel jumps to her feet in the space opened by her husband's gaping stare and sticks out her hand. "I'm Rachel," she says.

"Very pleased to meet you," Tyrell replies, shaking firmly.

"My sister-in-law," Naomi informs him, as if this might be a surprise, and then turns to Aaron. "And this is my fuckhead brother, Aaron," she says, but her voice is without rancor or sarcasm. Without mischief or satisfaction. It's as if she calls him a fuckhead in a concerned, almost fretful manner.

Aaron snaps to quickly and juts out his hand as well. "Aaron Perlman," he introduces himself in a soldierly fashion. "Pleasure."

"Pleased to meet you too," Tyrell insists.

"My sister's got quite a mouth on her," Aaron points out, maybe not so much of a compliment this time, more half an excuse and half a reprimand.

To which Tyrell replies, "So I've noticed." Smiling, in a pleasant sort of way, though his eyes, Rachel can see, are watchful.

And then there's only a splinter of silence before Naomi declares, "Supper's almost ready. I'm going to pour you a glass of wine."

20.

A Dinner Roll

Out of the oven, the chicken Kiev receives cooing accolades from Tyrell and Rachel, but not so Aaron. Naomi places it on the hot pad at the center of the table with her oven mitts on and invites Tyrell to carve it into slices, addressing him as "Boyfriend." Aaron looks on sullenly, causing Rachel to fill in for the empty spot he's occupying. "It smells delicious," she declares and gets busy helping Naomi with the vegetable dishes. Mashed potatoes seasoned with paprika and minced garlic, and asparagus served with a cream of mushroom sauce, looking as bright as fresh oil paint on a palette. Rachel notes the tins of Campbell's cream of mushroom soup lying in the garbage pail.

"It all smells so wonderful," she confirms again, sinking a large serving spoon into the corner of the mashed potatoes. Naomi is setting out a basket of dinner rolls and covering them with a striped tea towel to keep them warm as they sit down to eat. Tyrell assists Naomi with her chair in a gentlemanly fashion, forcing Aaron, who is midsit, to quickly hop over and follow suit with Rachel. "Thank you, Husband," Rachel offers him.

Naomi raises her glass of Chianti for a toast that serves as a blessing. "Blessed is he who creates the fruit of the earth. Or in this case, the fruit of the vine," she says with a smile. "L'Chaim."

"L'Chaim," Rachel echoes pleasantly.

Tyrell declines to attempt "L'Chaim" but is smiling when he says, "To your health." Aaron? Nothing. He just takes a deep swallow from his goblet. But as the dishes are passed and plates filled, he begins to raise himself from his silence. A friendly barracuda.

"So what do you do, Mr. Williams?" Aaron is interested to learn.

"He's a lawyer," Naomi answers for him. "Just graduated from Columbia Law School."

"Well." Tyrell smiles in modest correction. "Actually I'm not a lawyer yet. Not yet," he repeats. "I still have to pass the bar."

"Oh, but you *will* pass it," Naomi assures him. "I know you will. You're brilliant. He's brilliant," she assures all.

"No," Tyrell disagrees in a good-natured way, slicing his asparagus. "That is *not* true. Far from it."

"It *is* true," Naomi replies, then turns to Rachel with a confidential smile. "You should see him play chess."

"Oh? You play chess?" Aaron asks, as if this might interest him, the man who's played checkers his entire life.

"I play a bit of chess, sure," Tyrell admits.

"He practically put himself through law school with it," Naomi announces, and here's the chicken tuck of Aaron's chin jerk.

"You play for *money*?" he asks.

Tyrell must pick up on the ambivalence, because his answer is constrictive. "I've made a couple bucks," he confesses. "But I've lost a couple too. *More* than a couple." He smiles. "There are plenty of people whom I've played who are ten times better than me."

"He means the Russians," Naomi kibbitzes. "There's a whole crowd of all these old farts from Leningrad or wherever over in Washington Square. But you've nearly beaten what's-his-name," she reminds him. "The grand master."

"Yaakov," Tyrell says and frowns lightly.

"Right. That's him. *Yaakov.*" She pronounces the name as if it's the name of a new Soviet secret weapon. The Yaakov Bomb.

"Really. A grand master." Aaron grins with a touch of malice. "So how much did he take you for?"

"Nothing. Yaakov doesn't play for money. And I've never 'nearly' beaten him." Tyrell pokes his fork into the food on his plate. "Not by

a long shot. I had him on the run for a minute or two maybe, but that
was just luck."

"Okay, if you insist," Naomi surrenders. "But this from the man
who doesn't believe in luck."

"I agree," Rachel hears herself say. "I don't believe in luck either, Mr.
Williams."

"*True*," her husband confirms, chewing. "She doesn't. You never
hear her say, 'good luck,' my wife. Not even 'break a leg.'" And then,
"*So*," he says, chewing. "Mr. Williams." Swallows. "If you don't mind me
asking. How old are you?"

"He's thirty," Naomi answers.

"And who am I asking, *you*?" Aaron says to his sister. "I think if the
man is thirty years old, he can speak for himself."

"That's right. I think I can," Tyrell assures Naomi firmly. "I'm actually thirty-one," he says and takes a bite of his chicken. "This is delicious, Naomi," he tells her, eliciting a girly grin that might even qualify
as starry-eyed.

But Aaron is still stuck on Tyrell's age. "Thirty-one," he says with
a frown. "Isn't that a little late, you know, for just graduating college?"

"Well, not really college. Law school, I think, is considered to be
graduate studies," Tyrell corrects mildly, thoughtfully. "But you're right.
It *is* late." To this he nods in agreement. "I *started* late, you might say. I
had an undergrad degree from City College—"

"On *full* scholarship," Naomi interjects.

Tyrell simply smiles over the top of that fact. "In engineering," he
finishes. "Worked for a firm uptown for a while. But. I don't know." He
scratches his head, frowning. "Swimming in electrical schematics and
all, day after day? After a while, I was looking for a change. And *then*,"
he says, "Uncle Sam decided I should spend twenty-four months in
Korea with the Eighth Army, Second Infantry Division. It wasn't till
afterward that I went back to Columbia for law on the G.I. Bill."

"He was in combat," Naomi cuts in sharply, informing her brother with reverent relish. "Against the *Red Chinese.*" The words *Red Chinese* are spoken as if a more lethal opponent on earth cannot be imagined, though oddly her eyes are still smiling.

"Really?" says Aaron, eyes flat. A frown of stilted interest. "I didn't realize that, ya' know, *everybody* over there was actually *fighting.*"

A small, infinitesimal pause as Tyrell absorbs this remark before he answers. "Actually, you're correct about that, Mr. Perlman," he says. "I wasn't *sent* there to fight. I was *sent* there as a pack mule. The army didn't put Negro troops in the front lines," he says. "Instead they had us in the rear, hauling supplies and digging latrines. Dug a lot of latrines, I can tell you that," he recalls with only a tiny glimmer of polite bitterness.

"Aaron went to school on the G.I. Bill too," Rachel hears herself announcing, but that's all she can manage to say.

"Yeah, though not exactly for a *real* degree," Naomi points out. "Not exactly at Columbia University."

"No, well, that's true," Aaron agrees. An admission. "Not exactly that. Two semesters at N.Y.S. Applied Arts, Brooklyn."

"So you were in the service too, Mr. Perlman," Tyrell adds chivalrously, trying to keep things from disintegrating.

"The service? Yep," Sergeant Perlman answers. "For the *big* one. Duration plus six. Though I was stationed stateside. In California."

"A fortunate man," Tyrell says plainly.

Naomi, however, scoffs. "Yeah. Keeping Culver City safe for democracy."

"*Naomi,*" Rachel breathes.

"No, it's okay." Aaron raises his palm. "She's right. I wasn't exactly raising the flag on Iwo Jima." And then he makes his confession. "I was in the Three-Ninety-Fourth Quartermaster Detachment, Mr. Williams. Technical services. I coordinated logistics with the U.S.O. Victory Circuit on the West Coast."

"Sounds like fun to me," Tyrell offers.

"More fun than hand-to-hand combat." Naomi nods, scooping

another helping of the mashed potatoes onto Tyrell's plate. "Wouldn't you agree, Aaron?"

"Oh yeah. Much more fun," Aaron replies. "For me it was just hand-to-hand with the caterers," he says with a sharp downturn of his lip. "But I'm confused. Maybe somebody can explain to me how hauling supplies in the rear and, well, digging out latrines qualifies as combat duty."

"Aaron," says Rachel. "There's no reason to ask such personal questions."

"No, it's okay," his sister insists firmly. "I'm proud of how Tyrell served his country." Turning to Tyrell, she prompts him. "Tell him, Tyrell. Tell him about the Chongchon River."

Tyrell frowns. "Naomi."

"Please. He needs to know. How many times have you said that America's forgotten about the war in Korea, like it never happened. We *all* need to know," she says.

A breath. "Okay. If, uh, if that's what you want." Tyrell swallows some wine and scratches his head again, as if activating the memory. "The Second Infantry Division," he says. "We'd, uh, we pushed the NKs... I mean, the North Koreans... We'd pushed them back. Past the Thirty-Ninth Parallel and all the way to the border with China on the Yalu River. So we thought, okay, we had 'em pretty well whipped. That's what everybody believed, I guess. The brass even commenced what they called the 'Home-by-Christmas' offensive," he tells them. Rachel can see the pain of this memory drifting across the man's eyes. "But things don't always go according to plan in the army. Do they, Mr. Perlman?"

"They do *not*," Aaron must agree.

Tyrell takes a breath. "One night at the end of November... Well, it was a bit of a surprise, if I can put it that way, when a few hundred thousand Chinese regulars came screaming across the river with their bugles blowing. We were..." he starts to say and stops. Searching for the correct word perhaps as he shakes his head. "We were *overwhelmed*," he says. "Half the division was simply—*annihilated.*" It's the only word he can find to describe it. "Out of the forty-two men in our platoon, I was one of only *six* who made it out alive. The rest of them? I don't know. Maybe they're still there lying in those mountain fields. Nothing but bones by now, I suppose."

A dead silence reigns over the room. It settles as if those bones have been scattered across the table.

"Helluva story," Aaron admits quietly, staring into his wine before taking a frowning swallow. His face is flushed.

"Not a very happy story for the dinner table," Tyrell tells Naomi, as if to say, *I told you not to push me on it.*

Naomi absorbs this and sucks in a breath. "I'm gonna open that second bottle of wine," she announces.

The meal continues with the passing of side dishes and the refilling of glasses. But Rachel can see that her husband's face has darkened. His color has settled into a flush of male embarrassment. He's quit his interest in the food on his plate and pours more wine. "Mr. Williams," he begins, even though his sister hasn't finished talking about how she got her recipe for the chicken from *The Joy of Cooking.* "This old guy. 'Yaakov' you called him," Aaron begins. He speaks the name into the air as if to consider it more clearly. "The great grand master or whatever. He's a *Jew*?" Aaron wonders. "I mean, 'Yaakov.' It sounds like a Jew's name, am I right?"

"I really don't know, Mr. Perlman," Tyrell answers, tending to his plate. "I've never asked him."

"Oh, so you can't *tell*," Aaron concludes. "I mean, he doesn't have a huge schnozz or anything? He doesn't talk obsessively about how much money he's losing—but *oh*, that's *right*. He can't possibly be a Jew, can he, because with him, no money changes hands."

"What the fuck are you doing?" Naomi demands sharply over Tyrell's silence.

"*What?*" Aaron is just an innocent guy. "I'm just making conversation with your friend here, the lawyer. Oh, I'm sorry—the almost-a-lawyer. *You know,*" he says, returning to his plate with alacrity, cutting up a spear of asparagus, "I mean, what do I know from chess? I'm just a Jew from Flatbush. But Rachel's Uncle Fritz plays, doesn't he, sweetheart?" He doesn't wait for a response. "He tried to teach her how to play too, if memory serves, but she could never remember how the pieces moved."

Rachel tries to maintain a smile. "I don't have a mathematical mind," she admits.

"You're an *artist*, Naomi tells me," Tyrell suggests helpfully.

"Yeah, if she ever stops glaring at an empty canvas," Aaron answers for her, chewing as he cuts up more asparagus. Rachel feels it like a knife stab.

"Well, I could never paint *any* kind of picture," Tyrell declares. "That takes a special kind of talent that *I* do *not* possess."

"Naomi, I'm going to get a glass of water," Rachel says.

"Oh, let me." Her sister-in-law starts to rise, but Rachel waves her off.

"No, no, no. I'll get it." At the sink with her back to the table, she listens closely to the water gurgling into the glass from the tap. Her hand trembles as she drinks it. She is having a problem. An old problem. After going hungry in hiding, it's still painful for her to eat in public. She has managed to train herself away from it, but it can still turn up during moments of tension, and right now, she has a killing desire to start hiding food instead of eating it. She drinks the water down as Naomi appears with an empty platter and a few utensils greasy with sauce that she sets in the sink.

"You okay?" Naomi asks.

"Yes. You?"

Naomi shakes her head ruefully, turning on the tap to rinse the plate. "My brother. What a piece of fucking work."

"Should I make him take me home?"

"Nah, Tyrell can handle it. He's been handling bigoted assholes his whole life," she says with smothered anger. Rachel wonders: A bigoted asshole? Is *that* who she's married? Naomi shows her a forced smile. "Go. Sit back down. I'll be there in a minute. I just wanna get a jump on some of the cleanup."

Rachel assumes that it's Naomi's excuse to escape for a moment too and nods. But when Rachel returns to the table, she can't help but focus on the dinner rolls in a basket, and she thinks if she could only slip one into her sweater pocket, that might be enough. Just to know it's there. Just to know she won't starve. That she won't ever be starved again. Just a dinner roll, that's all. Then she eyes Aaron's wine goblet. He's just refilled it with the last of the Chianti. It'll make a mess of his slacks, but he deserves an embarrassing ride on the subway, so Rachel reaches for the basket of dinner rolls.

"*Shit!*" Aaron yelps as he leaps up from the table, his lap drenched by the overturned goblet.

"Oh my God, I am so *sorry*, Husband." Rachel is apologizing loudly, heatedly, but the deed is already done, the dinner roll has been expertly pocketed. And it would have been perfect, a flawless theft, if she had not been caught by a blink of Tyrell's eyes.

Naomi is on the job with a dish towel. "It's okay, it's okay." She clucks maternally at Aaron as if he's obviously overdoing it. "For god's sake, it's not the end of the fucking world. Besides, *you deserved it* for being such a first-class putz all night. Remember what Pop used to say? Ess, bench, sei a mensch." Eat, pray, and be a man! Not a putz.

Aaron grabs the towel from her and starts roughly brushing at the wet spot. "Yeah? Thanks for the reminder, Sis," he says acrimoniously. "Just tell me how this is going to look when I get on the fucking subway, huh? The man who's pissed himself."

"So take a taxi," says Naomi.

"Right. Money to burn." Aaron frowns, embarrassed at having to tamp dry the crotch of his slacks in front of another man. "*Take a taxi*," he smirks, shaking his head.

"Oh, for… *I'll give you the goddamned two dollars*, cheapskate!" Naomi detonates, her face bleached by the burst of anger. "Jesus *Christ!*"

The float of traffic noises from the street suddenly becomes very pronounced in the silence that follows. Aaron glares, jaw clenched. Then abruptly, he frowns and swipes at the stain on his trousers again. "Well, let's not bring *him* into this," he requests, then adds, "No offense meant, Mr. Williams."

"None taken," Tyrell assures him cleanly.

Aaron has had enough of mopping up and tosses down the dish towel with a huff, then sits, elbows on the table, fingers woven together. "I have a clumsy wife sometimes," he tells Tyrell without rancor, simply explaining one of the small banes of his fucking existence. "And I'm sorry if I've been offensive," he says as he refills his goblet from the bottle of white. "As my wife can testify, I'm sure, she married a jerk." He shrugs and then tips back the wine.

There's some problem with the I.R.T. at West Fourth, so they have to walk to Christopher Street and Sheridan Square to take the Broadway Local to 23rd. Not much is said. Aaron sits beside her on the subway with his coat closed over the wine stain. The local is slow and truculent. A rattling bucket of bolts, schlepping its sardined passengers from one stop to the next.

"I didn't do it on purpose," Rachel says finally.

But Aaron only looks at her as if he's really a mile or two away. "What?"

"I didn't spill the wine on you purposely," she lies.

"Okay," he shrugs. Willing to accept this.

The train lumbers into the 23rd Street station with a dull blast of thunder and starts to brake.

"This is us," Aaron announces blankly.

It's a ten-minute walk to their apartment building. As they cross Ninth Avenue, Rachel pulls the dinner roll out of the pocket of her sweater and drops it in the gutter for the pigeons to fight over.

"So why do *you* think your husband acted in such a hostile manner?" her shrink wonders aloud.

Rachel draws in smoke from her cigarette. "I don't know."

"Do you," the doctor asks, "believe he is bigoted? Racially speaking."

"No," she says. "Yes. I don't know. It shocked me. I'll admit this. I've never once heard him speak a single insulting word. How is it called? A *slur*," she says. "But I have noticed that he keeps a certain distance in place with the Negro men working at the restaurant. The gentleman who plays the piano. The doorman. He's often overtly chummy with them, like they're friends, but still there's a barrier he keeps up. It's a *fausse amitié*," she says. "According to his sister, their father was the same way."

The doctor nods without expression. "So you think that your husband's attitude may be inherited? Copying his father's behavior?"

"I never knew his father, so it's hard for me to say. But I *do* know that underneath their bickering, he really does worry about Naomi. He feels responsible for her. You know, not only is he the older brother, but with his father gone? He's the *man of the family*. Isn't that the expression? That's why Naomi tries so often to thwart him." Touching the cigarette to her lips. "And I think it frightened him. His sister with a Negro man? What would that mean for her future? Greenwich Village is one thing, but how will the rest of the world see it?"

"Is that how *you* see it?"

"No. The world is an ugly and dangerous place for everyone. People will do as they will do, for good or ill, no matter what color they are. But Aaron? He is still naive in this way. He still believes that a person can be safe in life. So perhaps his fears got the better of him? Though I believe he is terribly ashamed of himself for how he acted."

"He told you that?"

"Not in so many words." Exhales smoke. "But he is."

"So," the good doctor points out, "you didn't actually discuss it between you?"

"We did try," she tells him. "I told him that I didn't understand why he had tried to make Mr. Williams out to be anti-Semitic. Without any cause at all. As if he was simply digging out an excuse to dislike him."

"And"

"He said he didn't need an excuse. But. As I said, I think in the end, it was all much more about Aaron's relationship with Naomi than it was about Naomi's relationship with Mr. Williams."

"And what," the doctor wants to know, "is the effect of all this friction on Mrs. Perlman?"

A glance up. "His mother?"

"No. *You*, Rachel." The doctor lifts his eyebrows above the frame of his glasses. "*You*. The subject of our discussions here."

Rachel feels her stomach tighten. "I spilled his wine."

"On purpose?"

"Yes."

"Because he was being insulting?"

"No," she says. "Because I wanted to steal a dinner roll."

Dr. Solomon looks back at her, obviously patient.

She inhales smoke more deeply. "I was afraid," she says painfully, "that there wouldn't be enough food." She shifts. The chair she is filling feels suddenly painful to sit in. "It strikes me at times. I wanted to hide a piece of bread."

And now the doctor observes her with a great projection of sorrow. "I understand," he whispers.

But does he? Can he? She doubts it. Not really. He can't understand the agonizing urgency of it. U-boat Jews wandering Berlin without shelter, without food for days. Searching refuse bins for scraps. The gnawing anguish, the belly cramps, the terrible pains inflicted by one's own body in the absence of any nourishment. The imprint that starving makes on a person's body, on their soul. The shame it perpetrates on the young girl who still lives inside her.

Her mother believed in drawing. She had received a classical training at the Universität der Künste Berlin, where proper draftsmanship was considered an essential skill. Before she applied the first brushstroke from her palette, the entire composition was worked out in charcoal across the face of the Dead Layer. Perfect propositions meant perfect harmony. Eema believed in re-creating the music of the spheres in her art. But Rachel never had the patience for Pythagoras. Her mother would force her to lay down a sketch on the canvas, but it was never harmonious. It was rushed and rough, because it was the color she was hungry for. The paint wet on her brush swiping color across the surface.

Now, however, the colors of her desire have all grayed. After the Episode, they became mud and gravel and ashes. A night in a strait-jacket contaminated her desire. Color led her to insanity, and those smears of saffrons and scarlets and cobalt blues that have long since dried to her palette? They only serve to taunt her now.

She has put the canvas away. It wouldn't fit in any closets, so she had no choice but to slide it under the bed, where it lies in the dark, gathering clots of dust. She sits on the windowsill by the fire escape. Her coffee cup is in her hand. She is still dressed in her pajamas as she stares out the window. Parked cars jam the street as delivery trucks try to artfully navigate the narrow passage. The buildings look dusty in the undiluted morning glare as she sips at her cup. Aaron drinks his coffee with milk, but she cannot stand it that way and must have it black. People pass on the sidewalk below in an oddly aimless fashion, as if the light or the early morning chill has shrunk their ambitions for the day.

Aaron is at the table. For breakfast, she had poached him two eggs for his toast, though perhaps they're not so perfectly shaped. Aaron hasn't complained about their odd shapes, however. As long as they're messy when he puts his fork into them, that's all he cares about. He likes his toast soaked in yolk.

On his way out the door for work, he asks her, "Is my tie straight?"

Rachel adjusts it. "Yes, it's *you* that's crooked."

"Funny." He offers her a peck on the lips, and she takes it.

"Have you talked to Naomi?"

"No," says Aaron leadenly. "Have *you*?"

"She's not mad at you."

"No? Well, that's what she tells *you*, just to lure me into her trap. Then the next day, they find what's left of me in the East River."

"Tyrell seems like a very decent man. And I think they really care for one another."

"Terrific," he says. And then, "I'm only thinking of her, ya know. Naomi has lost her fucking mind with this guy? *Okay*, fine for now. But what's gonna happen in the future? That's all I'm saying. I'm trying to save her heartache is all. And *him too*," he declares. "Him too. He even *said* that his family was against him dating a white girl."

"Did he say that?"

"Sure. Weren't you listening? About his sister?"

"His family must be fearful for him."

"And they've a *right* to be, God bless 'em," Aaron declares as if his point has finally been proven. "They're fearful for *him*, just like I'm fearful for *her*." He says this, then huffs out a breath. "Look, I don't wanna talk about this right now, okay? You can berate me later. Right now, I gotta get to work before they let the salmon go bad."

"I'm not berating you. Just stop being so judgmental for once."

"*For once.* Great," Aaron says. "Okay, so *I'm* the big problem here, huh?"

"You know that Jews are not always considered to be 'white.' And I don't mean in the old country. I mean right here in America. Think about *that*."

"All right—you don't need to explain to me what it means to be a Jew in this country. I think I know that by now. My question to you is: What if he was German?"

Rachel's jawline tenses. "What is *that* supposed to mean?"

"It means: What if he was German? What if Naomi's new boyfriend was named Wilhelm instead of Williams?"

Rachel steps back from her husband. "*Aaron*," she murmurs, her expression darkening.

"I'm sorry. I know, I'm touching the taboo subject. I'm just the Jew from Flatbush, while you're the one who lived through hell. I have no right, I know that. But I'm also not the one who can't go down to the basement to ask the super to unclog the friggin' pipes because he's a goddamned *Kraut*."

"Go to hell," Rachel says flatly. And when Aaron realizes that maybe he's gone too far and tries to retract, she pushes him away.

"*Rachel*, look..."

"I said, *go to hell!*" She shouts at him this time. "Go! Go make sure your precious salmon doesn't go bad. *Go!*"

He gazes back at her, face pallid, then puffs a sigh. "Okay," he says and wiggles his finger in his ear as his face bloats with a frown. "Okay. Look, I'm sorry. I overstepped. It was unkind."

"*Unkind*?" Rachel turns back, her eyes hot and her face wet with tears. "You have no *conception* what it was like. *You don't know*," she blames him. "And once more, you don't *want* to know. You think you've *done* your duty," she cries, smearing away her tears. "You think you did your part. You married the poor refugee who'd escaped with her life and nothing more. And so that somehow absolves you from any guilt. Any guilt that while you were busy schtupping pretty shiksas in California, there were millions of Jews living in terror and despair! Millions shipped off in filthy boxcars like animals! Millions of Jews funneled into the gas chambers! *Including my mother!*"

Aaron stares at her, stunned. His face completely blank and devoid of color. But Rachel can do nothing but collapse into the chair and sob into her arms.

And then he is beside her. His voice is helpless, but his arms are there, enclosing her. "I'm a putz. I think we've established that. You married a putz, and I should be sorry for *you*. But *never*, Rachel. Please. Don't *ever* think that I married you out of guilt. I married you because you are the woman I love, and that is the only reason."

She turns her head and lets herself be enfolded by him, sobbing against his skinny polka-dot tie, wetting his clean white shirt. The grief, the drowning, unfathomable grief is too much. The grief of a victim, the grief of a betrayer, the grief of one who has survived. She carries all three. The image of the schoolgirl is buried in the corner of her mind. Her braids. Her burgundy beret. A child innocent as rain.

But Aaron is there. A wall for her to wail against. Finally, she manages to tell him, "You married me because I was the only one who would have you."

"That too," Aaron agrees and kisses her softly on her head. "That too."

"You should go," she tells him, sniffing. "Your salmon."

"The hell with the salmon," he answers, rocking her lightly. "The salmon can turn to shit for all I care. Let 'em eat pollack."

21.

Blitzkrieg in Washington Square

THE DAY IS NOT AS CHILLY AS IT HAS BEEN. A BREEZE BLOWS THE trash around Washington Square. The smell of dog poop scents the air, combining with the lightly vomitous perfume of the ginkgo trees. At the entrance to the South Square, the game tables are thickly settled by chess players huddling around their boards.

"Ain't no crime, brutha. Ain't no crime." Tyrell is grinning as he counts through the money he's just won from a skinny Negro youth in a plaid coat. "Next victim," he calls out. But then his expression stiffens as Rachel sits down on the bench opposite him.

"You're different here," she observes.

Tyrell observes her as if from a distance, then stuffs the money into the pocket of his short-waisted jacket. "Is that right? Different from what, Mrs. Perlman?"

"Different from when you were in Naomi's apartment. You speak differently. I didn't hear you say 'ain't' once while you were eating chicken Kiev."

And now he chuckles mildly to himself at this lady's nerve. "No, you did *not*," he must agree. "That's because I was around a bunch of white people."

"Otherwise, you say 'ain't'?"

"Otherwise, I'm myself."

"Tyrell-Who-Says-Ain't."

"Sometimes I'm him, yeah."

"Do you say it when you're with Naomi?"

"Are you driving at something, Mrs. Perlman?"

"Please call me Rachel."

"Nah, I don't think I will," he answers. "Are you trying to make a point?"

"I'm not," she answers. "I'm just curious. My guess is you're different with different people. I know something about that. I think it's a trait we share. Being an 'autseyder' we would call it in Yiddish. A person on the outer edge of things."

"Same in English. An outsider."

"Yes, the same."

Tyrell studies her for a moment with a kind of blunt, hammer-heavy gaze. "Look, Mrs. Perlman. We met *once*. That's it. Let's not pretend we're friends. Okay? If you don't mind, I've got bills to pay, and I've gotta make some money," he tells her. "So unless you've got five dollars you feel like parting with…" he says.

Rachel gazes back at him. She produces her cigarettes and then opens her bag and pulls out her matches. Lights up with a cupped match flame.

"Uh, Mrs. Perlman…"

"So you said five dollars?" she asks, cigarette fluttering from her lip as she frets through a wad of bills. "That's one, two," she counts.

Shaking his head with limited tolerance. "Mrs. Perlman."

"Three, four, and that's five." Digging coins from her change purse.

Tyrell stares at her thickly. "You're not serious," he tells her.

Offering it. "What? My money's no good here?"

Again a stare, and then, "All right." He nods. "All right, Mrs. Perlman. If this is the way you want it. Hold on to your money. I trust you to pay up when you lose."

"Okay," says she, depositing the bills and change into her coat pocket. "You must explain to me the use of the clock, though, before we begin."

His voice is bemused. "Oh, we're not using the clock, Mrs. Perlman.

You're in no way ready for the clock. Just a friendly little game." He snaps up two pawns, one white, one black, mixes them about, and holds out his fists. "Your choice," he tells her.

"This one," she says and points.

Tyrell opens the chosen fist, revealing a small white pawn. "You're white," he tells her. "That means you have the advantage."

They shake hands before beginning, because it's what opponents do apparently. American women don't shake hands, with men or even each other, but everybody in Germany is trained to do so from childhood, so Rachel thinks nothing of it. Also she likes his grip. Pleasantly firm. The games commences, but of course she is immediately lost, nudging pieces outward. What goes where?

"No, no," Tyrell corrects, half smiling with a kind of mildly alarmed indulgence. "That's *not*," he says, "how the knight moves."

"I know, but I can never remember correctly." Rachel frowns. "It's a capital L, isn't it? A knight moves like a capital L?"

"Two spaces, then one space at a corner angle."

"Ah, azoy dos iz rikhtik," she reminds herself. "So *two*," she says, repositioning the small wooden horse, "and then *one*."

Tyrell flattens his expression. "You sure you wanna do that?"

"Hmm. I don't know. Maybe not?"

The man grinds up a few words at the back of his jaw before he answers. "No. No, Mrs. Perlman. I assure you, you *don't* want to do that. Not unless it's your intention to lose your bishop. You see? Your knight's the only protection your bishop has from being taken by my queen."

"Okay. Well, that's too bad. But I moved. Vos iz geshen, iz geshen," she concludes, removing her bishop from its square and replacing it with Tyrell's queen.

"Aw, now *see*, you don't do that *either*," he corrects her. "You don't touch your opponent's pieces unless you're taking them. Not ever."

"Ah. Sorry. My mistake," Rachel says. "There's certainly no shortage of rules in this game."

Tyrell sighs. "Let's quit this, shall we, Mrs. Perlman? Just keep your money."

"Does that mean you're surrendering?"

"Resigning, not surrendering. And no. I'm not resigning. But this is getting ridiculous, don't you agree?"

"So do you despise my husband?"

Tyrell blinks, but other than that, he doesn't move. "*Despise?* No. I don't think I *despise* anyone."

"Even though he was terribly insulting to you? I would despise him if I were in your shoes."

"*Which*, by the way, Mrs. Perlman, you will never be."

"Of course. I *know* that," she answers. "I'm well aware of that fact."

"Are you?" he wonders doubtfully and gazes back at her. "You think, Mrs. Perlman," he says, "you think your husband insulted me? He did. But that ain't nothing. Nothing I'm not used to. I was born down south. And right now, if we were down *there*? You and me? *Well…*" He shrugs. "I guess you might have read in the newspapers what happens to a Negro if he so much as *speaks* to a white woman. That boy in Mississippi who was ripped to pieces? Fourteen years old. A child," he says, swallowing. "His momma kept the coffin open at his funeral just so people could bear witness to the pure barbarity of his murder."

"But we're not *in* Mississippi," she points out.

"No?" Tyrell frowns again. "Mrs. Perlman, this whole country's Mississippi. Don't you get that? North, south, makes no difference. This whole damn *country's* Mississippi."

"And do you think, Mr. Williams, that a Jew is welcome in Mississippi?"

He puffs his cheeks with a sigh. "I never said there wasn't enough to go around. I know about your—*your past.*"

"Oh, so you know that my mother was gassed to death? You know that I was hunted like an animal? Is that the past to which you refer, Mr. Williams?"

Tyrell looks back at her bluntly. "What do you want me to say? That you've suffered more than me? That I should be grateful that nobody ever stuck *me* in a concentration camp? Well, they *did* lynch my grandpa when I was a tyke, right in his own front yard."

"I'm sorry," Rachel says. "I didn't mean to make this a competition."

"No? I think maybe you did. But if not? Okay. Then you tell me, what *is* your intention here, Mrs. Perlman? What exactly did you expect to get for your five dollars?"

Suddenly Rachel feels her eyes heat with a sheen of tears. "I'm not sure. It's only that I must always be so normal. Such a good American. Such a good American housewife and a good Jewish girl. I too am expected to be grateful to God for my life. For the fact that I am living, and not ashes in a pit in Poland. I'm sorry. I just felt the need," she says and sniffs, "to talk to someone. Someone who was an outsider like me." She is opening her bag for the Kleenexes that she keeps there, but then Tyrell is offering her an immaculate cotton handkerchief. She accepts it, tamping her eyes. "Thank you."

He speaks not a word for a moment. Pigeons coo and flap their wings. And then he says, "So I've been curious about something."

Rachel raises her reddened eyes.

"When we were having supper at Naomi's place," he says, "you turned that wineglass over on your husband intentionally."

"Because he was making a fool of himself, you know?"

"Maybe he was, but that *ain't* why you did it, is it? You wanted to grab that roll from the basket. Why was that, Mrs. Perlman?"

She feels a drag of panic pull all expression from her face. "Because," she says but must start again. "Because I thought I could be hungry later."

"You thought?" Tyrell asks.

"Because I was *afraid* I would be hungry later," Rachel confesses.

"Because I was *desperately afraid* I would be hungry later." She stares blankly, then wipes the sting from one of her eyes.

Tyrell nods but does not relax his keen observation of her until a rather scruffy white beatnik kid appears with horn-rim glasses, uncombed hair, and a wisp of a beard on his chin. "Hey, Williams," the boy declares. "Yaakov's asking for a game."

"Excuse me, hot dog, but do you have eyes in your head? Can't you see I'm in the middle of my own game right now?"

"Really?" the kid asks dubiously. "Doesn't look like much."

"Now, that's an insult," Tyrell replies, but without much conviction.

"It's all right, Mr. Williams," Rachel inserts quickly, reclaiming herself. "He's right. I resign," she says and topples over her queen with a tap.

The boy barely smothers a laugh.

"That's your queen, Mrs. Perlman," Tyrell informs her. "When you resign, you tip over your king."

"Oops," says Rachel flatly and topples the king as well.

"So I guess you're open," the boy points out.

"And who are *you*? The great man's messenger boy?"

"Nah," says the kid with a sniff. "I just came over to bum a cig."

"Here," says Rachel, standing. "Take one of mine." She doesn't know if it's because he's being gentlemanly, but when she stands, Tyrell stands too.

"*Thanks*," says the boy enthusiastically as he accepts the cigarette. "Got a light?" he asks.

But Tyrell intervenes, shoving a book of matches into the boy's hand. "Keep 'em," he says in the same tone he might use to say *beat it*.

"Tell Mr. Yaakov that he should have a care playing Mr. Williams," Rachel informs the kid and then explains in a conspiratorial stage whisper. "*He knows how all the pieces move.*"

"Sure," the kid says, blinking at the crazy lady. "Thanks for the cig."

"You're an odd duck, Mrs. Perlman," Tyrell observes, not without some appreciation.

"So, Mr. Williams. If you're going to play the great man, may I observe?"

To which Tyrell shrugs. "It's a free country. So they say."

Pigeons flap and bustle around the edges of the gaming tables. The great man has a head like an old melon. Not a hair remains, only the tough, spotted rind. He surveys the board with a lurking superiority, as if he has already mapped out his victory and it's now only a matter of deploying the pieces.

"So I'm playing white?" Tyrell asks as he sits, considering the setup of the board facing him.

Yaakov lifts his eyes, his arms crossed over his sparrow's chest, his hands tucked under his armpits as if holding his rib cage together. "Vye naught?" he declares.

A crowd has coalesced around them. A circle of interested observers whom Rachel has joined. No one speaks or even dares to cough as the game begins with a clatter of pieces sped along by the thump of the time-clock buttons. It has the feeling of a prizefighter's match that's been sealed inside a mason jar. The speed with which the fingers fly and the pieces are marched across the board or snatched away is so astounding that it is like trying to focus on the view out a window on the Seventh Avenue Express bulleting down the track. Pawns, knights, bishops, are swept from the board in a rage of passive violence, their carcasses piled on the sidelines. Then Tyrell suddenly applies the brakes.

The great man has flicked a pawn two spaces forward. Not a very threatening move as far as Rachel can see, but it causes Tyrell to visibly stiffen. Keeping his gaze nailed to the board, he peels the foil from a stick of Wrigley's Spearmint and shoves it into his mouth, chewing hard at the back of his jaw. She can see the cool tension in his eyes as he decides to respond with a quick prance of his remaining knight. The great man, however, whose hands are once more tucked under his armpits, removes one hand long enough to shove his queen along a diagonal, and now Tyrell starts chewing again. Rachel tries to analyze the Russian's expression as he sits in a forward-leaning slouch, but he *has* no expression. Just the same, peeled-egg blankness. He doesn't even blink.

Tyrell stops chewing. His body hesitates, and then he acts. Plucking up his knight, he snatches one of the great man's pawns and replaces it. The Russian's hand shoots out and plunks *his* knight onto the middle of the board.

Rachel can see Tyrell's eyes racing. How many moves ahead is he calculating? How many *must* he be calculating to beat the great man's game? How many *can* he be? Another pawn moves. A bishop. A shift of the knight, and then, just when Rachel expects the board to explode, the great man pauses. There is no hesitation in his posture; he simply seems to momentarily harden into his slouch as if he has transformed into a pile of stones.

The onlookers tense. Someone takes a deep breath but then does not exhale it. Another clears a thorn of anxiety from his throat, but still the old man sits like a pillar. Has he died? Rachel begins to wonder. How long will everyone stand here before his corpse slumps over and disperses the pieces from the board with a crash? But then he stirs. He stirs, and without ceremony or comment, the Russian's hand shoots out and topples his king.

For a moment, it seems nobody can believe what they have just witnessed. Was it an accident? Did the great man reach for a bishop and inadvertently tip the wrong piece? It can't possibly be over, can it? Not just like that? The onlookers stare dumbly, still waiting for the next move. Even Tyrell looks stunned, or is he simply guarded? What kind of trap is this old Russki setting by resigning? It's only the great man himself who seems utterly unconcerned. "Nize game." He shrugs, with his hand glued under his armpits, his voice a quiet rasp of steel wool on an iron skillet. "Zo maybe you got spare steek of gum?"

22.

The World Is Stupid

WHOSE IDEA WAS IT TO GO TO A BAR FOR A DRINK? TYRELL'S OR hers? Didn't Tyrell say, "How 'bout a quick beer?" Yes. Rachel thinks so. And she had accepted, without thought, during the elation of his lightning victory over the grand master. If ever there had been an example of the word *Blitzkrieg* in the world of chess, that game had been it, she thinks. Blitzkrieg in Washington Square! So it must have been *his* idea to go for the beer. She was simply happy to accept. Then, walking west on Washington Place, she had started noting the glances. Quick, sidelong assessments, up and down, back and forth, from the eyes of fellow New Yorkers. Nothing spoken aloud, of course. Not even a frown. But the eyes snagging them like they were hooks. A Black man, a white woman.

Tyrell seemed oblivious to it. He was suddenly talkative. She had encouraged him to tell her about the game, how it had played out in his head, and he seemed, in fact, not to need much encouragement. "You know, I could *see it*," he tells her. "Yaakov's trap—classic Italian game, 'cause the man likes it quiet. But I could suddenly *see it*, six, maybe seven moves out."

When they cross West Fourth, a middle-aged couple passes by them from the opposite direction, and the quick probe of their eyes appears synchronized. Tyrell, however, doesn't even blink. Maybe it's that he is so accustomed to ignoring that kind of snap-judgment glance from people. A Black man, a white sidewalk.

There are no signs over any of the entrances to this bar. An upshot, he says, of its early days as a speakeasy. And the feeling now is that if you don't know how to get in, maybe you don't belong there.

Exclusive, she says.

He shrugs. But it's clear to her that he likes the idea of getting into an exclusive joint. Of an outsider belonging. He takes her into a courtyard and through an unobtrusive door. The Garden Door he calls it. Inside, the place is crowded with tables but not many patrons. "We're early," he tells her. "It's usually packed in here." And she can't tell whether he's disappointed or relieved.

"Grab a table," he says. "I'll get us a couple of drafts. Uh, you have a preference?"

"No," she tells him. "You pick."

She slips into a corner table tucked into a long upholstered banquette and takes out her cigarettes. The lighting is diffuse, intimate. The walls around her are plastered with the dust jackets of famous novels and portraits of famous writers. She lights up as Tyrell returns with two tall glasses.

He raises his beer as the foam sinks to the bottom in a stream of bubbles. "Cheers," he offers.

She raises her glass to meet the salute. "To the victor of Washington Square," she toasts, and Tyrell smiles in a modestly dignified way. He really is an excessively handsome man, this Mr. Williams. It's easy to see why Naomi is so crazy for him. But when Rachel tries to coax more about the game from him—How long have you been playing chess, Mr. Williams?—something has changed. Their connection has become more stilted, more self-conscious.

He shrugs and tells her how he first learned the game from his stepdad when he was six. He grins as he recalls the first time he beat the man. How his stepdad didn't speak to him for days, but then how Tyrell would spy him studying the chess books after supper, and finally the chess board came back out. "You're black." He imitates his stepdad's gruff voice. "And *I* thought—'Well, I believe I *know* that by now, Pap.'"

He laughs at the story, and so does Rachel. But something has definitely changed. For both of them. Sharing this booth, separated by beer glasses, suddenly words don't seem to come so easily. She inhales smoke and glances up at the rafter beams lined with framed book covers.

"You like this place," she says.

"Yeah, I guess it holds its appeal for me. I read all the time growing up. For a minute or two, when I was in high school, I even thought maybe I'd like to be a writer."

"*Really?*"

"Yep. Sent out some stories to some magazines. But, you know, they were all about growing up back in Chisolm," he says. "In any case, stories about Negroes from the neighborhood were not at the top of the list for publication," he says, and then he smiles without mirth. "Or maybe I just stank at writing. That could be true too.'" He shifts the concentration toward her. "So. You're an artist, I hear. A painter."

"That is what you hear?"

"Naomi says you're very talented."

"Naomi likes encouraging people."

"Yes," he must admit with half a smile as he pulls his pack of Chelseas from his shirt pocket. "She does at *that*." He lights up and then there's that silence again, awkward and gawky, separating them and yet coiled with its own brand of urgings. "Do you feel uncomfortable?" he asks her.

"Uncomfortable?"

"Sitting here in public. Sharing a booth with a Black man."

"No. I simply feel uncomfortable in the world. The oysvurf."

"More Yiddish," he half smiles tolerantly. "What's that one mean?"

"Like an autseyder, only worse. An outcast. An oysvurf is a person with a dead soul."

Tyrell looks concerned at this. He doesn't say anything, but what *can* someone say to that? And why did she say it in the first place? Maybe it's the beer. The beer she is drinking has hit her. Not like a hammer, but it's hit her. Or maybe it would be more accurate to say that it's mugged her. A popular word. It's given her a quick punch in the head and robbed her of her ability to properly defend herself against the world. She lights another cigarette, only to have Tyrell point out that she's got one burning in the ashtray.

The tables are filling in around them, and a comfortable grumble of conversation floats in with the growing cloud of cigarette smoke. She feels her mouth loosen. She's talking. Talking and talking, she can hear her own voice as if she's listening in from the next room. Eavesdropping on herself. What's more, she seems to be speaking any words that come to mind. Her eema. The greasy smell of oil paint. The solid wall of a white canvas. The Magen David slopped on across a bakery window in Berlin. The foggy existence of their U-boat days. The hiding places. The deprivation, the fear. The necessity of remaining invisible.

"So I have compulsions," she tells him. "For instance, I steal bread from the table. I must have a light burning to fall asleep," she says and looks at Tyrell, who is wearing an expression of quiet pity. "Don't look at me that way," Rachel tells him.

His expression does not change. "What way?"

"With pity. I hate pity. Not because I am too proud, but because I love it too much. Forget about consuming alcohol," she tells him and takes a swallow from her draft. "Pity is the superior intoxicant. I can get drunk on people's pity faster than on any beer. On any wine or whiskey." And then she says, "I'm sorry that my husband was offensive to you. He's not a bad man, just fearful."

Tyrell only shrugs in a small way. "Forget it. It was nothing, really, compared to what I get just walking down the street in Midtown. A Negro man in a suit and tie," he says. "I'm sure if I was wearing a door-man's livery or a chauffeur's cap, it would be dandy. But a nice suit with a nice tie and a solid shine on my shoes? It seems to incense a lot of white folks. Like I think I'm equal with them. Or worse, *better* than them."

"You sound embittered," Rachel observes.

Tyrell smokes. "Hard not to. I fight it, but it's tough." He shakes his head. "Maybe I'm *not* grateful enough for the life I have. My mother tells me I'm not, and she could be right. But what am I supposed to do? Here I am, sitting across from a white woman in a bar. In a place like *this*? In the Village? Maybe it's no big deal. *But.*"

"But?"

"But ask your husband if they'd let a Negro through the front door of the restaurant he manages."

Now Rachel frowns.

"Oh, maybe if I was Lena Horne, they might, but then only if I was on the arm of Walter Winchell. Otherwise, all the rest of us *colored folk* gotta enter through the service door, and that's *it*."

Rachel stares. Inhales smoke, then blows it out into a cloud that quickly dissolves.

"I used to think," he says, "that if I played along, you know? That if I was the good Negro. That if I served my country in the army. That if I went to college. That if I did all the right things to make myself the *right kind* of Black man, I'd break through. But that just *ain't* the case. And that's what keeps me angry, Mrs. Perlman. The stupidity of it."

Rachel wonders. "Do you say these things to Naomi?"

"Do I?"

"It's none of my business."

"No, but you're asking anyhow." He inhales smoke. "Sometimes. Mostly we pretend, though, like it's not a problem. Like there *is* no problem. Just like we did during supper that night. And sometimes when we're together, when it's just the two of us, I can even believe it."

Rachel absorbs this and then asks him, "Do you love her?"

"Love?"

"Are you in love with her?"

"Is she in love with me?"

"I don't know. Is she?"

"She says so," Tyrell replies.

"But you're not so sure?"

"I am mistrustful."

"Of her?"

"Of the word. Of the concept," he says. "But yes. I think I do. Love her."

"Good."

"Is it?" he says. "I wonder."

"Because she's white?"

"Because I'm not. Because sometimes I think that our *relationship* is more about her wanting to shock the people in her world. About thumbing her nose at her childhood. Her family. Her *brother*." He expels a cloud of smoke and shrugs. "And I get that. It's not like *my* people are too damn pleased about me seeing a white girl either. My aunties like to murder me every time the subject comes up. And it *does* come up," he says, his half smile returning. "My old man thinks I'm looking to get lynched. And my sister, Chloe, says that it means I must hate my own race. Or at least that's how the *white man* will see it—as evidence that even *Black* men think that Negro women aren't good enough for them."

"But none of that is true?" Rachel asks.

Tyrell fastens a look on her. "No. I met a woman who makes me feel good. And I wanted to be with her. That she was *white*?" He says this as if he's asking a question to the air. To the world. "It didn't matter. But I don't imagine..." he says next. "I don't imagine that we have much of a future. Greenwich Village is a quirky place. But it *ain't* the world. And the world is like a hammer always pounding away. Honestly? I'm not sure that I'm strong enough. Or that *she's* strong enough. That what we have between us is strong enough to survive the inevitable punishment. I mean, can you picture it?" he asks. "Naomi and me showing up on your mother-in-law's doorstep with a couple babies in the pram?"

"Only if you're raising them Jewish," Rachel tells him just to amuse. "And of course, you'd have to convert as well."

"Oh yeah?" That half smile.

"There *are* Black Jews. In Abyssinia, I think. Some came once to Berlin when I was a girl. They consider their royal line to be descended directly from King Solomon and the Queen of Sheba."

"*Well*," Tyrell says, carving a bit of ash from his cigarette on the rim of the ashtray. "I am not Abyssinian, nor to my knowledge am I descended from any kings or queens." He picks up his glass and downs the rest of his beer, leaving only a web of foam at the bottom. By this point, any ebullience at his victory over Yaakov has dissipated. "I should probably hit the trail," he decides.

But Rachel feels that she doesn't want him to go. Sitting here in this bar with him has taken her out of herself in a way that she finds liberating. She feels shielded from the judgment of the world in Tyrell's presence, regardless of how the world judges them sitting together in this booth. Perhaps that's why she makes her sudden confession. To keep him here. To keep the small bubble they are sharing intact, at least for a little longer. Or perhaps it is simply her *need* to confess that Tyrell has triggered. Her desire to purge herself of the shame she carries, one autseyder to another.

"I betrayed a young girl who was in hiding from the Nazis," she says, spilling out the words. "She was a Jewish girl *just like me*. And I sent her to her death."

The sentence separates them and entangles them both, as if she has just dumped a bale of barbed wire on the table. Tyrell's face is caught in a look of confusion and dread, as if maybe he hasn't quite heard what he's just heard. So she repeats herself. "A Jewish girl whom I picked out of a crowd in a café. A schoolgirl. I didn't know her name. I didn't know anything about her. Only that I felt, at that instant, as if she was my *opponent* in a terrible game, and that between us, the loser of the game was going to die."

Tyrell looks at her as if he is staring into the scene of a disaster. A car wreck. A train wreck. A plane wreck, where there are obviously no survivors.

Rachel comes home to find Aaron not manning the cash register at work like his father but sitting at the kitchen table drinking Ballantines and playing cards with, of all people? Cousin Ezra the Fucknik. "Hey there, buttercream," her husband greets her.

"What happened?" Rachel asks, hanging up her coat.

Aaron glances away from his cards. "What happened?"

"Why aren't you at work? Did another water main break?"

"Nope. Milton Berle walked into the joint, and suddenly Leo had to be the man in charge. So I said fuck it, let Uncle Milty deal with him, I'm going home. So I bumped into Ignoramus here, and he begged me to beat him in a couple hands of Michigan rummy."

"Begged?" says Ezra. "*Challenged* is more like it."

Rachel doles out a small kiss on the lips for Aaron and scrapes a chair up beside him. "Either way, it's more than I can ever do," she tells Ezra and sorts the cards in her husband's hand for him. "He never plays cards with me."

"So *why* do you taste like a brewery?" Aaron asks.

"I told you."

"No, don't think you did."

"Well, I had a beer today, if that's a crime. And *I* don't taste like a brewery any more than you do. Play your two sixes," she suggests.

Aaron flops down the cards and slips one from the draw. "I mean, who… *Why* were you drinking a beer?" And then he says it. "Never mind. Let me guess. *Naomi*."

Rachel doesn't lie; she simply doesn't correct him.

"Great." Aaron pulls a frown. "Now my *sister* is getting my *wife* schnozzled in the middle of the day."

"I am not *schnozzled*," Rachel replies. "You've got a pair of deuces."

"I can see that I've got a pair of deuces, thank you very much." And *she* can see that even the mention of Naomi has gotten under her husband's skin. "I don't know why she thinks it's okay to be knocking back a few just whenever the urge strikes her. Shouldn't she be working?"

"Why are you getting so upset?"

"I'm not getting upset. I just don't get it. Why can't Naomi just have a normal life, *huh*? Just a normal fucking life like everybody else?"

"Hey there, Sergeant Perlman," Ezra interjects. "Let's not get stupid over this, okay?" he suggests.

"Mind your own business, Ezra," Aaron snaps back. "Just for a change of pace." He stews in silence for a minute, then slaps down the pair of deuces. "Besides. You think *I'm* the one getting stupid? Of the two of us, who's down a hundred and twenty points?"

"A hundred and ten," Ezra corrects. "And I'm letting you win."

"Yeah? Well, how stupid is that?"

Ezra only shrugs. "Der oylam is a goylem," he answers. The world is stupid.

Rachel has extracted a cigarette from Aaron's pack of Luckies and reaches for the green glass ashtray. She lights up from Aaron's Zippo and peers at his hand again. She has a desire just to be nearer to him. Maybe because she feels guilty for lying to him, or rather *not telling him the truth* about Tyrell and the beers she drank. But why stir him up again? Let him be mad at Naomi instead of her; he'll get over it. She should be satisfied to allow the air to settle between them, because what she's really thinking about is her confession. The admission of her crime.

She was honestly shocked at how quickly Tyrell attempted to let her off the hook. Maybe it was the lawyer in him on the lookout for a defense, for a loophole. She had been no more than a child herself when it happened, he'd pointed out. How old was she? Only sixteen? That's still a child. A child suffering under a crushing amount of pressure. She was not the criminal in this situation. She was a child wrongly forced by an immoral adult to make a choice that she should never have been faced with. A choice between life and death.

Yes, Rachel had agreed. A terrible choice. Her life for a girl's death. Why? How is it that such unforgivable choices are given? Perhaps she'll never know. Or perhaps Ezra has actually provided the answer to her question. The simplest answer possible. Der oylam is a goylem.

The world is stupid.

23.

A Man Forgets His Wallet

Love. So complex. So organic, it can grow or die. It can drug a person, elate or poison them. Or both. Rachel thinks about her mother. Eema held love in contempt but never stopped hunting for it. Never stopped mixing it into her palette. It radiates from her portrait of the red muse.

Looking into the bathroom mirror that night, preparing for bed, Rachel can see her eema's face. Not from a spectral image but in her own reflection. In the eyes? The shape of the mouth? The cheekbones, less plump and more etched? The older she becomes, the more of her mother shows up in the mirror. She carries the resemblance as a burden of memory. She is responsible for maintaining not only her own face, but the face of her eema. The face of the dead. Dressed in her flannel nightgown, she rubs Phoebe Snow greaseless cold cream onto her skin, forming a mask, while Aaron noisily scrubs his teeth in his pajamas.

"Do you think that some women are born to be lesbian?" she asks him.

His mouth is foamy, and he unplugs the toothbrush long enough to spit some toothpaste and squint at her in confusion. "Do I *what*?"

Rachel repeats the question. "*Do you think* that some women are born to be lesbian? Or do you think being a lesbian is a decision?"

"How the hell should I know?" He returns to brushing with extra vigor and then spits. "And do you have to keep using that word?" He slurps water from his palm to rinse.

"*Lesbian?* Why, you think it's like a magical spell? If I speak the word, I become one?"

"Prob'ly not, but why risk it?" Aaron shrugs, wiping his hands, then balling up the hand towel to wipe his mouth.

Rachel starts removing the excess cream with a Kleenex. "In Yiddish, there's not even a word," she says.

"Really? And here I thought Yiddish had a word for everything," he tells her. He bares his teeth in the mirror to check that there's nothing been missed. "Why are you asking me this? Have you been reading one of those crazy Village rags again?"

"Just wondering."

"Okay. Well, ya got me. I've never known one in my life. I mean, not a lot of lesbians in Flatbush, I don't think. Though God knows I've met a couple of real ballbusters."

"You think lesbians are ballbusters?"

"I dunno, honey. You asked, I answered." He gulps a mouthful from the bottle of Listerine and winces at the burn, swishing it around as if he'd like to rinse the entire conversation from his mouth, then spits out. "Can we talk about something else, maybe?" he wonders. "Something less creepy, like the atom bomb or tuberculosis?" One final inspection of his bared teeth, then he gives Rachel a squeeze and a peck on the neck before he wanders out of the bathroom.

"You know, I use this bottle of Listerine too," she calls out after him. "Now it is full of my husband's germs."

"It's mouthwash," he calls back. "It *kills* germs. Read the label."

——◆——

In Berlin, life as a U-boat is an erratic journey. Unpredictable day to day, moment to moment. They are on the move again, Rashka and her eema. The Aryan whose root cellar they were hiding in has demanded more money. Either more money or permission to rape Rashka. He was a smelly old party comrade who ran a butcher shop above them. Rashka heard him make his proposition to her mother. He wasn't shy about it. "Either another three hundred," he said and tossed his head in Rashka's direction, "or a taste of the girl. But only if she's a virgin. It's bad enough I must dirty myself with a Jewess, so she must at least be chaste. I won't be soiled by a slut."

The look on her eema's face as the man spoke? It was like she was Lot's wife the instant before she calcified into a tower of salt.

"I'll get you the money," Eema said flatly, her voice losing all its tone. But Rashka knew she wouldn't. *Couldn't.*

Perhaps even the party comrade knew this, because he frowned morosely at Rashka standing in the corner of the cellar, arms clasped in front of her waist. "One or the other," he said, "when I come back tonight."

And so they had vacated the butcher's cellar immediately and were walking through their shoes again on Berlin's pavement. The winter had been cold but at least bereft of heavy snows, as if all of Germany's allotted snowfall had been sucked east to freeze the armies entrenched outside all those Russian cities they had not managed to conquer. It had given Rashka some little satisfaction that if *she* was cold, think of the thousands of good Nazi killers shivering in their boots in a Soviet icebox.

But only a little satisfaction.

Days and nights. Weeks turn to months. A fledgling Berliner spring is peeking through the gloom. By midday, the sun is yellow and bright and warming the streets. Winter recedes, revealing a shabby wartime town stripped of joy by shortages and surreptitiously disheartened by a growing yet unspoken fear. The unspoken fear of defeat that is underscored by the bombing raids launched by the so-called British Air Pirates. Though oddly, Rashka feels safest when the bombers invade the skies, sending the population scrambling underground. The U-Bahn stations become air raid shelters, and nobody much questions who's an Aryan and who might be a Jew when the world above them is being hammered by tons of high explosives.

But raids on Berlin continue to be spotty at this point, like occasional heart attacks. Gestapo men checking papers indiscriminately are more of a threat than bombs to U-boats. Berlin, after all, has been declared "Jew-free" by no lesser a personage than the Little Doctor himself, Reichsminister Goebbels. How embarrassing would it be for him to find that it's not quite the truth. This is her feter Fritz's little joke, spoken in a low whisper as they share a table in a café up the Friedrichstrasse. Eema, as usual, is mortified by his little jokes and glares as if she has just stepped on a nail but must keep quiet about it. Feter Fritz gives his niece a conspiratorial wink, sharing his little joke with her, even at Eema's expense. Those small moments of power over Eema? Rashka appreciates them, though without her uncle there, she is without a scrap of power. She is a piece of luggage that must be lugged.

And so it goes. From hour to hour, day to day, week to week. Rashka loses her sense of days. Monday? Tuesday? Thursday? Who knows? But her sense of hours, even of minutes passing, sharpens. Each hour spent in an attic, cellar, toolshed, or U-Bahn station is distinct. Each minute divergent from the rest, spent in silence inside a closet or an empty flat. Calculable and stowable. Sitting so very still so as not to prompt a floorboard to creak and alert the neighbors belowstairs. She has found a discreet silence in herself, a silence that is so powerful, she has *become* the silence and otherwise doesn't exist at all.

Her mother finds them shoes. They don't fit. They're too small and pinch Rashka's toes, but they're better than the shoes they have, which have separated at the soles and flop like lazy crocodile jaws. Also there's a woolen dress that's too big, but at least it's not going to tatters. Food is usually a few moldy potatoes often eaten raw with a package of Knackebrot, or—on the rarest of occasion—a wax-sealed pot of processed "meat." Sunlight is often something that is only remembered or hinted at through cracks in leather-faced blackout curtains or painted-over windowpanes. This ghost existence between the dimensions of oblivion and daily life carries them through summer and into the autumn when, in the course of two nights, the British RAF rains down the fiery lightning of Zeus upon Fortress Berlin. It's bombing on a new and devastating order that will soon become routine.

In two nights, the Café Romanisches is blasted to pieces. The Kaiser Wilhelm Memorial Church is reduced to the charred stump of its tower. The KaDeWe department store on the Ku'damm explodes when a downed bomber crashes through the roof. The vacant New Synagogue in the Oranienburger Strasse is crushed to jagged rubble. A gasworks in Neukölln ruptures in a gust of flame. The raids produce all these terrible landmarks of destruction, but what is more important to Rashka and Eema is that a Tommy incendiary strikes the building where they are held prisoner by their Jewishness and spills flaming thermite over the tar-paper rooftop. In the chaos of good Germans escaping the fire, even a pair of U-boaters manage to save themselves. They will find shelter on the second night of bombing by joining the thousands inside the thick concrete fortress of the Zoo Flak Tower. The 88-millimeter flak cannons on its fortified rooftop are like the hammer of God above them.

All these things Rashka is teaching herself to accept. Teaching herself to absorb them into the silence that is enlarging her from within, armoring her heart. Turning *her* into a fortress. Fortress Rokhl.

⌁

Aaron has called her at home. He's forgotten his wallet somewhere in the apartment. He could borrow a couple of bucks from Leo, but how wonderful would that be? God knows what might happen. Leo might start pulling out wads of cash from his twenty-four-karat money clip. "'What? Boychik? You need taxi fare?'" Aaron mimics. "So other than mooching a subway token off Smitty at the door, I got nothing." Not a crisis, but does she think maybe she could bring it by before she sees what's-his-name the shrink? It's probably on the bureau top. Or maybe it's still in the pair of pants he wore yesterday, the brown ones that he hung over the chair.

She finds it in neither of those places but on the floor of the bedroom. Yet she understands. A man out in the strife of the world without his wallet? It's emasculating. So she slips it into her purse.

Before her hour with Dr. Solomon, Rachel takes the I.R.T. Broadway Line uptown to the restaurant. "Good afternoon, Mr. Smith," she says to the doorman. He afternoon-ma'ams her in return, smiling blindly and tipping a salute off the peak of his cap. It's obvious that he does not recognize her as anyone but yet another white woman for whom he is hired to hold the door. Lunch rush is over, so the tables are mostly empty or being cleared by the busmen. A few show people from the Winter Garden sit at the bar drinking Kahlúa and coffees, kvetching over this or that review or casting call.

She is surprised, however, to find Leo installed at Table 27. It's early for him, isn't it?

"*Ketsl.*" He grins when he spots Rachel and kisses her on the cheek like an uncle. "Sit," he instructs in his graveled, intimate tone as he slips back into the booth. "You want some coffee? Or maybe a nice shot of cognac?"

"No. Thank you, Leo."

"Don't be silly. You need something. You're a bone. *Solly,*" he tells the balding waiter who has appeared to refill Leo's coffee cup. "Get Mrs. Perlman a cognac and slice of the French apple cake, will you?"

"Sure, Mr. Bloom," says Solly, finally back from Miami but without a tan, capping the dirty ashtray and leaving a clean one in its place. "And how are *you*, Mrs. P.?"

"I'm fine, Mr. Kolinsky, thank you. How are you?"

"Good, good," he says, quickly lighting Rachel's cigarette the instant she draws one from her pack.

"Thank you," Rachel tells him before he smilingly vacates.

"So out shopping?" Leo inquires. He is hunched forward, elbows on the table as he pops two fresh sugar cubes into his coffee.

"Shopping?"

He stirs his cup. "Yeah. Though I don't see any bags. God knows, when Gloria goes shopping, she needs a truck to carry it back." Shopping, Rachel realizes, is the only thing that Leo can conceive of a woman doing out and about in the city during the day. So she doesn't correct him.

"Uh, I didn't find anything I liked," she says. It also makes it easier to explain her arrival here. She can keep the forgotten wallet a secret and avoid wads of cash appearing from a golden money clip. "How *is* your wife, by the way?" His second wife, Gloria, is a trim, fierce woman in her forties with beauty-parlor blond hair and a smoky voice, mother of two out of three of his children.

Leo shrugs in mild despair. "Gloria? Upstate since October," he announces. "She likes the season up there. You know, the leaves and whatnot. And since the kids are gone, she goes up by herself. I could get run over by a bus, she don't care"—he grins crookedly—"so long as it don't interrupt her nature hikes. Suddenly, she's a crazy woman about nature. Completely tsedrait!" He takes a drink from his cup. Go figure. "So what's news with the lovely Mrs. Perlman, huh? Painting any masterpieces?"

Rachel swallows. She knows that Leo actually means well with this question. What could she paint if not a masterpiece, right? So talented. But she cannot even manage a spurious response. The question pains her. "No, not at the moment" is her only response. "But I have a question for *you*, Leo," she hears herself say. Honestly, she had no intention of bringing this up. No intention of trying to test Tyrell's theory. Maybe it's simply to deflect any further questions about masterpieces. Maybe it's that she happens to notice the young, dark-skinned man in the white busman's jacket clearing a table of dessert dishes and coffee cups. "Do you have a policy about seating Negroes?"

Leo looks like she just started speaking to him in gibberish. "Do I got a *what*?" he asks.

"A *policy*," Rachel repeat. "About seating Negroes."

"What kinda policy? I don't know what you're asking me here, ketsl. 'Policy'?" He smiles at the word. "What I gotta 'policy' for?"

"It's simple. If a Black man comes through the front door and asks to be seated? Would you seat him?"

"Well." Leo shrugs, frowns at the tablecloth, tugs his earlobe. A man trying to be diplomatic as well as evasive. "I don't know where this is coming from, sweetheart. You think I have a *policy* about what if a colored guy comes in for a table?" He puffs his cheeks and gives a slow shrug, as if it hurts his shoulders. "I suppose, if it's a private party, we take everybody in through the Forty-Sixth Street entrance anyhow, so I would say, what's the harm? One or two of the party members ain't exactly Caucasian? I say, *so what*? It's my place. I can do what I want."

"But a Black man couldn't get in through the Eighth Avenue door, if he and his wife, say, just wanted dinner before curtain time. Abe wouldn't seat them."

"Cognac and a slice of French apple cake for the lady," Solly announces in a pleasant rasp as he sets the snifter and plate in front of Rachel.

"Sol, remind Abe, would ya? The Goodricks are my party this evening, if I forget to mention."

"Will do, Mr. Blume," says Solly, and he is gone.

Rachel inhales a breath and repeats herself. "Abe wouldn't seat them."

Leo frowns as he sips from his coffee cup, then sets it down with a clink on his saucer. "Look, ketsl," he says. "You think I care about skin color? Black, white, yellow, purple? I don't care. God made the universe, so he made the coloreds too, as far as I'm concerned. But you gotta *understand*." And he says this carefully. As if he is cautious to put it in comprehensible terms. "It's the *public*. The customers," he explains. "Maybe *I don't* care about black, white, or purple, but the *public*? They do care.

"So if I tell Abe to seat some colored boy and his wife, then you know what happens? Every table around them gets up and leaves—fargreser a ayln out the door. And if I keep telling Abe to seat them, then pretty soon the colored boy and his wife are the only customers I got left, 'cause everybody else's standing on line outside Sardi's. Without the public, this room goes dark. Without this room, I'm on my way to the poorhouse, and *everybody's* outta work. Including, God forbid, your husband."

"All that," Rachel says, "because a Black man sits down at a table for some salmon soufflé?"

A shrug. The way of the world. "I don't make the rules. That I leave to God."

"So it's God who won't seat Negroes? Wasn't that the same thing the Nazis said about us? That God wanted to punish the Jews."

"I don't pretend to know, ketsl. I don't pretend to know. All I can say is that I do what I do to keep a roof over everybody's head." A shrug slumping his body slightly, opening his hands. "You should take a taste of that cognac. It's Courvoisier. Good stuff. Two bucks a pop."

Rachel picks up the snifter and runs her finger around the rim. "Thank you, Leo," she says. She gets it. Waste not, want not. Otherwise Solly's going to have to try to pour it back into the bottle with a funnel. So she takes a large swallow. It burns smoothly, like heated licorice.

But Leo's face has sagged. His expression is weighted, and the usual mask of gritty charm seems to have slipped as he leans forward carefully. His voice has gone low. "You gotta understand something," he says, the normal bemusement in his eyes drained. "I can't say what happened to you exactly. What you went through with the war and whatnot. I can't say 'cause I don't know. I wasn't there. I was *here* busting my tuchus trying to get this joint on its feet. But I've heard the stories.

"You gotta understand," he says, "that what *happened* to our people? What happened to *you*? It shouldn't have happened to a dog, much less a little girl like yourself. Entsetzlich! Utterly unspeakable. But nothing particularly new. The white man's been trying to drive the Jew into firepits for thousands of years. The Nat-zees?" he says, and he hangs the *t* onto the *z*. "They just did a better job of it than the rest. More efficient, like their accursed race. Four million, five million, six million? Who could survive it?

"So all I'm sayin' is… What you went through? It ain't nothing to be ashamed of," he tells her. "It means you beat the bastards at their game. All these jokers come back from the war with geegaws on their chest, this medal, that medal. None of that's important. It's life that's important. You're *alive*, ketsl," he says. "Don't let those farshaltn Nat-zees take that away from you. They tried to stamp you out, but you spit in their faces. Every breath you take, you spit in those evil butchers' faces. You know? You sent them to the devil! You're a Jew. You beat the white man's odds. *That*, to me?" he says. "Is something to celebrate."

Rachel gazes at him, gripping the snifter of brandy. Then Leo is suddenly turning to the aisle. "Hey, hey"—he grins—"it's the boss man himself." Rachel quickly wipes her eyes and collects herself back into one piece.

"Yeah, boss man of my ass," says Aaron. "Leo, Chef Boy-ar-dee in there wants you to come taste the chowder."

"What, I'm the cook now too?"

Aaron shrugs. "Whattaya want me to do? You made it into such a federal case about the Tabasco last week that he wants you to taste it before we start dishing it out."

"Fine." Leo surrenders with a frown. "Chief cook and bottle washer," he tells Rachel with a wink, back to his old self. "Sit," he tells Aaron. "Talk to your wife, why don't you?"

Aaron slumps into the booth. "So thanks for coming up, honey," he says confidentially. "You got it, right?"

"I got it." She nods and opens her bag, dispensing the forgotten wallet to its owner.

"Thanks," he whispers and shifts to stash it in his right rear trouser pocket. "So I see you got the French apple cake treatment," he observes.

"With the Courvoisier."

"Impressive. That's two bucks a pop."

"So I heard," Rachel says. He looks exhausted already, and the place hasn't even opened for dinner.

Dragging the plate of cake over to himself, Aaron picks up the fork and digs in blankly. "God, this thing is good," he says, chewing, but without any particular enthusiasm. "I could eat this forever."

And in that moment, she wants to seize him. She wants to give herself to him atop Table 27. To give him babies, to lose herself in him. But then she sees that schoolgirl with the burgundy beret has inserted herself into the booth beside him, the ragged little U-boat girl, who looks up hungrily with hollow-socketed eyes dark with death. *No cake for me?* those eyes ask.

24.

What's Done Is Done

HER SESSION WITH DR. SOLOMON? IT DOESN'T GO WELL. HE keeps asking her questions that she does not wish to answer. Have you thought of painting? Yes, I've thought of it. And? And I keep thinking about it.

"Really? Because it seems you're rather tangled up with other issues. Your husband. Your sister-in-law's boyfriend. Racism in our nation," he says.

"And racism isn't an important issue?"

"Of course it is. But," says the good doctor, "it's not helpful if you're using it as a distraction."

"Distraction?" As if the word makes no sense.

"A distraction from *other* troubling issues that you're facing."

Rachel pulls a face that indicates just how silly, how very, very silly such an idea sounds to her. "Oh. So you think I have something to *hide*, Dr. Solomon?"

"What I'm saying? And forgive the bluntness. But racist remarks from your husband did not put you into a hospital straitjacket."

"I think I'm not feeling very well, Doctor," Rachel suddenly says, eyes steaming as she glares at the rug. "You'll pardon me if we end early today."

At home, Rachel is confronted by the empty canvas. But that night, she says, "I've been thinking about what you said. If he was a German."

"Look, I overstepped."

"If it had been a German with Naomi. You're correct, I would have felt differently. But as far as that goes? Your comparison of my feelings about Germans to yours about Negroes?"

"I don't have 'feelings' about Negroes, *okay, honey?*"

"Negro people," she says, "did not send *anyone* to the gas chambers. In fact, *they* were once enslaved even as Jews were once enslaved."

"So I *apologized*," Aaron is telling her. "I'm sorry that they were slaves a hundred years ago, but it's not like I had anything to do with that."

"If I hate the Germans, it is only because Germans are murderers."

A shrug. "Okay. The Nazis certainly *were*, yes," Aaron offers. "No argument there. And I'm no great fan of the Krauts in general either. But seriously, do we have to make them *all* into Hitlers and Himmlers?"

"Why not? Of course, I know there were French Nazis too. And Dutch Nazis, and Hungarian Nazis, and English, and Italian, and Ukrainian, and even *American* Nazis. I know this. And they could all be complicit, or they could all be murderers themselves. Killing Jews has been a sport for centuries. Who doesn't know that? But only the Germans stoked the crematoria. Only *they* made it an industry."

"Look, what you went through? Losing what you did? It was"—he shakes his head over the inadequacy of words—"*horrific*. But does it mean that all Germans are murderers? The SS were criminals, true. No argument. But weren't they a *little* different from the regular dope on the street? That's all I'm sayin'. Must we make the building super out to be Julius Streicher?"

Rachel shakes her head and drops her eyes to the floor. Really, she is just waiting for Aaron to stop talking. If that ever happens. This is the big argument that Americans like to put forth. That there were *good* Germans. Even good *Nazis*, or at least Nazis who were not murderers. The scientists, for instance. The physicists. The anti-Communists. The *useful* Nazis, who were "denazified." Only America could come up with such a concept as "denazification." Those denazified Nazis have been exonerated to defend against the Communist onslaught. Exonerated, though not by her. Not for the first time she says, "You don't understand."

They change into their pajamas in the bedroom. Quietly. Not much conversation. In the bathroom, she asks her husband, "So what made you so threatened by Negroes?"

Aaron stops dead in the middle of brushing his teeth. Rachel is rubbing cold cream onto her face, waiting for an answer. Aaron returns to his scrubbing, but only for a second before he spits desolately into the bowl of the sink. "I'm not 'threatened,' as you put it, by Negroes, Rachel. I've got nothing against one race or another. I just want that said out loud for the record. And this guy Tyrell? He's probably a decent guy. It's only I'd rather not have him as a brother-in-law." He rinses his mouth with water from the tap and spits again, then pats his mouth dry with a towel.

"You think Naomi wants to marry him?"

"Who knows what in hell my crazy sister wants?" is Aaron's answer. "I just believe that everybody needs to stick with their own is all. *Jews marry Jews*," he declares, cutting the air with his hand as if he is giving it a chop, cutting through any wishy-washy confusion on the subject. "That's all I'm saying. Jews marry Jews and have little Jews. Let Blacks marry Blacks and have little Blacks. It's the way nature intended."

"And you know this how?" his wife wonders.

Aaron frowns at the question. "Look, can we drop this, please? I just wanted to say what I had to say, and that's it. I don't need to be interrogated in my own goddamned bathroom, thank you very much." Claiming ownership of the spot where he stands. *My own goddamned bathroom. My own goddamned living room.* It's his way of trying to assert a kind of masculine authority over the moment. She's learned this.

He drops down onto the bed, holding his cigarette as he picks up an old *LIFE* magazine with Sophia Loren on the cover and starts paging through, glowering. Rachel is on the bed beside him, her legs tucked under her. "You think your mother knows?"

Aaron huffs at the thought of this. "Well, no mushroom clouds over Flatbush, so my guess is *not*," he says, then shakes his head. "But who knows? Who can guess? I can't figure Ma out anymore. Since the old man passed, she seems to have gone off the rails."

Silence for a moment as Aaron gazes ahead.

Then Rachel inserts, "I'm sorry."

A blink. "Sorry? For what? That your husband's an ass?" he asks, parking his cigarette in the ashtray.

"Yes, I'm sorry about that too," she says, leaning over him to steal his cigarette. "But that's not what I meant. I'm sorry you feel so lost. I know how that is."

Aaron frowns. "I've got nothing against the guy, Rach. How many times I gotta say that? Mr. Almost-a-Lawyer is prob'ly better than buttered toast. I just don't want trouble. I don't want another big crisis to have to deal with. And I'd like to know *why?*" he asks the air, his voice rising. "*Why* the hell *Naomi* has to try to bust my balls all the time."

Rachel tamps out his cigarette in her ashtray, then hooks his arm around her and rests her head against his shoulder. She likes the feel of his muscles. The shape and firmness of his body. "She's competitive. She thinks your parents always discounted her opinion because she was the girl."

"She said that to you?"

"No. But isn't it true?"

"Well, it's not like *my* opinion ever counted for much either." He closes the magazine and tosses it wearily to the floor. It's clear that his mind is grinding over some old family dynamic, but he doesn't say more, and Rachel doesn't ask. A quiet descends. The cat hops onto the bed and winds into a ball at Rachel's feet, only to shoot away when the telephone rings. Rachel feels her heart jump. Aaron turns and looks in the direction of the noise, not with his normal annoyance at the intrusion of the phone at such a late hour but instead with quiet resignation.

"You want me to get it?" he actually asks.

They have dashed back into their clothes and met Naomi at the police precinct on Charles Street. She doesn't sound as wildly frantic as she had over the telephone but is now fortified by her shock and seething. Her hair is out of its ponytail and twirled off her neck into a tight French twist, and not only is she wearing the same black pencil dress that she had leant Rachel, under a stylish wrap, but she's wearing *cosmetics*. Lipstick. Eyebrows shaped by a pencil, but even with mascaraed lashes, her eyes are as dangerous as vats of acid. "Fucking *racists*," she keeps muttering. "Fucking *shithead racists. This isn't Alabama*, ya' know!" she rails at a passing officer, who blandly ignores her. But Rachel physically tightens her grip on her sister-in-law's arms. Naomi shouting at uniformed policemen unnerves her, even though summary execution by pistol is probably rare even in the Village.

Aaron, meanwhile, has separated himself, the head of the family taking charge, talking to the police on a man-to-man basis, and Rachel understands that it is her job to keep the lid on Naomi, to stop her from turning this bad-enough shtunk into the shtunk of nightmares. "He'll be out soon," Rachel is trying to assure her, because what else can she say? "Aaron is writing the check for his bail, no problem. He'll be out soon, I'm sure."

"That's not the *point*," Naomi answers, though she doesn't seem to be speaking to Rachel directly. "That's not the fucking *point*. They had no right to arrest him. He was fucking *defending himself*, for Chrissake!"

Aaron returns to them, hands in the pockets of his overcoat. "Twenty-five bucks," he announces, as if it's the cost of fixing a set of leaking pipes, anticipated, necessary, but still nothing to smile about. "We should go downstairs, I'm told. That's where they release offenders."

"Offenders?" Naomi takes issue with the word. "Is that what you're really calling him? An *offender*?"

"Sorry." Aaron surrenders quickly, showing his palms, as if addressing a ticking bomb. "That was their word. I just repeated it."

Naomi frowns, her eyes heating up with tears, blurring her mascara. "Never mind. *I'm* sorry," she admits. "You came all the way down here and paid his bail without arguing. Thank you," she says.

A shrug with his hands hung back in his coat pockets. "Hey, what else am I gonna do, huh? So let's get the hell outta here."

Downstairs, a door clanks as it's held open by a white officer, allowing Tyrell to exit. He looks bruised, not just in his face but in his soul maybe. As if he is threaded together by a tattered, burdensome rage suppressed by an equally burdensome weariness. His lip is split. His cheek has taken a punch. He's dressed for an evening out, a suit under a Brooks Brothers overcoat, but his tie is missing, and his shirt collar is ripped. Naomi breaks away from Rachel and Aaron, rushing to Tyrell and seizing him in an embrace.

"*Thank God*," she whispers aloud. "*Thank God*."

Tyrell hushes her consolingly. "I'm fine. I am," he keeps telling her. "Really." But his reaction to her embrace, Rachel notes, is reticent. He gives her a squeeze in return but then deftly separates himself from her.

Naomi does not resist, though she is unwilling to release him completely and wraps her arm around his, walking him forward. "We should sue those bastards at the restaurant," she's insisting. "And that cop too. We should sue the whole fucking department for false arrest!"

Tyrell pats her arm as if to quiet her as much as console her. "We'll talk about this later," he instructs. "I've got to sign for my belongings," he says. "I'll just be a minute." This gives him reason to peel away from her, leaving her drifting. Rachel steps up and hooks her with her arm, guiding her away from the heavy oak bureau manned by a middle-aged sergeant with a chalky face.

"Bastards," Naomi is whispering to the air, scowling. Rachel hands her a clean handkerchief. "Thanks." Naomi sniffs. "But I'll get mascara all over it."

"So who cares about that?" Rachel asks.

Naomi purses her lips and wipes her eyes, smearing black over the white cotton. "I feel so fucking helpless. Furious but so fucking helpless."

"Yes. I know that feeling. But for now, we concentrate on getting Tyrell away from this place. That's all. More can come later," Rachel says.

Naomi nods again. "Thank you for saying that. And for swooping in when I called. Especially you, Brother," she says to Aaron, "for footing the bill."

Aaron shrugs. "No big deal. What was I doing but sleeping anyhow?"

Tyrell appears, unloading the contents of a large kraft-paper envelope onto a windowsill. Slipping his wallet into his coat pockets. A fountain pen. "Missing a cufflink," he inventories with a slight grimace of pain. "Got a lighter but no cigarettes. One wristwatch with a busted crystal," he says, then shakes it against his ear. "No longer ticking."

"Fucking *crooks*," Naomi curses. But in any case, Tyrell seems to take it in stride.

"Thank you, Mr. Perlman," he says to Aaron in a heavy, formal tone, "for coming down here at this hour and for paying my bail." But it's a heavy thank-you. Not a comfortable one. "I'll get it back to you tomorrow."

"No rush," Aaron replies, waving off any need for haste. "*Really*. Whenever," he says.

"I had actually told Naomi to call my *sister*," the man points out thickly. "But I guess she called her brother instead," he says. This is a sideline scold directed toward Naomi.

"Well, whattaya gonna do?" Aaron shrugs. "Families stick together." In other words, Jews stick with Jews.

But Naomi leans in. "Let's just get the fuck outta here," she injects with an exhausted urgency. She has regained Tyrell's arm and gives it a tug.

It is raining by the time they exit onto the street. Not a downpour yet, but certainly a hefty sprinkle. There's a metal bucket by the door, though, containing a handful of forgotten umbrellas with a hand-printed sign that reads LOST AND FOUND. "Ah, now will you look at *this*?" Aaron sounds pleasantly surprised as he selects a long, black item. "You want one too, Mr. Williams?" he asks.

"No, thanks," Tyrell assures him. He lifts his arm free of Naomi and separates himself, squinting at the rain as he turns up the collar of his overcoat. "So, Mr. Perlman, do you think you could see that your sister gets home?"

"Home?" Aaron repeats, sliding open the umbrella.

But it's Naomi who jumps in. "Wait a minute. What do you mean, *see that I get home*? I'm not leaving you," Naomi insists, pained confusion rising in her voice. "Not after all this shit."

But Tyrell acts as if he's gone deaf to her. "If you wouldn't mind, Mr. Perlman."

"Uh. Sure," Aaron replies. "Sure."

"*Tyrell*," Naomi squawks, and only now does he acknowledge her.

"It's late," he tells her inflexibly, placing his hand on her arm. "I have to be up early, so I need to get home and get some sleep. And I'll sleep *better* knowing you're home safe."

"Me? What about *you* getting home safe."

"I'll be fine," he insists. "Really. I'll call you tomorrow," he promises and then quickly seals his exit with a kiss on Naomi's cheek before stepping off the curb and trotting across the street, dodging past the lights of a car.

Naomi calls out his name and advances a step as if to follow him, but Aaron drops his hand on her shoulder and draws her under the umbrella. "Let 'im go, Naomi" is all he says.

"You know, I *woulda called his sister* except she scares the holy shit out of me. And I guess now I embarrassed him. *Fuck!*" she spits.

"Look, what difference does it make?" Aaron is quick to reply. "The bail is paid, and the man's outta the clink. Beside, what's so embarrassing?"

"What's so embarrassing is that I put him in the debt of a white man."

"Oh, is *that* what I am?"

"You bet it's what you are. I shoulda just fuckin' called Chloe like he wanted me to."

And now Aaron is frustrated that she is refusing to cast him as the hero of this story as she should be. The man who got out of bed in the middle of the fucking night to answer her call for help. The man who shelled out the money, not just for the bail—twenty-five bucks, a week's rent—but for how many taxi rides? "Okay, okay. Let's forget about who called who, all right? What's done is done. Let's just *go*, for cryin' out loud."

Two days come and then go. It rains. Aaron goes to work, comes home, and goes back out to work. When Rachel arrives at Naomi's apartment in the middle of the afternoon, she finds that it has returned to its normal state of chaos, except now the ashtrays are overflowing, and there are new cigarette burns on the old blue sofa. Empty bottles of beer stand abandoned on surfaces like lonely sentinels, and the centerpiece of the coffee table is a half-empty fifth of Smirnoff's. "I started out mixing martinis," Naomi explains, "but then thought, *fuck it*, who needs vermouth? Just fuckin' cut out the middleman, right?"

She's a mess. Her eyes sleepless and swollen. Hair in an untidy ponytail. Barefooted. She's thrown on a pair of baggy old dungarees with the cuffs folded up the ankles and a stained wool pullover. She also smells, not just of vodka but of a kind of grimy misery. "You sure I can't get you something?" she asks Rachel. "I mean, it doesn't have to be alcoholic. I think I've got a soda in the fridge. Or maybe I could put on the kettle for tea or something." She looks toward her miniature apartment stove where a steel kettle rests atop a burner, but her expression is glazed. As if a journey to the stove is a distant concept.

"No, no," Rachel assures her. "Really, I'm fine."

Naomi nods blankly. "So I guess you must have figured it out by now," she says, her eyes dropping shamefully to the coffee mug of vodka in her hand. "Tyrell," she says, speaking the name, but then she must pause and swallow. "He broke things off."

Rachel takes in a breath and expels it.

Naomi frowns, eyes still downcast. "He said," she begins, but then must stop and start again. "He said what happened at the restaurant. The fistfight. The police. Getting arrested. It just made him *realize* that we had no future. Not in the long run. And that…that it wasn't fair to *me*," she whispers, her voice beginning to disintegrate into tears, "to keep things going." She sniffs hard. Smears at her eyes and then kicks back a swallow of vodka from her mug. "That's *it*." She shrugs. "So I've been downing the mashke ever since."

"You should eat," Rachel instructs. "It's not good for you. You should eat. I could fix you soup," she says and starts to move from the sofa. The truth is, she doesn't do well dealing with other people's grief. She would feel more comfortable avoiding empathy by diving into action, even it's only emptying a can of Campbell's chicken and rice into a saucepan. But Naomi restrains her escape from the sofa with a hand.

"No. Please. Nothing. I'd only throw it up anyhow."

At home, over T.V. dinners but with no T.V., Aaron gloats in a fatalistic manner. "Well, it was bound to happen, honey. Can't say as I'm surprised."

"Nor can you say you're unhappy with it."

A frowning nod. "Now that you mention it," he concedes.

"She was in such deep pain," Rachel laments. "I didn't know how to help her. What to say."

A flick of a shrug as he dips his fork into the vegetable medley. "She'll get over it," Aaron assures her. "She's tough."

"She was also drinking. Heavily."

Another shrug. Maybe this one is less comfortable. "Well. I dunno. There were hints that we had an aunt on Pop's side of the family who was a bit of a boozehound. But nobody ever talked about it much, at least not in front of us kids. And anyhow, she lived to be eighty-something, so how bad could it have been?"

25.

You Must Earn Your Keep

S HE DREAMS THAT THE POLICE COME BANGING ON THE DOOR IN
the middle of the night to arrest her. Aaron keeps saying, *I told
you not to cut up that newspaper at the library, and now look—the cops
are here. My mother's gonna hit the roof!* He's saying this as he opens
the door, dressed in his pajamas. In come two giant men, not in the
blue uniforms of the N.Y.P.D., but in the green of the Reich's Grüne
Polizei. She tries to hide under the bed, but they drag her out. She
keeps screaming. Gevalt geshreeyeh! But then Aaron is replaced by
Feter Fritz wearing his secondhand shmatte with his bamboo cane. *My
hands are tied, ziskeit,* he tells her. *Your name is on the list.*

Rachel wakes up with a floating anger in her chest. It swells her throat.
Thank God that Aaron is at the Fulton Market that morning, so Kibbitz
is the only one who must suffer her mood. Wisely, he exits through the
fire escape window at his first opportunity. She's been thinking about
the painting. Stewing over it. The red muse. It angers her that it has
been stolen from her. Yes, those are the words. Stolen from her. The
coffee she drinks only serves to underscore her anger. Not even the
Miltown is a match for it.

She takes the Seventh Avenue Local uptown. The gallery is housed
in an elegant Upper East Side monolith of polished sandstone. The
G. Albert Glass Gallery of Fifth Avenue, universally known as the
House of Glass. She is surprised to find that the door is unlocked when

she tugs on it. Aren't they concerned that any vagabond might steal
into the temple? She steps inside, feeling her heartbeat rise. What does
she think she'll find? La muse du rouge on the wall restored to glory?
But no. It's a Chagall. The true Jewish artist, he is called. After all,
he was born Moishe Segal of Vitebsk. And God knows how many
prints she has seen of his wistful gouaches and watercolors depicting
dreamy Yiddish motifs from the shtetlakh of his childhood, all neatly
framed in doctors' offices and dental waiting rooms from Midwood to
Washington Heights. Even her mother-in-law has a lithograph of *The
Three Candles* in a frame over the dining room table in Flatbush.

But the dream is not always airy pastel washes for mass-market
merchandising. A plummeting red rocket hangs on the wall. An angel's
descent exploding the scene. A fiery seraph—*L'ange tombant*. The
Falling Angel. It took him a quarter century to paint. She'd read this.
Stretching from the twenties till after the war, and every year—she can
see it, it's so apparent to her—every year the raging destruction of the
earth stained and ignited the colors of the angel as it descended, till its
wings were burning red. Till its body was gorgeous with blood.

Chagall was an innocent, her mother tells her, wearing her paint-
stained smock. *Naive as a child. It's amazing that he survived himself,
much less survived the war. But that was his luck. Always in the wrong place
but never at the wrong time.*

A college girl in a black turtleneck, her blond hair in a boyish garçon
bob, approaches Rachel as if she is something that needs sweeping back
out onto the sidewalk. "May I help you?"

"Yes. I want to see Mr. Glass," Rachel tells her.

"Mr. Glass is not available."

"Tell him, please, that I'm the niece of Mr. Landau?"

"I'm *sorry*, but Mr. Glass is not available."

"Tell him I'm the daughter of Lavinia Morgenstern. She knew
Chagall. When he was in Berlin. Tell him I'm here to see *The Red
Muse*."

"The red?"

"My mother's painting. I want to see it. Is it in the back room? I could just take a peek."

"Uh, *no*. No, that's not possible."

"Just a peek, nothing more."

"I'm sorry, what did you say your name was?"

"Rachel Perlman. That's my name now. In America, but once, I was Rokhl Morgenstern. He knows my uncle—Mr. Glass, that is. I've seen them together in the photograph."

"As I said, Mr. Glass is unavailable. I'm sorry, but there's nothing I can do for you."

"I think they must have struck a secret bargain."

"And *I* think I'll have to ask you to leave."

"So I'm being polite. I'm being polite," Rachel tells her. "But you must understand. He had no right, my uncle. He thought he was still the great Kunsthändler, making his deals, but he had no right. That painting, if it belongs to anyone, it belongs to me."

"Miss, this is private property," the girl says.

"She was a monster. Der Engel. But if she is anybody's monster, she is mine. I paid for her in full. And now, you think you can deny me? Pretend that I am nobody? I am the daughter of Lavinia Morgenstern! The founder of the Berolina Circle of Artists! A member of the Prussian Academy!" She hears herself shouting at this young slip of a girl, whose eyes are now bright with fear at the onslaught of the crazy lady.

"I can call the police! If you won't go, I can call the police."

"Call the police! *I am an artist.* Don't you understand that? An *artist*! I have my rights too! That painting is mine! So tell the exalted Mr. Glass that he made his deal with the wrong Jew! Tell him that!" Rachel shouts and then abandons the room, sweeping back onto the sidewalk, her face streaming in tears. She hears the door lock behind her to keep out the mad interloper. But she doesn't look back.

Their last hiding place as U-boats is a bicycle repair shop in Berlin-Kreuzberg. The owner of the shop is dead, his body buried in some frozen corner of the Ostfront, but the widow, Frau Huber, is making a little on the side to supplement her pension payments by hiding the odd Jew or two in her dead husband's vacant shop. The windows are painted over for the blackout. It's one long room down a set of steps in the Falckenstein Strasse. The place has a grimy feeling to it and an odor of wood rot and machine oil combined with the reek from the stinking night pail. So—*a palace!* They are gaunt, underfed, and street-worn like most all U-boats. But then that could describe most Berliners by this point of the war, so their very shabbiness affords them some lumpen-proletariat camouflage when they venture out into the beyond.

They sit in the Café Bollenmüller up the Friedrich, her mother tensed, overtly watchful. As usual, Eema has brought Rashka along because the sight of a hungry child is the only leverage available to her to influence price. She has explained this to Rashka. Explained that her job in this transaction is to look pitiful and underfed. A little waif. Sometimes it works, other times not. If the seller is a woman, then maybe such tactics have a better chance of depressing the cost of the counterfeit ration cards or some small identity document, like a postal card, or whatever it is she is hoping to purchase. But Rashka is never very talented at this, and this time when she tries to present a sympathetically heartbreaking face, her mother is disappointed in the outcome. "Never mind," says Eema. "You look like you're farshtopt." Constipated. Blocked. "Just sit and think about nothing."

Rashka attempts to follow this instruction as they sit this time in the perilous calm of a café morning, not buying but selling. Eema is trying to sell the last of her mother's jewelry. A white-gold bracelet studded with tiny diamonds. A piece that dates back to the imperial epoch of the Österreich. Rashka tries hard to think about nothing. Nothing but a zero. A void. But still, thoughts intrude. She cannot help but look at the faces. Aryan faces? They look not so much different than they did before Aryans existed. Only paler. Thinner.

She cannot help but play a game. Who is the crooked-over old man blowing the steam from his cup? A veteran of the last war, maybe? Unmarried. Bitter because he could not recover from his wounds. She would paint him in blue and black with yellow eyes. Then there's the younger woman with the middle-aged man. They seem hardly connected, staring separately into the air as they consume their coffee and bun. Yet there is some link chaining them together. A marriage where love has been left behind? She would paint him in greens from shoes to hat and her all in yellows with purple lips.

When the buyer arrives, it's a man. A black marketeer. The rumor is he was a gem cutter in Antwerp, a diamantaire, run out of the business because of underhanded trading. But who really knows? People like to make up stories. They like the world to fit together, especially when *nothing* fits together any longer. He's a frowning, unhappy specimen, with a sagging face and eyes as sharp as drawn knives. All it takes is a glance under the napkin at the table for him to instantly size up the value of any piece of merchandise. He mumbles a price. Eema looks displeased. She frowns, using her mouth only. Her eyes remain the shiny black rocks into which they have hardened. "Please. It must be worth more than that," she insists.

The man only shrugs. Maybe it is, maybe it isn't.

"Those are diamonds," Eema points out. "*Diamonds*," she repeats.

"So find somebody else to buy them if you think I'm cheating you," the man suggests.

"I'm only asking. A few more marks? Couldn't you see your way? For the sake of the child."

Really, Rashka despises being used as an object of pity in these transactions. She breaks away from her mother's dealing and returns to the stories she's telling herself in her head, all inspired by the crowd around them. A woman abandoned by her husband? A man sick with a disease that he pretends is not killing him? But then she catches the eye of another girl. Across the room is a schoolgirl not much younger than her. Velvety brown eyes, creamy skin with a cool ash-green underpainting. Her sable hair is woven into a braid, and she wears a burgundy beret. Sitting with a wrinkled old grandpa who is lost in the consumption of a bowl of soup, the girl dares to offer Rashka a tentative smile. Rashka dares to smile back.

She will never know the girl's name. This small exchange of childish smiles beyond the strictures of their isolation will compose the sum total of their communication. But yet. For that instant, Rashka can spot the lonely yearning they share. She can recognize herself. Another solitary heart.

Meanwhile the black marketeer is unmoved by her mother's plea. The offer is the offer, take it or leave it.

On the day they are arrested, the sky is bleak with ashen clouds and a low, white winter sun. They have entered the Bollenmüller. An accordion player is busy with a crowd-pleaser called "Du, du liegst mir im Herzen." Seated at a table in the rear, they spend precious pennies on ersatz coffee and a cup of warm skim milk. Rashka tries to drink the milk slowly, but she can't. It feels like everyone is watching her, so she downs it in a few gulps before it can be snatched away.

Meanwhile, the coupon seller they are waiting on is not appearing. Eema has tacked her eyes to the door, watching intently as the woman doesn't arrive. Rashka knows that the few marks Eema earned from the sale of the bracelet, that small amount, composes their entire fortune, and that after it is spent, there will be nothing left. Eema has recently instructed her to start praying. "For a miracle," Rashka is told. A miracle that will feed them, fit them with new shoes, mend the holes in their clothes. A miracle that will suddenly conjure them out of danger with a wave of a hand by the Master of the Universe. He parted the Red Sea for Moses, didn't he? Why not a small-in-comparison miracle for them?

When the door creaks open from the street, Eema is drawn forward in her chair as if caught in the pull of a magnet. A dowdy Berliner Frau has finally appeared and taken the small round table nearest the door. She is not as watchful, this Frau, as black marketeers normally are. There is also something insular about her expression. Her posture is tense, hunched, but she is focused on her hands instead of the room. When she does finally raise her eyes long enough to speak a word to the waiter, Rashka spots a scab on the Frau's lip and a purplish bruise shadowing the under-crescent of her eye.

"What's happened to her face, Eema?" she whispers to her mother, but her mother has already locked Rashka out of her course of action. Her daughter is no more now that the sad mannequin Eema can point to, hoping to shave a few marks off the cost out of sympathy.

"Stay here, and don't *move*. Understand?" her eema commands, then stands, marching toward the Frau. The two women huddle together, crowding the small table. Watching from this distance, Rashka can see how Eema has lost her looks. What a tattered rag her mother has become! It makes her feel ashamed and prompts her to look away. It is by this accident of embarrassment that she catches the red-haired woman's gaze. A gaze that is at once dangerous and intimate.

Rashka has no defense against the resolve of those eyes. She can only stare back, even as this beautiful creature crosses the café, seating herself at Rashka's table with a scrape of a chair.

"Hallöchen, Liebling," the woman says with a smile contouring her bright-red lips. "Did your mummy leave you all alone?"

Rashka is both terrified by the woman's arrival and oddly thrilled by the attention. So beautiful! Beautiful even as the seven worlds!

And then the memory strikes her.

How could she ever discard the memory of those eyes? The eyes of the girl posing on a dais in Eema's studio? Rashka's heart bumps heavily. It's obvious that the woman does not recognize her any longer, but for Rashka, it's like reclaiming an icy dream. The eyes of la muse du rouge. She thinks she should call over to her eema, but to say what? *She is here! The girl you painted!* But she doesn't do this, because she is trapped. She cannot speak.

The woman puts her hand on Rashka's arm and asks, "Where is your star, Liebchen?"

Her mother abruptly returns, and Rashka is confused by what happens next. The expression on the beautiful woman's face chills deeply. "*Lavinia*" is all she says.

Eema looks as if she has opened a door on a tiger. She lurches forward and seizes Rashka by the arm. "*Please,*" she whispers in a raw voice, her eyes gone round. "*For the child.*" A drop of hesitation colors the woman's eyes. But there is already an operation in motion. A trap snapping shut.

Men in trench coats appear out of nowhere, pointing pistols. "Geheime Staatspolizei!" they announce. A slim, blond man in a leather trench is pleasantly impatient. "Time to go, little mice," he declares. "Off to your new hole."

Night passes without sleep for Rashka. They have been loaded into the rear of a black touring sedan in an all-business manner by two Gestapo men and driven over the Weidendammer Brücke to this place. What was once the Jewish home for the elderly but is now designated by the SS as the Grosse Hamburger Strasse Lager. The attic space is crammed full of other captives—all Jews without stars. A starless galaxy of misery in a claustrophobic room. The moans, the snoring, the weeping. These are the noises that serve as Rashka's lullaby on the night before they are scheduled for transport. Transport to the *east*, they were told by the men who appeared in gray coveralls, sporting yellow Judenstern and red armbands. Die Ordneren! The Jewish lager orderlies. They stayed only long enough to distribute the placards to be worn about the neck.

Her mother has drifted away. If not into sleep then into some version of waking slumber that separates her from the reality of the world. Sometimes her eyes are open, and she is staring like the dead stare. Rashka does not wish to cry. She does not want to be a weeping child. She has, therefore, taken a tool in hand. On the back of the transport card, she is scratching out a likeness of herself with the nub of a pencil from her pocket. She has no mirror, so she uses the mirror of her mind to draw her face. A dark, scratchy cartoon of a ragamuffin. A scruffy animal with oily moons for eyes. If she is to wear this piece of cardboard, T for Transport, if this is to be the sum of her identity, a transported Jewess, then she will mark it. She will make it hers. With the final strokes, she scores a six-pointed star on the forehead.

The morning comes. The Jewish orderlies arrive shouting instructions, bellowing in a mix of German and Yiddish. "All those for transport! Stand! Form a queue! Move! Move!"

Rashka can tell that her eema is starting to panic. Not in a hysterical manner. She is, after all, an honored member of the Prussian Academy of Arts and founder of the Berolina Circle. She is too grand for tears and screaming. No, Eema's panic is interior. It stiffens her movements. Hunches her attention. Curdles the color in her eyes. Her grip on Rashka's hand is stone. The queue is proceeding. The shambling assembly of those marked for the east.

But then. Then at the door.

"Not this one," the ordner with the scared face commands. "Or this one," he instructs his underling with a scowl, shoving first Eema and then Rashka from the queue.

Instead of being sent to the trains, they are led down a pair of narrow stairwells into the cellar. The stone and mortar foundation that comprises the wall is a cold color, not quite gray, not quite brown. That's what Rashka concentrates on as they are shoved into a room where the windows have been bricked over. The door is steel, painted a greasy black. It clanks closed. Silence between mother and child. And then the door clanks open just as it had clanked shut.

Eema jumps to her feet as if she has been shot up by a spring. "*Fritz!*" she shouts and seizes her brother with such vehemence that she nearly topples them both off their feet. Feter must pry himself free from her grip. He is thin and pale in the face. Clad in the gray coverall of an ordner, he bears the Judenstern, and his sleeve is banded by a red armlet.

"Listen, listen to me, Vina," he is telling her in Yiddish. "I want you to keep your head, do you hear me? Keep your head! You must keep yourself in check no matter what."

"*In check?* What to do you mean, Fritzl?" Eema is searching her brother's eyes for understanding, but Feter Fritz is dodging her efforts. "What do you mean, I must keep myself in check. In check for *what*? What is *coming*?"

The door clanks again.

And there she is. So immaculately dressed. So carefully coiffed. A fashion plate from *Die Dame*. Her hair in a bright-red sweep over her collar like a roll of fire. And for her eyes? Two lit emeralds.

Eema's face drains of expression.

"No need to fear, Lavinia," the woman says. "Perhaps I am no longer your muse, but I can be your savior. Only you must cooperate. You must swallow your pride for once and do as you are told. You are *not* the mistress of *this* house."

———

Rachel ignites a cigarette and watches the smoke rise. It curls slowly upward. She is telling Dr. Solomon about her mother. How her mother suffered after the loss of her husband.

Maybe it wasn't love between them. Maybe there was no enduring romantic passion. But to lose a companion? The only companion she had chosen for herself? She suffered because she was alone.

"But she had you," the good doctor points out. "Her child."

Rachel smiles grimly. "Me? I was only a burden. She needed someone to share her love of art. To share her love of herself, really. To hold the mirror for her genius. But I could not do that. A child was a constant distraction. She made that very clear to me. And my uncle? His admiration was too tainted by his commercial interests. Selling Eema's genius by the pound, you know? Like a commodity. No, my mother was lonely. *Very* lonely. Until…"

The doctor waits patiently. Until?

"Until," says Rachel, "her muse appeared."

She returns home in a drizzle. The stairwell is stuffy with the dampness of the day as she plods upward. Opening the door to their apartment, she is met by the sight of her husband stuffed into the gossip bench, talking again to his sister. Rachel listens and notes how, as usual, Aaron's tone has changed now that his wife has intruded. He is more public in his summation, wrapping things up. "Okay, okay, yeah. So anyhow, like I said. I just wanted to say, ya know, that I was sorry that things didn't work out for you and Tyrell, and I'm sorry for being a jerk to the guy."

He's looking at Rachel as if to say: *See?* I'm not a complete putz. "And look. I know he gave you the dough to pay me back for the bond, but why don't you just hold on to it?" Suddenly Mr. Generosity. "I dunno, pay your rent on time. Go buy a couple cheesecakes at Lindy's or something. Give one to Ma next time she drops by. She's gotta close her mouth at least to eat." And then, "Look, I gotta go," he declares next. "Rachel just came home." Then, with a quick "'Kay, bye," he clamps the phone's receiver firmly into the cradle. "That was Naomi," he announces.

"Yes," says Rachel. "It sounds like she's doing better."

He shrugs. "I guess. I mean, *yeah*. She sounded pretty good. And you know how she is. One of these guys dumps her, she falls apart, but then in a couple days, she's off to the races again."

Rachel nods blankly. She feels detached from this conversation. "So now you're sorry for being a putz? Now that you can afford to be?"

Aaron scrunches up his expression. "Huh?"

Shaking her coat, she hangs it on the hall tree and steps out of her shoes. "Now that they've broken apart, and you no longer must worry about the race of future nieces and nephews. Now you can afford to apologize. That's all I'm saying."

"So." Her husband frowns. "Let me get this straight. First, I'm a putz who should apologize, and then when I *do*, I'm still a putz because it was too easy."

Rachel crosses to the refrigerator and pops it open. "Yep."

"So what you're *really* saying is the husband can't catch a fuckin' break."

She removes the last Ballantine and shuts the refrigerator door with a clunk. "We're out of beer," she announces. "You should go see your sweetheart at the liquor store."

⌐•═╤─

Rashka has been separated from her mother, deposited into a bland little room by a large SS man and left there seated in a chair. It is a harshly lit place with an old oak table at the center. On the wall? A framed photograph, not of the leader of the German Volk but of the SS-Reichsführer, Heinrich Himmler. A soft, puffy schoolmaster's face with pince-nez glasses. She is staring at the face when the door opens and the red-haired Fräulein sweeps in. Rashka stands as she's been trained to do when an adult enters the room, which seems to amuse the woman. She smiles as she occupies a chair like a throne and ignites a cigarette.

"You're so grown up, aren't you, Bissel? When last we saw each other, you were still a little brat. But look how you've blossomed. A little more meat on your bones and you might be attractive in a sprightly way."

Rashka does not know how to react to this. But the woman does not wait for a reaction. "Sit," she instructs. "Your momma and I have had a little talk."

Rashka sits obediently and waits.

"I've decided to take you on, Bissel," the woman tells her. "To take you on as my student," she says. "Isn't that good news?"

But Rashka is confused. A student? She swallows. "Pardon me, gnä' Fräulein?"

This response seems to aggravate the woman. "You didn't expect a *free ride*, did you?" she demands to know. "You're not here on a holiday, Bissel. You must earn your keep like anyone else. Like me. Like your uncle. Even Herr Kommandant Dirkweiler. Even *he* must work, so I hope you didn't expect to be treated differently."

Rashka swallows. "No, gnä' Fräulein."

"*Good*," the woman tells her, seemingly mollified. She expels smoke and inhales it smoothly back through her nostrils. "Because otherwise, I'll have you and your mother transported east," she explains. "But you're a good little goat, aren't you? Isn't that what your momma calls you, Bissel? Her little goat? Yes. I can see that you are. You'll do your best for us all."

When Rashka is returned to her mother, they have been moved to a different room. The Unterkunft Zimmer it's called. The room of accommodation, where Feter Fritz sleeps with the rest of the Jewish lager workers. "The gnä' Fräulein says I must work, Eema," she whispers to her mother on the straw mattress they share.

"Yes, Rokhl," her mother answers.

"That I must be her 'student.'"

"Yes, Rokhl," her mother says again. Her face gray. Her voice leaden.

"But I don't know what that means, Eema."

"It means that you are saving our lives, tsigele," her mother answers. "No matter what she asks of you—no matter how terrible it might feel—you must obey her. Do you understand that, child? You must obey her."

26.

The Good Hour

THE INEVITABLE TELEPHONE CALL COMES TO PASS. FETER, restrained. Not exactly apologetic but checking his tendencies toward embellishment and hyperbole. His subtle chutzpah curbed. He speaks of the future of art. At least the future of art where Rachel's work is concerned. He has an ace or two up his sleeve. Still a few contacts that might surprise her. With her talent and his kop for art business?

"So am I the only one who sees the possibilities?" he wonders. She cannot help but relax into his tenderly optimistic trap.

At home, her husband is not very thrilled to hear about any such possibility as doing business with her uncle. "So he'll take like a commission?"

"I suppose, yes."

"How much?"

"I don't know."

"Ten percent?" His voice raises. "Fif*teen* percent?"

"I don't *know*, Aaron. We didn't discuss it."

"No? Well, why not? I mean, let's face it—your *uncle*…" he says but doesn't finish the sentence. He doesn't have to.

"He says we'd have a contract." Which is true. This was the agreement when they spoke over the phone. Everything aboveboard. Everything in writing. That was the price of Feter's ticket back into Rachel's life. "That he'd have a lawyer draw it up so there'd be no confusion."

"Yeah, well. *Whose* lawyer? That's *my* question. One of those shysters downtown who specialize in chasing ambulances?"

"I don't know what that means," Rachel tells him.

"It means, honey, that we gotta be careful is all. I know, Fritz is your family, but we just gotta be careful. That's all I'm saying."

"And we will be. As it's said, we'll take one step before the next."

"Yeah," Aaron replies. "Is that what is said? Also one step at a time, that is said too, and you wanna know what else? Don't stick your head in the lion's mouth. This is also said."

"Are you upset," she asks, "because you don't trust Feter? Or are you upset by the idea that I might actually have some kind of career?"

"*Career?*" Aaron repeats the word. "What are you talking about, *career?*"

"That Feter Fritz might actually find a gallery willing to take me on. Willing to show my work."

Aaron frowns. "*Honey,*" he says. Trying not to sound smug as he explains the facts. But not trying very hard. "*What* artwork? What have you got? Not much as far as I can see. You got a bunch of little sketches. And you got a big, empty canvas without a spot of paint on it. That's all."

Rachel stares. She would like to hate him at this moment. She would like to, but how can she? He's only speaking the truth.

Daylight. She wakes to the sound of clanking. To bumping and banging. She shakes sleep from her mind and dons her pink chenille robe, following the noise out of the bedroom, where she discovers her husband seated at the kitchen table in his shirtsleeves, smoking a cigarette. "Ah, the lady of the house emerges," he says but in a loaded tone, as if he's talking to someone else and not her. Kneeling on the linoleum by the kitchen sink with a toolbox is? The German.

Rachel stops. Wraps her robe tightly across her chest.

"Mr. Bauer here came by to replace the trap in the sink," her husband informs her. "Apparently he's had a hard time catching anyone at home. So lucky I was up early."

"Good morning. Missus Perlman," the Boche says, as if he's as innocent as any dumb animal.

She frowns, feeling her heart thump. Her first instinct is to retreat to the bedroom and lock the door. But "Good morning," she mumbles in return. Pushing through the panic, she circles around her husband to an empty chair.

"I made coffee," Aaron says, nodding toward the stainless-steel percolator.

"*You* made coffee?"

"Somehow, I managed." Then he confesses. "Actually, it's only the instant stuff. I just stuck it in the percolator and poured in the water."

Rachel swallows. Blinks at her distorted reflection in the percolator's shiny stainless-steel skin.

"So Mr. Bauer here was telling me about how he came to America, honey," her husband enlightens her. Obviously he is trying to prove a point. Trying to teach her a lesson. "He comes from... What was the name of the town again, Mr. Bauer?"

"I come from Rengschburch in Bayerich, Mr. Perlman," the German declares. "I think in America it is called Regensburg. In Bavaria."

"And you said you immigrated here when? In forty-seven? Is that right?"

"Forty-*eight*," the German replies, squeaking his wrench around a pipe.

"Right, forty-eight," Aaron corrects himself. "That was the same year *you* came, Rachel, honey," he says, as if she needs reminding.

Rachel issues him a look as she filches one of his Luckies, igniting it from his Zippo. "And what did you *do*, Mr. Bauer, before you came?" she inquires, expelling smoke.

The German shoots her a quick glance, frowning. "*Before?*"

"Before you came to America. During the war? Was hast du während des Krieges gemacht?"

Another glance, another frown. He answers her in English. "I was a 'Sanitäter.' In the army, Missus Perlman. As I told to your husband. A medical soldier," he says.

"Right. A corpsman." Aaron offers clarification. "Or. Or a *medic*."

"Yes. Medic," the German confirms. "But only because I was—how is the word said? Forced into the army? Eingezogen."

"After he was conscripted," Rachel translates dully, expelling smoke.

"Oh yeah. *Drafted*," Aaron says. "Me too. I was drafted too. I ended up assigned to the Quartermaster Corps in California. Course it was the *Japs* who were our problem," he assures the German.

But the German only nods and grunts again, clunking about with a wrench before he announces, "That should finish the job, Mr. Perlman." Standing with a huff, he opens the tap on full. Water gushes. "The drain flow is now correct."

"Terrific," says Aaron and makes a point of shaking the German's hand. "Thanks a lot, Mr. Bauer."

"Oh yes," Rachel chimes sardonically. "Wir sind so glücklich, dass ein ehemaliger Reichssoldat unsere Pfeifen bewacht," she says.

The German looks at her warily. Then nods once with a half frown. "Missus Perlman."

After the German leaves, lugging his toolbox, Aaron shuts the apartment door behind him. "So ya see, Rach. Not so bad," he declares. "Not some mad-dog Nazi after all. Just another poor shlub who got drafted like everybody else." Grabbing his jacket from the back of the kitchen chair, he bounces a quick kiss off her temple. "Anyhow. I gotta get going. We're down two busboys, so *I'll* probably end up schlepping dirty dishes all afternoon." And then he says, "Aren't you supposed to go see what's-his-name today?"

Rachel raises an eyebrow. He's Mr. Absentminded when it comes to things like picking up milk or dry cleaning, but he seems to have her schedule with the psychiatrist engraved on his brain. "Yes. At three o'clock," she says.

Flapping his arm into his overcoat sleeve, he says, "Okay. Don't forget."

"Don't worry. I won't forget a thing," Rachel replies.

At the door, though, Aaron pauses. "By the way, what was it you said to the super right before he left?"

"Nothing," she answers with an innocent frown. "Just how lucky we are to have a former soldier of the Reich guarding our pipes."

Aaron looks pained. Releases a breath.

"So I understand, Aaron, what you're trying to prove," she tells him directly. "Shaking hands with that man. I understand that you're trying to help. Trying to show me that there's nothing to fear. The world is not so dangerous. Not all Germans are murderers. I understand," she repeats, "and I appreciate your effort. But here's the truth: The world *is* dangerous. And if to *me* every German is a messenger of death, it's only because that is what history has taught me."

Aaron sags slightly. Starts to speak but instead just shakes his head. "H'okay" is all he can utter, eyes dropping to the floor. "H'okay, I get it," though it's clear he doesn't want to. Flopping on his old snood, he says, "See ya later."

She watches the door close and hears her eema on the couch. *If you truly hope for him to understand you, Ruchel,* she says, *then you must show him your true self. Not housewife or refugee but the true person. Mais l'être humain authentique.*

She notes the shift of his eyes to the clock on the opposite side of the room. A small clock placed discreetly on a bookshelf ticking off the minutes of the therapeutic hour.

"Am I running out of time, Doctor?" Rachel asks.

The doctor does not answer this question. Instead he sniffs lightly and says, "I want you to think about something, Rachel. I want you to think about how you can express your emotions in your art. And I don't mean emotions on the surface. I mean the emotions you have trapped inside you. Down deep. The emotions that erupted the day at the department store counter."

Rachel is silent.

"I firmly believe you should return to painting. And I don't want to give up on the idea, even though you're resistant. It's important. Honestly, not only important to you. But important that it be known."

"Known?"

"The truth. The truth of what happened. It's been over a decade since the end of the war. I think it's time the truth be told."

"A decade?" says Rachel the stone. "Doctor, it might as well be a thousand decades. It's all ancient history. All anybody cares about now is the *bomb*. Who has the bomb? Who will get the bomb? The bomb and what's on television? *I Love Lucy*? No one cares about history or truth."

A pause. "Maybe not," Dr. Solomon is willing to concede. Then the leather of his chair creaks as he leans forward. "But if that's true, then all the more reason that you should wake them up, Rachel," he says. "As an *artist*. And dare I say it? As a *Jew*—or perhaps simply *as a human being*—you have a responsibility to share your story."

Rachel feels herself balancing on the point of a needle. "And with whom would you have me share it?"

Dr. Solomon shrugs. "With the world," he says.

"Is this really necessary?" Aaron is grousing into the bathroom mirror, tying his tie behind Rachel, who is rouging her lips in her slip. "An evening with the Fucknik on my only night off for a week?"

Rachel lifts the tube of Red Velvet, primps her lips to smooth the color. "You don't wish to go? Don't go. I'll say you're too busy."

"Oh yeah, sure," her husband snorts. "Like *that* wouldn't get back to my mother."

Rachel crinkles her brow. "What? *What* wouldn't get back?" she asks. "What are you talking about?"

"My mother, that's what I'm talking about."

"Your mother would really care if you miss coffee and dessert?" She mouths a tissue to remove the excess red.

"Care? If I skip an evening with my dear cousin Ezra, by lunch tomorrow, *his* mother's on the phone with *my* mother, drilling into her ear," and here Aaron drops into his sour-faced impression of his aunt Ruth's Brooklynese. "'Too *busy*? Too busy for *family*, I guess, but what can you do? For some, business comes first.' And then *kablooey*," he declares. "I just don't need the grief." He gives his hair a touch with the comb, then brushes past her into the bedroom to yank on his shoes.

Entering the Weinstein apartment upstairs, there's the matter of the mezuzah. Having a mezuzah fastened to your doorpost is a mitzvah in the eyes of God. But what to do if you're up from the Perlman apartment, where no such mitzvah is in evidence sanctifying even a single doorway? The Weinsteins' front-door mezuzah came from a trip to Jerusalem. The Hebrew words Shomer Dlatot, Keeper of the Doors, fashioned into its brass cylinder. Aaron always brushes past it with a tap, flicking away a kiss on two fingers with the same cursory routine as if he's kissing the cheek of ancient Bubbe Perlman.

Rachel usually follows in a hurry too, whisking past with a half gesture in her husband's wake. But this time, she's first through the door and skips it completely, covering herself by handing Daniela a half gallon of Newbrook vanilla ice cream in a carton. She catches the corner of Daniela's glance at the omission but keeps moving into the apartment. She could have pretended and offered up a counterfeit mitzvah, but she wants to be on the level with God. She has not yet forgiven Him, He should know.

The Weinstock children are asleep in the next room. Daniela invites Rachel to look in on them with her, as if it's an honor or a treat, but when she does, all Rachel sees are small heads poking out from blankets. Another mezuzah guards the bedroom door, and she does not challenge it by crossing the boundary.

In the living room, the coffee is going cold in the cups and the ice cream is melting into sugary pools on the plates of half-consumed slices of Daniela's homemade lemon pound cake. The room is lit by the foggy blue-white glow of the television screen, a Magnavox in a mahogany console. *I've Got a Secret.* That's the name of the show. Rachel finds it somewhat incomprehensible. A panel of celebrities, whom she is supposed to recognize but doesn't, are asking questions that are managed by some fellow in a bow tie. What are they supposed to be guessing? Secrets? She can't really follow.

"So what'd this gadget set you back anyway?" Aaron is asking, nodding toward the Magnavox like he's laying a trap.

"Normally? A hundred," Ezra informs him. "But Daniela's got a cousin on Utica Av'—so we got it for eighty."

"Eighty," Aaron repeats with a squinting frown. "*Still*," he concludes. "That ain't beans. But then who needs to eat, huh?" he wonders aloud.

"Aaron, you're being rude," his wife points out mildly.

"Just sayin', honey," Aaron responds. And then his expression balls up like a wad of paper as a commercial break interrupts the show's proceedings. "Ah, now, ya *see*? This is exactly what I hate about television," he announces. "Every how many minutes? A word from our sponsor."

Rachel glances at him, then back at the set. A few paid performers have come on the screen to sing that Winston tastes good like a—*bop, bop*—cigarette should. She and Aaron are sharing the green damask sofa. Her penny loafers are off and her feet curled under her. Ezra is planted in his chair, one sandal missing, massaging his toes through his socks, but Daniela has encamped on the floor, braced against the sofa. She is further along than Rachel realized and will need help getting up, because her belly is now swollen to the size of the moon. Her cheeks are flushed, and her face is round. She has lost all her angles. All her edges have vanished.

"I mean, do I really need this guy telling me that Winston brought flavor back to filter cigarettes?" Aaron rants. "Do I really need that information fed into my brain?" he asks aloud. "I don't smoke 'em and never will. I don't care what this schmo Moore has to say on the matter."

"My mother loves Garry Moore," Daniela injects. "She says he's cute as a button."

"Okay, well…" Aaron shrugs dismissively.

"So. You don't like the commercial shtick?" Ezra has the solution. "Close your eyes," he suggests, still working his toes. "Stick your fingers in your ears."

Aaron swallows, but Rachel can tell that the tension in his body is ratcheted upward. The unbearable boyish restlessness betrays itself in the flexing muscle along his jawline and the fidgeting cigarette. He bangs off ash into the ashtray they share.

The room is filled with the TV's chatter. Rachel looks around her. Everything is comfortable in the Weinstock apartment. Comfortable in the messy way that apartments with children can be. Toys picked up and dumped into a play basket. Children's books atop a stack of magazines. *Tawny Scrawny Lion. Clever Polly and the Stupid Wolf.* A basket of laundry, folded but not yet put away, tucked under the lamp table. The baby pictures in frames cluttering the wall.

Why is it so frightening for her, Aaron's desire for a child? Perhaps it's the same thing that frightens her so about painting. She is terrified by what might come out of her.

"Ah. *See*, here we go again," Rachel hears her husband complain. "Milk of magnesia. I'm trying to watch a show, and they're selling me milk of magnesia."

"*Shhh*," Rachel hushes. "I'm trying to hear." Although she really isn't listening. Someone has a secret? They're supposed to guess? And who *is* Boris Karloff? Everyone seems to know but her. She expels smoke. For a while, everyone stares dutifully at the screen. Aaron sighs as if he's constipated. His mind is so restless, he can't simply sit and watch. It's why he talks through movies even after people shush him. It's why he fits so well into the restaurant business, because in the kitchen or in the dining room during the dinner rush, his brain is kicked into high gear. Sitting and *watching* makes him crazy. That's the *real* reason they don't have a television. Finally, the program comes to an end, and he is ready with a frown.

"I mean, we've been sitting here for how long, staring at this little blue screen? At least with a movie you've got something to look at, ya know?"

But Rachel has stopped listening to her husband's bellyaching. She has noticed a certain expression on Daniela's face, as if all the woman's attention has suddenly inverted. Focused sharply inward. A knitting of the brow, slight at first but then forceful. A flatness of the line of her mouth, and then a crimp of pain. Daniela's hand, she sees, jumps quietly to her swollen belly. Instinctively, Rachel reaches across the sofa.

"*Daniela.*" She pronounces the name with polite concern, touching Daniela's arm.

"Oh boy," Daniela whispers aloud.

Ezra glances over to her. His shoulders slump. "Sweetheart?"

"That's a contraction," his wife declares with a certain solid forbearance.

It's taking too long! Telephoning the doctor, calling for a taxi, packing the suitcase that should have been packed already but wasn't, because weren't they supposed to have more time than this? More time before this impatient baby coming in such a crazy rush!

"The doctor's line is *busy*," Ezra reports, not panicking, just making the announcement, keeping the team informed. Tries again. "Still busy!"

Then there's the issue of the babysitter. Mrs. Bethel from the second floor has already gone to bed! Mrs. Seventy-Five-Year-Old Bethel who'd made a career of looking after the Weinstock children, to hear Ezra tell it. Anyway, when Ezra calls her to come up because the next baby is on its way, she seems to be taking her sweet time. So Rachel volunteers to stay, at least until the old lady can make it up the stairs. Just as well. She is starting to get very jumpy in the midst of this maternity emergency. Aaron has already bailed out, running downstairs to wait for the cab. At least that's his excuse, abandoning Rachel to this scene. Daniela is starting to grunt like one of the seals at the Central Park Zoo as she tries to swallow the pain of the contractions crashing through her in waves.

"The doctor's line is still busy!" Ezra reports again, except now he is shouting aloud, a note of panic threatening to strangle his voice.

"Leave me the number," Rachel declares. "I'll keep calling."

"Oh, *fuck!*" Daniela cries. It's shocking because it's the first time Rachel has ever heard her use profanity.

One of the children—the boy—comes wandering out of the bedroom, rubbing his sleepy eyes at the commotion. "Momma?" he asks. "Are you sick?"

"No, no, zeisele," Rachel answers for her, shepherding the child back into his room. "Momma is not sick. It's just that she's bringing your new baby sister or brother into the world."

"Does it hurt?" the boy asks innocently, taking Rachel gently by the hand. A gesture that nearly breaks her heart in two. That warm little trusting hand in hers.

"A little. But sometimes good things come out of a little hurt," she hears herself say. The boy hops back into his bed, and Rachel tucks him in. "So don't you worry, okay? You just go back to sleep and don't worry. Then tomorrow when you wake up, there'll be a new baby in the world."

"Okay," the boy replies and rolls into the worn fluff of his stuffed bunny.

She doesn't think about kissing him, but when she does, the sweetness of that little dark-haired head poking out from the covers is painfully perfect.

She reenters the living room as Aaron comes stomping up the stairs from below. "Taxi's here," he proclaims as if he's just saved the day. Mr.

Lone Ranger coming to the rescue. Daniella has her coat on, her belly sticking out. Aaron snatches up the suitcase from Ezra's hand. "*You*—help your wife. I'll schlep," he commands.

"At the good hour!" Rachel calls out after them as all three vacate the apartment, because what else can she say that isn't a jinx? But when she shuts the door, she is both relieved and bereft. She has shut the door against pain and contractions and motherhood threatening to spill out onto the rug. She feels utterly trapped in the loneliness of her own body. She crosses to the telephone and dials the doctor's number that Ezra had dashed across the message pad, and finally somebody picks up. She explains the emergency to the answering service and hangs up, suddenly exhausted by it all. Then dropping back onto the damask sofa, she lights a cigarette, inhaling the smoke deeply.

It's not too late, her eema tells her, seated at the sofa's opposite end. *I was older than you are now when you were born.* She exhales smoke, the amber cigarette holder in her hand. *Not that the process was any great pleasure, but I survived. Women survive*, she says.

"Except when they don't," Rachel says. She expels smoke but then snubs out her cigarette in the ceramic ashtray. Her eema has vanished with the last whistle of smoke, and Rachel is up. She returns to the children's bedroom and quietly creaks open the door. In the glow of the night-light, she observes the children snuggled into slumber, dressed in their footy pajamas, sleeping like rag dolls in a puzzle of blankets, the light describing the little moon circumferences of their heads. A quiet drift of traffic whispers through the window.

But then she hears something.

Something like a cow lowing. Not here but from deep down in the building. She pops the bedroom door closed behind her and recrosses the apartment with a sting of urgency. When she cracks open the door to the stairway, she hears it again, only much more prolonged and much more resolute, a thick moo of pain. Mrs. Bethel is hobbling up the steps, gripping the railing, her eyes bright as light bulbs behind her glasses.

"It's happening! It's happening!" she calls out with a slightly crazed tone. And it's true. The maternity party never made it to Aaron's waiting cab. They never made it to the foyer. The good hour has come right on the bottom of the steps.

"Press now, *press!*" she hears a male voice instructing as she is descending the steps. But it is not Ezra's voice, and it is certainly not Aaron's voice. It is a voice with an accent attached. It is, Rachel realizes with a clench of horror, the voice of the super. The voice of the *German*. She alights from the stairs slowly, as if alighting from a descending cloud. "Good! Good! It comes!" Herr Boche is announcing, hunched over Daniela's splayed legs. "The head appears!"

Daniela is huffing, sobbing, but her wailing has reworked its pitch. It is no longer the stilted keen of a woman in agony; it's the clean, arcing cry of a tiny infant in the super's large hands. Ezra is whipping off his sweater to swaddle it, repeating, "Oh my God, oh my God, oh my God," with teary, manic astonishment. Rachel can see the tiny head, still gooey and pink with the blood of its birth, tiny fingers grasping at the air. Tiny squinting eyes, but its mouth is open and bawling brightly with life.

"Geboren ist ein Mädchen!" A girl is born! The German announces it.

Ezra is presenting the baby girl to her mother, whose arms are outstretched, sobbing with shock and joy, her hair a sweaty nest, her face gleaming, as her husband delivers her new daughter into her arms. "Such a beautiful gem," she cries, "such a perfect, beautiful gem." Ezra is laughing now. The German is laughing, a sharp, shared cackle of glee, face-to-face, as they shake each other's blood-pinked hands.

Rachel stares. Aaron has finally managed to look up and spots his wife above them. "*Rach*," he shouts out. The wild smile on his face makes him look like he's having a seizure. "Can you *believe* it?" he wants to know. "Huh? The damnedest thing! Just like *that*—a *baby!*"

Daniela turns her head, smiling beatifically up at Rachel. Her eyes shimmer as the baby squalls, and Rachel hears her mother's voice from behind. *Life, tsigele*, she's saying. *It's life.*

And then Rachel looks at the super. Standing up. Standing back. His hands stained. He digs a handkerchief from his pocket and begins to wipe them. That is when he catches Rachel's eye, but he quickly looks away, donning a grin as the happy father slaps him on the back in a chummy manner. Ezra is grinning too as if he's deranged, his expression exploding with joy. "Thank you, Mr. Bauer! Thank you!" he's barking. The German continues to grin. But it makes no difference. Rachel can only believe that this is not the first time this Hun has wiped Jewish blood from his hands.

Beth Israel Hospital, First Avenue and 16th Street. Hallways of linoleum and fluorescent lights. Rachel stands in the viewing section of the maternity ward, separated by a large plate-glass window from the cluster of infants in hospital bassinets. People come and go around her, grinning as they wave through the glass. Cooing, delighted, it seems, at their own reflections. Tapping on the glass pane for attention. But Rachel stands there, staring. She is alone when Aaron returns with two paper cups of coffee. He is wearing his coat, no hat, his collar open and his tie undone. It must have started to rain outside, because his shoulders are dotted with raindrops, and he smells of it. "Where did you go?" she asks as she accepts the paper cup. "Timbuktu?"

"The coffee machine was out of order, so I had to go to a deli down the street. Probably tastes like drek, but at least it's hot."

Rachel sips. It does taste like drek, but it's not hot. Aaron drinks too but makes no comment. His interest is elsewhere, peering through the glass. He almost laughs. "Who knew the super is actually Dr. Kildare?"

Rachel says nothing.

"So. Look at *this*," Aaron says in amazement, gazing through the glass at the sea of babies tucked into their numbered basinets. Their blankets a wavy ocean of pink and blue. "Do we know which one is which?"

"Number seven, I think," Rachel replies.

Aaron nods. "Lucky number seven." The manic glee of the birth on the stairs has given way to a certain heaviness in him. "She's cute," he admits. "Has her father's receding hairline."

"They're all cute," Rachel says. "They're all beautiful." She falls silent for a moment but then remembers something she once heard. "Did you know?" she asks. "It is said that the Messiah is born into every generation."

His eyebrows lift wearily. "Is it? Said by who?"

"I don't know. The Sanhedrin? Whomever it is who says things. But it is said."

"Okay. But I gotta tell you, I don't think I see the Messiah in this particular batch. I mean, wouldn't there be a glow or something? The Star of Beth Israel twinkling over the kid's head?"

Rachel doesn't respond. She sips the bitter coffee.

You were a precious treasure, she hears her Eema say. Standing beside her as she recalls her in the flush of her success. *The day you were born, I thought you were a gift from God Himself. "Behold, I give before you this day the life and the good."*

"So what's gonna happen to us?" she hears Aaron ask her. It's a simple question. At least he makes it sound like it's a simple question. And maybe it is. Maybe it's just a simple matter of logistics. But Rachel has no answer for him.

27.

The Accuracy of Silence

D ANIELA RETURNS WITH THE BABY, A CRINKLY EYED LITTLE ELF-lette. They plan to name her Joanna Sara after Ezra's great-aunt of blessed memory. Rachel swallows but smiles. According to the Reich's Law on the Alteration of Family and Personal Names, every Jewish male had to adopt "Israel" as a middle name, and every Jewish female, "Sara." But Nazi policy has no place in the temple, where the rabbi calls out her name for it to be heard in Israel.

And let us say Aymen.

Rachel suffers through the prayer service, as she suffers through an excruciating twenty minutes in the infant's department of B. Altman's picking out a white knit layette—hat, sweater, and booties with pink trim. They visit the Weinstocks with fillet of sole and fish sticks for the kids carried from the restaurant. With a Lindy's cheesecake in a box. But neither she nor Aaron is much interested in staying long.

She sees the German super in the hallway once but hurries up the steps, pretending to be lost in the mail she has just collected from the box.

At the Museum of Modern Art, she stands in front of a Rothko. Before the war, the artist had become an American citizen because he feared that the U.S. government would deport Jews back to Europe. He changed his name from Markus to Mark, from Rothkowitz to Rothko, which still sounded Jewish maybe but wasn't the name over a delicatessen. And of his canvases? They grew huge and deep. He was quoted as saying that he had "imprisoned the most utter violence in every inch of their surface." He also said, "Silence is so accurate." A statement with which Rachel can only agree.

She would like to trap utter violence within the confines of a canvas. She would like to imprison it there, where it would live out its miserable existence in solitary confinement on the painted surface. But she also craves the accuracy of silence. Its perfect beauty, like the blank silence of an untouched canvas. The silence of a painting before it exists. So at home, she stares at the white canvas stretched across the wooden rectangular frame and tries to imagine how she could possibly capture an image of herself more silent than silence.

But then her mother is there, seated beside her on the sofa, dressed in her studio smock, her hands stained with colors, perfumed with linseed oil. *You think it's a barrier, I know. This white expanse. You think it's a wall, and you ask yourself: Do I have the strength to break through it? But the wall, Ruchel, is an illusion. It's not a barrier; it's simply a screen. A screen that's hiding the painting, which is already there, hidden behind it. You've already finished the painting in your head and in your heart,* she says. *Every stroke is already in place. All you need do is peel the whiteness away, and the truth of the work will be revealed.*

"And that is what I'm afraid of, Eema. It won't be a beautiful revelation. I'm terrified by that idea. I'm terrified of the ugliness that will come out of me. What kind of monstrosity I will release for all to see."

Tsigele. Listen to me. For once, please listen. Art is not always beautiful. There is horror and ugliness in the world that must be painted too. It is not beauty; it is truth that's at the heart of every true artist's work. So I say— paint your monstrosity. Better it live on the canvas than inside you.

"And once the truth is revealed, Eema? I will be hated and despised. I'll have no husband nor home. I'll lose everything I have and be shunned, an outcast. The police will find me sleeping in rags on a park bench with newspapers for a blanket and take me away." Her eyes are filling with tears. "And what's worse is I'll deserve it all."

Of course. My selfish child. Always thinking of herself, poor thing, her eema says, but not as an indictment. More like a sad, simple little fact. *You believe the monstrosity belongs to you alone? You're wrong, tsigele.*

A sob breaks over Rachel. "You don't know what I *did*, Eema. You don't know the *crime* I committed."

I don't care about crimes, Daughter. You're not listening. Your ears are blocked by your own self-pity. Look at that canvas, Rokhl. Look at it! Do you have the slightest conception of how I long for one more hour—one more moment—when I could touch a brush to my palette and paint even a single stroke? To feel the strength of that? But art is for the living, not the dead. So stand up and live, child. Your paintbrush is a weapon! Use it! Defend yourself against yourself.

Rachel liberates the easel from the hallway closet. The Woolsey standing floor easel, collapsed and stowed behind the vacuum. The tarp is there too, a shop tarp from a factory floor, saved from Aaron's days slaving for his uncle in the leather goods workshop, already stained with tanning solution before she stained it further with paint, though it still smells of both. The rusty tin of turpentine is under the sink, but her oil paints, her brushes, those are harder to find, till finally she remembers.

She must muscle out various boxes full of clothes and board games from Aaron's childhood, the lamps that came from Webster Avenue but need rewiring. The dusty debris that's too much trouble to pitch. Would her mother-in-law be upset if they threw out the tarnished brass floor lamp with the lion crest? Probably not, but why risk it? She shoves aside a box marked KIDS' BOOKS: AARON and finds it. The scuffed and paint-stained Winsor & Newton painter's box. Inside are the crusty tubes of oils, the bundle of wooden-handled brushes, the paint-stained palette and palette knives, the broad brushes for priming. They're all waiting for her. The smell rises into her nostrils like an ancient perfume released from a pharoah's vault.

The canvas she bought at Lee's Art Shop is already primed, but she still lays down a dry-brush underpainting of umber followed by the Dead Layer. La couche morte. She mixes it generously at the center of the palette. Then she must sit back. Oils require patience. They require a geological approach to time and art. Each layer must be permitted to crust and then harden, so she sits back and watches the color fix. She is still sitting on the sofa, wearing one of Aaron's old dress shirts as a smock, already blotted with paint, her hands already stained, her brushes soaking in turp, when the key turns in the lock. The door opens, and she hears Aaron before she sees him. "Holy mackerel, you spill the silver polish or something? It stinks in here."

And that's how it starts.

Aaron has always encouraged her to do what makes her happy, as long as maybe it doesn't smell up the place. Or as long as it doesn't interfere too much with eating a meal. Going out for a movie maybe. You know, everyday life. As long as they can still live everyday life, then it's fine, but really the *smell*, criminy.

"Open a window for cryin' out loud," he says. "Forget that all the heat will go right out the fucking windows. How can a person breathe, huh?"

"Paint. Smells." That's her reply.

"I guess that on that particular *point*, we agree," her husband tells her. Aaron slumps onto the sofa with an exhale of breath. They have not been doing so well since the birth of the Weinstock child. Most times, under daily pressures, something simply feels detached between them. Other times, though, it's a kind of stewing impatience, or even anger that heats up for an instant and then simmers away into silence. But now her husband looks bleached.

"You know, Rachel. I don't know what else to do," he tells her. He is sitting on one end of the sofa, and she is seated at the other end, holding Kibbitz hostage on her lap. "I try to make you happy. Well, maybe that's too much to imagine, but at least I try to make you less miserable. You wanted a cat? We got a cat. You wanted to buy expensive mail-order oil paints because the ones at the store weren't good enough? I say not a problem. Buy 'em. You deserve to have expensive oil paints. And then you need time to work on your painting and stuff? Great! It's not like I expect to have a meal cooked when I come home. So we live in a pigsty? Whattaya gonna do? You've got other priorities."

And that's how it starts.

"So you missed him," Dr. Solomon confirms.

"Yes."

"With the ashtray."

"I think the sugar bowl was close."

"And then you threw the toaster?"

"Yes."

"Did it break?"

"I don't know."

"Did you really intend to hit him with any of these objects?"

"He was gone by the time I threw the toaster."

"I see."

Rachel's eyes tear bleakly for a moment, and she wipes them. "No. I don't think I hoped to hit him. Not really," she says.

"And this argument. It started because?"

"Because it would kill me to wash a window. Because I open a can and dump it into a pot instead of cooking. Because I don't vacuum the drapes."

"Okay. So once *again*. Housework was the catalyst."

"Aaron thinks I am a bad housekeeper. He wishes he had married his mother instead."

"You said that to him?"

"He said it to *me*. Though," she admits, "maybe not exactly in such words."

"So I believe you *know* about my opinion concerning arguments over housework."

"They are never about housework," she reports, still a good little goat.

"That's correct. So after the argument, you left the apartment?"

"No. *He* left."

"And didn't come back?"

"There's a couch in Leo's office at the restaurant. A big, brown-leather, pleated chesterfield from the thirties. It wouldn't be the first time he slept there. Charades has always been his second home anyway. He keeps a shaving kit, suits, and fresh shirts there. When the waiters' union went on strike, he didn't come home for days."

A pause to examine her. "When was the last time you ate something?" the good doctor wants to know.

"Ate something? I don't know. I'm not hungry."

Her hair is stiff and flattened on one side while bristled on the other. She is still dressed in the same clothes that she was wearing under the painting smock. She hasn't changed since the day before yesterday. Her skin feels gritty against her blouse. Her mouth tastes of dead cigarette smoke. She had stopped at a diner on Lexington Avenue and swallowed a single cup of scalded black coffee, sitting at the counter with the crowd of men on their lunch break, wolfing down their sandwiches and meatloaf specials. The Wonder Bread deliveryman and the beat cop in their ill-fitting uniforms, and the middle-aged drummers with chapped faces, stopping off just long enough to stuff a B.L.T. into their mouths and gulp down coffee as they glare at the headlines of the daily papers.

"You look completely done in," the doctor observes.

"I don't want to talk about how I look. I didn't come all the way up here to talk about how I look."

"So tell me, Rachel. Do you feel you live... How did you say he put it? In a pigsty?"

"Do I?"

"Yes. Do *you?*"

She takes a breath. "The dirty windows or the dusty furniture, I simply don't see them. Or if I do see them, I simply don't care."

"And why do you think that is?"

She thinks of the Judenhaus in Berlin. The dirty hiding places in cellars and attics. As time passed, she no longer noticed the schmutz she lived in. Schmutz was her home.

The Eighth Avenue Express is not so crowded. Rachel sits across from a *Subway Sun* cartoon that contends: YOU MAY NOT GET TO HEAVEN— BUT YOU CAN LIVE IN NEW YORK! She is faced by her own dark reflection staring back from the train-car window. Could she imagine it to be the reflection of the mother of a child?

Back at the apartment, she goes into the bedroom and changes. Her hair tied back in a plain white scarf. An old striped work shirt of Aaron's with the sleeves rolled up under the hand-me-down apron from her mother-in-law. In the living room, she shoves the furniture to the corners and vacuums the rugs once, twice. She pulls everything down from the shelves and wipes them clean. Wipes the tabletops, the table legs, until she's coughing on dust. She chases cobwebs with the broom, fingers the dust rag into all cracks and crevices. Squirts the windows with Windex and wipes them with newsprint till she hears glass squeak.

Sweat slicks her skin. She hunts down spots on the rug with a bottle of Handy Andy spot remover, then rolls the rug to the wall. She yanks on the rubberized gloves and plunges the scrub brush into the soap pail of Spic and Span, scours the floorboards and linoleum on her hands and knees. She dumps the ashtray from the coffee table, washes it along with a coffee cup and saucer, and leaves them to dry in the dish drain. The counters are sponged, the pantry shelves. Sinks are sponged. The bathtub and toilet are pumiced clean with Old Dutch Cleanser, a crook-backed charwoman on the label chasing away dirt with a big stick. The tiles? Let Lysol do the dirty work! Even ovens can be cleaned with Easy-Off Oven Cleaner!

By the time she drops into one of the kitchen chairs and lights a cigarette, the striped shirt has blotted up so much sweat that it hangs on her like she's just jumped into a pool. She reaches for the glass garden-green ashtray, but of course it isn't there. She swept up its remains with the dustpan hours ago.

She eats a piece of cheese and a green apple for supper. Then steps into the shower. The hot water scalds the salty residue of the day's sweat from her skin. Cleanses her. Toweling dry, she does not bother with anything but her pink chenille robe, even though the room is chilly because she left open the window by the fire escape when she let out the cat. The sunset is a yellow bar the color of butter.

Opening up her battered box of paints, she lays out her palette in cold colors: a greasy blue, a hunter green, a squeeze of black for mid-night, and earthen colors: yellow and sulfur, and brown clay. A glob of titanium white as an anchor. At the center of the palette, she will mix her elements, the alchemist.

She drops her robe onto the floor and steps out of it.

The mirror from the bedroom door is leaned against a kitchen chair, footed by phone books. The canvas is positioned on the bridge of the easel. She stands naked and white, stripped of disguises. Bare to her past. She has screwed a pair of hundred-watt bulbs into the floor lamp and removed the shade, so it starkly illuminates her, throwing a black shadow across the floor.

She mixes an ashen-white flesh color on the palette and strikes the Dead Layer with paint.

Painting has sapped her. She feels chilled and emptied as she climbs back into the shower. There is nothing left in her. She has mixed all of herself into the paint she used to smear her naked image onto the stretched canvas. The paint will not wash off with water. If she is to clean herself of it, she must use turpentine and a rough rag or a scrub brush, but she does not. Instead she dresses in Aaron's plaid bathrobe that still retains his scent, her hair still damp, still dripping, her skin marked by her paints. That's when she hears the key, before the door to the apartment opens and shuts.

When she enters the living room from the bath, she finds her husband, hat still on his head, his coat hung over his arm, and his hands stuffed into his trouser pockets. He is examining the painting, his shoulders sunk. When he turns around to face her, his expression is drained, as if he's just finished staring at a car wreck.

"So," he says, his voice in neutral gear. "This is what you're painting?"

Rachel picks up a pack of Camels from the sofa and lights up using a matchbook from the restaurant. Fine Dining before Curtain Time! Expelling smoke, she drops onto the sofa. Cautious. Each keeping their distance. "Apparently it is," she answers him. Her brushes are soaking in the coffee can of turp. Chock full o' Nuts. Her palette is a chaos of paint, crusting over. But the paint on her canvas gleams. It will take days to dry thoroughly. To dry down to the bone of the canvas.

"And so the idea is…" Aaron begins. "The idea is that *people*…" he says. "People are gonna *see* this?"

Rachel exhales, gazing at her painted image. "It's not finished."

"Oh. So maybe you're still gonna paint some clothes on?"

Rachel slides her eyes over to her husband. For an instant, she mildly hates him. He's nothing but a Jew from Flatbush, worried about what the neighbors might think. What does he know of anything? *Of anything?* For an instant, she's sorry she missed him with the ashtray. But then his face softens. He releases a small but deflating breath, and she can see how lost he is. How utterly lost.

"I dunno, honey," he tells her in the same neutral voice, without a hint of rancor. "I think I might be in over my head with you."

PART THREE

The Red Angel

28.

The Catcher

THE NUMBERS ARE RIGID. A THOUSAND JEWS ORDERED FOR transport. A thousand will go. Not one less. Not one more. But the names? The names are fluid. And that is where Feter Fritz has found his value. It's the dirty work of negotiations and graft where Feter Fritz excels. He has carved out a small position for himself in the Gross Hamburger Strasse Lager and has even some small measure of power to determine whose name is typed onto which list—Paradise or Not Paradise—*or* if a name is rescued from the list completely. Of course, the entire quite delicate procedure can be overturned with a pencil stroke by Herr Kommandant Dirkweiler, who reigns like a petty god.

"Keep your head down," Feter tells Eema. "No disturbances. No arguments," he says, so Eema tries to contain herself in a cage of her own devices. And her little goat follows.

Keep everything in. Don't react. Don't expect. Eat what is given. Don't make noise.

But something shocking happens. Something terrifying for Rashka, though Feter Fritz seems to consider it a wild stroke of fortune. "She has an interest in your daughter," he informs Eema.

"An interest? What does this mean?"

But Feter Fritz isn't interested in answering this question. All he says is, "She has power here, Lavinia. Power with the Gestapo. Power over the lists in a way that I do not."

So he prepares Rashka. Coaches her on how she should behave

with the woman she now addresses as gnä' Fräulein. "Think of yourself as her pupil and she as your teacher," says Feter Fritz. "Let her talk, but don't be afraid to ask questions. She *likes* an interested pupil. Only be careful," he warns. "Under no circumstances should you question her judgment. Do you understand?"

Rashka can barely nod.

"It's a generous offer, ziskeit. She has influence here with these lunkhead Gestapo bulls. She'll make sure *your* name and your *mother's* name are kept off the transport lists."

Rashka turns to her mother. "This is what I must do, Eema?"

Her mother sighs with mournful resignation. "At least," she says, "if it keeps us off the trains…"

"But why? Why does she want *me*?" Rashka wants to know. She wishes to cry but holds it in. "What am I to her?"

A silence. Then Eema says, "She has no children of her own. Perhaps she thinks she's protecting you. Perhaps she wishes to punish me by stealing you away. Perhaps both."

"But *why*?" Rashka asks again. Though no answer to her question is forthcoming.

A café near the Anhalter Bahnhof. "A fresh hunting ground," the woman calls it. The two of them sit side by side at a table facing the door. Rashka's clothes are worn and stiff with the grime that comes with U-boat life. Her shoes battered, she wears a knit hat, but she has been given a new coat. A lovely wool coat with a fitch fur collar. A lady's coat. A "gift" from the gnä' Fräulein, so smartly clad and coiffed beside her. Black lace gloves and a matching lace veil over her eyes. Angelika Rosen, la muse rouge. Eema calls her Fräulein Rosen or simply "the lady," as in "You must do as the lady says," though Rashka has heard the other names given her. The Red Angel. The Angel of Death.

"Light me a cigarette," the gnä' Fräulein commands. Rashka knows how this is done because she used to light cigarettes for her eema when she was small. She strikes the match, sucking in air. The smoke fills her mouth, but she doesn't inhale. She whistles it out, careful to keep her lips pursed so she doesn't make the cigarette paper soggy.

"Two coffees, please, and a bun," the gnä' Fräulein tells the craggy old waiter, employing a sleekly imperious tone that is both superior and seductive. Then she turns to her pupil. Down to business. "So. Do you know who you are looking for, Bissel?" she asks.

"Jews," Rashka answers simply, because isn't that the truth of the matter?

But the gnä' Fräulein laughs lightly at the absurdity. "Well. If you mean beaked noses and heavy lips? Goggled eyes? Then *no*, Bissel. No. That's strictly rubbish. We aren't here to search for repulsive carica-tures. We are hunting the *invisible* Jew. A very elusive quarry," she says and expels a graceful drift of smoke from her cigarette.

Rashka can remember a pair of beautiful red suede gloves. Ten years before, when she was a child and the gnä' Fräulein was not so much older than Rashka is now. The gloves were immaculately stitched with scalloped cuffs. A gift from the artist to her muse, according to Eema, as if that would explain away the light brightening her mother's eyes. A light seldom bestowed upon her daughter.

The waiter reappears to deliver the coffees and a lumpy bun on a plate. Only old men are left in Berlin to wait at table. Rashka inhales the sweetish smell of the Feigenkaffee, ground from dried figs, and the slight chemical bake of the bun's ersatz flour.

"Eat," the woman tells her with a flick of her lace-gloved hand, so Rashka does so, attempting to refrain from wolfing down the bun, but she can't really stop herself. Soon the plate holds nothing but crumbs. Crumbs that she collects and licks from her fingers.

"*That's* the clue we're looking for," the gnä' Fräulein announces with a taste of disdain on her lips. "*There.* Exactly what you're doing now."

Rashka blinks. Swallows heavily.

"A little mongrel licking crumbs from her plate. Only starved little animals do that. It's a perfect signal."

Rashka blinks again. Is the woman angry with her? She sounds like she might be, and Feter Fritz warned her of the lady's temper. But then the gnä' Fräulein arches an eyebrow. "Wipe your fingers, child," she says in a tone that is nearly maternal. "And when you *look,*" she instructs, "look for *yourself* in the crowd. *You* are who we're hunting, Bissel. Not 'Jews.' Not 'U-boats.' *You.*"

There is a man too. Cronenberg is his name, though the gnä' Fräulein calls him Emil. Like the Fräulein herself, he has great freedoms. Great privileges. He is handsome like a wolf is handsome and blond as any Aryan might hope to be, though Rashka knows him to be a Jew. Like the gnä' Fräulein, he is a "Greifer." A catcher. A grabber. He favors the style of leather trench coat and snap-brim hat that Gestapo men often wear as an unofficial uniform and carries a police pistol in his coat pocket. He is quite brazenly obvious in his desire for his red-haired partner. On the other hand, he observes Rashka like she is a dog turd he must avoid stepping upon.

It is his job to make the arrests. The gnä' Fräulein searches out her prey, and the man steps in with his pistol. *Hands up, little mice! The cat is here, and the game is up!* He drives a glossy French automobile to ferry their prisoners back to Grosse Hamburger Strasse. It is through Emil that Rashka first hears of the term applied by the Gestapo to their little tribe of catchers. The Search Service. And for whom are they searching? Well, the gnä' Fräulein has already made that clear to Rashka. She is searching for herself.

By the end of the summer of 1944, things change drastically for all residents of the Grosse Hamburger Strasse when the Judenlager is moved to smaller quarters in the Schulstrasse. Transport after transport, trainload after trainload, even as the city suffers under bombing day and night, has depleted the camp's human inventory. There simply aren't enough Jews left to warrant such space. So orders were issued by Dirkweiler's bosses. The whole operation has been transferred from the former old age home to the Jewish Hospital in Berlin-Wedding.

An iron gate located at Schulstrasse 79 leads to the pathology building, where Jews are now confined to the morgue. Therefore, in order to cram the whole show into this new, congested space, the fat must be trimmed! The glut of Jews who are of no value to Kommandant Dirkweiler must be shipped out. The Gestapo is finished with many of the Jewish functionaries. Their services are no longer required, nor are the services of many of the orderlies. So a special transport to the Paradise lager is organized. Yet—a miracle! Feter's name is scratched from the list! Not by a miracle, really, but by the miracle worker, Angelika Rosen. "Perhaps," Rashka's eema posits, "she has not become so hard-hearted as to completely forget the past."

On the floor of the morgue, the Jews huddle, sleeping in an imitation of death. The cacophony of snores and snorts, however, indicates life. Rashka is pressed back to back with her eema. She can feel every twitch of her mother's body like it's her own, every spasm of sleep. When she hears the scuff of shoe leather on the tiles, her eyes pop open.

"*Feter*," she whispers with a small note of joy. Her uncle has crouched down beside her.

"Rokhl," he whispers in return, pressing a finger to his lips. And then he says, "Don't wake your mother."

Walking down the corridor beside Feter, she is hugging her shoulders with her arms against the chill of the cellar. Rashka is confused. "I don't understand," she is saying. "Why must I leave Eema?"

"Because it's the best thing for you," her uncle tells her.

"Because the gnä' Fräulein says I must?"

"There's a small room that's empty that she wants you to fill. You'll have better food. Warm blankets."

"But why?"

"Because the gnä' Fräulein says you must."

"I don't understand," Rashka repeats. "Why can't Eema come with me?"

"Your eema will be safe where she is," Feter Fritz assures her as they walk through the gray light. "Protected," he says.

"By *whom*?"

"You know by whom," he tells her.

"But how can that be? It's *you* who protects us, isn't it? Not her. Feter Fritz?"

"I had some influence once, zeisele," he explains without much sweetness. "But the Fräulein Angelika? She has the Herr Kommandant's ear. And that means power in this place. Real power. So at least for the time being," her uncle instructs her, "I suggest that you allow *her* to be your mother."

The room is no larger than an oversized closet. Four walls and one tiny window too high up to peer through. But at least there's a bare mattress with blankets and a flat striped pillow.

"Your new abode," Fräulein Angelika tells her. "Now, can you say thank you, Bissel?"

At night, the darkness drenches the room. Rashka huddles under the blanket and breathes. *Breathes* to stop herself from drowning.

Fräulein Angelika is standing at the entrance, leaning against the doorframe as she surveys Rashka's closet. "So. Not exactly a room at the

Adlon, I know. But it's clean. You won't catch any diseases from that filthy Jewish trash in the morgue."

"But. My eema. She is down there still, gnä' Fräulein," Rashka points out, causing the Fräulein to frown.

"That's the gratitude you're going to show me? I pull you off the dung heap, and all you can do is whine?"

"I'm sorry," Rashka says heavily, her ears flushing.

"Your mother understands the situation. Why can't you?"

"You spoke to Eema?" Rashka asks, feeling an odd nip of hope.

"I have," the gnä' Fräulein replies. "And she approves."

Confusion. "Approves of what?"

"Are you stupid, Bissel? Of what I'm *doing*. For *you*."

Rashka opens her mouth, but not a word escapes.

Frustrated, the gnä' Fräulein hurls down the sack she's kept tucked under her arm. Two fruit bar rations and a packet of Eckstein cigarettes spill out. "Why does one have children?" she demands to know.

As a sign of her newfound privilege, Rashka has been provided access to a bathtub. An old-fashioned tub filled with tepid water and suds from a chemical soap. But it feels luxurious. To be clean? To be clean after so long feeling filthy? She might as well be bathing in a golden basin inside a palace. She feels guilt, of course. To be so clean while Eema is left to the grime and muck. But she drowns the guilt in the soapy water. Next, she is dressed. Given better clothing. Nice clothing that is not frayed or nibbled by moths. A pearl-gray jumper. A crisp white blouse and a knit pullover the color of a pale rose. A black wool skirt with deep pleats, polished shoes that are not disintegrating, gray wool stockings without holes.

She has also been given cosmetics. Face powder with a puff. A tube of lip rouge. An eyebrow pencil and a tortoiseshell hand mirror. Holding the mirror, Rashka uses the pencil to turn the wall in her closet into her canvas. A small self-portrait rendered in eyebrow pencil. When she is discovered, however, the gnä' Fräulein is angry. Her face bleached. Her eyes stark.

"What are you *doing*?"

Rashka does not answer.

"Do you know how valuable a mirror is? A simple hand mirror? I give you things to beautify yourself, so maybe you won't look like a dirty little Jewess out on the streets. And *this* is how you waste my gifts?" Bending down, she smears her hand across Rashka's portrait, leaving it a greasy dark smudge. Then seizing Rashka by the hair, she forces the mirror into her face. "*Look!*" the gnä' Fräulein commands her. "Look at yourself! What do you see?"

Rashka gazes into her terrified reflection.

"I'll tell you what *I* see. What the *world* will see. A little kike sow! That's what!" And she slams Rashka's forehead into the wall. Her vision explodes into a shower of stars.

Rashka is in the rear of the auto. The shiny French touring car. Up front, the gnä' Fräulein is cavalierly smoking a cigarette, while behind the wheel is the slim blond man, Emil Cronenberg.

Rashka coughs. The smoke from the cigarette is drifting into the rear. When she coughs again, Angelika gives her a bored look but rolls down the passenger window a crack.

That's when Cronenberg tosses a glance over his shoulder into the back seat just long enough to leave Rashka with a frown of disapproval. "I don't know what in the hell you are doing, Lika, towing this bit of baggage!"

"She is my student," the woman answers him.

"Student?" He seems to be amused.

"I am the teacher. She is the student."

The man only snorts derisively. "All I have to say is she better not get underfoot. Because if she does, I'll stomp her. *You hear that, little baggage?*" he calls out.

She is too frightened to answer, but the gnä' Fräulein gives Rashka a knowing wink from the passenger seat.

"So where do you wish to start?" the man wants to know. He has lit a cigarette while he is driving from a gold-plated spirit lighter. "The Kranzler? Mortiz Doblin?"

"The Kranzler's played out for now, I think," Angelika replies. "And the service at the Doblin is abominable these days. Not to mention that the Himmelstorte tastes of horse shit. No, I say the Swedish Embassy this morning," she decides. "If it's profitable, we can stop at the Uhland Eck for lunch as a reward."

Cronenberg shrugs. "The embassy it is," he says, yielding.

"It's very easy, Bissel. All we need to do is sit here on our bench and let them come to us."

"Them?" Rashka asks.

"The Jews, Liebchen," she explains. "There are still Jews so stupid that they think that there are so-called neutral countries who will accept some shiny trinkets and give them a visa. Of course, that will never happen." She smiles. "So we let them go *in*. And then, when they come out looking dejected and paying no attention? That's when we *pounce*," the gnä' Fräulein tells her, explaining as if describing the rules of a children's game of cat and mouse for the playground.

But luck is not with the gnä' Fräulein. No U-boats are spotted. The man Cronenberg looks simply bored, smoking, while it's Fräulein Angelika who frets this way and that, unable to make herself comfortable. A hungry cat without a meal in sight. Finally, she scowls at her pretty diamond-studded watch. "This is pointless," she decides, exasperated at the lack of quarry. "Let's go for a coffee."

They find a place serving the usual ersatz. The gnä' Fräulein goes to use the toilet, leaving Rashka alone for the first time with the man Cronenberg.

"My God." The man sighs. "She is such a gorgeous monster," he says. Shakes his head. "It's really a crime." And then he turns to face Rashka. "Sorry I was so rough on you earlier," she is surprised to hear him say. "It's a show for her I put on. She likes to argue. Also, she's extremely jealous. It would do you no good if I sounded too happy to have another pretty face about."

Rashka is astonished. She has been eating a slice of cake that tastes of chemical filler, but still she is trying not to gobble it down like a waif. Trying not to gulp down her cup of warm skim milk. Trying to follow orders. Trying not to feel ashamed that she has tried to discreetly pocket a chunk of the cake for her eema. The next bite, she keeps telling herself. The next bite will be her last, and the rest she will take back to her mother. But the next bite is swallowed and so is the next after that. Until this man starts speaking.

"So what's your name, little baggage?" he asks her.

She must swallow the current mouthful of cake dry before she can answer. "Rashka Morgenstern."

The man nods as if he figured as much. "Good Jewish name," he whispers, as if this amuses him. "I'm Cronenberg," he tells her. "Emil Cronenberg."

"Yes. I know. And you're a Jew too."

"By blood," he answers. "Yes. And unfortunately, it's by blood we are all judged these days. Ah well. You must know the old saying: 'Neither cursing not laughing can alter the world,'" he recites. "You want a smoke?" he asks. "Here, have a taste," the man offers, proffering the cigarette he has just lit.

She stares at it. Then accepts. Inhales. He chuckles as she sputters smoke. "Head swimming, huh?" he says as he lights his own. "You'll get used to it. A person can get used to anything. We should know, correct?"

Rashka tries to ignore the sickly taste in her mouth as she tempts fate with another but less ambitious draw of smoke. This time, she manages to keep it down instead of choking it back up.

"She thinks you have talent, you know."

"She?"

"Your 'gnä' Fräulein,'" he tells her, retrieving the cigarette. "And maybe it's true. God knows, *she* has the talent. I could see that the first time I looked into her eyes. The animal instinct. Honestly? In your eyes, I don't see it. I don't see a killer in you. But maybe for you, it's different, hmm? If she says you have the 'doppeltes Gesicht,' then who am I to argue?" Doppeltes Gesicht. The Double Face.

"She frightens me," Rashka admits.

"She frightens everyone," the man also admits, removing a leather-bound flask from his coat. Unscrewing the cap, he takes a slug. "I think she frightens the Gestapo bulls as well. You want a drink?" he asks.

Rashka shakes her head tightly.

He nods. Then as he stares out at nothing, the bemusement in the man's voice dissolves. "Until the Tommies pummeled it, she favored cafés around the Gedächtniskirche," he says. "We Jews love our coffeehouses, don't we? At the Trumpf, I watched her jam the revolving door with her own body to keep her quarry trapped until I could come running with the pistol. After that? She got her own pistol. A Sauer Model 38." He says this and allows the smoke to drift from his lips. "You've heard what they call her, haven't you?" he asks, his eyes slitting.

"Yes," Rashka answers. "The Red Angel. The Angel of Death."

"But she doesn't care. I think she takes a certain pride in what they call her," he says. And then he asks her, his eyes landing on her, gaining weight. "So how old are you anyhow?"

How old? There are men who've asked her this question in a different way now. It makes her uncomfortable. She answers, but he only nods at the information. "I figured it was something like that," he tells her and whistles out smoke. "I figure my daughter's about that age too."

Rashka feels herself sit back. A daughter? Such a man and he has a daughter?

"Course, I don't know exactly. Last time I saw her, she was just a little pitsl in nappies." He says this, then something about him quiets, settles for a moment with his cigarette before he says, "If you want, you can make a run for it."

A blink. Rashka believes she must have imagined that this was said, but then the man glances back at her. "Did you hear me? I said you can make a run for it," he repeats casually. "There's the door," he points out. "You can go. I won't stop you. But you've got to do it now. Now," he repeats. "Before she comes back."

A kind of confused panic crackles through her. For an instant, her heart shimmers with the possibility. There's the door! Head out and run! That's all. Just run. But when she thinks about moving from her chair, something is wrong. She is paralyzed. Where would she go? How would she hide or feed herself? Mostly, how could she abandon Eema to the Gestapo? That's what she *should* be thinking. But she is shamed by the other question in her head. How could she abandon the gnä' Fräulein? After she has invested such faith in her?

A moment later, it makes no difference. The Fräulein returns to the table. She frowns suspiciously as she sits. "And what are you two plotters up to?" she wants to know.

The man Cronenberg returns to his usual frown. "Just have your coffee and let's get back on the street," he says. "It's getting late. Dirkweiler will think we've laid an egg."

Rashka receives grudging permission from the gnä' Fräulein to visit her eema down in the morgue. "For a few minutes if you must. Just don't bring any disease back with you," the woman commands. A chest infection has begun to circulate among the prisoners. Her mother is burdened by it. Eema lies on straw, coughing and sputtering, sweating and shivering under a thin cover. Rashka brings her something heavier. A wool horse blanket. She brings her tea in a steel thermos and bread with lard. Her mother has no stomach for the bread and is too weak to sit to drink the tea, so Rashka spoons it into her eema's mouth.

"She's very ill," Rashka tells the gnä' Fräulein.

"Yes?" The woman is clad in a silk dressing gown, showing a stockinged leg as she lounges on the davenport in the room that she shares with Cronenberg. She pages through a copy of a fashion magazine. Elegant watercolors of stylish women are on the cover of *Modenschau*.

"She has a fever."

"What do you want of me, Bissel?"

"Some medicine?"

"I can get you aspirin for her," the gnä' Fräulein is willing to concede.

Rashka is silent for a moment. The gnä' Fräulein looks up from her magazine. "*Yes?* Vo den?"

"I thought..." she starts to say.

"Yes? What? What did you think?"

"I thought," says Rashka, "you loved her."

The gnä' Fräulein glares darkly. Then turns back to her. "Would you like to look like this, Bissel?" she asks and turns fashion pages to face Rashka. "So elegant. Can you see yourself in such modern kleyd?"

Rashka doesn't know how to answer.

"You're a woman now, Bissel. Aren't you? I mean, you're on your cycle now."

Rashka's eyes search the air anxiously.

"Bissel?"

"Yes," Rashka says.

"Yes," the gnä' Fräulein confirms. "So you must know that men are looking at you."

Again, the uncertain silence.

"I wonder is all. Are you looking back?"

Rashka senses a pulse of danger. Shakes her head. "I don't..."

"You don't what? Know they are looking or look back?" The question has gained an edge. "It's all right. You're allowed to answer. In fact, I insist."

"I don't," says Rashka. "I don't know. And I don't look back."

"*Liar.*" The gnä' Fräulein defines her. "I've seen you with Emil. You look back at *him*. And he certainly looks at *you*."

Rashka is stunned. Her skin prickles, and she feels her belly hollow out.

"Do you deny it?" the woman asks her, flipping tightly through the magazine pages. "No? Good. At least now we have the truth between us," she says. "Do you know what the Stapo men call it here—to iron out a problem? It's when a problem is *flattened*. An unwanted wrinkle is pressed out. Do you know how easy it would be for me, Bissel, to iron you out? I need only have the NR erased from your name in the ledgers. Just two little letters." NR. Nicht registriert. Not Registered for Transport. "I could do it in a snap," she says, "and you would be on your merry way." The gnä' Fräulein allows this to sink in for a moment as Rashka stands frozen in her shoes. Finally, "I'll get the aspirin to your mother," she says. "Now, get out."

The night brings a terrifying bombing raid. An English bomber has dropped from the sky in flames and exploded into a street not so far away. The crash site is still smoking by morning, a tower of black rising upward. In fact, the city as a whole has assumed a pall of smoke that it wears like a shawl over its shoulders. The smell of it follows them even inside. Their little troika has returned to the café in the Friedrichstrasse. Cronenberg has gone outside to smoke. He does this sometimes, Rashka has noted, when the gnä' Fräulein is in a certain type of mood. Impatient and easily riled.

The Fräulein has her hair done up in a turban, because she recognizes that her red tresses are becoming too famous. Too easily identified among the U-boats. Rashka is seated beside her, but there is a problem. The gnä' Fräulein is not happy with her protégé. "I don't have you tagging along to eat cakes, Bissel," she tells Rashka. "Emil already thinks that I'm wasting my time. That I should throw you back to the rabble and let the next transport take you and your mother both. So you must produce *results*, *clear*? No more loafing," she scolds.

No more loafing. If Rashka Morgenstern is to be a catcher, she then must catch! She must grab! To save her life. To save the life of her mother, this is what she must do. Find a U-boat. Find herself in the face of another Jew. So can she be forgiven? Rashka begs of God. Can she be forgiven for what she is about to do? Cannot the Master of the Universe, praised be His holy name, step from her eema's prayer book and, in His limitless wisdom, see past her sin? Her crime? If she devotes herself to a lifetime of mitzvoth after this moment, can't her soul be cleansed?

"The girl in the corner," Rashka listens to herself say. She says this trying to keep her eyes dry. Trying to imitate resolve. It's the young schoolgirl with the sable braid and wine-red beret returned. The girl with whom Rashka had once exchanged an innocent wave. She is against the wall alone. The woman who was with her has left the table, so she has no adult attending her for protection. Just as Rashka had been, she is left alone without a mother. The girl allows her eyes to lurk about the café. She must search for danger by herself, shielded by nothing but a fragile bubble of anonymity.

But Rashka Morgenstern has just popped that bubble.

"Why *her*?" the Angel quizzes.

The schoolgirl happens to catch Rashka's eyes at that instant. She smiles without artifice. A small smile. But then the smile sinks. She looks unsure. Perhaps perplexed. But not alarmed. She is unaware that she has just been murdered.

Why her? "*Because*," Rashka the catcher replies, "she is me."

29.

Speak of the Wings

FIGHTING STRONG WINDS, AN AEROFLOT ILYUSHIN IL-12 MILI-tary transport, on route from Krasnoyarsk to Irkutsk in the Soviet Union, has plowed into the eastern slope of Mount Sivukha, approximately thirty kilometers from the Mana River. Of all aboard, no survivors.

Rachel clips the article from the paper while Aaron is at work. At home, an uneasy truce reigns. This is how it's been for the past several days since Aaron stopped sleeping at the restaurant and returned to their apartment, though not to their bed. He has been bunking on the couch. "Billeting" he calls it, like a soldier. They connect to one another only through the points of routine. She serves breakfast; he eats it. She washes the dishes or doesn't. He doesn't complain about the dirty dishes, but neither does he touch the sponge or the bottle of Ivory Liquid.

Her painting sits on the easel. The oils have dried enough for her to pick up her brush again, but she hasn't. She has cleaned her brushes in the kitchen sink but not used them. Aaron complains that he can't sleep lying on the couch with her naked portrait staring at him, so Rachel has draped it with a sheet like a ghost. The ghost of herself. They don't really touch each other, not as wife and husband might. They touch only logistically. Passing to enter the bathroom, to get to the sink to spit out toothpaste. Nor do they talk about what has gone wrong. What is *going* wrong. Probably because neither one can really say what exactly is going wrong, only that it is. So they live not quite like roommates but like business partners in their marriage.

Morning. Rachel wakes, having sweated through her pajamas. From the next room, she hears music. Nat King Cole singing "A Blossom Fell." She finds that Aaron has not left his bedclothes for her to strip from the couch as usual but has folded them neatly. Good Soldier Perlman. In fact, he is already dressed and wearing his necktie and suit jacket, sitting at the kitchen table with a coffee cup beside the percolator that dribbles steam from its spout. He looks up at her from his copy of the *Herald Tribune*. "There's coffee," he tells her.

Rachel approaches the table. Sits. Lights a cigarette from Aaron's pack. The sharpness digs into the back of her throat. She sighs out smoke.

Darkness. After midnight. She had given Aaron the bed because she is painting, and he hadn't argued. She can hear him snoring turbulently. An unshaded lamp burns, and the cat snoozes in a ball at one end of the sofa while Rachel sits on the opposite end, drilling into the past cemented in her own head.

Two decades before, on the day of the Nazis' anti-Jewish boycott, brown-shirted storm troopers defaced hundreds of Jewish shops across the city. She was only a child, inside Ehrenberg's Konditorei. Only a child staring out as a giant ogre in his dung-brown uniform slopped a paintbrush across the outside of the shop's window.

She sees it before she paints it.

But the light is switched on, and the glare hits the canvas like a soft punch. She sees it like it's been there all along, invisible until she follows the dots of a constellation. It propels Rachel forward off the sofa. Compels her to squeeze cadmium yellow from its tube onto the palette and smash a brush into the blob of greasy color before whipping up the dirty turp standing in the coffee can. She wants it wet; she wants it oozing and dripping. Muddy and desecrated to match her memory. A zodiac unto itself. A constellation now of a single star. The Shield of

David, six points dribbling down the face of the canvas, clothing her nakedness.

And now she must let it dry. She must allow her paint to settle into the canvas before she can finish. Naomi had slipped a couple of her cannabis roll-ups into Rachel's bag, so she sits by the window with the sash cracked open and smokes a juju, thinking of the schoolgirl with the sable plaits and the burgundy beret. Tears cool her cheek. A young girl entering Birkenau? It was a toss-up, wasn't it? Many went straight to the gas. Most did. Rachel can see the girl standing in front of her. "What happened to you?" she asks. "Tell me the truth. Did I murder you?"

But she keeps the truth to herself, this girl. And then she is gone, leaving Rachel gazing at the canvas before replacing the sheet over her easel. When Aaron comes out, she is shoving a casserole dish into the oven.

"Jeez, what's that smell?" Aaron wants to know, entering in his bathrobe and pj's. "You smoking those clove cigarettes that Naomi thinks are so beatnik?"

"Yes," she lies. But his attention is diverted.

"So Halloween's long gone, but we still got the ghost here haunting us, huh?" he says, surveying the shrouded easel. Rachel only pours out coffee from the percolator, but then he is behind her. "So do I at least still get a good-morning kiss, or have we suspended that practice?" he asks.

She turns and looks into his face. The pain, the uncertainty behind his flippancy. He's asking for mercy, so she gives him a kiss. Something more than a peck, but without heat. A kiss to satisfy the practice.

In Berlin, the transports continued till the end. Even as the thunder of the Red Army artillery drifted closer from the east, the transports continued. Lorries to the trains. Trains to the camps. The track rails were kept polished by use. For a moment, the schoolgirl joins them at the supper table. Aaron is busy with his favorite subject. Work. Something about Leo arguing with the owner of the Stork Club. Rachel is not paying attention. She's looking at the peas that her husband has actually taken the time to remove, pea by pea, from his helping of casserole and crowd into a pea ghetto on the side of his plate.

That's when the schoolgirl makes her appearance. Filling a chair. Gazing with empty eyes. Rachel wonders. If she survived the ramp where the trains were unloaded and the first Selektion began, it was just as likely that she starved, died of disease or an infected wound, or simply was sent to the Kremas on a whim by some SS doctor in a white coat. Or she froze to death on her pallet or dropped dead during a never-ending roll call on the Appellplatz. In Auschwitz-Birkenau, there were plenty of ways to die.

There's another headline at the bottom of the page of Aaron's discarded newspaper. A U.S.A.F. B-29 Superfortress has crashed into a suburb in California, killing all aboard. She separates the page of newsprint and folds it into a square that she slips inside the basket of magazines next to the sofa. She will save it for her clippings book.

That night, the telephone rings. It's after supper, and she is at the kitchen table with a cigarette, smoke hanging over the coffee cup that she's poured but left untouched. Aaron is reading *National Geographic*, sitting with it on the sofa when the phone starts to ring. On the third ring, he looks up. "Telephone, honey," he informs her.

She crosses to the gossip bench and picks it up. "Hello?"

"Rashka," she hears a familiar voice answer.

Aaron is mouthing: *Who is it?* Rachel turns away from him and looks blindly at the wall. A calendar from the Gruber Refrigeration Supply Company of Forest Hills, Queens, featuring an illustration of a giant red monkey pecking on a typewriter. "What's *happened*, Feter?" she asks.

"Happened?" her uncle echoes the word. "Has something happened?"

"I don't know. You sound as if it has."

"Well, I sound as I sound, Rokhl," he says dismissively, impatient to move past explanations. "I need to you see you. Tomorrow."

"Why?" she asks.

"*Why?*"

"Yes, Feter, *why?*"

"Because," he decides to admit. "Something's happened."

Once more, the meeting place is planned for none of her uncle's usual niches. Instead, it's the Automat. It's the Horn & Hardart's at Trinity Place across from the chapel graveyard. When she first arrived in the States, she was astonished by the existence of such a spot. The outside decorated like a Bohemian Weinstube from a fairy tale. And inside! She had never seen such a wonderland. Drop a coin into a slot, and pop open a small brass-framed window for a plate of steaming cheese-baked macaroni, a bowl of freshly creamed spinach, a chicken salad on rye bread with lettuce, or a tall slice of lemon meringue pie. Magic! The cafeteria steam table offered Salisbury steak, fish cakes, freshly carved ham, roast beef, and corned beef. The interior gleamed with bright light. The tile floor was shiny white. The tables were scrubbed spotless, and the customers poured in.

Now she finds the space to be a shabby ghost of itself. The customer population is sporadic. Wilted housewives in their department store hats at the end of shopping. Clots of shopgirls, stenographers, and secretaries forking up dishes of pear and cottage cheese or Jell-O salads, shedding their heels under the table. Stooped salesmen on their lunch break fortifying themselves on roast turkey and gravy with ruby-colored cranberry sauce and a glob of mashed potatoes on the side.

For nostalgia's sake, she slides a nickel into a slot and removes a slice of lemon meringue. But when she sits down with it, picking up her fork, she pauses. The meringue has gone hard, crusty brown and dotted with beads of grease.

"Ziskeit!" she hears and sets down the fork. Feter seizes her hands and kisses them as he scrapes into the chair opposite. "Meyn kind!" is what he says. He is still in his tweeds, and his necktie is straight, and his hair is combed, yet he looks exhausted. Also, she notes, the bamboo cane is missing from the ensemble.

"Feter" is all she says before he interrupts her.

"Rashka. You must listen to me," he insists. "What I am about to tell you may shock you. It may frighten you. But you must remain strong."

Silence. She sees that for all his surface bravado, the brash persona he is wearing like a cloak is utterly fabricated. His eyes betray a dread-filled panic.

"I hope you'll forgive me, but…" He must pause here to fortify himself. For effect? "But I lied to you." The confession. "Lied about *me*, about your eema's painting." And then he says, "I asked you for money for that gonif pawnbroker? You turned me down. I understood why," he is assuring her with great sympathy. His shoulders are hunched forward.

"A person can't give what they do not have. But *I*," he says, shaking his head—and here something begins to alter. A crack in the sheen of the performance when his eyes go overtly frantic in his head. "I couldn't let it go. *I couldn't.* So I went to someone else," he confesses. "I've managed to generate a few connections to the art world, even here in this meshugana metropolis," he insists with a certain manic egoism. "*Oh, yes*. The name Fritz Landau is still known to a handful of discerning souls, my dear. On that you can rely."

Rachel's gaze is probing. Both distressed and wary. Is he having a breakdown? A stroke? Should she consider finding a pay phone for the ambulance?

"So I went," he says solemnly, almost reverently, as if speaking of the Temple, "to the House of Glass."

Silence.

"You doubt this?" he demands to know in a tone that is laced with both indignation and fear. Of course he must be able to read her face.

"You doubt that your old uncle could still retain a shred of dignity with such a prestigious operation?"

"No. In fact, I don't doubt it, Feter." She does not mention Naomi's photograph. It would only push him further toward the edge: *What?* I am to be *spied upon*, Daughter?

"I just want the truth," she replies carefully.

"The truth? And what is *that*?" He snorts. Frowns. He closes his eyes for a moment and massages the side of his head with his fingers. Then he looks away from her. Bites his lips for an instant, eyes gone raw. What inner trauma is he staring at? Is it a breakdown, or is it an act? "Very well," he decides. "Truth is what you desire, then it is truth you shall receive. I met," he says, "with David Glass. Yes. The exalted one. The great man himself." He breathes out. "I explained to him what I knew."

"What you knew?"

"*And*, as it happened? What I knew was *valuable*. I was promised a commission," he says. "A commission for your eema's painting, ziskeit," he declares and swallows. Swallows hard. The blush of performance is leaking away from him. The color draining from his cheeks, exposing la couche morte beneath. The Dead Layer. "I convinced the man that if he buys for pennies, he could sell for a fortune. I would take no more than a modest percentage. Honestly, I was a bit amazed how quickly he agreed. But then it struck me that he must already *have* a buyer *in mind*. I simply never conceived that the buyer could be…" He stops. Unable to speak the name. His gaze goes hollow. "She married a rich man, of course. She's Mrs. Irving Mendelbaum now."

Rachel repeats the name vacantly. "Mendelbaum."

"Yes." He nods with leaden eyes. And then he says, "You recall the proverb, ziskeit? 'Speak of wings and the angel appears.'"

Silence.

And then her uncle says, "She's alive" in a toneless voice.

Rachel feels her face heat, her nerves vibrate. "No. No, she's not."

"Rashka... She is."

"No. No, you said yourself that she was dead. That she had hanged herself in a Russian cell."

"*That* was the lie," Feter informs her.

"No, this is the lie. What you are saying. She's not alive. *You're* lying, Feter. Eema always said you couldn't help yourself. That lies were too easy for you."

Feter is shaking his head. "Not this time."

"She *died*, Feter. Elle est morte!"

"Rashka." He makes her name sound like such a pitiable thing. "The truth is different. If someone was found hanged in a Soviet cell, it wasn't her. She is here. In New York. Very much alive. And she wants to see you."

30.

All Because of Her Little Goat

THE DAY IS COLD, BUT THE ORCHARD CAFÉ IS WARM. RASHKA breathes in the scent of perfume that clouds the air around the gnä' Fräulein, who has ordered them two coffees. No more warm milk; she is not a child. *Just look at yourself in the mirror, Bissel.* That's what the gnä' Fräulein tells her. Womanhood is upon her. The blessing and the curse of it. "Give me your face," the woman tells her, crooking her finger, gesturing for Rashka to turn toward her. Rashka shifts in her chair. "Closer," says the gnä' Fräulein. Rashka pokes her face slightly forward. There is something in the gnä' Fräulein's hand. A tube of lipstick that pops softly when it's uncapped. "Now, give me your lips, like so," she says and puckers lightly to demonstrate.

Rashka feels nervous. The color of the lipstick in the tube is red, bright as blood. Very few women in Berlin have such luxuries available, and besides, don't the Nazis detest cosmetics on good German women? But the color is so rich. She feels a pang of hunger for it as she obeys the command of the gnä' Fräulein. The feel is waxy but thick as it's applied. A smooth roll on the flesh of her lips. Upper lip. Then lower lip. The same slightly sticky velvety roll.

"Now do as I do," the gnä' Fräulein tells her and primps her lips together. Rashka obeys. The gnä' Fräulein observes her and then nods. "Yes," she says and holds up the small mirror in the shell-shaped powder puff case. Rashka stares at the color ripening her mouth in the reflection.

Rachel is walking aimlessly. Shoulders crouched. Head down and bumping into people. *Hey, lady! Watch it! Open your eyes, why don't you! Jeez, are you blind?* The words bounce off. She doesn't care. She is fleeing herself, but no matter how fast she bores ahead, no matter how many steps she puts behind her, she is still a prisoner of her own body, of her own mind, of her own history.

Stepping off a curb, she stumbles, and a car horn blares irately over a scream of brakes. She glares at the car's chrome bumper. The driver is shouting curses at her, but she shrugs them off. The car suddenly swings around her with an angry gun of its engine and is replaced by another car blaring its horn. At this point, like a sleepwalker coming awake, she blinks. Shakes herself. Standing at the curb is the schoolgirl with the sable braids and the wine-colored beret, watching her as always from the silence of death.

"Hey, sweetheart. Move out of the fuckin' street, for Chrissake!"

This time, she obeys the demand of the driver and steps back up onto the sidewalk. The girl has vanished.

"You should go see a fuckin' *shrink*, crazy bitch!" she hears the driver suggest, followed by another gun of another engine.

There's a telephone booth on the corner. Rachel is making a call as people pass by indifferently. The phone receiver in her hand, she inserts a nickel. She listens to the clatter of the dial as it rotates backward with each number. A truck rumbles past the booth as the drone of each ring precedes a dull clack of connection. But Dr. Solomon? He is not available. This is what the woman from his answering service tells her. Can she take a message?

Yes. The Red Angel is not dead. She is alive.

The answering service woman is confused. "I beg your pardon? Could you repeat that, please? The angel who?"

Rachel hangs up. Stares through the glass of the booth. Waiting for her across the street under the lamp of the United States Realty Building is the schoolgirl again. Watching.

Feter Fritz had given her the particulars. The time, the location, all arranged. She takes the Eighth Avenue Independent uptown. Entering Central Park, she feels cold. A deep, shivering chill. She digs out her bottle of Miltown to warm her, but her hands are shaking, and when she attempts to open the bottle, it slips from her grip, spilling the pills in all directions. "Scheisse!" she cries out. She could try to pick them up, kneel down on her hands and knees to retrieve them pill by pill, but that feels too humiliating, so she simply abandons the mess.

Off the Central Drive, there's a statue called *Eagles and Prey*. A small goat trapped in a crevice is devoured alive by a pair of ravenous eagles. This is where she finds the bench. The spot where Feter has instructed her to wait. This is the third cigarette she has smoked, lit from the ember of the last. The butts of the first two lie flat on the sidewalk, crushed by the toe of her saddle shoe. Her eyes close. Who is she expecting? A ghost scissored from her memory? A fury from her nightmares? A bloody archangel, fiery in her naked hunger, spreading her ragged wings?

Speak of the wings and the angel appears.

"Good morning, Bissel," she hears.

The shock is flooding. It matches the jolt from a frayed electrical plug, a cold pulse of electricity fed into the body, vibrating her bones. It sweeps through the whole of her. But then she simply stares into the still-beautiful face.

A transport. It's raining that day. The day Rashka loses her mother. Two lorries leave for the Grunewald rail station. Rashka is aware of this transport; who is not? But it is not until the gnä' Fräulein appears that she feels a horror fill her to overflowing.

"I put your feter on the train."

Confusion.

"The train?"

"To Poland. Your feter. Your feter and your eema both."

The pain of a thousand needles surges through Rashka's body. Her eyes burn. Her mouth opens, but no words come. No words at all.

"It's for your own good, Bissel. Your uncle? Really, he was doomed from the start. Even *he* knew that. And your mother? Your mother, Bissel, she was holding you back," the gnä' Fräulein insists. "She was a drag on you," the woman says. "An *impediment*. You can see this, can't you, Bissel? I'm sure you can. For us to...*to do our work*, we must be free of impediments. So you must be strong, Bissel. No tears," she commands, wiping away the tears that are streaming down Rashka's cheeks. "You must be hard like stone."

"I *don't* understand," Rashka whispers, her voice raw. "You *promised*. You promised to keep her *safe!*" Suddenly, she is shouting like a mad demon. The whole of her being feels aflame. "*You promised! You promised!*" And then she sees stars as the gnä' Fräulein slaps her across the face with the back of her fist.

"You! How can you *dare* speak to me so? I've kept you alive. Do you think that Dirkweiler cared one shit about another insignificant Jewish sow? It was *me* who kept you off the trains. Not your beloved feter. *Me!* No one else! Me alone! And this is how I'm repaid? With your childish *anger?*"

Rashka feels the blood dripping from her nose. Tastes it on her lips.

"Do you think I have taken on the burden of your life for my own well-being? A stupid little fish to keep swimming? *No.* This is for *your* good, not mine. Can you comprehend what I've done? I have saved your life. I chose you over your mother. Though now I think maybe I should have put you both on the train and saved myself the heartache."

These are the woman's last words on that day.

The next morning comes, and Rashka is aroused with a kick. "Come, Bissel," says the gnä' Fräulein flatly. "Time to earn your keep."

The bombing is worse now. The Tommies by night, the Amies by day. Masses of gleaming silver wings streaking through the blue of the sky. The wine restaurant that the gnä' Fräulein had picked for the day has evacuated to the nearest U-Bahn tunnel, which is now thickly crowded with Berliners intent on surviving the latest onslaught. Above them, the guns of the Zoo Flak Tower begin to pound the air, and a fresh swell of people invade the tunnel, but in the crowd, the gnä' Fräulein is suddenly gone. Separated from Rashka and the man Cronenberg. The tunnel stinks of fear and of soapless Berliners. Faces are numb-looking. Numb to any illusion of victory piped out through the loudspeakers of the Propaganda Ministry. Numb to the daily ration of destruction. Numb to the crush of defeat.

Rashka is numb as well. She tries to imagine where her eema is. In a slave camp somewhere east? Is she hungry? Frightened? Cold? Does she believe that Rashka has abandoned her? Rashka herself feels beyond tears. She has isolated her soul within her body. Now she simply breathes in and out. Her heart simply continues to beat without pur-pose, when abruptly, she feels a hand invade the inside of her coat. It's Cronenberg. For an instant, it feels like a violation. But then the hand is withdrawn. He has stuffed her coat with an envelope. She glares at the man's face in confusion, but Cronenberg's eyes are level.

"That's money and papers," he tells her. "Enough for train fare and some food along the way. Also, a bomb pass with a false name. Your building was bombed out. Your father's at the front. You'll be on your way to join your family in the town of Furtwangen in the Schwarzwald. That ought to put you far enough west of the Russians when they come."

She is too shocked to answer him.

"Not much of a plan. Might not work. But it's the best I could manage," he tells her. "When the raid ends, leave by the opposite stair-well. I'll make sure she doesn't catch up with you. So good luck, little baggage," he says, and then he is gone.

"I know it was me who asked for this meeting," says the Angel, "but I almost did not come." She tells this to Rachel on the park bench as if she is speaking more to herself. They are separated on the bench by an empty middle space of a little less than a foot. That's all. "I thought you might be laying a trap for me." She frowns off at the trees for a moment before she speaks. "That you might have some misguided desire for vengeance."

"You must mean for justice."

"Justice?" The Angel turns with a half smile. "Let's not get in over our heads, child. Justice." She repeats the word. "*True* justice. Don't you believe that might sink us both?" She breathes in smoke and then releases it. "That's why I decided to take the risk. I thought, if I am guilty of anything, then surely she is guilty too."

Rachel turns away from those huntress eyes and stares at the walk. The spent cigarettes and daily sweep of litter, from which the ashes of a nameless, braided schoolgirl have risen on the breeze and assembled themselves. The girl stands before Rachel as she must have once stood before the death chamber of the Krematorium. Stripped to her flesh, staring still with terror yellowing her eyes. And then she melts in a drizzle of wind.

"So why can't we dispose of this nonsense, hmm? I did what I did, and I'll tell you why. It began as all tragedies begin. With a mitzvah, of course. When I was first arrested, I tried to spare my parents. They were vulnerable. Helpless. I did my best to save them. Them *and myself*," she admits. "I confess to that much. I was trying to save myself as well. I had an instinct for self-preservation, but is that a crime? Every animal has the instinct for life, and only the human animal lays blame to it. But what can be said? Did you know there was money paid for Jews?" she asks. "Two hundred marks, Dirkweiler paid me. Two hundred marks per Jew. That's what they paid me for *you*. I admit it. You and your mother. Four hundred Reichsmarks you earned me. So don't expect to get high and mighty with me, child," she instructs. "You were pocket money." She pauses to ignite a cigarette from a gold-plated case.

"Why aren't you dead?" Rachel asks aloud.

"I beg your pardon?"

"I said, why aren't you dead?" she repeats. "You committed suicide in a Russian jail," Rachel points out. "So why aren't you dead?"

And the Angel shows her an ugly, humorless smile. "When the Red Army entered Berlin, Dirkweiler blew his own brains out. The lager disintegrated. Berlin disintegrated. Emil and I had slipped into the city at night during a raid, but we split up after the Russians crossed the Teltowkanal, and I didn't see him again. I hid until the Russians found me like the Russians found most women," she says. "It was brutal and debasing. But then I acquired a protector. A major in the NKVD. He was ugly and smelled of onions, but he could make things happen. It was he who had the rumor spread that I had been arrested and hanged myself.

"It was all nonsense. I was never arrested. What crime had I committed after all? But it worked. It saved me from the zealots rooting out so-called war criminals. What dreck. One does what one must to survive, and that is a crime? *You* did what you did because you thought it would keep you alive, didn't you, Bissel? When you spied that little Mädchen with the braids in the café that morning? You did what you did to stay off the transports. To keep yourself alive. To keep your mother alive. I understand. Your *mother* understood. That's why she gave you up."

Rachel glares darkly at her.

"Ah, such a look. You didn't know, Bissel?" she taunts. "Mummy never told her little Schatzi? Well, then *I* will tell. I asked her permission. Your uncle Fritz had some power over the transport lists, yes, but it was limited. Dirkweiler could overrule any decision at any time. But I had the power to influence the Herr Kommandant himself. No one netted him Jews like I did, not even Emil. *But.* Before I brought you into the *business.* Shall we call it that? Before then, I wanted your mother to agree. I simply refused to allow her to *pretend* that I had stolen you from her. You were a gift, Bissel. Your eema gave you to me. Just as she had given me to your uncle since she was too cowardly to pursue her *own* feelings for me. She had a *reputation*. She had a *child*. It was hard for a woman to survive in the art world. So I understood. But I did not forgive. How does a person ever really forgive betrayal?" She crushes out her cigarette. "I have done some digging on you, Bissel. Isn't that how it is called? Digging? You are married."

"Yes," says Rachel.

"But no children?"

Rachel says nothing.

"No? Your husband would like things differently, perhaps? Never mind. No need to answer. I can see it in your face. My advice, Bissel, is stand to your ground. How is it said? 'Stick to your guns.' The world does not have to be an unhappy place. Can you learn that, do you think? There are beautiful things to be had. To be enjoyed. If there is any lesson I can still teach you, perhaps it could be this: the world resents the unhappy but indulges those who know how to take joy from their surroundings."

And suddenly the Angel issues a laugh. "I'm sorry," she says. "I don't mean to laugh. It's only that here I am *preaching*. The last thing you expected from me, I'm sure. You must have hoped I would break to pieces in front of you. Come apart like a doll. But be honest, will you?"

Rachel grinds out words. "You have my mother's painting."

"Yes. So I do. And—I believe I have the story correct, yes? Your Feter Fritz discovered it with a *pawnbroker?*" She pronounces the word with amused disdain. "How astonishing. It makes one suspect the hand of fate, doesn't it? I sometimes sit and gaze at it, wondering if I could really have ever been so young. With so much fire. Your mother was a genius. She captured the essence of youth. Of desire."

"And is this why we are *here?*" Rachel wishes to know. Is it for her to gloat? *Kvell* is the word she uses.

"What? *No.* I asked your uncle to arrange things not so I could kvell

over a thing. But so I could offer you help. I want to *help* you, Bissel,"
she declares.

"*Help?* From the one they called Red Angel?"

The Angel's expression flattens. "Don't use that name."

"Why not? It was who you were. The Red Angel of Death. And
help from her was always poison."

"So I am to be blamed now for staying alive? For doing what was
necessary? I thought you learned what courage survival took. I thought
I had taught you that at least. But now you sound like a pitiful victim.
The poor little Jewess who can never remove the Judenstern after it was
sewn over her heart."

Rachel shivers. With rage? With fear? With grief? She can speak
only to spit a curse. Black sorrow she wishes upon the woman.

But the Angel is unimpressed. She shakes her head, disappointed,
even as tears like ice are running down Rachel's cheeks. "Ah, Bissel,"
she laments. "In so einem Gewirr bist du," the woman declares. Such
a tangle you are in. Then she is digging into her alligator handbag for
an expensive linen handkerchief. "You were a delicate child, so your
mother always said. 'Rokhl? She is a delicate little bird,' is what she told
me. Wipe your eyes," she instructs, offering the linen square.

But Rachel refuses the offer, uses her palms to smear at her tears.
"You cannot speak to me so. Ir zent nisht meyn muter," she burns. You
are not my mother.

"No," the Angel admits, frowning lightly as she returns the handkerchief to her purse. "No. But I *could* be."

Rachel's glare goes jagged. She coughs, covering her mouth.

"I *could* be," the Angel repeats. "I'm a very wealthy woman, Bissel.
My late husband, Irving, was called 'the Concrete King,' and believe me,
in New York City, the king of concrete was a very good thing to be. I
could *help* you," she presses. "Ikh ken helfn du."

"*You?* Help *me?*"

"Is that so absurd? I have no children of my own. And your uncle tells me now that you are an *artist*. That you have inherited your eema's talent."

Rachel stares.

"I could *help* you if you'd allow it. I know many people in the art world," she says. "I am well known as a collector. I have many connections I could share with you."

"Such as David Glass," Rachel notes leadenly.

"David? *Yes*, why not David? He has a good eye and is always interested in emerging talent."

"I went to his gallery looking for Eema's painting. The girl there acted as if I was demented."

"Pfft!" The Angel dismisses this. There is a certain manic hunger creeping into her voice. Into her eyes. "That makes no difference. I spend *plenty* with the Glass Gallery. Plenty. So believe me, what I ask for, I will get. Oh yes. But Glass is only *one* gallery. It's a big city. There are any number I could call on. Many debts I could collect."

But Rachel has no reply to the bribe she is being offered. The bait laid by the Angel for her trap. "You made me into a murderer," she announces and watches the woman's face freeze, cut off in midbreath from her busy spree of possibilities. "I am the crime that you committed," Rachel tells her. "And now you think you can buy my forgiveness? That I will sell myself like you did?"

The Angel's expression levels. "I may have sold myself, Bissel, but never cheaply. Never for mediocre gains. I know more about you than you might guess. Your marriage to a man who makes pennies? No children. No future. A few paintings sold from a nameless gallery years ago. And *then*? Clapped into an asylum. My, what would your eema think of that? Her poor daughter? 'What a waste,' she would say."

"Do not speak for her!" Rachel shouts, the rage like a blast of steam. "Don't you dare speak for her! You *murdered* my mother!"

"I *loved* your mother," the Angel shouts back. Painfully, as if her own words have cut her heart from her breast. "*I* was the one betrayed!

She betrayed *me*! For you! For her *child*. Didn't you ever figure that out? It wasn't *the world*. It wasn't her high-and-mighty reputation. It was *you*. The child! We couldn't be together because of *you*! I was nineteen years old, Bissel. I would have given her myself in every way, but instead she gave me up! Passed me on to her brother all because of her *little goat*!"

The sky cracks open at that moment, and the rain that follows the thunder falls like a lead curtain. A man with a newspaper evacuates his bench, dashing away with his paper over his head. The Angel contains herself. Reassembles herself from her outburst and raises her umbrella.

"Ah. Now comes the flood," she announces and then offers, "Shall we share my shirem?"

Rachel squints through the soaking downpour. She has felt a poison bubbling through her, but now it is on a full roil. She barely makes it off the bench before she heaves the whole boiling mess onto the grass, splattering the sculpture's granite base with vomit. The sickness of it all coming up. The murderous eagles must be outraged at the affront, their slaughter interrupted. She spits.

The Red Angel has risen from her seat. She is standing there under the umbrella's black crown, shoulders back, victorious now, a smug pity forming her expression. She thinks she won. She gazes down at Rachel as she says, "You think you are so special in your guilt, Bissel? It is so precious to you? So precious that it sickens you, but you cannot vomit it out because you do not want to. You want to keep it down in your belly where it can boil. But your guilt does not make you special.

"That girl in that farshtunken café off the Friedrich? With her silly plaits and beret? She was a casualty of war," the Angel informs her. "Like tens of millions of others across the breadth of this farshtunken world. There was nothing special about her. Just as there was nothing special about your so-called crime. Yet you must make it so. You must make it such a terrible transgression that it stops you from living. You hide behind it, hide from life. But you need not. You *can* move beyond it."

Rachel stares at the woman as the rain begins to soak into her.

Those hard green eyes. The muscle twitches along the line of the woman's jaw.

"See yourself in my mirror, Bissel," the Angel tells her. "I am your reflection, just as you are mine." She reaches out. Reaches out to touch Rachel on the arm, but Rachel bats the attempt away.

"It's *you* who sickens me." She wipes her mouth on her sleeve and swallows her breath. "It is you. *You* are the sickness," she declares. "It's too bad the rumor wasn't true. That you *didn't* hang yourself ten years ago. Think of how much air you have stolen since then, just by breathing. Think of how much space you've purloined by staying alive. Space that should have belonged to someone else. Someone human."

"Bissel," the Angel says.

"You are nothing but disease! A plague that infects everyone you have ever touched!"

The Angel seizes her arm, her eyes jagged. "*Rashka.*"

Rachel tugs to regain her arm. "Let go! You have no claim on me."

"I'm *dying*," the woman shouts, her voice suddenly a croak.

Rachel freezes. She sees the raw bewilderment at such a fact in the Angel's face.

"I'm dying," she repeats.

"Another lie," says Rachel.

"No. No, simply the truth. I have cancer of the blood." The muscles twitch again along her jaw. "There is no cure," she says. "Only death is the cure."

Rachel breathes. She shrugs her arm free from the Angel's grip, and this time, there is no resistance.

"It's why I bought your mother's painting. It's why, when I was informed of your uncle's part in its discovery, I revealed myself to him as its new owner. But not because of him or the painting either. Because I wanted to know about *you*. And when he told me you had your mother's gift with the paintbrush?" She breathes out. "This is why I wanted him to push you. To produce your own work while I still have the time to act.

I will buy whatever you produce, Bissel, and *pay plenty* for it. I still will, don't you see? I could give you the career that your mother had!"

Rachel stares, but then turns and walks away. She walks away with her head up as the rain pours down, soaking through her. She hears the woman crying out her name behind her. But she does not turn. She does not slow. She feels the rain washing through her.

In the shower, the water is scalding.

Seated at the kitchen table, holding the cat in her lap, Rachel watches the smoke rise from the cigarette. She has replaced the green glass ashtray that she threw on the floor with a red plastic item sporting the word FIRE in white block letters—unbreakable. She is dressed in a pullover and dungarees, her feet in wool socks, her hair still damp. A change in the wind rattles the window behind her. She absorbs the rattle. Evicts the cat from her lap and crosses into the closet beside the bedroom.

From behind the vacuum cleaner, she retrieves the shopping bag from B. Altman that hides her scrapbook of clippings. She opens it to the last entry. A United Airlines jet called the "Mainliner Denver" was destroyed in midair when a hidden bomb exploded in the luggage compartment. The creased newsprint is bumpy with library paste.

The rain has dwindled to a cold drizzle, but Rachel has not bothered to wear a coat as she opens the foyer door and steps out onto the stoop. She does not run but keeps a steady pace, trotting down the steps. The air smells lightly of smoke as she descends the steps to the cellar where the trash bins are located. Dented garbage receptacles, grimy and smelling, the street number slopped on the sides with black paint.

The blackness of the clouds has grayed. A thin flow of thunder drifts above her head as she lifts the lid on the middle can with a light clank of metal. Then drops in the bag. Goodbye to it. Goodbye to her book of scraps. Her history of disaster plummeting from the sky like a falling angel. Dumped now into the trash. Goodbye. She clamps down the lid.

Shedding the shroud from her easel, Rachel stares into the canvas. A dark rectangle. But under the skim of black, her own image emerges like a pale pentimento. Naked and glaring. The Magen David dripping down into her eyes.

She lets her head drift lightly to one side. And then she is moving. It doesn't take long to assemble her palette. Lead white. Zinc white. Titanium. Lamp black. Alizarine crimson.

On the day she was taken, the girl with the burgundy beret did not cry. She did not scream. The terror in her eyes was banked by obedience. The girl is curled into a white fetal sphere and inserted into the womb of the painting. And there is something mysterious that Rachel searches for now as she paints the girl's face in miniature. An attempt at life. Deuteronomy commands it. *Behold, I give before you this day the life and the good, the death and the evil, blessing and curse; and you shall choose life, so that you will live, you and your seed.*

When Aaron comes home, he's brought one of the restaurant's doggy bags with him, a little greasy at the bottom. "The red snapper was pretty good at lunch," he says. "Thought I'd bring some home." He passes behind her and heads for the oven. "What should I set the temp at to warm it up?"

Rachel looks at her husband's face, the crooked half grin. The hopeful boyishness in his eyes that shines through even his exhaustion.

She bursts into tears. He reacts with confusion at first. "Hey, what's wrong? What did I do now?" Then his brow crinkles. "Honey, what is it? Whatssa matter?"

Is she hurt? Is she bleeding somewhere, what? But then he sees the painting.

The image of his wife behind the black curtain and then the

gestating ghost of a child. His face crunches up. His eyes narrow. He's on his feet, holding onto Rachel, who's hugging his waist. All he manages to say is, "What the…"

"It's my crime, Husband," she whispers. "My precious crime."

That night. That night in bed, Rachel grasps him before he can even turn off his bedside lamp. They are artless with each other, clumsy in their coupling, but it makes no difference. The crush is all that's important. Rachel is on her back. The springs squeak. The mattress is ungiving, unforgiving. She uses Aaron as an anchor to keep her pinned. She grips his curls like she might like to rip them out from his head.

It's hard to keep track. To be sure that she will make him pull out in time. Hard to focus on anything but the hard pulse between them. She is thinking but not thinking. "Fire" is all she is thinking. The fire consuming her. The fire defining her. Reducing her will to ashes. And when suddenly his body arches and spasms, it's too late to think. It's too late and she lets him flood her, with nothing between to separate them.

31.

Shemp Howard Is Dead

THE DAYS ARE GROWING COLDER. RACHEL WITNESSES DANIELA changing a diaper, and she watches with disbelief. The safety pins. The pail full of smelly diapers. The small, naked baby squiggling at the center of attention, eyes goggling with curiosity. Daniela is planning for her mikveh after childbirth. The Jewish Women's Club has made her an appointment at a mikveh on the Upper West Side. A ritual bath and a cleansing of the soul. It sounds so inviting to Rachel. To be so well cleansed.

At home, Rachel throws up in the toilet. She washes her mouth in the sink. Gargles with a cup full of Listerine and flushes the evidence into the plumbing. When Aaron asks if she's okay, knotting his tie in her vanity mirror, she tells him she shouldn't have eaten his leftover kung pao shrimp from the fridge. He accepts this explanation without question, stubbing out his cigarette in the seashell ashtray. "Kung pao," he says, frowning. "Not for amateurs. You should let the professionals handle it, sweetheart."

She takes the train to the Village. She finds Naomi is less of a mess in that she is no longer teary. No longer wearing a ragged sweatshirt with stains and has started bathing and washing her hair again. The long chestnut ponytail is still hanging down her back. But life is not perfect. Much less than perfect. Naomi makes that clear. She pulls out the bottle of wine, but Rachel finds she doesn't have a taste for it and declines to join her. Naomi doesn't seem to care. About that or much of anything. She dirties ashtrays, lights cigarettes, and sighs out smoke, her eyes clouded, staring, ringed with sleepless purple shadows.

Perhaps Rachel has come to say something, to make an intimate announcement. To use her sister-in-law as practice, as a test case for her news. To run it up the flagpole and see who salutes, isn't that the expression? But she can see that Naomi is deaf to the world, so she keeps her announcement to herself.

Snow flurries sweep mindlessly around the park at Washington Square, but the game squares are still filled by players, wrapped in coats and sweaters, shivering against the chill of the concrete benches. She finds the scruffy white beatnik kid with the dirty horn-rims and uncombed hair. He's wearing an earthy brown jacket from an army surplus store and must be freezing. His breath frosts, for heaven's sake. "Haven't seen him," the kid tells her when she asks about Tyrell. "Not since Yaakov kicked the bucket."

Rachel is surprised. The grand master?

"Yeah," the boy tells her. "Middle of a game, just keeled over, *boom*. Heart attack," the kid cites. "Pieces flew everyplace."

Crossing the square, Rachel sits on the wall around the fountain, facing Washington Arch, and lights a cigarette. She is surprised when she hears his voice.

"Hello, Mrs. Perlman."

She turns her head. "Hello, Mr. Williams."

"What are you doing here?"

"Looking for you, actually," she admits.

He stands with his hands jammed into the pockets of his coat. "Well," he says and looks away as if the pigeons bobbing around them have caught his interest. "If you're here because Naomi sent you, Mrs. Perlman…"

"I'm not. She doesn't know I'm here. Nobody knows."

Now he faces her with a mild frown. "So why then?"

"Won't you sit, Mr. Williams? It's hurting my neck looking up at you."

His expression says he'd rather not. But maybe he's just too well mannered, so he sits, leaving a few steps separating them.

"I'm sorry to hear about Mr. Yaakov," she says. "About his heart attack."

The frown stays. "How'd you know about *that*?"

"The boy with the glasses told me."

"Pete," says Tyrell.

"What?"

"That's the name of the kid with the glasses. Pete."

"Were you there when he died?" she asks.

"*There?* I was *playing* him," Tyrell says with a small snort at grim fate. "We were in the middle of a *game*."

"A rematch?"

"I guess you could call it that."

"It must have upset you."

He shrugs at this. Maybe, maybe not. "It's not like I'd never seen a person die before."

"The boy said that chess pieces flew everywhere."

"Yeah, well. That's true. What's also true is that I was getting creamed. Lucky for me, the old man dropped dead before I had to resign." He says this and then removes a chess piece from his pocket. The black king.

"This was yours?"

"Nah. This was *his*."

"Oh. So you were white," says Rachel.

And now Tyrell surrenders half a smile. "Yeah. I was white."

"And this is your trophy?"

"Not trophy," Tyrell decides, absently twirling the king by its crown. "More like a memento mori I guess you could call it." A talisman of the dead.

Rachel pauses and expels smoke from her cigarette before she says, "Naomi is still very devastated," she says.

Tyrell expels a heavy-bottomed sigh. "Mrs. Perlman…"

"Please call me Rachel."

"She doesn't *understand*." He's certain on this point.

"No? She's very smart."

"Not about *this*. Naomi is wonderful. Beautiful. Brilliant. Yes, I know. But she has *no idea* what it would be like for us in the long term. What it would be like for us out of the bubble we're in. Here, things are easier. *Possible*. But the world is not Greenwich Village."

"No. The world is Mississippi."

"Exactly," Tyrell agrees.

Rachel agrees. She nods lightly, but she has started staring blankly at the pavement.

"Rachel?" he asks.

She looks up at the sound of her name. "Ikh bin mit kind," she says aloud.

Tyrell blinks. Shakes his head as if he's gone deaf maybe. "I'm sorry, what did you just say?"

"I'm with child," Rachel repeats, this time in English. "I'm going to have a baby, and I've told no one. Not even my husband."

Tyrell looks flummoxed. "Yet you're telling *me*?"

"I tell you because you will understand why I'm so terrified. I'm terrified because the world is Mississippi and sometimes worse. Because it eats children alive. Poisons them. Burns them up and casts their ashes into the pits." She shakes her head, smears the dampness from her eyes. "It's just so strange. And so frightening. To have another human being, *separate from you*, yet growing *inside* you."

"You should tell your husband," says Tyrell. "He's got a right to know."

She nods. "Yes. I'm sure you're correct," she agrees. Then, "What time is it?" she asks and then balks at the answer. "Oh, I have to go. I have an appointment. Thank you for listening to me. And for your understanding."

"Sure," Tyrell tells her. "Sure." Covering it all.

"And you should think about calling Naomi. I believe the two of you need each other. More than you are willing to see."

He straightens. Expels a breath. Gazes off toward the tall marble arch. "Yeah," he answers quietly. "Sometimes... I dunno. Sometimes I think that's true. How stupid are people in love, Mrs. Perlman," he wonders.

She sticks out her hand to shake, like at the end of the chess game. He takes it.

"How stupid is the world, Mr. Williams," she answers.

It's been how long? A week since their argument in the Orchard Café? But the telephone call came, as Rachel knew it would. "Nisht gefonfit, Feter!" she'd insisted. No hedging. No double-talk. She wanted an apology.

So here they are, not at one of her feter's usual preserves but at the Bickford's on East 23rd Street. Bickford's, where the grisly yellow fluorescent lighting competes with the daylight washing through the tall glass windows. Rachel is reserved. Maybe *she* is here for his apology, but what is *he* here for? The coffee steams in a cheap ceramic Bickford's cup. It tastes overcooked and slightly vinegary. A skim of oil greases the dark-brown surface with a purplish rainbow. Feter dumps sugar into it, gulping it down, drinking it like a punishment. He speaks to her now in Yiddish.

"I must make an admission, Rokhl." Du bist geven gerekht. "You were correct," he says. "I was attempting to exploit your talent. It's true, and I only hope you can forgive me," he tells her. "But it is also true that you have your mother's gift. And I do believe," he says carefully, "that for *your* good, and yes, for *my good as well*—I can find a gallery for your work."

Her tolerance for Feter's schéma grandiose is limited. But she cannot deny a weak, dizzy hope at such a possibility, even now. Therefore, she must be clear. "What exactly are you proposing, Feter? A business relationship?"

A business relationship? A partnership, he thinks, is a better word.

"As you had with Eema?"

He shrugs lightly with open palms. "Would that be so intolerable?"

Rachel breathes deeply. "So. You haven't said a word," she observes.

"Haven't I?" he wonders.

"You haven't asked me a thing. But maybe you don't need to. Are you still connected, you and her?"

His face grays. "We were not 'connected' as you put it, no. I simply played the role of her messenger."

"So you don't speak?"

"We do not," he admits thinly.

"Do you know she is dying?"

"Yes," he answers. "But who isn't, Rashka, my dear? Who isn't?"

Days pass. A gush of cold air blows in as Rachel opens the kitchen window. Kibbitz leaps out on the prowl. Snowflakes dance through the air. She hesitates for an instant longer, then shoves the sash closed.

"Hey, Shemp Howard is dead."

"Who?"

Aaron is seated at the table over his breakfast, a grapefruit, since he's been putting on a little weight, he thinks. "Shemp Howard." He repeats the name. "He was one of the original Stooges."

A shrug. "I have no idea what you're saying."

"The Three Stooges. You *know*," he insists, as if she *should* know. As if who could possibly *not* know. "Once, there was a fourth stooge?" he says. But then gives up, surrendering the paper. "Anyhow. Here, you can read all about it. I gotta get my ass in gear." He stretches from the lower back up, extending his arms and yawning out a spacious breath. Then he's up, heading for the bedroom to tie his tie, singing along to the radio to "Sixteen Tons" in a faux bass voice. "Ya dig sixteen tons—whattaya get? Another day older and a cherry-red Corvette…"

But Rachel is not listening. She has suddenly seized the page of obituaries. A headline and picture.

Mrs. Angel Mendelbaum, wife to Mr. Irving Mendelbaum of the construction firm of Mendelbaum & Sons, sadly fell to her death yesterday morning from the terrace of the couple's penthouse apartment on East 91st Street and Fifth Avenue. Mrs. Mendelbaum was alone at the time of the accident. Born in Berlin, Germany, she became a naturalized U.S. citizen in 1947 and will be remembered as a generous supporter of Jewish charities as well as a patroness of the arts.

Staring at the photograph, Rachel hears the voice and looks up at the face.

You didn't imagine that I was going to allow myself to be victimized by the ravages of a disease, did you, Bissel?

The woman who fills the chair across from her is not the matron Rachel faced in the park. She is the gnä' Fräulein, in lace gloves and fine fabrics. She has resurrected herself as the exquisite murderess from the Prenzlauer Berg. The Red Angel of Berlin, her vanity intact even after death. And then she is gone. Her final murder victim was herself.

Aaron reappears, flapping his arms into his jacket, and belches lightly. "Oy, that grapefruit is so full of acid," he complains, but she isn't really listening to him until he steals the piece of toast from her plate.

"*Thief,* that's my toast."

"Sue me," he suggests, chewing. "You know, my pop had the same breakfast every day for forty million years. One poached egg on toast with pickled herring. That and a glass of prune juice." He says this and downs the last swallows of coffee from his cup.

"Coffee won't help a sour stomach," she points out.

He shrugs. Whattaya gonna do? "Life is suffering. I gotta run."

"I'm pregnant," she says. The words fall out.

32.

For the World That Will Come

THE FROST IS STICKING TO THE WINDOWPANE. A THOUSAND intricate stars of frost. It's mesmerizing.

"So," he begins. On his way out. Lights his Lucky from the gas burner and huffs smoke. "You've got an appointment today, right? With the doctor?"

"Yes. Two o'clock."

"Should I come with?"

"Should you?" Rachel sounds slightly too surprised. "I don't know. Why?"

"I don't know either," he says. "This is the first time I'm having a baby too, ya know. I got no idea what the hell I'm supposed to be doing. *Go* with my wife to the obstetrician? *Don't* go with my wife to the obstetrician? So I ask you."

"Because I'm the expert."

"Well, in this case, you're the star of the show, honey," he says, stubbing out her cigarette for her. A habit he's developed to curb her smoking, because his mother read an article in *Reader's Digest*. "I'm just playing a bit part. The guy who walks on in Act Three and says, 'Your Majesty! The heir to the throne is born!'"

"I don't know *what* you are saying, as usual. But the doctor's only a few blocks away. I can walk."

"No, no," Aaron begins to insist. "No *walking*, thank you very much. Take a cab."

"A cab costs money."

"So what's money? Who cares? No slipping on the icy sidewalks for the pregnant lady, please," he tells her, bending over to kiss her on the head. "I gotta go."

"You don't want breakfast? I'll get up and make you breakfast."

"Nah. No time. Don't worry. I'll grab a sack of cashews on the way in," he tells her, sliding on his overcoat from the coat tree. "There's a guy with a cart on the way to the train."

As he adjusts the fit of the jacket's shoulders, he bends forward. "Okay, so I'm going this time for real," he says, coming back to dispense a final kiss, a big smack on the cheek. Then he pops on his hat and is heading out. "Chinese tonight," he declares. "I promise, nothing too spicy. Some chicken and broccoli or something."

"Sure," she says, when she is pinched by a pulse of need and calls his name. "*Aaron?*"

"That's me."

He's stopped. But now she's not sure what to say. Suddenly, she feels embarrassed by the impulse, so what she says is, "I'll have an egg roll."

"Okey-dokey," her husband says. "Egg rolls on the side. I'll see you at the doctor's at two. There—I made the decision," he announces. "Take care of the heir."

"I will," Rachel says back. And then, "Aaron?"

He stops once more, eyebrows raised. "Yes, honey?"

"I'm not the star of the show," she tells him and lays her hand on the swell of her belly. "The star is inside me."

Aaron looks back at her for a second. "Okay," he says. "I'll remember that. See you at two."

She nods. Then listens as the door closes behind him.

Turning back to the window, Rachel gazes at the icy galaxy of snowflakes clinging to the glass. Each unique. Each fragile, fleeting in the brightness of daylight.

The cat curls around her ankles, and she scoops him up, transports him to the sofa, where she deposits him on the couch. At twelve weeks, she is just starting to show. Her belly is a small, round bump that stops her pedal pushers from properly fitting.

On the wall, her painting hangs without a frame. Hangs from a pair of nails, a little crooked because she's never been good at straight lines. Aaron does not complain. She has agreed to him moving the sofa to face the opposite direction, so that the painting does not give him the evil eye, though now and again, she spots him gazing at it as if he's staring into the darkness of a cave. A cave that has opened up in their living room.

It becomes late in the afternoon, and she has dozed off on the sofa after her return from the appointment with the obstetrician. A woman no less! Dr. Eileen Kushner, a middle-aged practitioner with calm eyes and competent hands. She calls Rachel "Mami," as in, Now breathe deeply for me, Mami.

Aaron remains uncomfortable around a female physician and keeps wondering whether they should go see Dr. Grauberger in Brooklyn, "Just to be on the safe side?" But Rachel likes Dr. Kushner, and who needs to schlep all the way out to Avenue P in Midwood?

The door buzzer rouses her from her nap. The copy of *ARTnews* she had been paging through has fallen on the floor. She shakes herself awake and wobbles toward the door only to find that it's the German super standing there with an oversized wooden crate he has hauled up from below.

Rachel's eyes go wide. "What? What is this?"

"Just delivered for you, Mrs. Perlman. A man on a truck." The stencil on the crate's exterior reads: G. ALBERT GLASS GALLERY, FIFTH AVE, NEW YORK.

"Shall I open it up for you?" the German wants to know. "The crate?"

It takes some work with a hammer from his tool belt, prying out nails with the claw. Rachel keeps her distance, standing with her arms folded. But after a few minutes, the large rectangle emerges packed in straw and wrapped with kraft paper. Rachel glares heavily at the shape as the German collects the scraps of crate wood. "There you are, Missus Perlman," he tells her, hovering, and she realizes he must be waiting for a tip.

"Oh. Um. Let me get my purse," she says, avoiding eye contact, but the German is shaking his head no. Nothing is required, he tells her in German. The sound of his soft, slushy Bayerischer Sprechstil stops her in place. She is surprised by the painful expression on the man's face.

"For all of it, I am sorry, Mrs. Perlman," he tells her. "For all of what was done. It is so painful to carry the knowledge of such terrible happenings. But I was always only a medical soldier." He wants her to know. "This I swear to. I had three wounds on the battlefield. A bullet is still with me. But I only ever treated wounded men. Never hurting other soldiers. Never hurting Jews. Never hurting anyone," he says. His eyes are wet. Beseeching. And she can see it. The wounds he carries. She can see them reflected in his eyes.

Rachel breathes. Swallows. But then releases a tight nod.

A beat passes between them. The man frowns. The pain in his face closes over. "Let me know if there is more to be fixed for your apartment," he says, avoiding eye contact, and makes for the door. But as he opens it to exit, Rachel speaks.

"Thank you," she chokes out. "Mr. Bauer."

He blinks back at her. Uncertain.

"For your help with the crate," she explains.

The German purses his lips flatly. Nods, then steps out, closing the door behind him. She wipes her eyes and turns her attention to the straw-packed rectangle, and then her mother is there, in her painting smock, excited. Eyes dazzling. *Tsigele. Quickly*, she is commanding, her hands clasped tightly together. *Oh, please! Quickly*.

A painting rests against the wall, the nesting material torn away. The figure before her throbs off the canvas. A sensual inferno of red pigments.

The long, willowy body. The sweeping red tresses, like a fire blowing through a forest, and the beatific face with the hungry leopard's eyes. Rachel glares at it as if staring straight into a firepit.

A square envelope contains a card with a small explanation written by hand in German: *For you, Bissel. Who else but you?*

There's a scrape of a key in a lock. The door pops open, and in comes Aaron carrying a paper sack. "Okay, I got you the sesame chicken with broccoli," he announces happily. His voice is always a happy one these days. The overcrowded subway, the city, the dirty sidewalks, the price of fucking everything? Happy. The restaurant, the customers, the cook, and the bottle washers, all of it happy. Even complaining about Leo is a happy subject.

"Also, two egg rolls," he says. "If you don't want both, I'll have the other. Oh, and I don't know if I said? I promised Ezra we'd come up tonight after supper." See! Even dessert with the Fucknik watching T.V. is a joy. Aaron is smiling. The father-to-be. He smiles with puzzlement at the mess of packing materials and the canvas leaned against the wall. "So what's this?" he wonders.

"This," she says, "is my mother's painting." She has tears standing in her eyes.

Aaron's smile grows a bit more serious. "Really?" He stops, turns to stare at it. She can see the wheels turning in his head as he surveys the brutal desire in every brushstroke. The blood boiling through the paint. Maybe he's finally starting to get it. Why his wife is the woman she is. "Wow," he breathes. And then, "Where'd it come from? I mean, is this *it*?" he asks. "The thing itself, I mean. From the pawnshop?"

"Yes."

Aaron, poor man. It's obvious he understands just enough about what's going on here to *know* that he doesn't understand what's going on here. "Sooo…I don't get it." He concedes. "How did it end up here? Your uncle finally pull a rabbit out of his hat or something"

"Yes," Rachel decides to tells him. "Feter Fritz." She will burn the card. When she is alone, she will light it off the stove and let it burn away in the sink. Eingeäschert. Reduced to ash. "That's what happened. The rabbit from the hat." Which isn't entirely a lie.

"Holy mackerel, *honey*," says her husband sweetly, caringly, and squishes her shoulder against him. Maybe he's just noticed her teary eyes, and as for the rest? What difference does it make? She laughs lightly at her own tears as she wipes them with her palms.

At night. Aaron is in the other room still gabbing on the phone with Naomi.

Her sister-in-law rejoiced over the news. "Oh my God, I'll be Mume Naomi!" she cried, laughing through tears. She was on her way out when they appeared at her door. Her hair was out of its ponytail, a chestnut mane down past her shoulders. Kohl eyeliner, red lips, and fishnet stockings. Tyrell had called her. He'd passed his bar exam. They'd made a date to meet at a place on MacDougal called the Gaslight. A beatnik dive! Aaron was still smiling. "Well. Give 'im our regards," he told her. Happy!

And on Webster Avenue in Flatbush? Her mother-in-law had REJOICED in capital letters, as if Rachel had just delivered the Messiah into her lap! *You sweet thing! You sweet, sweet thing!* Hugging the stuffing out of her. The entire mishpocha of the Perlman tribe rejoices at such news and will not quit rejoicing. The phone stays hot. Rachel gets calls from aunts, uncles, cousins, and friends of the family. The whole of Flatbush and then some, like they're planning a ticker-tape parade.

She hears Aaron telling Naomi over the phone, "Oh, who knows?" His voice is lazy with affection. "Boy? Girl? We're just gonna pick a name off the labels of the spice rack over the stove. Yeah, Allspice Perlman, Nutmeg Perlman. *Pepper* Perlman. Actually, that one's not so bad. I should write that down."

She bestows a kiss on his head. She is tired early, she finds, so she had made ready for bed, changing into her flannel pajamas.

"Hold on, the pregnant lady's saying good night," he says. Then, palm clamped over the phone, "who couldn't guess," he says. "She wants to have us over for dinner again with Mr. Now-I'm-a-Lawyer. I said my wife handles our social calendar. You wanna talk to her?"

"Tell her I'll call her tomorrow. We'll find a date." And now she bends forward and gives him a kiss on the lips.

In the bedroom, the curtains are closed to the street, and Rachel has not snapped on her night-light but instead lies on the bed cocooned by the darkness.

She once felt so alone in the darkness and afraid of it overwhelming her. But tonight, she feels no fear. She is not alone, not even in her own body. She starts to light a cigarette but then stops herself. Lets herself sink into the darkness instead. And then the springs groan, she smells smoke, and she sees Eema sitting on the corner of the bed, a Gitanes Brune inserted into an amber resin cigarette holder. Her eyes shine.

So here we are, you and I, her mother says.

"Yes," Rachel whispers into the darkness. "Here we are."

So. You're the artist now, tsigele, she declares. *And soon enough? A mother.* A soft shake of her head. *Children. You know they're a curse,* she says. Though even in death, there is a smile touching her lips.

That night as Aaron sleeps beside her, Rachel feels the shape of his body beside her. A man. Her husband. A Jew from Flatbush whose child she is bearing. A second heartbeat inside her mimicking her own. Sometimes she believes she can feel it. Could her eema feel it too? she wonders. When the founder of the Berolina Circle was carrying her child, could she feel her child's heartbeat even before birth? Such a small and fragile thing, an infant's heartbeat. Hardly more than the swish of a butterfly's wings. And yet how it reverberates. A child full of possibilities. Full of difficulties. Carrying the future.

Outside, the West Side freight line passes, shuddering down its tracks, pursuing the night to its final boundary.

Dawn at the kitchen table. First light is streaking the lower quarters of the sky, a raw pinkish glow. Rachel lights a cigarette. Smoke rises. Kibbitz meows for attention, and she scoops him up into her arms. She can smell the spirits in the jar where her brushes are soaking. As she hugs the cat to her breast, the tears come. Grief and liberation. She sobs without constraint but not without purpose. It's the cleansing purpose of the mikveh, washing through her. She sobs for her mother. She sobs for the millions. She sobs in grief for the world that has vanished, just as she sobs in hope for the child she carries and for the world that will come.

Author's Note

Shadows of Berlin stemmed from my desire to dramatically explore the post-war consequences of the Holocaust, not only for those who suffered under the Nazis and lost family to the murder machine, but also for those who lived in safety an ocean away while six million perished. So I created Rashka Morgenstern. Rashka is a young Jewish Berliner who has outlived the terror of war but carries her trauma with her like baggage as she crosses the Atlantic to a new life as a refugee in America. In New York City, Rashka becomes Rachel, and in 1950, she marries Aaron Perlman, a man who spent the war in the catering corps in California, while Europe was being reduced to cinders.

It's through these two characters and their families (past and present) that I dig into the potent dynamics of guilt and regret, culpability and consequence that still shape the character of people's lives ten years after the war has ended. I wanted to investigate how a traumatic experience, on both a massive and minor scale, can invest itself in the hearts of those who survive it for the rest of their lives. How "survivor's guilt" can impact a person's continued existence—overtly, in the case of Rachel, and more subtly, in the case of her husband. But profoundly so in both cases.

At home, Rachel complains that her husband can never understand the depth of her grief or how she endured the tragedies of surviving Berlin. But neither does she fully understand or appreciate Aaron's own struggles with his guilt and shame, that even though he spent the standard "duration plus six" in the army, he never spent a moment in harm's way.

Nothing separates their two perspectives more than the issue of children. They both entered into their marriage to fill voids in their lives. Aaron needed to be a hero—a savior—and who better to save than a survivor of Hitler's campaign of extermination? Rachel needed, in her way, to *be* saved. Not only from her past, but from herself and her own clear sense of culpability. But children? The idea terrified her. For her husband, Aaron, children were a responsibility. Being Rachel's "savior" wasn't enough. He had to look "forward." He had to produce progeny as a duty to the future. Only producing a child justified his own existence. But Rachel was so traumatized that she can only look backward. How could someone so damaged ever produce something so beautiful as a child? It's only when she was finally forced to confront the dimensions of her guilt and culpability that she was compelled to answer a single simple question. Can the past be redeemed by the future? It is the central question of Rachel and Aaron's marriage, and of the novel itself.

Reading Group Guide

1. Aaron is extremely impatient for children. Why is Rachel reluctant to start a family? Does Aaron respect her reasoning?

2. Rachel's uncle, Feter Fritz, is an important character in Rachel's life. Yet he is often manipulative and self-serving in his behavior toward her. Why do you think she puts up with him and continues to go out of her way to maintain his affections?

3. In many ways, Rachel resists thinking of herself as traumatized. What prevents her from feeling "worthy" of her struggles with mental health?

4. Characterize the Red Angel. Did your opinion of Angelika change as you learned more of her story? In Rachel's position, would you have accepted her help in New York City ten years after the end of the war?

5. What does Aaron expect Rachel to get from her appointments with her therapist? What does she actually achieve through therapy?

6. What is the root of the rivalry between Aaron and his cousin Ezra? What does the character of their rivalry say about Aaron? How does Rachel react to their rivalry?

7. Had you heard of Jews living as U-boats during the war before reading the book? How did hiding in plain sight provide safety, and how did it increase danger?

8. Compare Rachel's and Aaron's relationships to Judaism. How do they deal with the differences in their experiences?

9. Why does Rachel become so invested in Naomi and Tyrell's relationship? Do you think she helps them?

10. Rachel feels responsible for carrying on the legacy of the many Jews who lost their lives, including her mother. What actions does she take to fulfill this responsibility? How do you contribute to the legacy of your ancestors?

A Conversation with the Author

Where did the idea for *Shadows of Berlin* come from? Where do you start when writing a new book?

I had been very interested in the idea of survivor's guilt, and I wanted to explore the aftereffects of trauma and what the living owe to the memory of the dead.

All your books have dealt with World War II in some way. What brings you back to this era in history?

I have been interested in the Second World War since childhood. On a personal note, my father served in the army during the war. More broadly, I believe the war shaped the world we live in today. And we are still dealing with many problems the war created or failed to address. So I believe it remains relevant and very fertile ground for fiction.

While we come to understand Angelika, the narrative does not forgive her actions. Do you think it matters *why* people do bad things? Should it change the consequences they face?

I have always searched out the "gray" areas of my characters' actions and intentions. No one is totally good or totally bad in my books; no one rides for free. Everyone must pay a price for their actions. I don't expect readers to feel any particular sympathy for Angelika. In the end, she was still a murderer. But I do hope readers are moved to discuss the relationship between trauma, power, and personal actions and their consequences and come to their own conclusions.

Rachel's development of her self-portrait is vividly rendered. How would you compare her artistic process to your own?

In some ways, they represent two very different approaches to art. Rachel paints to both honor her mother's death and forgive her mother's abuses. Also to forgive herself. There is a great desperation fueling Rachel's painting.

My writing, on the other hand, is less of a compulsion and more of a vocation. (Though I can never imagine myself quitting the habit!) And yet? At a basic level, both Rachel and I are compelled to create. Growing up, I had a strong interest in both history and art and thought I might become a historical illustrator. But writing eventually won me over. Still, Rachel and I share the joys and trepidations of creating a whole out of nothing—whether we are faced with an empty canvas or a blank page.

When they meet, Rachel is still a refugee in a Lower East Side residence hotel. Aaron is at loose ends, unsure of his direction after the army. Rachel is in need of security, and Aaron is a young man in search of purpose. Why, as the author, would you say they fell in love? What are their greatest challenges to their marriage?

They fell in love because they both felt lost, and marriage seemed a perfect refuge for them. But Rachel has secrets that disrupt the "normal" life she is supposed to be leading. Her heart is a secret, even to herself. And as the book opens, after seven years of marriage, things are not so simple between them. Aaron likes married life, though marriage to a former displaced person is not as easy as he might have imagined it. She's a refugee from the ash pit of Europe, lovely and feline and exotic—and broken. He thought he was saving her, of course. A Jew from Flatbush making the ultimate American mitzvah—saving the persecuted waif from her own brutalized past. But as it turns out, maybe he's not the savior he thought he might have become. Maybe he needs some saving himself.

And as the story spins, both Rachel and her husband must deal with their own brands of guilt. Rachel's guilt is triggered by her horrific experiences during the war and by the lengths she was forced to go to in order to stay alive. And Aaron's guilt is that of one of the multitude of American Jews who, while the chimneys of Auschwitz smoked, lived lives sheltered by democracy, safe from the atrocities perpetrated across the ocean. All this is wrapped up into Aaron's desire for children and Rachel's resistance.

Though Rachel finds a sense of equilibrium at the end of the book, she is not "cured" of her trauma. What do you most want readers to take away from this representation of her emotional health struggles?

I don't think that grief and guilt are easily overcome. A person can spend a lifetime coping with them. But this is a story of survival and redemption. It's a story of the trauma, of self-preservation, and of betrayal and remorse. But in the end, I do want the reader to believe that it is also a story of hope. Because hope is a vital regenerative force.

Acknowledgments

Writing and then publishing a novel is always a team effort. There have been many people involved in bringing this book to the shelves, and I owe them all my deepest thanks and appreciation.

My everlasting gratitude goes out to my agent, the best of the best, Rebecca Gradinger of Fletcher and Company, whose commitment and hard work I depend on in every project I undertake. As always, her insights were keen and her patience immeasurable. Thank you, Rebecca. I could not have done this without you.

I also want to express my deepest gratitude to my wonderful editor at Sourcebooks Landmark, Shana Drehs. I am so indebted to you, Shana, for your unwavering support and understanding. Thank you for your encouragement and for your dedication—and most of all, for your faith in this book. It has been a real pleasure working with you.

I also wish to thank the Sourcebooks Landmark team, whose hard work and commitment have been utterly invaluable. My gratitude goes out to my marketing team for their smart and creative promotional strategies: executive director of marketing Molly Waxman, director of retail marketing & creative services Valerie Pierce, and marketing manager Cristina Arreola. I must also express my thanks to senior production editor Jessica Thelander for expertly riding herd on the book's production, to art director Heather VenHuizen and creative director Kelly Lawler for their terrific cover-to-cover design, and to the entire Sourcebooks Landmark sales staff for their commitment to getting the book on the shelves. Thank you to all who have dedicated long hours of heavy lifting in order to bring *Shadows of Berlin* to readers.

My affection and appreciation goes out to those who supported me along the way. Many thanks to Christy Fletcher, founder of Fletcher and Company, who, three books and many years ago, was the first agent to express an interest in my work. Also to Kelly Karczewski of Fletcher and Company, for her priceless professional support. Thank you to my amazing writing consultant, Carol Edelstein of "A Gallery of Readers," and to Liz Resnick for her invaluable insights as an early reader. And for their expert advice on finding the correct word in Yiddish, my thanks to Prof. Haim Gunner and to Prof. Alyssa Quint.

Also, my warmest gratitude goes out to my fellow writers for their support, in person and over social media: Jillian Cantor, Dean Cycon, Kathleen Grissom, Pam Jenoff, Dan Levy, Erika Marks, Emily Neuberger, Julie Ries, Erika Robuck, Jennifer Rosner, Anika Scott, Pat Stacy, Leah Weiss, Kate Whouley, and Andria Williams.

Finally, I cannot forget my family, who not only supported me throughout the process but provided me with respite and encouragement: my boys, Cameron Gemmell and Alexander Pavlova-Gillham.

And as always, from the depth of my heart, I am thankful to my life's partner and wife, Ludmilla Pavlova-Gillham, who is still my touchstone in all things and to whom I have dedicated this book.

About the Author

David R. Gillham is a *New York Times* bestselling author. He studied screenwriting at the University of Southern California before becoming a novelist. After moving to New York City, Gillham spent more than a decade in the book business, and he now lives with his family in western Massachusetts.